Chartist Fiction

Chartist Fiction

Thomas Doubleday,
The Political Pilgrim's Progress

Thomas Martin Wheeler,
Sunshine and Shadow

Edited by

Ian Haywood

Ashgate

Aldershot • Brookfield USA • Singapore • Sydney

© Ian Haywood, 1999

Published by
Ashgate Publishing Limited
Gower House
Croft Road
Aldershot
Hants GU11 3HR
England

Ashgate Publishing Company
Old Post Road
Brookfield
Vermont 05036–9704
USA

Ashgate website: http://www.ashgate.com

British Library Cataloguing in Publication Data

Chartist Fiction
   1. Doubleday, Thomas. *Political Pilgrim's Progress.*
   2. Wheeler, Thomas Martin. *Sunshine and Shadow.* 3. English
   fiction—19th century—History and criticism. 4. Chartism in
   literature.
   I. Haywood, Ian, 1958–
   823.8'09358

Library of Congress Cataloging-in-Publication Data

Chartist fiction/edited by Ian Haywood.
     Includes bibliographical references.
   ISBN 1–84014–648–6 (acid-free paper)
    1. Great Britain—Social conditions—19th century—Fiction.
2. Social problems—Great Britain—Fiction. 3. Labor movement—Great
Britain—Fiction. 4. Political fiction, English. 5. Chartism—Fiction.
6. Utopias—Fiction. I. Haywood, Ian, 1958–   . II. Doubleday, Thomas,
1790–1870. *Political pilgrim's progress.* III. Wheeler, Thomas Martin.
Sunshine and shadow.
PR1309.S63C47   1999
823'.8035821—dc21   99–42754
                                                        CIP

ISBN 1 84014 648 6

This book is printed on acid free paper

Printed and bound in Great Britain by MPG Books Ltd, Bodmin, Cornwall

Contents

The Nineteenth Century
General Editors' Preface

The aim of this series is to reflect, develop and extend the great burgeoning of interest in the nineteenth century that has been an inevitable feature of recent decades, as that former epoch has come more sharply into focus as a locus for our understanding not only of the past but of the contours of our modernity. Though it is dedicated principally to the publication of original monographs and symposia in literature, history, cultural analysis, and associated fields, there will be a salient role for reprints of significant text from, or about, the period. Our overarching policy is to address the spectrum of nineteenth-century studies without exception, achieving the widest scope in chronology, approach and range of concern. This, we believe, distinguishes our project from comparable ones, and means, for example, that in the relevant areas of scholarship we both recognize and cut innovatively across such parameters as those suggested by the designations 'Romantic' and 'Victorian'. We welcome new ideas, while valuing tradition. It is hoped that the world which predates yet so forcibly predicts and engages our own will emerge in parts, as a whole, and in the lively currents of debate and change that are so manifest an aspect of its intellectual, artistic and social landscape.

Vincent Newey
Joanne Shattock

University of Leicester

To my son David

General Introduction

This is the second volume in a series of reprints of Chartist fiction. The first volume, *The Literature of Struggle: An Anthology of Chartist Fiction*, came out in 1995. In the intervening period I have been pleased to discover an enthusiastic and expanding scholarly interest in this neglected area of literary and cultural history. In order to acknowledge the work of colleagues in Britain, North America and elsewhere, I include a bibliography of relevant publications and research at the end of this introduction. I also hope to encourage interested newcomers from literary and historical backgrounds to pursue new agendas. The most exciting aspect of investigating radical nineteenth-century literature is the interdisciplinary nature of the work. It is impossible to understand the forms and themes of such fiction without an examination of the appropriate political and cultural contexts. While such an approach probably illuminates all literary texts, Chartist fiction by definition has a particularly close relationship with the fortunes of the Chartist and labour movement. This productive intimacy is reflected in the fact that Chartist literature has now become an established, if minority, concern of labour history. As I argued in *The Literature of Struggle*, the Chartists were writing themselves into history on many different but ultimately connected levels. In order to prove themselves worthy of political representation, it was a vital task to also conquer the realm of symbolic representation. This arena of radical 'expression' included convivial anniversaries and social gatherings, songs, toasts, collective reading, funeral orations and a vigorous investment in radical 'spectacle': marches, rallies, and a remarkable array of flags and banners. While the focus in this book is on imaginative fiction, the wider symbolic, ritualistic and ceremonial life of popular radicalism is a rich field for further research.[1]

When I was gathering material for *The Literature of Struggle*, I decided that the only way I could show the range and variety of Chartist fiction produced between the late 1830s and the early 1850s was to include as many texts as possible. Inevitably, this meant choosing a high number of short stories and 'sampling' long narratives through the use of extracts. While it was important and appropriate to use the anthology to reflect the popularity of short fiction amongst Chartist authors (the short story was the genre best suited to publication in Chartist newspapers and periodicals), the aim of this volume and its successor is to reprint three longer tales in their entirety. The process of selection was not made easy by the small but impressive range of stories. In addition to the two works in this volume, we only have to turn to the prolific career of Ernest Jones to locate several full-length novels: *The Romance of a*

People (1847), *De Brassiere* (1851) and the series of tales given the title *Woman's Wrongs* (1852; reissued 1855). Thomas Frost wrote *The Secret* (1850), and the field expands enormously once we include the remarkable output of George W. M. Reynolds. In the end, I decided to reprint Doubleday's *The Political Pilgrim's Progress* (1839), Wheeler's *Sunshine and Shadow* (1849-50) and Jones's *Woman's Wrongs* for their intrinsic interest and because excerpts from some of the other works were included in *The Literature of Struggle*.

It is in these longer works that Chartist fiction most directly competed and interacted with its mainstream rival, the Victorian novel. But this does not mean that Chartist novels simply aspired to the status of bourgeois fiction, as they also derived inspiration and aesthetic energy from traditional and commercialized popular fictional forms. At the risk of imposing a false coherence on a series of divergent texts, we can see the Chartist novel and novelette as an amalgam of four genres and traditions: the serialized novel; the 'improving', respectable, didactic Evangelical tale; the sensational, melodramatic, Gothic 'penny dreadful'; and the radical pamphlet and journal. Of course there are other discourses at work in the texts, but identifying these dominant influences helps us to see that Chartist fiction was a response and a resistance to a unique set of cultural pressures and opportunities. As Raymond Williams has argued, from the 1830s onwards, it was state policy to fight the radical press with commercialism rather than censorship or repression, hence the relaxation of newspaper taxes.[2] Yet David Vincent, the historian of popular literacy, finds it ironic that the first major triumphs of this new bourgeois era of depoliticized 'popular leisure' should be Edward Lloyd and George W. M. Reynolds, two radicals.[3] Reynolds is the most stunning example of the radical conquest of the marketplace of popular Victorian fiction, and it is gratifying to see that there is now available a modern (if abridged) reprint of Reynolds's best-selling masterpiece, *The Mysteries of London*.[4] But Ernest Jones's decision to reissue *Woman's Wrongs* in penny format is also testimony to the popular demand for radicalized mass fiction. This genre functioned as an alternative to both mainstream serialized fiction and the cheap, 'useful' knowledge of Evangelical periodicals. Yet at the same time as they might exploit the new resources of cheap fiction, Chartist authors could choose to operate within the relatively autonomous orbit of Chartist publications, shielded from the populist imperatives of commodification. This level of cultural protectionism provided a degree of aesthetic freedom and the chance to experiment with new forms of politicized fiction. Two of the best examples of this innovation are the stories included in this volume. I offer some detailed comments on each text in the respective introductions, but some preliminary comparative points can be made here.

It is tempting to read Thomas Doubleday's *The Political Pilgrim's Progress* and Thomas Martin Wheeler's *Sunshine and Shadow* as symptomatic of the fortunes of Chartism. The stories function like bookends of the movement. In form, content and intention they seem to be polar opposites. The former is a

Utopian vision of victory in the heady days of the first Chartist Convention; the latter takes stock of the defeats of 1848. While Radical and his family enter the City of Reform, Arthur Morton flees into exile. Doubleday demolishes corrupt institutions with a Swiftian flair; Wheeler is troubled by Chartism's failures. The earlier text combines Bunyanesque allegory with political caricature; the later text utilizes varieties of realism such as reportage and the *Bildungsroman*. Where the former is avowedly physical force, the latter praises the restraint of Chartist leaders in preventing a bloody confrontation with the Whig state. The mood and method of the two texts help us to plot the parabolic curve of Chartist history.

But there are also similarities. Both stories are pristine Chartist productions, serialized in leading Chartist newspapers and written by activists. Doubleday was a popular Newcastle radical, while Wheeler declared his credentials beneath the title of each weekly instalment: 'Late Secretary to the National Charter Association and the National Land Company'. Wheeler wrote *Sunshine and Shadow* while he was living at O'Connorville, the first Chartist settlement. Both stories draw on the cultural and ideological core of Chartism's values: the quest of the respectable worker for independence and liberty, 'bread, knowledge and freedom'. On the negative side, the stories also illuminate the basis of this vision in patriarchal notions of gender roles (though Wheeler also challenges Victorian orthodoxies about sexual morality) and in persistent anti-Semitism. These qualities make any assessment of the stories both troubling and challenging.

Notes

1. See: James Epstein, *Radical Expression: Political Language, Ritual and Symbol in England, 1790-1830* (Oxford: Oxford University Press, 1994); Paul Pickering, *Chartism and the Chartists in Manchester and Salford* (Basingstoke: Macmillan, 1995), Part Two; James Vernon, *Politics and the People. A Study in English Political Culture, c. 1815-1867* (Cambridge: Cambridge University Press, 1993), pp. 119-26 .

2. Raymond Williams, 'The press and popular culture: an historical perspective', in George Boyce, James Curran and Pauline Wingate, eds, *Newspaper History from the Seventeenth Century to the Present Day* (London: Constable, 1978), and 'Radical and/or respectable', in Richard Boston, ed., *The Press We Deserve* (London: Routledge and Kegan Paul, 1970). See also James Curran and Jean Seaton, *Power Without Responsibility: The press and broadcasting in Britain* (London and New York: Routledge, 1997), chapter 1 *passim*; Kevin Gilmartin, *Print Politics* (Cambridge: Cambridge University Press, 1996).

3. David Vincent, *Literacy and Popular Culture in England 1750-1914* (Cambridge: Cambridge University Press, 1989), p. 251.

4. George W. M. Reynolds, *The Mysteries of London*, ed. Trefor Thomas (Keele, Staffordshire: Keele University Press, 1996).

Studies of Chartist fiction

Most of the books, articles and essays cited in the first section below deal in the main with the following full-length Chartist narratives:

Thomas Doubleday, *The Political Pilgrim's Progress* (*Northern Liberator*, 1839);

Thomas Cooper, *Wise Saws and Modern Instances* (1845), a collection of short tales;

Thomas Frost, *The Secret* (*National Instructor*, 1850);

Ernest Jones, *The Romance of a People* (*The Labourer*, 1847), *De Brassiere: A Democratic Romance* (*Notes to the People*, 1851), *Woman's Wrongs* (*Notes to the People*, 1852);

Thomas Martin Wheeler, *Sunshine and Shadow* (*Northern Star*, 1849-50).

Somewhat surprisingly, the remarkable George W. M. Reynolds, author of the best-selling *The Mysteries of London* (1844-48), and a leading figure in 'late' Chartism, does not figure in most of the criticism on Chartist fiction. However, Reynolds has received a good deal of attention from scholars of Victorian popular politics and culture. Given his emerging importance for our understanding of radical fiction in the mid-nineteenth century, I have appended a separate section for Reynolds.

Ashraf, Mary, *Introduction to Working-Class Literature in Britain: Part Two. Prose* (Berlin, 1979), pp. 64-71. This is a very rare book, though it is available at the Marx Memorial Library in London. It is most useful for the way it places Chartist fiction as the beginning of a tradition of working-class novels.

Devereux, Steve, 'Chartism and popular fiction' in John Lucas, ed., *Writing and Radicalism* (Harlow: Longman, 1996). Devereux argues that the attempt by Chartist authors to appropriate popular narrative forms such as sentimental romance was only partially successful. The bourgeois origins of such generic influences ultimately undermined or diffused the radical message.

Harvie, Christopher, *The Centre of Things. Political Fiction in Britain from Disraeli to the Present* (London: Unwin Hyman, 1991), pp. 16-18. A brief discussion which provides a mainstream literary context for Chartist texts.

Haywood, Ian, *Working-Class Fiction: From Chartism to 'Trainspotting'* (Plymouth: Northcote House/British Council, 1997), chapter 1, which discusses Wheeler and Thomas Cooper.

Klaus, H. Gustav, *The Literature of Labour: Two Hundred Years of Working-Class Writing* (Brighton: Harvester, 1985), chapter 3. Klaus is much more enthusiastic than his left-wing precursors about the agitational value of Chartist fiction, even if he is mildly critical of the melodramatic, aristocratic type of class enemy in some of the novels. Klaus can be credited with reviving the reputation of Chartist narratives.

Kovalev, Y. V., Introduction to *An Anthology of Chartist Fiction* (Moscow, 1956); translated into English as 'The Literature of Chartism', *Victorian Studies*, **2** (2), 1958. Kovalev is less keen on Chartist fiction than poetry, but he is still to be credited for keeping the memory of the fiction alive.

Mitchell, Jack B., 'Aesthetic Problems of the Development of the Proletarian-Revolutionary Novel in Nineteenth-Century Britain', in David Craig, ed., *Marxists on Literature* (Harmondsworth: Penguin, 1975). Mitchell, like Vicinus, takes the line that Chartist fiction failed to live up to the standards of Engels's 'triumph of realism', though it made important progress in forcing working-class experience into literary tradition.

Randall, Tim, 'Towards a Cultural Democracy: Chartist Literature 1837-1860' (Ph.D., University of Sussex, 1994). The most comprehensive survey of Chartist fiction to date, this is a valuable bibliographical resource for scholars, though it tends to be rather negative about the achievements of Jones and Reynolds.

Roberts, Stephen, 'Thomas Cooper: Radical and Poet, c. 1830-1860' (M.Litt., University of Birmingham, 1986). Written by a historian, this is the best source for background information on Cooper's career as a Chartist lecturer and writer. See in particular chapters 10-13 which cover Cooper's published and unpublished fiction.

Schwarzkopf, Jutta, *Women in the Chartist Movement* (Basingstoke: Macmillan, 1991), chapter 2. As a feminist labour historian, Schwarzkopf is critical of the domesticated roles allotted to women characters in Chartist fiction, which she sees as cultural evidence of the patriarchal ideology of the Chartist movement.

Vicinus, Martha, *The Industrial Muse: A Study of Nineteenth Century British Working Class Literature* (London: Croom Helm, 1974), chapter 3. See also her essay 'Chartist Fiction and the Development of Class-Based Literature', in H. Gustav Klaus, ed., *The Socialist Novel in Britain: Towards the Recovery of a Tradition* (Brighton: Harvester, 1982). Vicinus believes that the importance of Chartist fiction was its ambitious attempt to find alternative literary means to disseminate a radical, class-conscious culture to an emerging popular urban readership. However, this ambition did not produce works of great literary merit. For Vicinus, Chartist fiction is weakened by didacticism, schematic plotting and thin characterization.

George W. M. Reynolds

The best summary of Reynolds's life and works can be found in three sources: E. F. Bleiler, Introduction and Bibliography in the reprint of Reynolds's *Wagner the Wehr-wolf* (New York: Dover, 1975); Louis James and John Saville, entry for 'G. W. M. Reynolds' in Joyce Bellamy and John Saville, eds, *Dictionary of*

Labour Biography (London: Macmillan, 1976), vol. 3, pp. 146-51; Rohan McWilliam, 'The Mysteries of G. W. M. Reynolds: radicalism and melodrama in Victorian Britain' in Malcolm Chase and Ian Dyck, eds, *Living and Learning. Essays in Honour of J. F. C. Harrison* (Aldershot: Scolar Press, 1996). Also useful is Trefor Thomas's Introduction to his abridged reissue of the first series of *The Mysteries of London* (Keele, Staffordshire: Keele University Press, 1996), particularly his discussion of Reynolds's working methods. Reynolds's reputation has also been recuperated by labour historians working on 'late' Chartism: see McWilliam, 'The Mysteries of George W. Reynolds'; Patrick Joyce, *Democratic Subjects: The self and the social in nineteenth-century England* (Cambridge: Cambridge University Press, 1994), p. 82 and his *Visions of the People: Industrial England and the Question of Class 1848-1914* (Cambridge: Cambridge University Press, 1991), pp. 65-74; Margot Finn, *After Chartism. Class and nation in English radical politics 1848-1874* (Cambridge: Cambridge University Press, 1993), p. 112.

Reynolds's work is also discussed in the following studies:

Bayuk Rosenman, Ellen, 'Spectacular Women: *The Mysteries of London* and the Female Body', *Victorian Studies*, **40** (1), Autumn 1996, pp. 31-64.

Berridge, Virginia, 'Popular Sunday papers and mid-Victorian society', in George Boyce, James Curran and Pauline Wingate, eds, *Newspaper History from the Seventeenth Century to the Present Day* (London: Constable, 1978). This essay is a distillation of Berridge's dissertation, 'Popular journalism and working-class attitudes 1854-1886: A study of *Reynolds's Newspaper*, *Lloyd's Weekly Newspaper* and *The Weekly Times* (D. Phil, University of London, 1976), which is worth consulting separately.

Dalziel, Margaret, *Popular Fiction 100 Years Ago: An Unexplored Tract of Literary History* (London: Cohen and West, 1957).

Gallagher, Catherine, *The Industrial Reformation of English Fiction. Social Discourse and Narrative Form 1832-1867* (1985; Chicago and London: University of Chicago Press, 1988), pp. 131-4.

Haywood, Ian, 'George W. M. Reynolds and the radicalization of Victorian serial fiction', *Media History*, **4** (2), Winter 1998, pp. 121-39.

Himmelfarb, Gertrude, *The Idea of Poverty. England in the Early Industrial Age* (London: Faber and Faber, 1984), chapter 18.

Humpherys, Anne, 'G. W. M. Reynolds: Popular Literature and Popular Politics', *Victorian Periodicals Review*, **16**, 1983, pp. 78-89, reprinted in Joel H. Weiner, *Innovators and Preachers. The Role of the Editor in Victorian England* (London and Westport, CT: Greenwood Press, 1985).

Humpherys, Anne, 'Popular Narrative and Political Discourse in *Reynolds's Weekly Newspaper*', in Laurel Brake, Aled Jones and Lionel Madden, eds, *Investigating Victorian Journalism* (London: Macmillan, 1990).

Humpherys, Anne, 'Generic Strands and Urban Twists: The Victorian Mysteries

Novel', *Victorian Studies*, **34** (4), Summer 1991, pp. 463-72.

James, Louis, *Fiction for the Working Man 1830-1850: A study of the literature produced for the working classes in early Victorian urban England* (1963; London: Penguin University Books, 1973).

Kestner, Joseph, *Protest and Reform. The British Social Narrative by Women 1827-1867* (London: Methuen, 1985).

Maxwell, Richard, *The Mysteries of Paris and London* (Charlottesville and London: University Press of Virginia, 1992).

Neuberg, Victor, *Popular Literature: A history and guide from the beginning of printing to the year 1897* (London: The Woburn Press, 1977).

Punter, David, *The Literature of Terror*, 2nd edn, 2 vols (London: Longman, 1996), vol. 1, pp. 145-63.

Vicinus, Martha, *The Industrial Muse. A Study of Nineteenth Century British Working Class Literature* (London: Croom Helm, 1974).

Williams, Raymond, 'Forms of English Fiction in 1848', in Frances Barker, ed., *Literature, Politics and Theory* (London: Methuen, 1986).

The Political Pilgrim's Progress

Thomas Doubleday

Editor's introduction

The Political Pilgrim's Progress appeared anonymously in the radical Newcastle newspaper, the *Northern Liberator*, between January and March 1839. It was reissued in pamphlet form in May 1839 as part of an occasional series of *Northern Liberator* reprints. The pamphlet version was priced at sixpence and reproduced exactly the original text, including 'seven beautiful woodcuts' which it has not been possible to include here.[1] To describe these illustrations as 'beautiful' is publishers' hyperbole, but they are clear evidence of the populist appeal of the narrative. Despite the relatively high price, the reprint shows that a strong local demand existed for this blend of agitational political satire and radical mythology. Some 6000 copies were sold, making *The Political Pilgrim's Progress* a local bestseller.[2] Given the fact that the *Northern Liberator* had a national circulation, we can also assume that the tale found an eager radical readership well beyond the north-east of England. The timing of the story's original publication coincided with the first Chartist convention, and the story was obviously designed to play its part in defining the scope and direction of Chartist policy and politics. But that aim does not explain why the story took the form it did. In order to understand more fully the intriguing generic features of *The Political Pilgrim's Progress*, we need to investigate the interrelationship between radical culture and political forces during this period. This will involve a consideration of personnel, productive processes and the various transformations of the political discourse of reform.

The genesis and evolution of the *Northern Liberator* tells us much about the value that radicals placed upon the printed medium during a time of resurgent reform agitation. The paper was founded by the American-born journalist and entrepreneur Augustus Hardin Beaumont (1798-1838) in October 1837, the same year that the London Working Men's Association launched the six-point Charter. Beaumont became a radical in the early 1830s after a chequered career as a plantation owner in Jamaica. He settled in Newcastle and quickly established a reputation for radical leadership. He was asked to stand for the city in the 1837 general election as a Radical and later the same year set up the *Northern Liberator* to support 'ultra' democracy. He therefore helped to maintain Newcastle's status as a powerhouse of radical and republican politics. He was assisted in his task by two other highly rated local radicals: the Mayor of Morpeth, furrier and philosopher Robert Blakey (1795-1878), and the writer and activist Thomas Doubleday (1790-1870). The paper emblazoned on its front page the twin goals of freedom of the press and universal suffrage. In its early months the paper's main cause was opposition to the new Poor Law, which was fiercely contested in the north of England.[3] It also sponsored meetings to raise funds for industrial struggles such as the Glasgow cotton-spinners' strike. The peak of Beaumont's influence was probably the huge anti-Poor Law meeting which took place on New Year's Day 1838, and at which Doubleday and Joseph Rayner Stephens spoke. At this juncture Beaumont announced he was leaving to join the rebels fighting British rule in Canada. He sold the paper to Blakey, who steered its politics more firmly towards Chartism. Beaumont never made the journey, as he died in January 1838.[4]

He left behind him a paper fully committed to its radical role of promoting and organizing Chartist and radical agitation in the north-east. Though it collapsed in December 1840, the *Northern Liberator* is a classic example of the operation of the radical press in the early nineteenth century. In addition to advertising and reporting radical meetings and events, the paper contained domestic and foreign news, outspoken editorials, theatre and book reviews, and a regular smattering of literature, including poems, stories and satirical sketches. The paper's published circulation figures of 4000 undoubtedly underestimates the number of readers, as the customs of reading aloud and collaborative purchase were common in radical and working-class circles.[5] One recent study estimates ten readers for each sale, and the *Northern Liberator*'s stamped price of 4½d. (while typical) was high even for prosperous artisans.[6] The same mode of consumption probably applied to the reprint series.[7] The close relationship between the producers and the readers of the paper was generated by the shared political causes, the dual role of the editors as both writers and activists (Doubleday and Blakey feature regularly as speakers in the reports of meetings), and the fostering of a sense of a collective purpose, will and destiny (a feeling strengthened by the paper's preferred attribution, 'the Writers of the *Northern Liberator*').

It was precisely this ability of the radical press to forge a practical class consciousness and collective political culture that was so feared by the State. It is now widely accepted that the reduction of the stamp duty to a penny in 1836 was a measure aimed at forcing up the costs of newspapers and ending the counter-hegemony of the unstamped radical press.[8] The extent to which capitalist market forces destroyed the *Northern Liberator* has yet to be ascertained; the fact that it ended its days as a freesheet could be evidence of desperate measures to restore circulation.[9] Given that the running costs of radical papers were low and enabled them to break even with fairly modest circulations,[10] it may be more likely that the paper was crippled by Blakey's netting a hefty fine for a leader in which he affirmed 'Right of Resistance to Constituted Authorities'.[11] The wider picture at this time shows an explosion of Chartist and radical publications, though later in the century changes in technology did mean that large amounts of capital were needed to start up a popular paper. According to Raymond Williams, the form of the 'popular' press changed several times in the course of the century. Initially it was synonymous with the radical press of Cobbett and the unstamped wars: supporting the cause of the people against a corrupt aristocratic state. From the 1840s an 'intermediary' stage arose with the advent of mass circulation Sunday weeklies based on a diet of sensationalism and crime mingled with radical politics, shown most strikingly in *Lloyd's Weekly News* and *Reynolds's Newspaper*. In the later portion of the century the modern, depoliticized 'tabloid' approach became dominant.[12] Using Williams's model, the *Northern Liberator* was obviously 'popular' in the first sense, but the presence of *The Political Pilgrim's Progress* (and, as we shall see, other satirical fictions) indicates that an appeal was also being made to the reader's appetite for 'popular' narrative. This was far from being a dominant discourse in the radical press at the time, but it nevertheless made a significant contribution to the formation of radical consciousness, as *The Literature of Struggle* series will hopefully demonstrate.

The inclusion of literary narrative in the paper probably owed much to Doubleday and Blakey, who already had reputations as writers. Indeed, Doubleday is credited as the author of *The Political Pilgrim's Progress* by H. Gustav Klaus in his brief but important discussion of the tale.[13] A comparison of the narrative with attributed Doubleday journalism does provide persuasive textual evidence for this provenance.[14] The decision to remain anonymous may have been a legal camouflage, considering the story's wincing satire of government policy and institutions. But Blakey was also a seasoned radical journalist, having written in the early post-war years for Wooler's *Black Dwarf* and Cobbett's *Political Register*. Until further evidence is forthcoming I will assume for convenience that Doubleday is the author, though it is quite likely that Blakey collaborated to some degree, not least in the tale's offensive anti-Semitism, a point I will return to later. A brief outline of Doubleday's career is therefore apposite at this stage.[15]

Thomas Doubleday was the son of a Newcastle soap manufacturer. Under the influence of an uncle who was a classical scholar, Doubleday soon acquired a passion for scholarship and writing which easily outweighed his interest in business. At the same time as a number of his early literary pieces were published he also became a convert to radical politics. He achieved a regional prominence as secretary of the Northern Political Union during the Reform Bill crisis of 1832, and at one point a warrant for his arrest was issued. Once the bill became law he joined the radical campaign for universal suffrage, and made the natural progression to Chartism in the late 1830s. He was actively involved in two unsuccessful attempts to set up a radical newspaper in Newcastle, but eventually teamed up with Blakey to produce the *Northern Liberator*. As well as writing propaganda pieces for the paper, he was a popular local political figure. He spoke at the huge anti-Poor Law rally on New Year's Day 1838, and chaired a 'monster' Chartist meeting on Newcastle Town Moor in June 1838. In early 1839 two celebratory dinners were held in his honour.[16] During the tense summer months of that year, when the Chartists debated 'ulterior measures', Doubleday may have been part of the *Northern Liberator's* involvement in an insurrectionary plot.[17] Although like many Chartist leaders he publicly dissociated himself from recommending physical force as an aggressive tactic (recourse to arms for defensive purposes was, however, frequently mentioned), there is a conspicuous and witty denigration of moral force in *The Political Pilgrim's Progress*. As the General Convention of the Industrious Classes convened in London in February 1839, the character of Radical took possession of a musket in preparation for the battle with Political Apollyon. It may be the case that Doubleday turned to religious fable and satire as cloaks for an otherwise inflammatory message. As noted earlier, Blakey was prosecuted for an outspoken defence of the right to arm.

The period during which Doubleday was associated with the *Northern Liberator* may well have been the peak of his political career. After 1840 the family business collapsed and Doubleday sought a salaried post, eventually becoming registrar of births, deaths and marriages for a local parish. He played a consistent but minor role in reform politics, lending his support to Joseph Cowen's Northern Reform Union in the 1850s. Most of his political energies went into his writing: his output included contributions to numerous newspapers (including Cowen's *Northern Tribune*), agitprop, essays (some of which were collected in book form), biography and political economy.[18] Though not from an artisan background, Doubleday can be seen in Gramsci's terms as an 'organic' intellectual, one of the growing number of semi-professional ideologues of the radical movement. His role model was Cobbett, whom Blakey also admired.[19] Doubleday inherited Cobbett's analysis of Old Corruption and the whole apparatus of his demonology, including rabid anti-Semitism. The grossest villains in *The Political Pilgrim's Progress* are not aristocrats but moneylenders, typified by the stage Jew. Any reading of the tale must take account of this 'darker' side of popular radicalism.[20] When George Jacob Holyoake summed up Doubleday's achievements for the *Dictionary of National Biography* in 1888, anti-Semitism was simply not mentioned: 'He was a remarkable instance of the combination of ardent and refined literary tastes with strong and outspoken political principles.'[21] While there is much to admire in *The Political Pilgrim's Progress*, the indulgence in Jew-baiting is a glaring eyesore across the surface of the narrative. In my discussion of the tale I try to tackle this problem directly rather than sweeping it conveniently into the generalized discourse of 'outspoken political principles'.

The original model for the narrative is of course John Bunyan's classic allegory, *The Pilgrim's Progress*, first published in 1678.[22] By the early nineteenth century this work came second only to the Bible as the most widely owned book in British households. According to E. P. Thompson, it ranked alongside Paine's *Rights of Man* as a 'foundation text' of the English working class.[23] Thompson argues that the book's influence stemmed from its inherently democratic values; it tells the story of a poor man 'clothed with rags' who against all the odds achieves salvation and grace. Bunyan's Dissenting religious beliefs and anti-aristocratic politics reinforced the radical critique of Old Corruption. He refers to providence as 'that hand/That pulls the strong down, and makes weak ones stand' (p. 36). The Chartist 'rebel' John James Bezer is surely not untypical in his vivid recollection of the work's inspirational effect on his formative education:

> My own dear Bunyan! if it hadn't been for you, I should have gone mad, I think, before I was ten years old! Even as it was, the other books and teachings I was bored with, had such a terrible influence on me, that somehow or other, I was always nourishing the idea that 'Giant Despair' had got hold of me, and that I should never get out of his 'Doubting Castle.' Yet I read, ay, and *fed* with such delight as I cannot *now* describe — though I think I could *then*. Glorious Bunyan, you too were a 'Rebel,' and I love you *doubly* for *that*.[24]

The formal qualities of Bunyan's allegory were as important as the story's explicit and implicit values. The narrative structure provided a quasi-*Bildungsroman* form that could easily be secularized into a paradigm for working-class autobiography. The tale also offered a Utopian model for both thinking and writing about the journey to the promised land: from poverty to riches, ignorance to enlightenment, disenfranchisement to liberty. Additionally, the populist dimensions of the story ensured its continuing appeal and accessibility. Apart from the obvious debt to the Bible, the tale borrows from the generic features of heroic romance. Christian has exciting adventures and fights a courageous battle against the supernatural adversary Apollyon, the dragon to Christian's St George. The landscape is also derived from fairy-tale and romance, with menacing natural wastelands, Delectable Mountains and a visionary city that resembles an enchanted castle. There are numerous encounters with a large cast of walk-on strangers who have comic and colourful allegorical names such as By-Ends and Save-All. But another reason why the common reader could identify with Christian's journey is that the fantasy is grounded in native, English experience. The path Christian pursues takes him down English country lanes; Vanity Fair is both a medley of vices and a version of a real country fair. Christian is waylaid by smug, sophistical trimmers whose language of compromise anticipates the post-1688 bourgeois settlement. Most importantly, as Q. D. Leavis pointed out over half a century ago, Bunyan wrote the tale in vernacular, regional English, the 'idiom of common speech'.[25] These naturalistic and nationalistic connotations of Bunyan's language have been appreciated at least since the Romantic period, when Southey referred to the tale's 'clear stream of current English'.[26] It was as if Bunyan anticipated the Wordsworthian democratization of literary language. In the words of a recent editor of the text, 'fine speaking is repeatedly associated with hypocrisy, and both, often, with elevated social status'.[27] For Leavis, the story glows with the vital, Protestant values of freedom of conscience and individual self-improvement: 'one is in contact through [Bunyan] with a genuine culture'. Aspiring artisan autodidacts in the late eighteenth and early nineteenth centuries could turn to Bunyan, Defoe and the Bible as 'no bad substitutes for a formal education'. It is clear that Leavis regards this period as a golden age of serious, 'solid' popular reading that fell into terminal decline with the advent of industrialized, mass literary production, state education and 'popular taste'.[28] In the mid-nineteenth century, so this argument goes, 'popular' fiction becomes 'light' fiction, debased by commercialism. As noted above, more recent critics also believe that a dissociation of radical sensibility occurred in the period concurrent with Chartism. Contact with that 'genuine culture' of common experience was lost, distorted or commodified.

In *The Political Pilgrim's Progress*, however, we see Bunyan's influence in full flow. Moreover, it is the combative rather than consolatory aspects of the fantasy that are emphasized. As E. P. Thompson noted, 'when the context is hopeful and mass agitations arise, the active energies of the tradition are most apparent'.[29] *The Political Pilgrim's Progress*'s implied readership certainly includes Leavis's Bunyan-loving respectable artisan, as the concluding Utopian vision makes clear: '*here* every man possessing common industry was able to earn an ample livelihood, and bring up his family in ease and comfort' (p. 58). But the narrative does more than substitute political for religious allegory. The first few paragraphs make it abundantly clear that the tale will be a full-frontal satirical assault on contemporary social, political and cultural institutions. The pilgrim's detached, naive point of view is exploited for its capacity to defamiliarize contemporary experience:

> The city had a great profusion of guilded domes, and fanes, and its
> appearance at a distance, especially under the subdued rays of a setting
> sun, was the most imposing and striking imaginable. Its people seemed
> active, industrious, and enterprising; but there appeared a singular
> custom amongst them, which greatly marred their social happiness and
> unanimity, and this was, that nearly one half of the inhabitants made a
> practice of putting their hands into the pockets of the other half, and
> taking their money from them. (p. 17)

The obvious literary debt here is to Swift. It is not coincidental that the companion piece to *The Political Pilgrim's Progress* was entitled *The Political Tale of a Tub*.[30] The *Northern Liberator*'s writers often had recourse to Swiftian imagery and savagery to denounce their political enemies. For instance, in the controversy surrounding the infamous *Book of Murder* by 'Marcus', the paper turned that text's Swiftian method against itself.[31] The influence of the English satirical tradition on nineteenth-century radical discourse has possibly been undervalued. Radicals of the age of Doubleday and Blakey had lived through the great period of scatalogical Regency satire.[32] One of the striking qualities of *The Political Pilgrim's Progress* is the adaptation of this satirical inheritance to a new political situation, the emergence of Chartism.

These literary borrowings also evoke a sense of longer historical evolution which has now reached a critical juncture. This perspective reflects that peculiar, distinctive quality of English radicalism in this period, the adherence to constitutionalism.[33] The City of Reform may await the arrival of Radical and his family, but the City already exists. The rights and freedoms that flourish there have been lost and need rediscovery. Radical's journey is nostalgic, a return to a mythic past before the Norman Yoke imposed aristocratic rule. *The Political Pilgrim's Progress* is a vibrant demonstration of the continuing ability of constitutionalist nostalgia to fire the radical imagination in the nineteenth century. The key reference here is again Cobbett, but even with the new forces of industrial capitalism looming large on the horizon (the Evangelical Mr Staytape is a cotton lord), the Paradise Regained of pre-capitalist artisan splendour continued to resurface in texts such as W. J. Linton's *Bob Thin; or the Poorhouse Fugitive* (1845), Fergus O'Connor's writings on Chartist settlements and, much later, William Morris's medievalized fantasies of non-alienated labour. Indeed, the basic aim of the Charter could be seen as freeing the artisan from repressive and intrusive state policies. The communitarian basis of such a political vision is also envisaged in *The Political Pilgrim's Progress*; even though Owenism is mocked for its supposed sexual irregularity, the City of Reform is less a city than an organic community, the English people restored to their 'natural' condition.[34] The final few pages of *The Political Pilgrim's Progress* constitute a checklist of radical causes and solutions.

Within this collective framework the narrative foregrounds particular abuses that reflect the author's pet hatreds and intellectual specialisms. While the repressive state apparatus of the Whigs is paraded in front of the reader in all its grotesque grandeur, it is the unseen power of financial institutions which merits special attention. The Utopian quest of Radical is countered by the Dystopian ascendancy of paper money. The debt that Doubleday owed to Cobbett is once again manifest here. Cobbett believed that Pitt's introduction of paper currency during the Napoleonic wars fuelled speculation, national debt, high taxes and the mortgaging of the nation's future wealth to stockjobbers, fundholders and bankers. Only a democratically elected government could demolish this rotten edifice of parasitism. Without a reform of the State, 'real' money would remain another lost freedom. Cobbett predicted accurately that Peel's Currency Bill of 1819, which promised the restoration of metal currency within a few years, would lead to a crash rather than an improvement. In Doubleday's writings on political economy, 1819 is memorable for Peel's bill rather than Peterloo.[35] *The Political Pilgrim's Progress* transforms this radical critique of finance into a demonology of skulduggery and mystifying jargon which reaches its apotheosis in the monstrous Political Apollyon. This creature is not an allegory of the denial of political rights; it is an embodiment of the tools of financial power: paper money and the enigmatic symbols of the stock market. Radical's defeat of Political Apollyon represents more than a thinly veiled argument for physical force Chartism (the cowardly Moral Force dies in the first encounter). The victory is a Cobbettite fantasy which warns the reader that political reform will be ineffectual without the reform of unelected financial institutions, the powerbase of capitalism. Significantly, the final conflict is fought right outside the gates of the City of Reform. The reader familiar with Bunyan would know that it was possible to fail at the last moment. It may be the case that Chartism responded to such pressures by including withdrawal of savings (intended to create a run on the banks, a threat used effectively in the Reform Bill agitation) as one of the unused 'ulterior measures' of the summer of 1839. But the Cobbettite analysis of capitalist oppression remained on the margins of radical discourse. Perhaps the conception of the ruling class as a swindling coalition of aristocrats and financiers was regarded as populist, old-fashioned and too remote from the common experience of Whig power (it would not be easy to explain the evil of workhouses by invoking 'omnium' or 'scrip', and Doubleday does not attempt this when Radical and his family are thrown into the Castle of Despair). But seen from the present day, the idea that real power resides in unregulated, unelected financial institutions seems depressingly accurate. Political Apollyon bestrides the world like a colossus.

The same degree of respect cannot be accorded to the anti-Semitic tone of the demonology, regardless of its acceptability at the time. The personification of usury and greed is the creeping, disreputable Jew of traditional caricature, complete with a pantomime accent. The underlying reasons for the revival of popular anti-Semitism in nineteenth-century radicalism needs further research. Not that radicals were the only culprits, of course. Doubleday's racism may have been bolstered by the success of Dickens's *Oliver Twist* (1837-38). But Fagin is a low-life crook, not a spokesman for the banks. In *The Political Pilgrim's Progress* the Jew figures are constructed as the shuffling operatives and physically repulsive representatives of the financial system (though we never see the non-Jewish members of this conspiracy). The Jewish characters have no precedent in Bunyan or Swift. The Jewish villains are the racist stereotypes of Cobbett, synonymous with exploitation and unscrupulous accumulation. The *Northern Liberator* became markedly anti-Semitic when Doubleday and Blakey took over the paper. Anti-Semitism is present in some of the paper's editorials and in reports of Doubleday's speeches.[36] But the most lurid treatment of the offensive against Jews is to be found in *The Political Tale of a Tub*, first published in the *Northern Liberator* in late 1839 and issued separately in 1840. A reworking of the Swiftian original, it charts the political history of Britain from the Glorious Revolution of 1688 to the present. The original roles of Peter, Martin and Jack (who represent the Catholic, Anglican and Dissenting religions) are replaced by Bill (Tory), Charley (Whig) and Dick (radicalism, the people). The real problems begin when Bill tries to pay off debts incurred in the Napoleonic wars. He mortgages his father John Bull's estate to Mordecai the Jew. Before long Mordecai and his tribe have made themselves at home on the estate:

> They drank his wine; intrigued with his servant girls; lamed his horses; shot his game; criticized his housekeeping; bribed his butler; and swore that bowlegged Moses, the eldest son of one of them, should marry Lord Bill's daughter. (p. 66)

The infestation remains when Charley comes to power. Charley introduces the 'bloodhound' or Rural Police Bill as a desperate act 'to preserve the throats of himself and Jews, who now filled the hall' (p. 84). With the chronology now up to date, the narrative becomes Utopian as the United States intervenes in the situation by undermining paper currency and installing Dick in government (the authors claim at the outset that paper money with its 'sorceries, delusions and devilries' [p. iv] is the villain of the story). Dick's first act is to expel the Jews. The scenes that follow can only be described as a pogrom, a fantasy of ethnic cleansing. Dick encourages the tenants of the estate to take revenge for all the years of exploitation:

> The word was no sooner spoken than it was done; every human being on the estate seemed to enjoy the drumming out of these usurious, swindling and blasphemous rascals who had so long fed upon their vitals ... such a hunt commenced as the Bull estate never saw. The tenants seemed to rack their invention how to revenge themselves on villainous usurers. One fellow they tied between two pigs and set them to pull opposite ways; another they tarred and feathered ... the remainder, after being pelted with rotten eggs and garbage, and kicked, and buffeted, and worried, and pummelled nearly to death, got off the estate. (pp. 88-9)

This makes *The Political Pilgrim's Progress* seem tame.[37] Although Radical and his son use abusive language and threaten violence, the exclusion of Jews from the City of Reform is simply noted as a fact (Jews were not legally emancipated until 1858). Similarly, neither tale attempts to explain the Jewish dominance of financial power; it is simply assumed to be a racial instinct. There is insufficient space here to trace the actual social evolution of Jews in Britain in the early nineteenth century. The extent to which the perceived preponderance of Jews in money-lending institutions had a basis in reality has yet to be proven.[38] A useful sociological line of investigation may be to apply Weber's notion of 'pariah capitalism' to the situation. This is the process whereby a socially and politically excluded group can only excel or serve the State in disreputable or unpopular forms of economic activity, a clear 'double standard'.[39] This social process could explain the motivation of popular anti-Semitism at this time, though it could never excuse it. Nor was it the case that all radicals accepted the stereotype of the grasping usurer. George W. M. Reynolds was one of the few radicals of the period to outspokenly attack anti-Semitism: 'Talk of the usury of the Jews — look at the usury practised by Christians! Look at the rapacity of Christian lawyers!' This attack, launched from the pages of his hugely popular serial *The Mysteries of London* in 1847, earned Reynolds the praise of the *Jewish Chronicle*.[40] But the depressing reality is that anti-Semitism remained an ingrained if minor feature of mainstream Chartist discourse. Wheeler's *Sunshine and Shadow* is also tainted by its presence.[41] It seems that the radical version of popular nationalism could not dispense with the need for the absolute Other.

But there are other casualties of the nationalist vision. Radical dismisses Mr Cant Humanity's concern for West Indian slavery as pious hypocrisy: 'I postpone my interest in black people two thousand miles off' (p. 22). Radical is sceptical about any scheme of reform which will not allow him to support his wife and family. His incorruptibility is based firmly on partriarchal principles. At first sight, the fact that his wife and children accompany him may seem an improvement on Bunyan:

> Now he had not run far from his own door, but his wife and children perceiving it began to cry after him to return; but the man put his finger in his ears, and ran on crying, 'Life, eternal life.' So he looked not back behind him, but fled towards the middle of the plain. (p. 41)

The Political Pilgrims' Progress would therefore be an accurate title for the story if it were not for the fact that Radical's wife is an insubstantial, silent and often invisible character. She is most conspicuous (and most needed by the narrative) in the Castle of Despair episode, which grotesquely exposes the way the workhouse system separated family members. With this anti-Poor Law statement out of the way, Radical's wife fades into the background. She never participates in the numerous verbal encounters which punctuate the journey. When physical force is required her stereotypically feminine weakness contrasts with her son's courage (the other children are rarely mentioned). He is the fledgling warrior who proves his masculine prowess by chasing off the Jew and acting as his father's lieutenant in the combat with Political Apollyon. In order to intensify the allegorical recommendation of physical force, the story presents the character Moral Force as an effeminate wimp:

> *Moral-force.*—I hope to make my way amongst the intelligent and educated, by dint of soft persuasion, and a copious flow of tender tears.
> *Radical.*—I am afraid you are relying on a broken reed.
> *Moral-force.*—I think otherwise. But, pray what is that long thing you are carrying in your hand?
> *Radical.*—That is a musket and bayonet given to me by the good Shepherds of the Delectable Mountains, who said I was not to use it but when severely pressed for life and limb. Look at it; it is in capital order.
> *Moral-force.*—No, thank you; I cannot endure brute force. (p. 38)

The phallic humour is one of the more *risqué* satirical moments.

If some aspects of *The Political Pilgrim's Progress*'s political vision are severely compromised by present-day standards, other features of its narrative method are fruitful territory for the contemporary critic. In particular, the story's foregrounding of symbols, inscriptions, rituals, spectacles and songs reveals a self-consciousness about the political power of writing, art and culture. The story does more than subject the 'occult art' of politics (p. 17) to the radical process of decoding, debunking and demystifying. Corrupt or ineffectual symbols are counterpointed by radical symbols. Radical is converted when 'two or three men came into the *City of Plunder*, bearing in their hands certain inscriptions' (p. 18). Immediately after Radical is dragged out of the Slough of Despond by two strangers who 'held in their hands the *Charter of Freedom*' (p. 20) he meets Mr Cant Humanity who 'was heavily laden with petitions, remonstrances, and projects' (p. 21). Talkatives's obfuscating verbosity follows Radical's song of freedom. Similarly, when Radical has dismissed Temporary and Expediency, who 'had their pockets all stuffed with papers, containing plans for different ways to arrive at the immortal city, than that which had long been established', he bursts into song (p. 36). A good deal of paper circulates through the narrative, most of it symbolizing intellectual and moral bankruptcy. Ironically, this phoney paper economy includes newspapers. In Scientific-place Radical sees 'thousands of sheets flying in the air, like flakes of snow, and eagerly seized on by the people below' (p. 44). The apotheosis of bogus paper power is of course paper money. In the City of Reform there is 'no such thing as a stock exchange, or a saving bank, or a bank note' (p. 59).

Radical's view of Benthamite rationalism is that 'codification may be a very fine thing' but all abstract thought must be judged by results on the ground: 'Radical had a natural dislike to all obscure, cloudy and mysterious talk' (p. 27). When he is in a 'cloudy' place, the Delectable mountains, he is shown the reformers' monument and the temple of constitutional law, shrines of radical constitutionalism. These contrast with the false 'column of Reform', which represents sham-radicalism, and with the 'huge and strange' Marcus monument. So memorialism is both celebrated and undermined. In the City of Reform there is 'no erecting of monuments to men who, if remembered at all, ought to be remembered only to their shame' (p. 58). Public culture must be democratic.

With its glaring weaknesses and intriguing strengths, *The Political Pilgrim's Progress* is a testimony to the rich contradictions which energized radical discourse in the Chartist period.

Notes

1. See the advert on the front page of the *Northern Liberator*, 9 May 1839. The pamphlet version can be found in the British Library.
2. Joan Hugman, paper delivered at the Chartism Day conference, Birmingham University, 12 September 1998.
3. The extent of this opposition can be judged by the fact that Robert Blakey published a letter on the front page of the *Newcastle Standard* (18 March 1837) attacking the operations of the Morpeth Poor Law Guardians, even though he was himself a member. I am grateful to Joan Hugman for directing me to this source.
4. The source for information about Beaumont is William H. Maehl's entry in Joseph O. Boylen and Norbert J. Gossman, eds, *Biographical*

Dictionary of Modern British Radicals. Volume 2. 1830-1870 (Brighton: Harvester, 1984).

5. See the entry for the *Northern Liberator* in Royden Harrison, Gillian B. Woolven and Robert Duncan, *The Warwick Guide to British Labour Periodicals 1790-1870: A Check List* (Brighton: Harvester, 1977).

6. James Curran and Jean Seaton, *Power Without Responsibility: The press and broadcasting in Britain* (London and New York: Routledge, 1997), chapter 1 *passim.*

7. The three *Northern Liberator* reprints I have located are: *Northern Lights* (1838), a collection of miscellaneous pieces by Doubleday (initialled 'T.D.') and others; *The Political Pilgrim's Progress* (1839); and *The Political Tale of a Tub. With Annotations Critical and Explanatory by the Right Hon. Sir John Cam Hobhouse, Bart., MP., etc. and John Bowring Lld., F.S.S. A.S.S. etc.* (1840). The pamphlets are attributed to 'The Writers of the Northern Liberator' rather than individual authors. All three were published at the office of the *Northern Liberator* by its printer John Bell.

8. See Curran and Seaton, *Power Without Responsibility*, for the most recent confirmation. Other relevant sources include: Raymond Williams, 'Radical and/or respectable', in Richard Boston, ed., *The Press We Deserve* (London: Routledge and Kegan Paul, 1970); Virginia Berridge, 'Popular Sunday papers and mid-Victorian society', in George Boyce, James Curran and Pauline Wingate, eds, *Newspaper History from the Seventeenth Century to the Present Day* (London: Constable, 1978); David Vincent, *Literacy and Popular Culture in England 1750-1914* (Cambridge: Cambridge University Press, 1989); Kevin Gilmartin, *Print Politics* (Cambridge: Cambridge University Press, 1996).

9. Robert Blakey merged the *Northern Tribune* with the *London Champion* in May 1840 but this failed to save the paper and it closed abruptly in December 1840, despite its strong base of support in the Northern Political Union.

10. Curran and Seaton, *Power Without Responsibility*, p. 17.

11. Information about Blakey from D. J. Rowe's entry in Boylen and Gossman, eds, *Biographical Dictionary of Modern British Radicals*. See also Dorothy Thompson, *The Chartists: Popular Politics in the Industrial Revolution* (Aldershot: Wildwood House, 1984), pp. 165-6.

12. Raymond Williams, 'The press and popular culture: an historical perspective', in Boyce, Curran and Wingate, eds, *Newspaper History from the Seventeenth Century to the Present Day.*

13. H. Gustav Klaus, *The Literature of Labour. 200 Years of Working Class Writing* (Brighton: Harvester, 1985), pp. 51-2.

14. For example, 'The Three Bastilles' by 'T.D.' in *Northern Lights* uses the same satirical vocabulary as *The Political Pilgrim's Progress*, such as 'Paperkite Buildings' for the Stock Exchange.

15. For information about Doubleday I have used: R. C. Gammage, *History of the Chartist Movement 1837-1854* (1894; rptd London: Merlin Press, 1976); George Jacob Holyoake's entry on Doubleday in the *Dictionary of National Biography*, vol. 15 (1888); W. E. Adams, *Memoirs of a Social Atom* (1903; rptd New York: Augustus M. Kelley, 1968); William H. Maehl's entry on Doubleday in Boylen and Gossman, eds, *Biographical Dictionary of Modern British Radicals*; Dorothy Thompson, *The Chartists*.

16. *Northern Liberator*, 30 March 1839; 6 April 1839.

17. The claim is made by the Thomas Ainge Devyr in *The Odd Book of the Nineteenth Century* (1882; rptd New York and London: Garland, 1986); see chapters 11-13. Devyr was an Irish nationalist and a reporter for the *Northern Liberator*. He remembers Doubleday and Blakey as 'men [who] would have saved England' (p. 159). Devyr claims that 60,000 pikes were sold in the summer of 1839, and that insurrectionary plans were still being made in early 1840. While Devyr's reputation as a reliable historical source has been questioned, Dorothy Thompson shows that Newcastle was not alone in plotting armed uprisings. See D. Thompson, *The Early Chartists* (London and Basingstoke: Macmillan, 1971), pp. 18-26. Devyr fled to America to avoid arrest.

18. The British Library has 24 items by Doubleday, one indication of the extensiveness of his writings.

19. In an essay with the wonderful title 'Is Aristocratic or Democratic Society most Favourable to Mental Excellence' Doubleday praises Cobbett as 'the most sagacious observer, the finest political writer, the most honest man, and sincere patriot, that, perhaps, [England] ever produced, or may produce for centuries to come'. See *The Touchstone: A Series of Letters on Social, Literary, and Political Subjects* (London, 1863), p. 92.

20. I refer here to W. D. Rubinstein's well-known essay 'British Radicalism and the 'Dark Side' of Populism', in *Elites and the Wealthy in Modern Britain* (Brighton: Harvester, 1987).

21. *Dictionary of National Biography*, vol. 15, pp. 255-6.

22. John Bunyan, *The Pilgrim's Progress* (Harmondsworth: Penguin, 1975). Subsequent page references are put in parentheses.

23. Bunyan's importance for the formation of working-class consciouness is discussed by E. P. Thompson in *The Making of the English Working Class* (1963; Harmondsworth: Penguin, 1977), pp. 34-8. Louis James notes that Evangelical reformers overcame their distaste for fiction by using 'weak imitations' of Bunyan to target working-class readers. See L. James, *Fiction for the Working Man 1830-1850* (1963; Harmondsworth: Penguin, 1974), p. 142.

24. John James Bezer, *The Autobiography of One of the Chartist Rebels of 1848*, in David Vincent, ed., *Testaments of Radicalism. Memoirs of Working Class Politicians 1790-1885* (London: Europa, 1977), p. 167.

Thomas Cooper remembered *Pilgrim's Progress* as 'my book of books' in his autobiography. See T. Cooper, *Life of Thomas Cooper: Written by Himself* (London: Hodder and Stoughton, 1872), p. 22. Those radicals who inclined towards freethinking and infidelism made a point of rejecting Bunyan's influence. See Francis Place, *The Autobiography of Francis Place*, ed. Mary Thale (Cambridge: Cambridge University Press, 1972), p. 46.

25.   Q. D. Leavis, *Fiction and The Reading Public* (1932; Harmondsworth: Peregrine Books, 1979), p. 89.

26.   Southey is quoted in the Introduction to *The Pilgrim's Progress*, ed. N. H. Keeble (Oxford: Oxford University Press, 1998), p. xx.

27.   Ibid.

28.   Q. D. Leavis, *Fiction and The Reading Public*, pp. 91, 101.

29.   E. P. Thompson, *The Making of the English Working Class*, p. 37.

30.   *The Political Tale of a Tub* was serialized in the *Northern Liberator* between 18 October and 13 December, 1839, and reissued in pamphlet form in February 1840 as *The Political Tale of a Tub. With Annotations Critical and Explanatory by the Right Hon. Sir John Cam Hobhouse, Bart., MP., etc. and John Bowring Lld., F.S.S. A.S.S. etc.* The connection of Hobhouse and Bowring to the *Northern Liberator* is intriguing but as yet has not been traced.

31.   *The Book of Murder* by 'Marcus' was in circulation in late 1838 (as evidence of this, Joseph Rayner Stephens declaimed it in some of his speeches at that time). The pamplet is a Malthusian and Poor Law satire which advocates gassing every child after the second-born as a method of population control (in Ireland only one child is allowed), a clear borrowing from Swift's *A Modest Proposal*. Its authorship is still disputed (see the forthcoming reprint of Marcus in Gregory Claey's series of Chartist tracts to be published by Pickering in 2000). The *Northern Liberator* was typical of many outraged radical responses to Marcus, claiming the text was a vicious Whig attack on the poor. It covered the issue extensively in early 1839. One of its rebuttals (2 March 1839) took the form of an illustrated mock-lecture 'Marcus Unveiled', in which the virtues of carbonic-acid gassing are demonstrated by a scientist to a respectable audience. The scene and the accompanying woodcut were recycled in *The Political Tale of a Tub*. Ironically, *The Book of Murder* was probably a radical, anti-Whig satire. The putative author is one of the three Poor Law Commissioners, and the Address to the Reader places the blame for starvation on the 'rapacity of capitalists' (p. 7).

32.   One possible source for *The Political Pilgrim' Progress* could be an 1820 satire entitled *The New Pilgrim's Progress; or, A Journey to Jerusalem* (London: printed for W. Wright, 1820). This is one of the numerous skits on the Queen Caroline affair. The story is told from a loyalist, anti-Caroline point of view, and focuses on her sexual indiscretions. For the

influence of Augustan satire on radicals in the post-war period, see Ian Dyck, *William Cobbett and rural popular culture* (Cambridge: Cambridge University Press, 1992), p. 23.

33.   The literature on this topic is large. See, for example: E. P. Thompson, *The Making of the English Working Class*, chapter 4 *passim*; Gareth Stedman-Jones, 'Rethinking Chartism', in *Languages of Class* (Cambridge: Cambridge University Press, 1983); Patrick Joyce, *Visions of the People: Industrial England and the Question of Class 1848-1914* (Cambridge: Cambridge University Press, 1991) and *Democratic Subjects: The self and the social in nineteenth-century England* (Cambridge: Cambridge University Press, 1994); James Vernon, *Politics and the People: A Study in English Political Culture, c. 1815-1867* (Cambridge: Cambridge University Press, 1993); *idem*, ed., *Re-reading the Constitution: New Narratives in the Political History of England's Long Nineteenth Century* (Cambridge: Cambridge University Press, 1996); James Epstein, *Radical Expression: Political Language, Ritual and Symbol in England, 1790-1830* (Oxford: Oxford University Press, 1994); John Belchem, *Popular Radicalism in Nineteenth Century Britain* (New York: St Martin's Press, 1995).

34.   See Anne Janowitz, *Lyric and Labour in the Romantic Tradition* (Cambridge: Cambridge University Press, 1998) for a recent study of the communitarian influence on radical writing. For Cobbett, see Ian Dyck, *William Cobbett and rural popular culture*.

35.   Doubleday also attacks Peel's bill for having the support of Ricardo, a 'rich Jew stock-jobber'. See T. Doubleday, *A Financial, Monetary and Statistical History of England, from the Revolution of 1688 to the Present Times* (London: Effingham Wilson, 1847), p. 243. Doubleday's most Cobbettite treatment of this theme is an essay, 'Has the system of paper credit been beneficial to those who adopted it?', included in *The Touchstone*.

36.   For example, at the celebratory dinner in Doubleday's honour in April 1839, he alarmed the young women in the audience by describing their fiancés as 'mortgaged to the Jew swindlers, and not one shilling of [their] earnings shall you enjoy till Shylock has had his pound of flesh'. A leader in November 1840 accuses the *Times* of being 'the organ of THE JEWS'. See the *Northern Liberator*, 6 April 1839; 7 November 1840.

37.   Hobhouse's comment on this scene is intriguing but over-clever: 'Prejudice of the most violent sort peeps out in every sentence; so much so, I think, as in some measure to neutralise itself' (p. 45).

38.   The best introduction to this topic is W. D. Rubinstein's detailed survey of the Jewish presence in Britain, *A History of the Jews in the English-Speaking World: Great Britain* (Basingstoke: Macmillan, 1996), chapters 1-2. The Rothschilds were very prominent bankers who provided some of the finance for the Napoleonic wars. Lionel Rothschild (1808-79) also

campaigned for emancipation of the Jews in Britain. The 'Epistle Dedicatory' of *The Political Tale of a Tub* praises the American President van Buren for his 'holy war against the ever-damned Jew' (p. v). This refers to the fact that in the late 1830s van Buren tried to wrest control of government finances away from private banks.

39.   Max Weber, *Economy and Society. An Outline of Interpretive Sociology*, eds Guenther Roth and Claus Wittich, 3 vols (New York: Bedminster Press, 1968), vol 2, p. 614. See also Max Weber, *The Protestant Ethic and the Spirit of Capitalism* (1930; London: Unwin University Books, 1974), in which Weber argues that 'pariah capitalism' was a pre-modern form of 'speculatively oriented adventurous capitalism' which progressive (bourgeois) Puritan capitalists associated with aristocratic monopolies, wars and government contracts, in contradistinction to the 'rational organization of labour and capital' (pp. 39, 165-6, 271). Radical anti-Semitism may have flowed from the belief that this backward, irrational form of capitalism was still dominant; Cobbett, of course, believed that an even earlier stage of capitalist development existed which was less exploitative.

40.   *Jewish Chronicle*, 19 March 1847, pp. 101-2.

41.   See Editor's introduction to *Sunshine and Shadow*, n. 13. One measure of the currency of anti-Semitism in the radical movement is the use of anti-Semitic slogans on Chartist banners. An illustration of this is the rally in Manchester which celebrated the release of Peter MacDouall and John Watkins from prison in August 1840. The 'splendid banner of the Wigan Association' included a picture of the British Lion trampling on 'Starvation Bastiles, Debts, Funds, Jew Jobbers, Aristocracy, Shopocracy, White Slavery, and State Paupers'. See the *Northern Star*, 22 August 1840. This account of the rally is reprinted in Dorothy Thompson, *The Early Chartists*, pp. 139-74. While there has been some excellent work in recent years on Chartist flags and banners, the issue of anti-Semitism has been neglected. See Paul Pickering, *Chartism and the Chartists in Manchester and Salford* (Basingstoke: Macmillan, 1995), part 2; James Vernon, *Politics and the People*, pp. 119-26.

The Political Pilgrim's Progress

PART I

As we one day were indulging in a kind of political reverie, on the severe and multiplied miseries and distresses of this country, we insensibly fell into a most profound nap, and we dreamed a dream of a deep and lively interest.

We thought we saw a large and populous city, called the "CITY OF PLUNDER." Its edifices and buildings were of the most mottled and varied description; some splendid palaces, and others mean hovels of mud. The city had a great profusion of guilded domes, and fanes, and its appearance at a distance, especially under the subdued rays of a setting sun, was the most imposing and striking imaginable. Its people seemed active, industrious, and enterprising; but there appeared a singular custom amongst them, which greatly marred their social happiness and unanimity, and this was, that nearly one half of the inhabitants made a practice of putting their hands into the pockets of the other half, and taking their money from them. There was *law*, indeed, for this singular custom; but then, upon enquiry, it was found that this law had been made exclusively by the persons who claimed the exercise of this odd privilege. This law was fortified by a thing called "*government*," which professed an intense interest in the happiness and welfare of the people, but stoutly maintained, at the same time, that they were not able to take care of their own concerns, but that it had a singular knack and skill in this occult art. This thing "*government*" always vehemently affirmed that the mode of making one half of the people work for and support the other half, was the very perfection of human wisdom. Once every year it called divers persons together into a certain building in the city, and they concocted various public declarations and ordinances, which were promulgated, with great pomp, to the people touching this great truth; and which declarations and ordinances contained rules, both general and particular, how one division of the people might take the money from the other, and on this account these public acts were designated with the imposing epithets of the "wisdom of parliament".

It became obvious, however, that this custom amongst the inhabitants did not operate favourably upon their social condition. One half of the people were doomed to a state of misery, vice, and want, while the other part, who took their money from them, were rioting in wickedness, sensuality, and ostentatious splendour. Murmurings and discontents prevailed to a considerable extent; but the thing called "*government*" always declared that these evils were necessary ones, and that to complain and remonstrance was a grievous sin committed against another sacred thing, called "the constitution by law established." Divers confabulations, called "*debates*" ensued on the disputed topics; and some part of the city always indulged the hope that these outpourings of the lips would be followed by some decided advantages to the whole of the people; but in this they had been cruelly disappointed.

Now we saw in our dream that two or three strange men came into the *City of Plunder*, bearing in their hands certain inscriptions, and called the especial attention of that portion of the people who were plundered to the import of these inscriptions. These persons pointed to a distant city, called the "City of Reform," where the people lived under just and equal laws enacted by themselves, and enjoyed to the full all the fruits of their own labour and skill. When these strangers had explicitly stated their views, we thought we saw a strong labouring man with his wife and ragged children, express a determination no longer to live in the "City of Plunder," but to set out for the "City of Reform," under the guidance and direction of the strangers. His name was *Radical*, and he had a weighty load on his back, which he had endured for many years, and which materially impaired his strength, and absorbed his resources, in spite of all his efforts.— The strangers made him fully aware of the dangers and difficulties of the journey; but he was not disheartened; on the contrary, he cheered up the spirits of his wife and children by singing the following ditty.—

> Where'er we shall our pathway take—
> Thro' wood, thro' wild, thro' bush, thro' brake—
> Our honesty shall be our stay,
> And virtue guide us on our way.
>
> By night, by day; by wild, by wood;
> By rock, by desert and by flood;
> Beneath the ever-beaming ray,
> Or when the night o'ercasts the day;
>
> 'Mid tempests wild; 'mid savage cares,
> That echo to ten thousand waves;
> Still in our cause shall be our trust;
> Death hath no terors for the just!
>
> 'Mid perils we our course may bend,
> But Providence shall be our friend.
> Hell is beneath for those who fall;
> God, for the good, is over all.

When Radical's intention became generally known in the "*City of Plunder*," it created a considerable sensation. The party who had long enjoyed the privilege of putting their hands into their neighbour's pockets, were composed of two sects, one called the "*outs*" and the other the "*ins*!"—They cordially hated and abused each other, except when the other inhabitants of the city complained, and then these sects were hand in glove. Now the "outs" and the "ins" had various consultations about Radical's departure for the "City of Reform." The "outs" maintained that there was no such city as that of "Reform;" on the contrary, it was the "City of Destruction," and the people who lived in it were called "destructives," "revolutionists," and "rebels;" while the "ins" thought there *might be* such a city as "Reform," but it was at such a long distance, and the road was so intricate and beset with brambles and thorns, that it was dangerous for any one to set out on such a journey just at *this peculiar time.* They did not like to deny the existence of this renowned city, but at the present time they were comfortably off themselves, and thought the people who complained, were labouring under an impatience of change. They, the "ins," solemnly declared that the whole people of the city, that if they found themselves not so comfortably situated as they thought their merits demanded, they would have no great objections to set out with Radical to the new country; but for the present they felt no *great* disposition to change.

When Radical and his family were leaving the city, they met with with Mr. Worldlywiseman, who was just on his way to his daily occupation. He enquired of Radical the end and object of his journey, and expressed surprise to see so formal a preparation for another country. The following dialogue then took place between the Pilgrim and him.

Worldlywiseman.—Pray, Radical, what has made you so discontented with your lot in the "City of Plunder," as to induce you to leave the place of your nativity, and where you have spent so many years of your life?

Radical.—Why, Sir, the motive is an urgent one. I have for a long time been compelled to bear this load upon my back, and I am not only, therefore, prevented from making my wife and family so comfortable as I could wish, but I am subjected to much real personal suffering besides. I am anxious, on this account, to seek for a little ease.

Worldlywiseman.—Ease, did you say? Why, sir, you are just going the road to misery and disappointment. Rolling stones gather no moss. Agitation and change are two things I heartily detest; they are completely subversive of our worldly happiness and respectability. I would never recommend them to any friend of mine.

Radical.—Well, Sir, no change can be a change for the worse to me. I am half starved myself; my wife and children cry for bread, and I have none to give them; and you see, with your own eyes, our helpless and ragged condition. I know from bitter experience that my stationary habits of life have hither brought no moss to me.

Worldlywiseman.—You common people are always so discontented and repining that there is no satisfying you. All men cannot be rich, Providence has ordered matters otherwise; therefore, you should learn patience, and humility; happiness, let me tell you, lies in the mind; and if you will only be prevailed upon to think yourself happy, you will soon find the sharp sting is taken out of your temporary evils.

Radical.—Part of this may be true, but hunger and nakedness are but indifferent stimulants to the virtues of patience and humility. I do not wish to be rich, in the ordinary sense of the word. I wish to have a just and reasonable compensation for my labour, and to have the privilege of keeping what I do earn for the use of my wife and children. I should like to change places with you in society, and then, perhaps, you would see how comfort and happiness are to be promoted under the circumstances I am placed in.

Worldlywiseman.—Oh! that is quite a different thing; I see you are bitten with the rabid mania of the day. Good bye, and a pleasant journey to you. I see my friend, Mr. Lickspittle, has an order for me.

After Radical and his family lost sight of Mr. Worldlywiseman, they bent their steps towards a flat and swampy district. Here it became difficult and tiresome to travel. The load on the Political Pilgrim's back began to feel exceedingly heavy, and his wife and children rather lagged behind. As they moved slowly forward they came in sight of an immense bog, called "the Political Slough of Despond." This was an appalling and disheartening object; and yet is was necessary to pass right through it before they could regain the right path to the "City of Reform." The scenery and objects around were the most dreary and melancholy imaginable. One immense swampy marsh presented itself, with only here and there a little tuft of vegetable life, just sufficient to beguile the hapless wanderer into a fatal security of a sure footing. The heavens seemed to frown upon the whole aspect, and to mark it out as an especial object of vengeance and hate. The sloping edges of the Slough were thickly crowded with reptiles, and obnoxious and troublesome vermin of all kinds, together with gibbets, skulls, and dead men's bones. Indeed, this Slough was the natural receptacle of every thing filthy and impure from the "City of Plunder," and was not susceptible of the slightest improvement from human skill. Radical had to prepare himself to go through it, together with his wife and family, and the prospect was dreary and disconsolate enough, for there was no one to assist or comfort. However, he took courage, and ventured into the Slough, taking all possible care to lend his wife and children every degree of assistance. The struggle was an arduous one, the whole family appearing at one time to be near the point of perishing, but they were supported by a voice from the opposite side of the Slough, counselling them to persevere, and be of good heart, till assistance could be rendered. When Radical and his family got near to the opposite side, they espied two men standing near the edge, close to a guide post, which had the words written on it, "the straight road to the City of Reform." These two individuals held in their hands the *Charter of Freedom*, which every inhabitant of that famous city has presented to him when he becomes a citizen of it. These two strangers lent Radical their aid to get out of the Slough, and attended to the comfort of his wife and family.

We saw in our dream that when the Political Pilgrim and his family got in some measure comforted, they set out on their journey, and directed their steps towards the City of Reform. They had a heavy and long hill to climb, and as they were bending their steps upwards, they met a man in great haste coming down the hill, and making his way towards the City of Plunder. He had a singular dress, spoke in soft and tender accents, and seemed to feel a deep interest in the object of his mission. His name was Mr. Cant Humanity, and he was heavily laden with petitions, remonstrances, and projects, for the immediate abolition of all kinds of misery and oppression amongst people of a black colour. When Radical saw him, he civilly moved his hat, and asked him if he could relieve him, or give him some advice, for the prosecution of his journey; when the following dialogues took place:—

Mr. Cant Humanity.—My dear friend, gladly would I advise you, for deeply do I feel interested in your welfare, and that of all the human race besides—but to give men advice is sometimes no easy matter!

Radical.—How so, Sir?

Mr. Cant Humanity.—Why, my dear friend, when men have fixed their affections upon pursuits, which after all, may only be built on clouds, and are the dreams of an excited and heated fancy, to undeceive or to reason with, looks like an injury—and, God forbid, I should appear harsh to any man—oh! no! I am too sensible of the frailty of our common nature.

Radical.—Sir, I assure you that no advice you can give, will be received as an injury by me! I am bound for the City of Reform. Can you assist me on my road?

Mr. Cant Humanity.—We are all brethren, and must, when we can, assist each other. You are bound, you say, for the City of Reform. Alas! my dear friend, words are not things. Can you be, or are you sure, that such a city as you speak of exists; or, if you were then, are you sure that you would have changed your situation for the better?

Radical.—Why should I doubt it, Sir. No one has ever yet denied the reality of the city; though some certainly do say, it cannot be reached, and others, that if it were, it is all a cheat!

Mr. Cant Humanity.—My dear brother, I do not presume to decide, but deceptions are abroad, and beset us on all sides. We are erring creatures, and to be content with our own lot, and to try to better that of others, is our safest course in this vale of tears. Many persons, you are aware, have set out in search of the city you mention, but none have yet reached it; many have never returned, and those who have returned, have rued the hour they set out—added burthens, and diminished respectability, have been the fruits.

Radical.—How so, Sir ?

Mr. Cant Humanity.—How so, my friend, Radical? Why, is it not easy to see *how*? You set out on this endless, toilsome, journey, with your wife and children. You are, as you say — and from my heart I regret it — heavily laden. Even so, you fall by the way as all your predecessors have done, and how do you return? worn out — stripped of all — shoeless, hatless, coatless — your poor wife dying broken hearted, — your children foot-sore, all of you covered with mud, and no one to sympathise with you. My dear brother, I respect your motives, but doubt your understanding. Leave this fruitless quest and try something tangible. Now, there are the poor blacks in the West Indies, no one doubts their degraded state, let us rescue them — and then —

Radical.—Sir, I can pity suffering wherever it be; but I must confess, my humanity begins at home. When I see my poor children and wife and feel my burthen, preventing me doing my duty by them, as I wish to do, I postpone my interest in black people two thousand miles off. No, Sir, I must go on. Can you assist me?

Mr. Cant Humanity.—Gladly would I do so, my dear friend, were it in my power, but man's means and time, are limited; we must submit to the decree of Providence. See all these documents, they all relate to state corporeal and spiritual of the poor Negro. Here is enough for one man, and this is only a small part of this great work!

Radical.—I am sorry you can do nothing for us Sir, but I do not despair.

Mr Cant Humanity.—Oh! by no means. I have no doubt your intentions are good, but I fear they are impracticable. I shall be happy to hear from you, and now wish you a good journey; be cautious, my dear friend, as to every step you take.

Now we see in our dream that when Mr. Cant Humanity had left Radical and his family, that the latter directed their steps towards a wicket-gate, at the entrance of which stood a small porter's lodge, at which they ventured to enquire the road to the City of Reform. It was kept by one Mr. Sincerity, who gladly directed the Pilgrim to the right path, and gave him such assistance and counsel as he required. Radical had not travelled far till he met with two men, going to the City of Plunder, whose names were *Obstinate* and *Pliable*. They had both been so far on their journey to the City of Reform, but from divers reasons had turned their backs on it, and longed to return to their old quarters. *Obstinate* did not like to do as other men did, to think as other men thought, nor act in consort with other men; and *Pliable* became easily persuaded to change his course, whenever the slightest difficulty fell in the way. They both knocked at the wicket-gate, but there was no entrance for them.

PART II

Now we saw in our dream that Radical and his family were getting much enfeebled in their journey, and their means of living becoming scanty.—They were constrained, therefore, to ask subsistence by the way. This came to the knowledge of some official people in the neighbourhood, who carried the information to a large castle, called the "Castle of Despair," in which three despots resided, who were appointed by the ruling authorities in the City of Plunder, to oppress, and cruelly use, the poor, the aged, and unfortunate. This formidable castle, with its whole establishment of scouts and runners, was instituted for the express purpose of reducing the people of this country to live on a coarser kind of food, in order that their spirit might be humbled and broken, and that the idle and profligate might obtain more plunder from the industrious and virtuous. This griping system was considered, by the philosophers of the City of Plunder, to be a master stroke of policy; for it was strenuously maintained that all former legislators had greatly erred in supposing that good and substantial living was favourable to virtue, industry, and social happiness; whereas it was now clearly demonstrated, that to raise the national character to a truly "liberal" pitch, men must live on seaweed and grains, be clothed in rags, and dwell in mud cabins without an article of furniture.

This castle was notorious throughout the whole country for cruelty and crime. Those unfortunate persons who became inmates of it, were fed on the most loathsome food, not fit for even pigs to eat; they were subjected to severe and ignominious labour; men were separated from their wives, and their children from both; young women were shorn of their hair; a prison dress was put on every unfortunate victim; and their bodies, when dead, were given for dissection. Crimes of all sorts abounded in the Castle of Despair. It was one black and offensive sink of inconceivable enormities; and the owners of the domain were only one degree removed from devils incarnate.

We thought we saw Radical and his family taken up to the Castle of Despair, and brought before the three despots, when the following dialogue followed:—

Despots. What is your name, from whence do you come, and whither are you going?

Radical. My name is Radical, I come from the City of Plunder, and am on my way to the City of Reform.

Despots. You are lazy and profligate, and consequently discontented and fond of change. Your rags and numerous brats are a sure indication of your thoughtlessness and improvidence.

Radical. I am not aware of being lazy, profligate, or improvident. I laboured incessantly twelve hours every day in the week, lived on the most humble fare, spent nothing in the way of indulgence, and yet I could not keep my wife and family with the commonest articles of food and clothing out of my wages.

Despots. You committed an error in the first step of life. You took a wife before you had obtained a fortune to keep her, and you have gone on since peopling the world without placing yourself under that wholesome "moral restraint" which we teach, as the great and infallible preservative against misery and want.

Radical. I am not aware that I have violated any law, either of God or man, in taking to myself a wife. I see no reason why working men, whose labour creates every necessary and luxury of life, should be denied the pleasures and comforts of home.

Despots. You are impertinent, sir. We shall make you more civil before you leave us. You must be put on the tread-mill to grind oats for your gruel, your wife must be separated from you, and we shall place your children under the care of our matrons.

We saw in our dream that the three despots ordered Radical and his family to be brought into the castle, and immediately subjected to the cruel discipline of the place. The hair was shaved off his wife's head, his children sent to the care of some horrid unnatural wretches, and himself compelled to run with a bag of sand upon his back up and down stairs so many times a day; all this was inflicted to learn him to be industrious, careful, prudent, and moral. But the horrors he and his family endured were not the most galling parts of his sufferings. The moans, and cries, and lamentations, of the other inmates of the castle, afflicted him fully as much as his own personal troubles, and trials. During every hour of the night and day, the cries of suffering were heard, and the sun rose o'er the distant mountains only to mark one point in the endless circle of human woe.

By a fortunate concurrence of circumstances, Radical was enabled to have a few minutes interview with his wife. A concocted plan of escape was agreed on, and she contrived matters so as to get her children acquainted with the scheme. They and their mother made their escape, and the Pilgrim himself soon followed. Nothing could exceed the joy of the family when all were collected together, even under the most trying circumstances. They all wandered at night, and slept in the woods by day, lest they should be discovered by the scouts of the castle. At length, they reached a part of the roads out of the liberties of the Castle of Despair, and Radical's heart was so melted, that he burst forth with the following song:—

> Though rough and wild my way may be,
> I shall not grieve, whilst I am free,
> Nor o'er my journey's toll repine,
> While flowers, and fields, and skies, are mine.
>
> He, who can breathe the mountain air
> Whilst there is life shall not despair;
> The thirsty man shall find a spring,
> And wend along his way and sing;
>
> That God, who, in the wilderness;
> His chosen People still could bless,
> Shall help me with his hand divine,
> And give his aid to me and mine.
>
> The wild fruits and the cedars shade,
> Not for a few were given or made;
> The wild vine and the palm tree tall,
> By him who sowed were meant for all.
>
> Tho' poor and scant our fare may be,
> I'll toil and hope, for I am free,

I'll take content what nature gave,
Nor o'er despair, whilst not a slave.

After this the Pilgrim proceeded on his journey, but he had not got far from the Castle of Despair, till he fell in with one *Talkative*, who was an important personage at all public meetings, and who said he was going towards the City of Reform.—Radical was glad of a companion, and he and *Talkative* joined in the crack as they progressed on their journey.

Talkative.—I presume, Sir, that you have not read much as to the constitutionality of an enlightened and philanthropic modification of our legislative enactments. Good government, in its abstract essence, is a scientific occultation; the quintessence of intellectuality; the infinite perfectibility of social aggregation; the happy centralization of representative power; the combined volitions of emancipated intellects; the regulated development of political conglomerations; the united combination of universal sympathies; the infallible dispenser of transcendental advantages; the primeval precursor of indefinite domestic amelioration; the creative foster-father of national energies; the practical application of scientific codification; the concentrated momentum of extatic and sublimated humanity; the glorious effulgence of refined libertinism; the unextinguishable blaze of ardent and patriotic devolution; the patibulary horrification[1] of judicial excellence; the harmonious adaptation of civil and fraternal enterprises; the soft and modulated accentuation of the public voice; the peaceable incorruptibility of political elevation; the dulcet titilations of refined and senatorial speechifications; the legal logomachies[2] of liberal institutions; and the enlightened pathology of the body corporate. This is what I call a proper definition of good government.

Radical.—I must confess my inability to follow you in these learned matters; but my humble notion of a good government is, that it will let working men, like myself, enjoy the fruits of their industry.

Talkative.—Allow me, my kind Sir, to illustrate your position, with a scientific exemplification. This subject is redundant with rational investigation. Exorbitant fiscal exactions tend to produce national haemorrhage; to induce a social hemiplegia;[3] to effect an attenuated liquification of the state juices; to cause a constipated obstruction of the commercial ducts; to produce a squalid squamification[4] of national impoverishment; to check the insensible secretions of individual enterprise; to dilapidate and disperse the industrial accumulations of commerce; to check the creative power of productive capital; to weaken the concentrated energies of labour; to foster the bilious belchings of state corruptionists; to encourage the rapacious rascalities of fiscal extortioners; and to throw over the whole land the dark and shadowy mantle of chaotic obscuration.

Radical.—You seem well versed in the subject; but what I wish to see is, that I may have some share in the making—

Talkative.—Of the laws; begging your pardon for the interruption; but I have so long paid undivided attention to this subject, that whenever I hear it mentioned, I have luminous vivifications of its innate importance. The electoral extension of the suffrage, is the sagacious extension of political wisdom; it is the condensed superiority of legislative acumen; it is the prescriptive inheritance of patriotic individuality; it is the polarity of utilitarianism; and it is the bright and etherial effervescence of the general will.

Now, we saw that Radical was, in some degree, confounded with this eloquent torrent of his new companion, and he appeared not willing to provoke any further discussion. They both trudged forward on their journey, and in a short time overtook another traveller to the city of Reform, whose name was *Vanity. Talkative* and he soon scraped acquaintanceship, and entered into an animated debate on public matters. The Pilgrim and his family, however, left them to their own discussion, and took a night's shelter in a neat cottage by the way side, kept by one *Common Sense*, who was always of great service to all travellers. After supper, which had been plainly served, and during which his host made Radical drink a glass or two of fine home-brewed ale, the children having gone to bed with their mother, who was dreadfully fatigued with the journey, the following dialogue took place.

Common Sense.—Now, Radical, I should like to know your ideas as to this journey of your's, for I must tell you, that amongst your fellow-travellers are all sorts of notions and tales, as to this City of Reform. There was a family passed here last week, who called themselves the "transcendentals."[5] They travelled in a sort of curricle, and had a footman behind them; and when I asked them what they expected to find at the City of Reform, they told me that it was a city in the middle of which was a great square, in the centre of which was a statue of one Jeremy Bentham,[6] and that the streets were classified and codified in way surprising to think of. Well, they went on, and were followed by another odd fantastical man with great whiskers and mustachoes, who called himself Republican. He insisted that the City of Reform was governed by a Town Council of men who stood with their heels uppermost more wisely than upon their feet, and that nobody could enter it unless he stood the fire of a battery of guns loaded with oyster shells, of which the fishwomen of the city yearly accumulated great quantities.[7] Now, I want to hear your ideas.

Radical.—Truly, sir, I cannot understand the merits of either transcendental or republican. I have read somewhere that in the ancient republics they sometimes banished men by votes written on oyster shells, and for aught I know, codification may be a very fine thing. But to tell you my sincere opinion, I look at what a government *does*, not at what it is called. I have learned by bitter experience, that under the *name* and *form* of *liberty*, oppression the most horrid and tyrannical may take place. In short, sir, that government is best which takes least from the people, no matter what its *name* may be. A republic that took *fifty millions* would be an intolerable tyranny; a dictator who took only five would be a tolerably good governor. A free government is best, because there is security for its continuance, but all governments must be judged by what they *do*, not by name and form. In the City of Reform I hear there are hardly any taxes, and that satisfies me. That is my creed, sir.

Common Sense. And a plain creed it is. This creed of your's, Radical, pleases me better than anything I have heard for a long time. There is practical sense, there — so now good night, and pleasant dreams to both.

When morning arrived we saw in our dream that Radical and his wife and children being much revived and in high spirits, set out on their journey. Common Sense had given them much useful advice and many valuable directions, which they were determined to follow. In fact, there was something so winning in the tone and manner of their host, that Radical could not avoid putting implicit faith in all he said, so clear were his counsels, attended always with reasons so convincing. Radical had a natural dislike to all obscure, cloudy, mysterious talk, which experience taught him always boded some mischief or other. Consequently, he was delighted with the conversation of Common Sense, which, though plain, was lucid to a high degree.

As Radical was proceeding on his journey, ruminating on his entertainer's wholesome advice, he met a very ill-looking man coming down the hill. He was rather shabbily and dirtily dressed, though he had some rich rings on his fingers, and a gold-headed cane in his hand. He had a shuffling gait, and wore a long frowzy beard, which seemed to be rarely combed and never washed; from his skin a very disgusting effluvium seemed to be given off. He had greasy, dark complexion; a nose very hooked; and black round eyes, beneath black eyebrows. The rest of his hair was grizzly.

On seeing Radical he stopped and accosted him at first in a whining tone. "Where are you going, broder?" said he in an outlandish dialect. Radical now saw he was a Jew, but civilly answered "to the City of Reform."

Jew. Vat you say, the Shitty of Reform? ah! fat do you mean dat devilsh place yonder (pointing up the road)? Broder, you must be out of your sheven senses to tink of such a ting.

Radical. Begging your pardon, Mr. Solomons, or whatever be your name, I am no such thing, I am bound that way, and for the City of Reform.

Jew. Reform! shitty of tieves, I shay. Why, do you know they have no such ting as a stock exchange there, and don't know, de cursed fools and rogues, fat a bleshing it is to have a national debt, and pay de devidends.

Radical. Truly I have heard as much.

Jew. Fy, do you know, the dam ninnies won't understand you if you ask de prishe of scrip or omnium — dey absolutely don't know what conshols mean.[8]

Radical. I am absolutely, as you say, very glad to hear it, Mr. Solomons.

Jew. Glad to hear it. Oh! you spoliator of the children of Israel. I tell you day are all tieves — you will be robbed. I will take my sholemn oath I heard one of dem swear if they had a national debt the rogues would not pay it.

Radical. Faith, Mr. Solomons, I am of their opinion, and that, to tell you a bit of the truth, old Shadrach,[9] is one principal cause of my going. I have worked long enough to pay swindling "national debts" as you impudently call them, you blaspheming old usurer.

Jew. Stop tief, stop tief — he is running away wid my dividends — I apprehend you for yon spoliator — you shall keep de national faith! you shall, by de beard of Aaron!

Here the Jew held up his cane menacingly to Radical, when the eldest boy, who was about fourteen, gave the Israelite such a salute across the fingers with a stout cudgel he had cut by the way, that the gold-headed cane was demolished, and the Jew hobbled down the hill as fast as possible, wringing his hand and tearing his beard with the other in a way pitiful to behold. Radical first looked after him with pity, but recollecting how he had assisted in strapping his burden to his back patted his boy's head, and went on as merrily as before.

PART III

We saw in our dream that the Pilgrim progressed in his journey till he came to where there was a vast assemblage of people, and considerable excitement amongst them. This proved to be what was called an Election for members to sit in the House of Parliament in the City of Plunder. Two parties, the *Ins* and the *Outs*, were keenly contesting the town. Both made feeling appeals to the inhabitants, professed a zealous regard for their best interests, and both were sure of success. As soon as it became generally known that *Radical* had made his appearance in the town, he was waited upon by the respective candidates for his vote and interest. The parties were decked out with ribbons; blue was the colour of the *Ins*, who commonly went under the denomination of *Liberals*; and buff that of the *Outs*, who were known by the term *Tory*, or *Conservative*.

Ins.—Oh, my good friend *Radical*, how are you? glad to see you; hope *Mrs Radical* and all the young *Radicals* are Radically sound in mind and limb. Piping times these, my buck. Devilish troublesome gentry these old pimpled-nosed, corrupt, jobbing, vagabondish, Tories. We know you hate these fellows, my little hearty, and that you will support *liberal* measures and *liberal* men. Shall we have the honour of your vote and interest for *Mr. Scapegrace*, our member? He is a right true fellow, we'll warrant him.

Radical.—I have a great load of taxes on my back, as you may see; my wife and children are in rags in consequence of its weight. Now, will you lighten my load considerably, or take it off my back altogether? If you will do this, I will give you all the support I can.

Ins.—Why, my dear Sir, you must know that taxes are necessary things in all states. No doubt they press upon the resources of this great empire, and depress capital; but still they are a necessary evil. Our party intend to make great changes in taxation. If the burden presses too heavy upon your *right* shoulder, they will shift it more towards the *left*; and this you will find a great comfort indeed. As to taking off the load altogether, why, my dear Sir, it would prove a dangerous thing indeed, to change the channels of so much capital.

Radical.—I do not comprehend what you mean by *capital* and *resources*; but what I want is the load off my back; and if a man will not promise to ease me of it, I will never give him a vote.

The party now left the Pilgrim, and the *Outs* made their advances for his vote and interest.

Outs.—Good morning, *Radical*, we wait upon you to solicit your vote for our glorious Constitution of Church and State. These vile Whigs, with their endless commissions, and liberal measures, promise soon not to leave a single stone of the venerable fabric of our National Temple standing upon another. We beg to introduce *Mr. Bellweather* to your notice, as a Conservative from his very birth, and true and sound in doctrine to the back bone.

Radical.—Will you vote to take the load off my shoulders? If you will do that I will give you my vote, without asking any questions about this curious fabric of the Constitution you talk about.

Outs.—We would be glad to gratify you in this particular, only we are convinced that the load is a great benefit to you. You would feel very awkward and uneasy without it. Your constitution has accommodated itself to your burthen, and your burthen to it. We could easily demonstrate to you how it tends to keep your body in good order; without it you would run all to grease in a month, grow nervous, and die of melancholy.

Radical.—I will not keep you waiting. My mind is made up. If you will not ease me of my load, then I shall have nothing to say to you.

Now, we saw in our dream, that the Pilgrim and his family left this scene of contention, and espied on their journey a guide post at a short distance, on which were inscribed the words, "direct road to the Delectable Mountains." He and his wife and children then turned into this narrow lane, which became very rugged and precipitous as they advanced. As he moved upwards, however, the prospect became delightful; he saw beautiful gardens, orchards, vineyards, and cooling fountains of water; there were also Shepherds there to give relief and counsel to strangers and way-faring men. The names of these Shepherds were *Knowledge*, *Experience*, *Watchful*, and *Prudence*, and they took *Radical* and his wife and children, and treated them with great kindness and hospitality. In the morning the Pilgrim was taken out by the Shepherd to be indulged with a distant view of the City of Reform, which he distinctly saw, though at a great distance. The Shepherds then took *Radical* to a more distant part of these mountains, and bid him look over the awfully precipitous and rugged rocks. This was denominated the Hill of *Error*; and at its base were to be seen an immense number of bones and skulls of men who had fallen over the rocks, and dashed to pieces. The Guides then took the Pilgrim to an opposite part of the Mountains, to a Hill called *Caution*; and from it they discerned a number of men walking amongst tombs, who seemed to be blind. These men stumbled into a narrow path that led to the grounds of the Castle of Despair, were seized by the three Despots, who put out their eyes, and sent them here to wander, during the remaining part of their life, amongst the remains of the dead.

After taking some refreshment, the whole party set out again to see the grand monument upon the top of the Mountains, made of the finest marble, and which contained the names of a great number of the most illustrious individuals who had travelled to the City of Reform. Amongst the vast multitude of these worthies, *Radical* distinctly read the names of Alfred the Great, Egbert, Sir William Gascoigne, Fortesque, Coke, Bacon, Hale, Sir Thomas More, Hampden, Pym, Sydney, Locke, Harrington, Marvell, Shippen, Hollis, Milton, Vane, Fairfax, Prynne, Selden, Bolingbroke, Chatham, Tooke, Paine, Cobbett, and Cartwright.[10]

After this, we thought we saw the Shepherds take the Pilgrim to a side of a mountain, in which was a door. It was opened—the most hideous cries of wickedness and woe issued out of it. Pilgrim inquired what this meant; and was informed it was the place of punishment for perfidious, and cruel tyrants, who trampled upon the liberties of the people, and reduced them to beggary and want.

The Shepherds then took the Pilgrim to another part of the mountains on which a splendid temple had been built. In the building were to be seen all the ancient records respecting the City of Reform. Magna Charta, and the Bill of Rights, were both framed in gold. Here were all the most famous works of the Constitutional Lawyers, beautifully bound; so that by the reading of these valuable and precious books, *Radical* would obtain really useful knowledge, and be able to see the whole frame work of the law, that was acknowledged in the famous City of Reform, to which he was travelling. When these curiosities had been all examined, the Shepherds then took *Radical* into the *armoury*, which contained specimens of the weapons which all true Pilgrims should have, when they set out on their journey. These weapons were divided into two kinds, *physical* and *moral*; but the Shepherds convinced the Pilgrim, that the latter kind were not of the slightest use without the former. The *physical* weapons were guns, pistols, cannon, bayonets, pikes, &c., which the law of the City of Reform compelled every citizen to have in his possession, to defend his country and his rights from ruthless invasion. The *moral* armoury consisted of the breastplate of truth, the helmet of zeal, the shield of prudence, the sword of knowledge, and the shoes of perseverance, that never wear out.

Now, we saw that when these kind Shepherds had shown the Pilgrim every thing worthy of notice on the *Delectable Mountains*, *Radical* prepared himself for the further prosecution of his journey. The hospitable guides furnished him and his wife and children, with many necessary articles for their future comfort; and, in particular, gave the Pilgrim some very good advice. They furnished him with a plan of his journey, cautioned him against the seductive wiles of the flatterer, in the enchanted grounds; and, finally, bade him a good journey.

When the Pilgrim had reached the bottom of the mountains, he came to a tall column, which bore the inscription: "The column of Reform." On inquiry, it was found that this pillar was raised by a zealous Pilgrim of noble birth, who came as far as the *Delectable Mountains*, on his way to the City of Reform; but from the steep ascent of these mountains, he would not go up, but brought many artificers from the City of Plunder to build a column, from the top of which the City of Reform might be discerned; and by this expedient the labour of ascending the mountains would be avoided. But after this structure was erected, it was found of no earthly use whatever, for no Pilgrim could see the happy city from its top. This failure prayed so intensely upon the mind of its noble projector, that he grew faint-hearted, said he was troubled with "a great pressure from without," and that he would go no further towards the City of Reform. When this became known, the scouts of the *Castle of Despair* laid hands upon him, and carried him to the Despots of that ignominious establishment.

Now, we saw in our dream, that the Political Pilgrim and his family came near to the town of *Love-gain*, situate in the County of *Covetousness*. This town was nearly encircled with hills, called by the people the hills of *Lucre*; and as they were journeying through it, they overtook three men who said they were on their way to the City of Reform; but they did not like to travel so fast as some people did. Their names were *Hold-the-World*, *Money-love*, and *Save-all*. They had all been educated at a great public school in that neighbourhood, kept by a Mr. *Gripe'em*, who was admirably skilled to the science of getting money by violence, cunning, flattery, lying, sneaking, putting on the outward form of religion, and pretending to an intense love of the public weal. These travellers went at a snail's pace, and earnestly counselled *Radical* not to travel so quickly; but the Pilgrim heeded them not, but went on his way, repeating the following lines:—

Though to another land I go,
    Yet hope shall keep my spirit warm;
Through summer's heat, through winter's snow,
    My courage aid, my fears disarm.
What is to come—let fortune tell;
    The sorrows I have left—I know,
And feel that I have left them well,
    Though to another land I go.

Though to another land I go,
    They widely err who say I roam,
The bondsman hath no country. No;
    The free alone possess a home,
He who would have the heav'ns to smile
    Must leave or lay his tyrants low;
And this shall be my stay the while,
    Though to another land I go.

> Though to another land I go,
>   Why should my bosom heavy be;
> When, sweeter than the roses blow,
>   Love and contentment go with me?
> When those I love the best, I see,
>   As I would ever have them show,
> Why should I fail to share their glee,
>   Though to another land I go?

When Pilgrim had departed from the City of *Love-gain*, he came into a beautiful and extended plain, and at the further end of it stood a huge and strange monument. It was dark, tedious, and gloomy, in the extreme. At the top of it there were the representations of two human faces, but of the most hellish aspect. The column was engraved all over with various emblems of crime and wickedness, and near its base were inscribed in large iron letters, "To perpetuate the infamy of the Marcus, and Peter Thimble school of Politics, whose writings have outraged decency, common sense, and humanity."[11] This monument excited a deep interest in the minds of *Radical* and his family, and as they left it, they congratulated themselves that they had grace to shun all such wicked and unnatural counsels.

After the traversing of this plain, the roads to the happy city lay through a very narrow, dark, and repulsive looking valley, called the *Valley of Humiliation.* At the entrance to it *Radical* met a man, who said his name was *Discontent*; that he had come so far on his road to the City of Reform; but that he was fully bent in going no further, for he did not like to go through this *Valley of Humiliation.*

Radical.—Why do you object to go through this valley?

Discontent.—My principal reason is, that I shall disoblige all my near and kind friends, as *Mr. Pride, Mr. Arrogance, Mr. Self-Conceit, Mr. Worldly-Glory, Mr. Fashion*, and many others, of great respectability, who would incessantly revile and ridicule me for making such a fool of myself, as to go through this disagreeable valley.

Radical.—What need you regard the opinion of these men? I have long renounced all connection with them; and I feel myself not the less happy and comfortable on that account.

Discontent.—I begin to consider things differently from what I did. I think that patriotism is a low, sneaking, pitiful business; and that the bold hectoring tone about public liberty, and such like, brings upon a man the ridicule of all around him. We never see any of the rich, and mighty, and wise, follow this way of life. Nothing but low, base, ill-bred people, make a noise about the public good.

Radical.—Well, this may be your opinion now, but I shall not be driven from my purpose. I shall enter into the Valley, and I hope I shall come out triumphant.

Now we saw that *Radical* and his wife and children, had dreadful conflicts to encounter in passing through this valley. Many a time and oft were he and his family threatened with utter extermination. At length he reached the end, and was cheered by the reflections of self-respect that he had so boldly withstood all the trials and temptations that were thrown in his path.

Here *Radical* was suddenly intercepted by two men who almost ran against him, at a sharp turn of the road. One was dressed in a blue surtout and white hat, and looked like a half-pay colonel; the other was a little, fat, red-faced, bald-headed, man, in a snuff-coloured coat, and looked like a manufacturer. The colonel carried a little penny loaf stuck on the end of his cane, and a Corn Law Catechism in his hand;[12] his name was *Colonel Windmill*, and the name of the little man was *Mr. Will-o'-wisp*. They got hold of *Radical* by the arm, and the following somewhat obstreperous and odd dialogue ensued.

Windmill.—Hilloa! *Radical*, where the devil are you going to at that rate, singing ditties all the way? We heard your song well enough — don't, now, be in too great a haste.

Will-o'-wisp.—Haste! We've got something to please you — no need to go a step further now!

Radical.—Really, gentlemen, I am glad to hear it. What is it?

Windmill.—Do you see that penny cake on the top of my cane?

Radical.—It's so small I can hardly see it, Sir!

Windmill.—That's it. I mean to make it into one as large as your head in the twinkling of a bedpost. What do you think of that my hearty? Ha! ha! ha! No complaint after that I should guess, eh?

Will-o'-wisp.—Ha! ha! ha! No physical force after that — eh?

Radical.—Really, gentlemen, I hardly understand you! A large loaf for a penny is better than an invisible muffin; but how is the flour to be got to make it?

Windmill.—Got? Ha! ha! ha! You're not up to that quite — eh? We mean to offer a large bounty for cheap flour, my boy.

Will-o'-wisp.—That's it, my hearty!

Radical.—A bounty for cheap flour! What? if a man offers me flour for three shillings, am I to offer him a bounty of two shillings to let me have it for eighteen pence?

Windmill.—Pah! Don't peddle amongst figures; figures are inconvenient, misleading things.

Radical.—But, gentlemen, I want to know where the bounty money is to come from?

Windmill.—Psha! Never mind that, so that we get it!

Radical.—Truly, gentlemen, I must go on my journey; a large loaf bought with a bounty won't ease me of my burden.

Windmill.—You will never feel it after, 'pon my honour.

Will-o'-wisp.—You never will, 'pon my honour!

Radical.—That won't do! No, no, Sirs, I know better than that, and so now I wish you good morning.

Radical then went on his way — the two muttering "Pertinacious ignorance!" and "Deplorable want of educational illumination!" *Radical* heard this; he, however, took no notice, but went on, singing as before.

PART IV

We saw that after Pilgrim had left this part of the country he came to the town of *Economy*, situate in the county of *Delusion*. This town was famous for its political exhibitions; for during the whole year there were always some jugglers, rope dancers, mountebanks, fortune-tellers, and caravans full of wild and curious beasts. On the day *Radical* and his family entered the town, there was a mortal rivalship between two establishments. The one had a splendid caravan, in which, amongst other things, there was a yellow Canadian dwarf;[13] and the other had a company of prize fighters and fire eaters, under the direction of one Slashing Harry, well known in that part of the country as a first rate vomiter forth of fire and smoke. This fierce contest engrossed the undivided attention of the whole town; and nothing was talked about but the respective merits of the two sets of showmen.

The master of the caravan, in which was the Canadian dwarf, was particularly zealous and noisy. He dwelt with extatic raptures on the merits of his establishment. The dwarf had cost a great deal of money, for he was not like his tribe in general, he required nice and expensive keeping. The master descanted also upon the incomparable curiosity combined in his own person; that he was double jointed; that his skin was all scaly, like as if studded with black diamonds; and that he had all the assumed dignity of a man of full stature. He also endeavoured to amuse the company with a brief narrative of his wonderful travels, particularly into a country called *Canada*, where he accomplished very surprising things, such as journeying along the banks of a great river there, looking at himself in some splendid mirrors, bought for the express purpose, and issuing forth proclamations which no one would heed nor comprehend. The showman then enumerated the other rare animals he had in his menagerie; but particularly dwelt upon his stock of reptiles, which were the most splendid ever collected under one roof. He had the hissing serpent, the salamander that eats fire, and the repulsive double-hooded snake, only found in the dark places of the earth, full of horrid cruelty. Here was, in fact, a complete Noah's Ark upon a limited scale; every thing rare and curious from the heavens above and the earth beneath.

Harry, the Harlequin, we saw, was equally zealous for his own interest. He succeeded, in some measure, in drowning the pretensions of his rival, by his loud and obstreperous manner. He maintained that his *corps dramatique* were the most renowned in Europe. He had fools and buffoons, and jugglers, and fire eaters, and mountebanks, and quacks, and fortune-tellers, and rope dancers, and diviners, and enchanters, and soothsayers, and sorcerers, and necromancers, and pantomimic actors, of the very first-rate genius; and the minor parts of his incomparable establishment would be found equally excellent and perfect. As to the Canadian dwarf, he was all humbug together; a regular pig in a poke; and his travels were not worth a cobbler's curse. Harry, the Harlequin, then showed the people how he could eat fire, and vomit smoke, in long, thick, and spiral columns. He then produced his specimen of the impoverishing effects of slavery, by exhibiting his half-starved and cruelly worked negro upon the stage. This was received with loud acclamations by the bystanders, and his establishment was filled to the brim with the idle and the curious.

We saw in our dream that Pilgrim went down a very pleasant valley, where he overtook a man apparently going in the same direction as himself. His name was *Mr. Pedantry*, a great man for educating mankind, and who had a great desire to see the City of Reform. He and *Radical* entered warmly into conversation; and the day proving very hot and sultry, they sat down by a fine spring of water, to enjoy a mutual interchange of opinion and sentiment.

Pedantry.—I think you will agree with me, my friend, that every national system of amelioration ought to be based on a systematical and comprehensive plan of intellectual cultivation. Ignorance is the *primum mobile*[14] of the vicious principle; and while it is allowed to flourish in unbrageous[15] revelry, the more elevated and refined principles of the inner man, cannot be allowed sufficient scope for their determinate action.

Radical.—Knowledge is good for all purposes, and conditions of life. It is of great use for a man like myself, with a wife and family, to know how I may feed, clothe, and instruct them properly.

Pedantry.—True, my good Sir; but still you must give the preponderating influence to the intellectuality of the scheme, and not be solely guided in your standard of value by the grosser ingredients of mere matter. How ravishing and extatic to roam unfettered over the vast and boundless regions of mental invention.

Radical.—No doubt it must be very delightful for those who have time and leisure for such contemplations; but knowledge and talent are no more intended by Providence to be universal, than riches and honours. What I want is sufficient remuneration for my labour, which will enable me to attend to my family, and have a little leisure to reflect upon the great objects of a social being's destiny, both as it regards time and eternity.

Pedantry.—Very good, my friend, as far as it goes; but to dwell upon the sublimities of science ought to be the grand object of every Pilgrim to the City of Reform. You could not relish the social inter-communications of refined civilization, except by a comprehensive expansion of mentality.

Radical.—I should vastly approve of my own, and my wife and children's stomachs being expanded with plenty of good victuals first. My notions of education and knowledge have an intimate sympathy with my back and belly.

Pedantry.—This I consider a lamentable feature of the times. The sensual appetency preponderates over the intellectual energies; and thus a material idiocracy is produced. You will never be able to appreciate the excellencies of legislative sagacity, without you throw off the lethargic influences of the bodily frame. You are, perhaps, unacquainted with the mysteries of gravitation?

Radical.—I know a little of that subject. I know that a good piece of English roast beef drops very pleasantly into one's stomach, when one can catch such a dainty.

Pedantry.—You misunderstood me. I allude to the principle of gravitation in a vacuum.

Radical.—So do I. In the vacuum of starvation the beef drops gratefully to the bottom.

Pedantry.—You are all body together, and no mind. The sensorial system is too conspicuously developed; and a gentle titilation of the *mucus membrane*, leads you into the mazes of political error. I must leave you to your gross and material propensities.

Now we saw that *Pedantry* and the Pilgrim separated, and the latter, with his wife and family, went up a hill, in the middle of which the party overtook two men, apparently travelling very slowly towards the City of Reform. Their names were *Temporary* and *Expediency*. They seemed very happy and plausible kind of persons, and of a free and easy disposition. They entered into conversation with *Radical*, and endeavoured to persuade him not to travel so quickly, for they had discovered a shorter route to the city, and Pilgrims might safely indulge themselves with more leisure in prosecuting their journeys. They had their pockets all stuffed with papers, containing plans for different ways to arrive at the immortal city, than that which had long been established. Pilgrim, however, did not think it prudent to delay his journey, by stopping to examine all those voluminous details; but quietly bade the two men a good morning; and with great glee struck up the following lines:—

> There's strength within the arm;
>   Within the feet there's speed;
> There's courage in the heart
>   To dare a warlike deed.
> The sword is on the thigh;
>   The helmet on the head;
> Just God is up on high;
>   Then what is there to dread?
>
> When Honesty's the guide,
>   There's cheer for the opprest;
> There's firmness in the eye
>   When virtue's in the breast;
> The blade to quit the sheath

For Freedom need not fear;
For when she asks for aid,
    There's one above to hear.

Be peril in the path;
    Be death upon the way;
When liberty's the prize,
    What to the brave are they?
The steel is in my hand;
    Before me is my foe;
And for freedom, God himself
    Shall help to strike the blow.

As the Pilgrim advanced in his journey he came to a large house, in which resided an opulent merchant, who carried on his business in the City of Plunder. His name was *Mr. Staytape*, and he manufactured buckram[16] to a great extent. This kind of profession was a great favourite with many of the philosophic politicians in the City of Plunder, so much so that several of the more profound and sanguine of these speculative men entertained lively hopes that the whole of the inhabitants of the city would be learned in time to live entirely upon cotton fuz which blew off as mere waste in the manufacture of this staple commodity. The cultivation of the soil and the rearing of cattle were considered as low, grovelling, and profitless pursuits, totally unworthy of a liberal people, panting after the renovation of their social system. It was one of the leading tenets of this new philosophy that until the people really get themselves properly accustomed to the daily use of the fuz, they might be partially fed with the grosser articles of grain and flesh from other neighbouring countries, and this would enable the whole of the City of Plunder to become an immense workshop for such articles of buckram as other countries might fancy to take. These deep subjects engrossed the undivided attention of the learned, and universities were founded, and professors appointed, to shed this new light over the dark and benighted huts of the land.

Mr. Staytape had extensive workshops not far distant from his house. Here were employed an immense number of people of both sexes, and of all ages; and as Pilgrim looked through the works, he felt deeply sorrowful for the miserable condition of these unfortunate persons. The whole building groaned under the yoke of outraged humanity; and one race of human beings after another were hurried off the stage of life, in the noontide of their existence, to administer to the wants and luxuries of *Mr. Staytape's* family. But he was considered a good kind of man for all this. *Mr. Staytape* attended all public meetings for the "amelioration of the species," and the advancement of "universal philanthropy"; gave handsome donations to all places of religious devotion; and was President of the societies for the "suppression of vice," for "repressing cruelties to animals," and "for administering relief to the houseless poor."[17]

We saw that *Radical* gave but a passing glance at these strange scenes; for his mind was intently bent on pursuing his journey with all possible alacrity and speed. He approached a neat cottage by the way side, kept by one *Mr. Good-heart*, who kindly gave him and his family some good beef and beer to relieve their pressing hunger. As the Pilgrim went forward he overtook a weak and feeble-looking person, who said he was going to the City of Reform, and that his name was *Moral-force*. On a near approach, *Radical* found him an emasculated person, with down instead of hair for his beard, his eyes full of tears, and a shrill and feeble voice like a child's. *Radical* wished to have a little talk with him.

Radical.—Are you going to the City of Reform?

Moral-force.—Yes, I am.

Radical.—You seem but ill provided for such a long, tedious, and dangerous journey.

Moral-force.—I hope to make my way amongst the intelligent and educated, by dint of soft persuasion, and a copious flow of tender tears.

Radical.—I am afraid you are relying on a broken reed.

Moral-force.—I think otherwise. But, pray what is that long thing you are carrying in your hand?

Radical.—That is a musket and bayonet given to me by the good Shepherds of the Delectable Mountains, who said I was not to use it but when severely pressed for life and limb. Look at it; it is in capital order.

Moral-force.—No, thank you; I cannot endure brute force. My weapons are those of reason, and not gunpowder and lead. Pray keep the muzzle of the gun from me, for I am afraid it goes off; do keep it away!

Radical.—There is no danger; but, look! do you see yon horrid thing who is making his way towards us, with rapid and impatient strides?

Moral-force.—Yes, I do; who can it be?

Radical.—It is, I verily believe, the fell fiend, *Political Apollyon*, the patron of corruption and tyranny, and the owner of the whole City of Plunder. Now be firm!

Here *Political Apollyon* made his appearance to *Radical* and *Moral-force*. He was hideous to behold. He had wings like a dragon, scales like a fish, was full of running sores, and fire and brimstone came out of his mouth. He began in the most authoritative air to question the Pilgrims.

Apollyon.—From whence come you, and whither are you going?

Radical.—I have come from the City of Plunder, and I am going to the City of Reform.

Apollyon.—You are all my subjects, and have left my dominions without my consent.

Radical.—True, I was born in your City; but you were a severe task-master; your wages were toil and starvation; and you considered us made for no higher purpose than to administer to your wants and pleasures. I came, therefore, to the determination to leave your service, and seek out a better country.

On hearing this plain and determined speech of *Radical*, the monster *Apollyon* seemed convulsed with a sudden fit of inexpressible rage and vengeance. His eyes shot forth livid fire — from his mouth issued a thin suffocating smoke for breath — upon his chin were long scattered bristles having the semblance of a beard, and these appeared instinct with actual life as he ground his teeth together, and coiled and twisted themselves like snakes. At this terrible apparition the woman and children were terribly alarmed, and fell down on their knees to pray for the father and husband. They also besought *Moral-force* to interfere, and, if possible, still the wrath of the horrid monster who stood bent on bloody work. *Moral-force*, however, slunk behind, and seemed in as great a state of trepidation as the rest. *Radical*, however, still stood firm, deliberately cocking the musket with which the Shepherds had furnished him, and imagining that the sight of it would cool his antagonist, but in this he was disappointed — as appeared in the sequel.

On seeing his firmness, the monster expanded and then contracted his wings two or three times with a great noise like that made by the sails of a windmill in a sudden tempest, and prepared to draw a huge crooked scymeter that hung by his side. In doing this *Radical* had presence of mind to observe that the substance of his wings appeared to consist of layers, like huge feathers, composed of a thin paper-like substance, mottled with black marks of irregular forms like the *black* letter of an old Bible or statute, such as **FIVE-TEN** and so on; and as he twisted his limbs, he saw layers of the same substance under the scales of his skin-like armour. Seeing the monster drawing his sword, he at once pointed his musket, when the other making a wonderful bound up from the ground exclaimed — "Nay, then wretch, perdition be upon thee," and half flew and half ran right at *Radical*, hoping to cleave him to the chin at the first stroke. *Radical*, however, was too nimble for him, and by a rapid leap aside let him pass, which he did, giving *Moral-force* a severe wound with the sweep of his weapon, and almost crushing the children, who ran screaming with affright.

This sight roused *Radical*, who being unused either to fire-arms or such encounters, was naturally in great perturbation, and taking the best aim he could, he fired at the monster. Had *Radical* been a good marksman, the battle would have been ended by that shot, aimed as it was at the monster's back, which was unarmed and defenceless; but being unused to fire-arms, he missed the fiend altogether, shooting through one of his expanded wings, from which the shot dislodged an immense quantity of the paper plumage which fell around like leaves in autumn. The monster's movements were evidently disconcerted by this. He attempted to bound as before but failed as a fowl does when one wing is clipped. His vengeance, however, seemed increased, and with horrid imprecations and curses, blaspheming Christ, his Apostles and Saints, and calling on Lucifer for aid, he again made at *Radical* with his falchion in one hand and a shield in the other, on which appeared in strange characters the motto LEGAL TENDER[18] — which *Radical* took to be magical or cabalistical characters. The screams and prayers of the woman and children were now terrific, for they believed that of a verity *Radical's* last hour was come, and he himself put up a short prayer to Heaven to support him through the worst. He, however, stood firm, and warding with his discharged gun the blow aimed at his head, he with the sword which the Shepherds had recommended to him, which was so bright, it shone like a mirror — dealt so well aimed a blow at the shield that he fairly split it in two — when it appeared to be stuffed with the same paper-like substance which also composed the wings of the monster, — and the monster gave back, slightly wounded in the arm.

On seeing this the children took heart, and the eldest boy shouted out "father the villain is turning very white, take courage and we shall win;" — and on this he came to his father's side with a huge branch of a tree he had found, determined, if he could, to entangle the monster's heels, and this he did so successfully, that Radical easily avoided a heavy blow aimed at him by the Fiend, who had now taken his sword in both hands, and seizing the opportunity gave him such a back handed cut across the loins, that he pierced clean through the monster's armour, and not only drew blood, but strewed the ground with an enormous number of the same paper-looking leaves, some of which had inscribed STOCK, others EXCHEQUER BILLS, and others SAVING SCRIP.[19] On feeling this dreadful blow, the monster gave a despairing howl so shockingly discordant, and issued so fetid a stench, that the very birds fell down, and Radical was well nigh suffocated with it. The brute, however, would wait no further combat, but seizing Moral-force as in a last effort of revenge, dashed his head against the ground and then fled, uttering shocking blasphemies in some unknown tongue, taking an eastward course in his flight.

Great were now the congratulations of Radical and his wife and children, and heartily grateful were they that they had taken the weapons offered by the good Shepherds. Radical endeavoured to revive poor Moral-force, but it was lost labour, the fiend's last dreadful blow having evidently scattered some of the brain upon the ground. Radical, therefore, putting up his sword and reloading his musket, went on his way, proceeding very carefully for fear of a surprise by the horrid monster at some other turn of the road.

PART V

Now we saw in our dream that *Radical* had to go through a long and dreary wilderness, and at its termination there stood a very large and populous town called *Vanity*; at which there was a fair held every day in the year; and from this cause, the town went generally under the name of *Vanity-fair*. All Pilgrims to the City of Reform had to go through this fair; and the records of the place show, that many thousands of Pilgrims have, from time to time, perished amidst the trials and indulgences of this renowned city. The place is very ancient, so much so, that the precise time of its foundation cannot be settled by the most profound and accurate antiquarians. The city is, however, tributary to the City of Plunder; and is supported out of the revenues of that town. General history and tradition affirm that many thousands of years ago, Beelzebub, and his two archangels, Tyranny and Corruption, laid the foundation of this notorious city, for the express purpose of way-laying Pilgrims to the City of Reform, against the interests of which, they always manifested the most deadly and revengeful hatred. The city was laid out in the most artful manner to seduce and bewilder the minds of unwary and simple men; and contained a vast number of persons engaged in public amusements and traffic. Here every thing was to be found which could gratify the senses, and captivate the fancy.

When *Radical* had arrived within the gates of the city, he was delighted to find his former kind friend *Common-sense*, who had come here to discharge one of his public duties, namely, to guide Pilgrims through the intricate labyrinths of this town. This meeting was the most provident thing that could have happened for poor *Radical*, and his wife and children, who were deeply impressed with the idea that they would never find out the right road in this crowded place. *Common-sense* admonished the Pilgrim to rely with implicit confidence on him; to go with him whithersoever he went; and to conduct himself in all respects as he wished and desired. *Radical* promised complete submission. *Common-sense* then said he would show him through a great part of this city, for he knew every hole and corner of it; and he was wishful to let him see the extent of this snare set in his way, in order that his pleasures might be increased when he had escaped from it.

Now we saw that after these introductory admonitions had been given, *Common-sense* took the Pilgrim and his family into a large open square, where there was a vast crowd of persons, and a man was handing round to eager applicants several things considered of inestimable value in this place, such as honorary offices, knighthoods, dukedoms, earldoms, marquisites, baronetcies, privileges, quarterings,[20] heraldic titles, escutcheons,[21] coats of arms, orders, crests, crosses, decorations, emblems, stars, ribbons, garters, devices, mottos, guards, offices, salaries, commissionerships, honours, titles, governorships, clerical benefices, pluralities, prebendaries,[22] royal grants, &c. &c. The anxiety to obtain these fine things was the most intense imaginable. *Common-sense* then showed *Radical* the plan of the *City of Vanity-fair*. It had a great many streets, but they all terminated in this spacious centre; like the spokes of a wheel in the nave. The principal of these streets were, *Corruption-street*, *Guzzle-row*, *Scientific-place*, *Bribery-street*, *Usury-terrace*, *Courtly-circus*, *Quack-quadrant*, *Paperkite-buildings* and *Prostitute-alley*.

Common-sense intimated to *Radical* that he would take him through these places, and let him see what they contained; taking care at the same time to remind him of the injunctions he had previously laid upon him, to be cautious and circumspect in all his words, thoughts and actions.

When the Pilgrim had left this street or circus, *Common-sense* took him to *Guzzle-row*, a noted part of the city, frequented by all keen and successful politicians belonging to the City of Plunder. Here are a vast variety of houses of entertainment for political thieves, burglars, adventurers, and pick-pockets, who have an unconquerable aversion to working honestly for their daily bread. They are busily intent upon gratifying their bodily senses, having plenty of victuals, strong liquors, lewd women, and being completely masters of their own time. The landlords, as they are called, entertain them with the most pernicious and destructive drinks, which charm the indolent, makes the starving and half-famished sot view his rags and nakedness with stupid indifference, and drivels away his time in senseless laughter and dull jokes. His daily beverage sets his brain on fire, burns up his entrails, drowns his cares, makes him indifferent to the cries of his children for food, their shivering colds, and empty home; and finally, brings upon him loss of appetite, fevers, jaundice, consumption, palsies, diseased liver, dropsies, and death. It is from these establishments that a great deal of the revenues of the City of Plunder are derived; and the proprietors of them have a licence from the ruling powers there to sell, "wholesome and retail," this Stygian comfort[23] to the people. Here Pilgrim had to witness all the filthy actions, and hear the vile language of nasty drabs, and the lowest hell-rakes; and be also subjected to all the stench, and squalour, and noise, and impertinence, and vulgar ribaldry, from the most shameless and abandoned of mankind.

Common-sense then conducted the Pilgrim to *Courtly-circus*, where wealth, fashion, and political intrigue resided. The residents here were all worldly minded, ambitious, and voluptuous, but entirely devoid of merit. Their great aim is to obtain specious palaces, delicious gardens, fine horses, magnificent coaches, splendid furniture, beautiful women, well filled cellars, tables covered with all manner of dainties, judicious cooks, fine music, servants in splendid liveries, who are to show nimbleness without hurry, dispatch without noise, and the most perfect and slavish attention to orders. The residents here, to fill up their vacant time, have numerous blacklegs, bawds, gamblers, pick-pockets, and blackguards of all kinds and degrees. *Common-sense* then pointed out, as a resident in this street, a personage who goes under the designation of a *man of honour*. He considers himself different from other men, as possessing a *principle* and rule of action which the vulgar herd have not. This distinguished principle is like the gout, hereditary in his family; and all his children are born with it.—It is greatly strengthened by reading and conversation of a certain description. A man of honour must live up to the rules and maxims of honour, which are a set of laws he must think, and talk, and act by. Here he must be very conscientious, and always pretend to preface the public good to his own. He must not tell lies, nor openly defraud, nor insult, nor put up with an affront, except under very particular and special circumstances. He is always considered the pink of impartiality, and, of course, a man of sense; for it would be little short of a contradiction of terms to say that a man of honour was a fool. There is, however, a certain latitude allowed him. He may bilk his creditor, he may keep a mistress or a bawd, he may sponge about on society at large; but still his *honour* is not violated. He must always be judge in his own case; and if any injury should be done to himself, his friend, his servant, his horse, his dog, or any thing which enjoys his honourable protection, he must have the satisfaction of a gentleman, or man of honour.

Pilgrim was now informed by his guide of another class of persons who resided a good deal about this *Courtly-circus*; these were gentlemen soldiers. They are made familiar with the engines of death and destruction, with the shouts of victory, and the groans of the dying and dead. These men are often dressed in the most ridiculous manner. Coarse cloth, dyed a scarlet or red colour, ornamented with bits of things in imitation of gold and silver lace, with a fantastic cap, ornamented with red and white cock feathers. A piece of calf's skin is placed over some of their staves of wood, to make a noise, and at the sound of this he marches to perform many ridiculous tricks; and be placed under the drill of Serjeant Kite, who raps him over the knuckles with a gold-headed cane for awkwardness. Along with the gentlemen soldiers *Radical* was shown the gentlemen parsons. These were very dandily dressed gentry in black, who swore they were "successors of the Apostles" and were "called by the Holy Ghost to the cure of souls." Many of them had cures of souls in various parts of the country, where they seldom ever went, but employed poor journeymen soul-curers to do their work for them, whilst they feasted in the City of Plunder! They were excellent at a pious game called *Whist*, by which they sometimes got large sums of money from the gentlemen soldiers and others; and besides the Scriptures, were well read in a publication called the *Racing Calendar*,[24] and also a thing called *old port wine*, for which they seemed to have a religious veneration. Though their office was to destroy the trade of the gentlemen soldiers, which they professed to hold in abhorrence, they were the best of friends in the world — and if *Radical* had been cut down by the men in red, the men in black would have put up a thanksgiving for this "glorious victory!"

After the Pilgrim had left this street, *Common-sense* took him into another called *Scientific-place*, a most splendid and imposing part of this vast city, so far as outward appearances go. Here were assembled all the philosophers, poets, historians, men of letters, antiquarians, astronomers, geologists, periodical writers, newspaper editors, and the whole race who live by their pens and their wits, and whose names are to be handed down to future ages.—Pilgrim's first impression was, that these splendid houses were all the property of the different literary crafts who resided in them; but *Common-sense* undeceived him on this point, and told him that these men had generally no property of their own, but were fed and kept by other rich individuals for particular purposes who lived in the City of Plunder. "Indeed," said *Common-sense*, "to convince you of this, we shall go into this splendid house and see its various inmates." Here they rang a bell, and a dirty, sooty, old woman, blind of an eye, and with a broken nose, opened the door. They were shewn into a room, on the door of which was painted, in white letters, James Foolscap, Esq., L.L.D., F.R.S., M.R.S.A.,

M.W.S., &c. The party found Dr. Foolscap in this room writing, with a wife and four young children. There was scarcely any furniture in the room; and the children were crying aloud for bread. They were hushed into silence by their mother, who appeared a young, pretty-looking person, with a very interesting expression of deep melancholy upon her countenance, evidently the effect of heart-rending anxiety and care. *Dr. Foolscap* was very communicative and told *Common-sense* that he was very busy with an essay, which was to be placed under the patronage of *Lord Gripem*, "on the Principles of Productive Capital; with an Appendix, shewing how the Progress of Population Trenches upon the Means of Subsistence." This work would, the writer hoped, place this interesting problem in its true light, and also be productive of great honour and benefit to himself. *Dr. Foolscap* mentioned that he had also been, for a considerable time, employed with some political dissertations for the use of the *Honourable Timothy Numskull*, a great politician in the House of Parliament, which was now sitting in the City of Plunder. These dissertations were of the most varied kind; but the principal of them was one relative to the important duty of the poor paying every attention to *industry and economy*. This paper was to form the groundwork of some comprehensive and stringent legislative enactments in the City of Plunder. *Dr. Foolscap* mentioned that he was to receive one guinea for this document when properly illustrated with the necessary statistical tables. On leaving, the Doctor delicately asked if the party could give him a pair of old shoes, as he had not a pair of any kind to go over the door with.

Common-Sense took the Pilgrim to another house in *Scientific-place*, where a very venerable looking personage resided. He kept a respectable establishment, wore a large bushy wig, and spoke as one having authority. This was *Mr. Quarto,* the author. *Common-sense* told the Pilgrim the gentleman they now saw was paid so much a year by a leading squad of politicians in the City of Plunder, who owned a periodical publication which appeared four times a year, and the leading object of which was to perpetrate the old custom in that place of one man putting his hands into the pockets of his neighbour. *Mr. Quarto* had just finished an essay "on the State of Parties," in which he demonstrated that the party called the *Ins* were the most degraded, ignorant, snuffy, old blackguards that ever existed, and that the *Outs* were the very pinks of wisdom and patriotism. This publication was considered of the greatest importance to certain members of the legislature in the City of Plunder; for without it they could not know either how to act or how to speak on public questions. *Mr. Quarto* had also the privilege of reviewing books, for which the authors or publishers of them paid him in proportion to the length and eulogistic nature of his critiques. But the most interesting thing to Pilgrim in this *Scientific-place* was the vast number of newspapers. Here were seen, at particular hours of each day, thousands of sheets flying in the air, like flakes of snow, and eagerly seized on by the people round about. These immense establishments were generally the property of political partizans; but nothing could be a more heinous offence than to call in question their complete and perfect independence of any influence whatever. They laboured only for the happiness of the people; were the great refiners and educators of mankind, and the sedulous guardians of public and private morality. Each of these newspaper's concerns was conducted by a man who went under the generic name of *Mr. We*, who was always considered a very important person, full of knowledge of all kinds, knew more than any body else, and held a pen as sharp as a lancet. *Common-sense* had a cousin (five degrees removed) one of these *Mr. We's*, and he took the Pilgrim up to an attic, seven stories high, to see him. He was a thin, blear-eyed man, much marked with the small-pox, and apparently about fifty years of age. He had a wife and family; but kept a couple of mistresses besides. He drank a bottle of brandy a day; besides a fair proportion of porter and ale. He had been thrice a bankrupt, and was well known at every sponging house in the city. He was a great glutton, and the most barefaced and consummate liar in the place. But he had a great reverence for religion, and when *Common-sense* and *Radical* were with him, he was just finishing, what he termed, a very powerful "leading article," on "*the moral degradation of the lower orders.*"

When *Radical* and *Common-Sense* came out of this building, the following dialogue took place:—

Radical.—You surprise me very much with such an exposure of the newspaper press. I had been led to entertain much more favourable opinions of its character, than I now find that circumstances will warrant.

Common-sense.—It is base, corrupt, and unprincipled, beyond all comparison. It is founded on avarice; it is the propagator of delusion; it lives on hypocrisy and fraud; it is the abettor of oppression and violence in all shapes and forms; it is a deadly enemy to real public liberty; it is the prolific source of national degradation and impotency; it is the zealous and willing advocate of powerful guilt against defenceless innocence; it sows, with a prolific hand, the seeds of intellectual imbecility and corruption throughout the whole land; and it openly and shamelessly glories in its own prostitution and venality.

Radical.—Do the newspaper editors not believe what they write? I often peruse passages in which expressions such as these occur; "these are contrary to *our principles*," "an honest journalist," "our defence of enlightened and liberal institutions," "our advocating the best interest of the people." &c., &c. Now these expressions must, I would fain hope, rest upon something like honesty of purpose amongst men.

Common-sense.—No such thing. These fellows have no principles but one, how to sell themselves to the devil at the highest price. There is nothing they will not say or do, to obtain money! With a score of exceptions there would be neither injustice nor injury inflicted if all the *Mr. We's* in the kingdom were hanged by the neck tomorrow morning. But come further down this *Scientific-street*, and have a peep at the *Philosophical Bazaar*.

Now, we saw in our dream, Pilgrim and *Common-sense* went into a spacious
court, lighted from the top by numerous domes. Here were a large motley group
of persons, talking loudly on various topics, giving themselves great airs of
importance, and manifesting intense zeal and rivalship in the distribution of
their respective wares. This was called "*the Philosophical Bazaar of Useful
Knowledge,*" and was quite a pet institution with many politicians in the City
of Plunder, for divers ends and purposes. The establishment was divided into
numerous compartments. Some of the proprietors or occupiers of these were
dressed in the ordinary habit of the country; others had large gowns and wigs,
and a portion were equipped like hucksters and pedlars. *Common-sense* and
Pilgrim stood a while at a stall where a loud, boisterous, vulgar, ragamuffin
kind of a fellow (well known as a great doctor in the City of Plunder), was
holding forth. He was delivering a lecture to an odd-looking group of hearers,
on twenty-seven new species of what he called "*Precursor lice,*" which he had
just discovered, in immense swarms on the inhabitants of *Emerald Isle*, a
country tributary to the City of Plunder.[25] The lecturer explained the great
difference between the present animals and the "*repeal,*" the "*emancipation,*"
and the "*rint*" lice. The "Precursors" had longer tails, several more legs, and bit
with more ferocious keenness than the other kinds. The Doctor, on concluding
his lecture, distributed his handbills. *Radical* was surprised to find they were
in rhyme; but *Common-sense* told him to be thankful for either rhyme or reason
at the city of *Vanity-fair*!

> When a nation grows sick, and is likely to die,
> To me for advice and for physic apply;
> Eschew the empiric,[26] the humbug, and quack,
> But open your purse, when I open my pack;
> For this is its virtue—there's nothing that's in't
> Can bear to shew face till you've paid up your "rint."
>
> For folks that are ill, and can't stomach their rations,
> I've prescribed, with success, my bran-new corporations.[27]
> For who can be other than hungry and bare;
> When he's under the away of an orange Lord Mayor?
> "Corporations (quoth Pat) to cure hunger and cowld!
> "Better give us some prog[28] to put into the owld!"
>
> Oh, bother! that's blarney! such blarney's a sin;
> If you won't believe me, then go ask Mr Finn;
> Of hunger in Eyreland I'm sure he won't hear,
> Since I got him his place of a thousand a year!
> And for cowld, sure, there's not such a thing about town
> To be felt, since I bought Dickey Shiel his silk gown!

Are you not axy[29] yet? then I'll bet you three crowns
I've a plan that will cure both your ups and your downs;
I'll make you a railroad, and ne'er a hill in it,
That shall whisk you along thirty miles to the minute;
And who'll then belave (let them say it who will)
That in Eyreland reform has come to a stand-still?

Buy Precursory Pills!—good for grumbling souls!
They'll cure all your ills, if you've got any bowels;
They'll sharpen your teeth, make your appetite kane,
If you've got any beef to partake of I mane;
Buy Precursor cathartics! I, surely, may say!
For "precursor" manes only a "clearing the way."

My name's Doctor Dan, from the lakes of Killarney,
And, remember, I deal both in physic and blarney!
Eschew the empiric, the humbug, and quack,
But open your purse, when I open my pack;
For this is its nature—there's nothing that's in't
Can bear to shew face till you've paid up your "rint."

At the further end of the Bazaar stood a splendid collection of natural objects of great variety and interest. It comprised specimens of hair out of a peculiar species of bull's tails; variegated flies, lops, and bugs; black and white snails; camel's dung from the desert; a phial full of cuckoo's spittle; cushy kye, from the Harmalyam mountains;[30] two white mice with red eyes; a piece of black cinder out of a burning mountain; the entire back bone of a red herring; a white pebble, considered nearly as old as the world itself; a front tooth of a jackass; four rats' tails of different lengths; a stuffed sucking pig, in an elegant glass case; a lump of fairy's butter;[31] six green and speckled caterpillars; four sparrows' eggs; two geese feet; four moths, and two speckled butterflies; several tadpoles, preserved in spirits; three cods' heads; with many other articles of great curiosity. Now we saw the Pilgrim and *Common-sense* were eagerly importuned to purchase those interesting objects; and the dealers in them maintained that they were a sovereign remedy for all political troubles whatever. With an accurate knowledge of these works of nature, there was no need for a man to trouble himself about going to the City of Reform; for this would prove the real saving knowledge, and would fill his belly and clothe his back. Several of the learned men then surrounded *Common-sense* and Pilgrim, and almost insisted that the latter should go no further on his journey. The following dialogue between the *Professors* and *Radical* then took place:—

Professors.—Allow us, my good sir, to impress upon your attention the absolute necessity of your remaining with us, for some time at least, in order that your mind may be cultivated and enlarged with the elements of true knowledge and science.

Radical.—I am fully bent on pressing forward in my journey. What you call knowledge has no immediate nor necessary connection with my social condition and happiness. I know I have too little for my labour, am kept poor and degraded, my wife and children are in rags, and myself, politically speaking, an outcast.

Professors.—But only listen to us for a moment. Our various departments of knowledge are so delightful and improving, that you will soon find that deep sense of degradation you speak of entirely leave you, and you will be raised to respectability and renown, by the lessons of wisdom we shall teach you.

Radical.—I consider your opinions arrant delusion. You are a parcel of exquisite coxcombs. You employ learning to enslave and degrade mankind, not to elevate them or make them socially happy or comfortable. You have always been the ready dupes and instruments of wicked and tyrannical men; and teach any thing but that which is really useful and beneficial for the mass of the people to know.

Here there arose a violent clamour from all parts of the Bazaar and the whole race of learned Professors, were highly indignant at the plainness of *Radical*'s remarks upon their sacred callings. Some began to hoot, and spit upon *Common-sense*, and the Pilgrim; and a considerable crowd gathered around them both, and followed them to the end of *Scientific-place*, pouring out torrents of low invective and ribaldry, on their uncultivated and boorish natures, and their disrespect for true knowledge and science.

PART VI

Now we saw in our dream that *Common-sense* took the Pilgrim to a place of refreshment after the strange sights the latter had witnessed; and when this was done, the guide took him to see *Bribery-street*, one of the most important and crowded thoroughfares in the whole city. The pressure of the multitude was great, as this was an important public day, the election and chairing of a Member of Parliament for the City of Plunder. The candidate was met at the entrance to the street, carried on the shoulders of the electors, and followed by an immense and noisy crowd, who hurrahed and shouted with might and main, in answer to which the member kindly and politely bowed his head several times in succession. This was considered an act of great condescension, grace, and humility; and an infallible sign that he was endowed with much wisdom and uprightness of purpose. His name was *Numskull*, and he was descended from an ancient family in the neighbourhood, whose connections were very numerous. As the Pilgrim advanced down the street, the scene began to deepen in interest and political profligacy. Hundreds of houses were opened for eating and drinking, and the electors were reeling about the streets in a state of savage and beastly intoxication. Some had been retained in their residences for a whole week together, and never allowed to go over the door, nor see the light of the sun; and so well plied had they been with drink, that they thought the time only one night. But eating and drinking were not the only means that Members of Parliament employed to promote their electioneering views. A vast number of electors obtained considerable sums of money, whilst others got places, and situations for their sons and relatives in exchange for their "vote and interest."

Common-sense did not fail to point out to *Radical* the evil consequences of this system of bribery; and to show him how the liberties and happiness of the natives of the City of Plunder, were subverted by those unconstitutional practices. The Pilgrim implicitly acquiesced in every word his guide uttered.

After *Common-sense* and the Pilgrim had left *Bribery-street*, they bent their steps to *Quack-quadrant*, a part of the city that had been vastly enlarged, beautified, and improved, within these few years. Here the sight was indeed both curious and imposing. The number of persons engaged in promoting the happiness of mankind and removing all their social and political troubles, was great beyond conception; and the harmony that prevailed amongst them was a pleasing feature of their society. They, however, walked very quick, looked wild, and had their eyes fixed on particular objects. *Common-sense* took *Radical* to one part of the *Quadrant*, which was occupied by a great doctor in the Science of Quackery, who was dressed in a long cotton robe, a muslin turban, and beautifully figured gingham inexpressibles.[32] He was demonstrating to a crowded audience, how all the evils of state could be removed by making certain things in our own country, and sending them, when made, away to other distant climes — and this was the true secret of all national wealth, to give neighbouring countries, whatever you can make at home; and the more naked and pennyless you leave the workers at home the more rich will the nation become. This was loudly applauded by the company. The next person the strangers met with, was a great lord for the City of Plunder, who comes here at stated intervals to deliver lectures to the people, who, he said, were all very ignorant, and extremely liable to delusion. He pointed out some very striking analogies between the body politic and the body corporate, and showed that reason clearly indicated that the one should be treated in the same way as the other. If the people were grumbling, discontented, quarrelsome, and noisy, it was a clear proof that more irritating and inflammatory humours in the body, gripes in the bowels, vertigoes[33] and delirium in the head, crude exestuations in the stomach,[34] frothy discharges of mucus from the chops,[35] and irregularities by laxatives, astringents,[36] sedatives, and absorbents. But he preferred the laxative system beyond all others. It might be turned into a perfect mine of national wealth. He would recommend the whole people to be well scoured in their intestines for a considerable period, as the cheapest method of properly manuring the soil, and enabling it to yield treble its present quantum of produce. Nay, he had no doubt, but in the due course of time, the whole people would get into the method of evacuating gold sovereigns, so that the voice of want and misery would never be heard more!

Common-sense and *Radical* were interrupted in hearing a more detailed account of this wonderful projector, by an immense crowd of other schemers, parading the whole length of *Quack-quadrant*, accompanied with a loud blowing of tin trumpets, and rams' horns. These men were engaged in a new and extensive undertaking for the renovation of the species. The appearance of the whole assembly was marked and striking. There were great numbers of persons with long and sad countenances, broad brimmed hats, buttonless coats, and with a cunning arch look of sinister design conspicuously spread over the whole physiognomy. Some were running up and down with long tin cases; maps, plans, sketches, estimates, elevations, designs, spirit levels, theodolites, chains, compasses, scales, ink bottles, tape-lines, &c. &c. The grand scheme of these men, who were now especially patronized, at the City of Plunder, by both parties, the *Ins* and *Outs*, was to level the globe, and to set carriages to run on the level plains, to carry the rich at *thirty miles* the hour, and to gratify and "ameliorate" the poor, by allowing them to look at the wonderful exhibition. The advantages to be derived from this plan was, that the sight of such a "vast improvement" would ultimately fill the bellies, clothe the backs of and shelter the millions, without any assistance, either from themselves of any one else. *Common-sense* and the Pilgrim were solicited by the leading projectors to get into some of their sliding machines; but they positively refused, and bent their steps to another part of the *Quadrant*.

A little lower down, they found a great crowd of persons about a man with green spectacles, a wooden leg, and a prodigious hump on his back. He was delivering an oration on a New Moral System of the Universe, where all were to live in a state of inconceivable peace, happiness, and contentment.[37] He endeavoured to demonstrate that there was no need to travel to the City of Reform, for all men had to consult *nature*, in the conduct of other animals around us, and regulate our conduct accordingly. Dogs afforded the best illustration. There was always the greatest harmony and peace in their society when they had *community* of property; for if one had a bone, and another had none, there was sure to be growling, and snarling, and fighting. Men, therefore, ought to have no personal property; but should all contrive matters so as to lap out of one trough. The lecturer was going on to show his deluded hearers, that the same principles applied to the intercourse of the sexes; and that wives were the great bane of society! Here *Common-sense* and *Radical* became so disgusted with his follies and blasphemies, that they abruptly left *Quack-quadrant* altogether.

At the further end *Quack-quadrant* was a most extensive and dreary looking burial ground, and near it a very large building, with iron bars at its windows for the reception of lunatics. The number of residents who died ere their heads were "tipp'd with grey,"[38] was very great; and the reverses of fortune, speculations, embarrassments, disappointed hopes, and broken hearts, of the traders of this noted place, drive thousands to madness, and confirmed idiotism. The sight of these two establishments made a deep impression upon the

Pilgrim, and more than anything he had witnessed, pointed out the necessity of his making more vigorous efforts in future, to get to a place of safety.

The Pilgrim now expressed a desire to depart from the city, and that he felt a little exhausted by the labour he had undergone in his examination of it. *Common-sense* was anxious, however, that he should see *Paperkite-buildings*, which were near at hand. To this *Radical* assented. Here the people seemed to talk an altogether new language, different from anything that Pilgrim had hitherto heard in this metropolis. There was an everlasting chatter, like the incessant crowings of a rookery, about stocks, funds, omnium, scrip, debentures, rentes, metaliques, discounts, premiums, exchequer bills, shares, accounts, balances, advances, consols, India stock, bank stock, exchanges, settling days, bear and bull account, lame ducks, pressures, panics, long annuities, bar gold, bullion, coin, mint prices, &c. &c.[39] The agitation and anxiety amongst the moving throng of *Buildings* were exceedingly interesting. The people were all exchanging bits of paper one with another; and this act was designated by the phrase of "the circulating medium," on which many large volumes of books had been written, and which was considered as an occult science in that part of the country. These papers differed one from another, in size, shape, texture, and embellishments. Some had figures of sheep suspended by the middle with a blanket; ships riding at anchor; a lady sitting with a long pole in her hand, and a lion crouching at her feet; views of iron bridges, church steeples, and court houses. But the newest design of note upon "change" was that of a bull popping his head out of a china shop, which was considered as an extremely expressive representation of the nature and offices of the instrument. The artist who executed it had been presented with a splendid necessary utensil made of the most refined and brittle clay of the country. The leading principle of occupation of the people in *Paperkite-buildings* was that they enticed men to take their notes, and to pay them something valuable for them, and then to keep out these notes from their own residences as long as they can. Here *Common-sense* pointed out to the Pilgrim the whole machinery, and how detrimental it was to the freedom and happiness of all nations.

On leaving this place, *Common-sense*, and his companion, *Radical*, found themselves at the entrance of *Usury-row*, and determined to have a peep, notwithstanding the place looked *very dirty* and had a remarkably disgusting *odour* about it. At this they soon ceased to wonder, for they found the place swarming with Jews of every description and grade. Here, in a corner, was a dealer in *old clothes*, there, in another, an equally honest buyer, and seller, and changer of *old pictures*. Here were money changers, and money lenders of all sorts and sizes, from the dealer in foreign coins, and buyers of old silver, to the loan monger, the Leviathan stock jobber, and the hawker of shares of Real del Monte Mines, Equitable loan fund societies, Railways to the moon and every conceivable scheme,[40] whether above ground or under it. At last, they were stopped by a fellow with a long beard, who, taking *Common-sense* by the button, earnestly begged him, and his astonished companion, to take, as he called it, "a slishe of de new loan for 1839!" "Here, (said he) is de scrip! vat you hesitate for? Only a trifle—*two, tree, four, hundred tousand pounds!*" *Radical* assured the Jew he had not in the world *four thousand pence*, when, to his utter astonishment, he found that was to make *no difference!* "Bah! what you say about poverty? (said the Jew) nonsense! I tell you de scrip is at a good premium already, and rising like de smoke, so all you have to do is to order your broker to shell and pocket *de difference* on settling day!" "But who must I sell to," said *Radical*. "Vy, to de first fool you meet wid monish in his pocket," replied the Jew, with a leer and a wink. *Radical* could make nothing of this; so turning to *Common-sense*, he asked, if this were a *loan*, to *whom* the money was *lent?* The Jew, however, would have the talk to himself; "lent (said he) vy, to de grand Chancellor of de Exchequer, de great and de profound Rabbi, Spring Rische?"[41] But how come you to lend to him? asked *Radical*. "Why, for to shave the contry to be sure!" rejoined Smouch. "Save our country! (exclaimed *Radical*) in that case, it is our duty to give, *not to lend*, and at a surious interest!" "To be sure! (said *Common-sense*) look at Puffendorf, and Grotius,[42] and every civilian; a country, in its *need*, can command LIFE as well as MONEY." "Bah! (said the Jew) bah! nonshense! no one *shaves* his contry for *nothing*, now a days! We must have the interest, aye, and de principal into the bargain! because why; you know out of your *gains*, you can MAKE ANODER LOAN and SHAVE your contry AGAIN! besides getting *rich*, as all *shavers* of de contry should do! Dat is the plan! — ha! ha!"

Common-sense was so disgusted with this villain, that he fairly turned upon his heel, and taking *Radical* by the arm, walked out of the place, muttering, "that fellow would grace a lamp-post, at all events!"

Trudging along in a pelt after this adventure, *Radical* and his friend suddenly came upon a place very different in appearance from *Usury-row*. It was a charming retired spot with a narrow avenue, but growing wider as they walked down. Before the houses were pretty gardens, planted with flowering shrubs and odoriferous plants and flowers; sweet briar, double blossom thoru, savine, heart's ease, lily of the valley, rue, marygold, orange thyme, thorn apple, batchelor's buttons, sweet William, sensitive plant, bee-orchids, monk's-hood, and love-in-a-mist.[43] Every house had a jasmine arbour leading to the back door. In front, hung cages with turtle doves, billing and cooing; Indian sparrows, and breeding canaries. The windows were all furnished with *Venetian* blinds, to keep out the too saucy sunshine; and, in some, the sound of music and singing was heard; in others, the inhabitants seemed not to be up, though it was now afternoon. *Radical* observed that all the doors were painted green, had no knockers, and mostly stood a little open, as did the garden gates also. "Bless me! (said *Common-sense*) this must be *Prostitute-place*, surely; but we shall soon find that out! And now, *Radical*, take care to remember you have a *wife and family* with you!" "I shall hardly *forget that*," quoth Radical, archly. "Well; we shall adventure," says *Common-sense*, and without ceremony, he marches into a house of a very elegant exterior, followed by Radical, who began to think this was very "free and easy" sort of work. On entering they were accosted by a very nice old lady, who said they were just in the nick of time to hear the greatest treat in the world, for *Lady Diana Trapes*, who was famous in the fashionable world for her musical and comic talents, was just going to give them an "*aria*," accompanied by herself on the Spanish guitar; the nice old lady then begged them to walk up stairs, and on *Radical* hesitating and looking rather sheepish, assured them that the besides Lady Di, there were only her three nieces, the Misses Skipjack, their companion, Miss Pliable, the Honourable Mrs Straddle, Lady Polly Prude, and the Dutchess of Graveairs; together with Sir Harry Helldrake, Jack Jauntish, M.P., Colonel Cully, the Duke of Dunder, and Lord Longbow! In short, it was quite a "*select*" party!

On their entrance, *Radical* and *Common-sense* found the party very much at their ease, having just finished their lunch. Some were lolling about on sofas sipping noyeau,[44] cherry brandy, and other liqueurs, and recommending them to the ladies who seemed "nothing loath." Others were tittering in a corner over some scandal in a newspaper; a brace were enjoying a port-folio of rare coloured prints; and *Lord Longbow* was helping *Lady Di* to tune her instrument. "How did you *vote* last night *Jauntish*?" said *Lady Polly Prude*, "Not with these odious Radicals I hope!" "Can't say 'pon honour!" was the answer, "got so much champagne with a devilled gizzard at Bellamy's[45] — that, curse me, if I know how I voted!" "Well, if you voted *wrong*, you know you need not speak to ME again; (said the *Honourable Mrs. Straddle*) that's all!" *Radical* stared at this, and was going to ask if *Members of Parliament voted to please ladies*, but *Common-sense* motioned him to be quiet. "I'm sick of hearing of these Radicals (said the *Duke of Dunder*.) *Colonel*, why don't you cut them down at once?" "Give the word, my *Lord Duke* — (rejoined the *Colonel*) — and *we* are ready 'pon honour!" "They deserve *twice* as much, the odious wretches!" (said *Miss Skipjack*.) "*We* can't kill men *twice* over, like *you* ladies!" said the *Colonel*. *Lady Di* was now ready to sing; so playing a prelude on her guitar, and leering with a pair of black eyes full of comic archness at *Jack Jauntish*, she sung as follows:—

> If a child you would please
>   Give it tuckers and bibs
> Politicians delight
>   But is satires and squibs.
> Your wits are still running
>   On humour and joke;
> Your soldier loves nothing
>   Like thunder and smoke.
> But if ladies to charm
>   You e'er have in your eye,
> Believe me there's nought
>   Like a charming white lie;

And to sport a white lie
  Who so ready as he
Who the host of his lifetime
  Has been an M.P.!

CHORUS
Has been a M.P.—been an M.P.;
Who the best of his lifetime
Has been an M.P.

With a lie comes a smile,
  Or it sticks in the throat;
And who wants a smile
  That e'er canvass'd a vote
With the smile goes a bow,
  Or it is'nt for good;
And who e'er lack'd a bow
  That on hustings has stood
But he, smile, and bow,
  Will all fail to delight,
If the breath be not sweet,
  And the teeth be not white;
And from the teeth outwards
  How pleasant is he
Who the best of his lifetime
  Has been an M.P!

CHORUS
Has been a M.P.—been an M.P.;
Who the best of his lifetime
Has been an M.P.

When *Lady Di* had concluded, a very pretty young lady seeing *Radical* was a stranger, and hearing his name, condescendingly entered into conversation with him. "Was he fond of music?" she asked in a voice that was really very charming, particularly when in company with an eye, the fascination of which, *Common-sense* said, was hardly inferior to that of the rattlesnake! *Radical* could only say he was quite ignorant of the science. Oh! so much the better! she of all things loved natural and wild music! and especially the *Aeolian harp*, of which she had in her *Boudoir* one of the most splendid ever seen! She should be "so *happy* to have *his* opinion of it!" *Radical* hardly knew what to say in reply to this kind offer; but *Common-sense* saw it was time to be off; so making an excuse, they trooped down stairs, and in such a hurry, that they had nearly run over another party of fashionables who were coming up, fresh from the Parliament house!

PART VII

Now, we saw that *Radical* and his family made preparations for immediately leaving the City of Vanity-fair; and *Common-sense* made himself useful in assisting him on his journey. When the Pilgrim had advanced a short way out of the town he cast his eyes back to it, and on looking at its showy and splendid domes, and recollecting all the enticing things in it, he felt a peculiar stupor steal insensibly over him. He was now upon the enchanted ground, a place where many a resolute Pilgrim had been overpowered with a drowsiness that ended in death. *Common-sense* reminded him of the dangerous pass; and, therefore, *Radical* was, in some measure, prepared to struggle against the intoxicating influence. He had to make great efforts to keep up his wife's resolution, which had been more severely shaken by the scenes in Vanity-fair than his own. After a determined struggle they all got safely off the enchanted ground, and arrived at a small cottage by the way-side, kept by a *Mr. Good-intent*, who comforted and directed Pilgrims when exhausted with their perilous journies. This worthy host informed the Pilgrim that he was now only two day's journey from the City of Reform, whose battlements and towers he would see from the top of the hill, a short distance from the cottage. But he also told him that he would have another severe battle to fight before he actually arrived at the City; but he had no doubt that he would prove victorious.

Radical was now within one step of the attainment of all his hopes; but that, though short, was, he knew, doomed to be sharp. Before him was the long wished for *City of Reform*. Like Bruce, when he reached the sources of the Nile; like Lander, when he sailed down the embouchure of the Niger; like Cortes, when reaching the western-most boundaries of Darien, he looked with astonished eye over the blue and boundless Pacific,[46] *Radical* beheld the lofty and noble towers and glittering spires of the city with a sensation of awe and rapture. The former, however, predominated; for on the plain on which he now stood, and across which he now looked, was to be fought the last terrible conflict with *Political Apollyon*, who, he was warned by *Common-sense*, would here confront him for the last time, with all the power which *desperation* could call to his aid. In fact, this was so well known that the walls and turrets of the city, which looked upon the plain, were covered with spectators of every grade anxious to see the issue of the contest. From a horrid looking fastness on the right it was generally expected the monster would issue to try his last desperate change. This fastness was called Change Alley Fastness. It was a *deep, gloomy,* craggy glen, infested with venomous snakes of all kinds, which fed upon the poisonous herbs with which it was over-run; the trees were loaded with unwholesome ivy, and covered with fungi, and wet moss, and mildew, the offspring of the corrupt, marshy ground which constituted the bottom. It was, in short, a place that few persons possessed of prudence cared to go near; and here it was supposed the monster *Apollyon* waited in ambush, having got his armour refitted, to attack *Radical* in crossing the plain to the city gate, which was called "*Pilgrim's Gate.*" *Radical* had been warned by *Common-sense* that the monster might probably bring auxiliaries to help to crush him, and saw that it was prudent to take every precaution that could be thought of before-hand. He, therefore, loaded the musket which the good shepherds had given him with two or three balls, instead of one, and an extra charge of gunpowder. He also loaded both his pistols, and sharpened, and loosened in its sheath, his well-tempered sword, which had shattered *Apollyon's* shield and drawn his blood in their first skirmish, when *Moral-force* met his death so unexpectedly. He also called his eldest boy, whom the journey had now made bold and hardy, and made him march close by his side to be ready for any emergency.

A loud buzz from the thickly crowded walls of the city, at last announced the approach of the horrid monster *Apollyon*. He was mounted on a huge and gigantic horse, of a strange pyebald hue. This monstrous brute was named "DEBT," and moved unwieldily along, making the very earth tremble. Out of his nostrils came a thick, heavy smoke, and his hoofs, clad in huge iron shoes, ploughed up the plain, devastating everything as he moved on. *Radical*, with great presence of mind, however, observed that the brute shyed at two or three objects in passing, and concluded that he was less easy to be brought to a steady charge than the monster on his back could wish. On his back sat *Apollyon*, armed with spear and sword, his eyes burning like red coals, and hot breath coming from his mouth, but his wings were not expanded as before, he, probably, remembering how he suffered on the occasion. As the monster drew near, *Radical* formed his plan, and giving his son one of his pistols and the sword, he sent him round behind a little knoll on the other side, bidding him, when the monster was opposite, fire his pistol boldly from his place of ambush.

As the monster drew near, *Radical* saw, with great apprehension, that he had an auxiliary on one side. It was a lean, gaunt, immensely tall skeleton-looking bearded figure, with what seemed a purse in one hand and a dagger in the other. The name of this tall, withered wretch was *Bribery*, and he was always ready to assist the monster *Apollyon* by fair means or foul. He kept close by the monster's steed, and *Radical*, seeing such odds against him, began almost to think he was lost. However, putting up a prayer to God, he stood his ground, with his bayonet fixed, awaiting the onset as best he might, and keeping a steady eye on his foes to enable him to parry or avoid the terrible thrust of the horrid monster's deadly spear. At this critical moment, the boy, true to his father's commands, fired his pistol suddenly, when the enormous brute on which *Apollyon* rode suddenly wheeled, and in doing so completely overwhelmed the gaunt wretch *Bribery*, and stumbling over him, came completely down on his knees to the apparent dismay of his rider, who used spur and bridle furiously to make him rise again. This, however, the unwieldy brute could not do so quickly, but that *Radical* seeing *Apollyon's* attention engaged, drew very near, and fired his musket right into the belly of the unwieldy steed, which, giving a horrid snort and plunge, rolled over on one side. *Radical* boldly seizing the opportunity, gashed with his bayonet the belly of the brute, "DEBT," out of which rushed a stream of blood so noisome and hot that it burned up the herbage like volcanic lava, and sent up suffocating vapours, which, by their pungency, forced *Radical* to retreat a little for breath! He perceived, however, to his great joy, that *Apollyon* was completely entangled by the fall of DEBT, and was going to reload his piece as fast as possible, when his attention was drawn by the cries of his son who invoked his father's assistance as in great terror. And well he might, for the boy was attacked by a burly fellow called *Treachery*, who had skulked on the other side of the monster, and thus avoided *Radical's* view. He was a huge, burly, and ugly wretch, with a very loud and threatening voice, and dressed in a loathsome manner, with a bloody *death's head and cross bones* painted on his breast which gave him an appearance shocking in the extreme. This wretch had made at the boy, who though in terrible alarm and far over-matched, kept him bravely at bay with his sword as well as he could. *Radical* lost no time, but coming rapidly up to him, with his pistol blew his brains completely out, just in time to save his boy who was on the point of falling a victim to the villain who thus met his reward. *Radical*, however rejoiced, had still no time to lose. The monster *Apollyon* was making tremendous efforts to free himself from his fallen steed. He was expanding his wings with all his might, and in no long time would have disengaged himself from this entanglement. *Radical* lost no time, but loading his well-proved piece as heavily as it would bear, came as near as he dared, and taking deliberate aim shot the monster through both wings, lodging, at the same time, a ball in his body just under the shoulder. This shot, as before, dislodged from the wings as well as the body of *Apollyon*, tremendous quantities of the paper-like feathers with which they were clothed, and so terrible had been the shot that in some places the lean ribs of the monster were plainly to be seen where the feathery covering had been blown off. The bellowings of the monster were now frightful, but his efforts gradually relaxing, *Radical* saw he was mortally wounded and his strength rapidly sinking. Drawing cautiously near, therefore, he succeeded in giving him repeated stabs; under which, roaring as a whale does when struck with lances of his pursuers, he at last sunk motionless and expired upon the body of his dead steed, *Debt*, which, after all, instead of aiding him had given *Radical* the Victory. *Radical* fell down upon his knees and thanked God who had thus brought him through his last trial in triumph and unhurt.

After the Pilgrim and his family had recovered from the excitement of this combat, they bent forward towards the City of Reform, which was just in sight. At a short distance they came to a most delightful country, whose air was deliciously sweet and balmy, whose fields were adorned with a profusion of flowers and aromatic plants, and its woods resounded to the notes of thousands of winged warblers. Here there was the prospect of everything desirable. At the entrance to the City the Pilgrim and his wife and family were met by the leading authorities of the place, who welcomed the party to their new residence, and complimented them upon the resolution and courage they had, one and all, manifested, during their long and perilous journey. Ample provisions were immediately obtained, a comfortable house procured, and the whole party clad with useful and becoming garments suitable to a working man's station in life.

When *Radical* and his family had thus got settled in the City of Reform, they all experienced a visible change in the whole circle of their domestic circumstances and enjoyments. Direct taxes were unknown; and the only thing in the shape of an impost was a small duty laid upon a few articles of foreign importation. Here every man breathed the air of freedom. No corrupt influence exerted; no loss of business or labour for giving your vote as your judgement might dictate; no man pursing politics, as a trade or profession, *to live by*; no fraudulent schemes with high-sounding names, to cheat the working man out of half the produce of his labour or his skill; no pensioners upon the public bounty, rolling in wealth, and bursting with vanity and insolence; no deprivation of civil rights on account of poverty; no distinctions between the rich and the poor, as to the administration of justice; no denial of the working man of his right to a decent subsistence out of the soil when aged and infirm, or deprived of the means of getting employment; no shutting him up in Giant Despair's Castle, starving him to death, separating him from his wife, and his children from both; no mortgaging of the citizen's labour and skill, to endless posterity, by public debts; no men employed by the government under the pretence of keeping the public peace, but with the real object of acting as spies upon the conduct of every man who may make himself obnoxious, by his boldness and public spirit, to the members of the Government; no herds of base, low-minded, sycophantish, creatures, who dare not even speak in a whisper on public affairs; no sending men to legislate for the natives of this renowned city, whose only recommendation is that they are rich, or connected with rich people; no men chosen to fill high and important public offices merely on the strength of their hereditary wisdom; no transporting men to distant climes for killing a wild bird or animal of any kind; no votes for members of the truly reformed legislature openly bought and sold; no schemes for checking the numbers of mankind, or for destroying their helpless and innocent children, to make more room for the idle and unprincipled part of the community; no means of ignorance and quackery gaining the ascendency over wisdom and integrity, in the conducting of public business; no legislative confessions that corruption is as well known to exist in the government as that "the sun is to be seen at noon day;" no succumbing to foreign nations which it is a bounden duty to keep in awe and subjection; no putting up with insults on the national character or honour from the sheer influence of national profligacy; no erecting of monuments to men who, if remembered at all, ought to be remembered only to their shame; no usurious, scheming, fraudulent, vagabonds, invested with power or influence over the public weal, none of these things were here. On the contrary, *here* every man possessing common industry was able to earn an ample livelihood, and bring up his family in ease and comfort; here the name of taxgatherer was unknown, and even the office of the *overseer* was almost a *sinecure*; here was no standing army, no police spies, no yeomanry, but the whole male population, from twenty to fifty years of age, were armed, and served in turn in the National Militia, and the only civil functionaries were the judge, the magistrate, the sheriff, the high constable, and the petty constable; here every man could, if he pleased, shoot a hare or a pheasant, unfound fault with, if he took care not to damage fences or growing crops; here was no such thing as a stock exchange, or a saving bank, or a bank note for any sum under FIFTY pounds, or a stock jobber, or a Jew, or a depositor, but men having money to lend, lent to traders on security; here was hardly any occasion for a bankrupt court or list, the occurrence being comparatively rare; here every man ate beef, mutton, veal, port, or bacon every day, and every man brewed his own strong beer, from the labourer to the lord; here the linen was spun at home, for the most part, and was so strong that it would out-last *one hundred* times the quantity of flimsy cotton; here the furniture of every man was made of solid oak, mahogany, or rosewood, and not of mere fir deal-boards veneered over with the appearance of mahogany as thin as a wafer; here, in short, all men spent a life of honest but happy industry, and lived generally to a good old age. Such was the CITY OF REFORM. And now, behold! our dream changed on a sudden, and we beheld *Radical* surrounded by his children and grandchildren, his head as white as snow, and they all kneeled down around his bed and praised God, with him, who had brought them there to happiness, and preserved their grandfather through all his dangers, even through that last bloody conflict with the beast *Apollyon* and his associates; and the old man then gave them his last blessing, and lay back, in his bed, and departed without a sigh! May our latter end be like his! AMEN.

Notes

1. *Patibulary*: pertaining to the gallows.
2. *Logomachies*: disputes over words.
3. *Hemiplegia*: paralysis of one side of the body.
4. *Squamification*: producing sores or scabs.
5. *"Transcendentals"*: a contemporary nickname for the Utilitarians or philosophical radicals.
6. *Jeremy Bentham*: (1745-1832), Utilitarian philosopher and social reformer. His rationalist approach to social problems is satirized in the text as cold and inhumane.
7. *Guns loaded with oyster shells*: as Radical himself indicates, this satirical vignette of a republican presumably has a classical basis, though it has not been traced.
8. The specialized vocabulary of the Stock Exchange and banking is mercilessly satirized in the narrative.

Scrip: a document issued in lieu of money, or a receipt for shares in a commercial venture. Perhaps unintentionally, this is also an ironic reference, as another, more familiar meaning of the word refers to the purse carried by pilgrims in which alms or charitable donations were carried.

Omnium: the total value of a stock.

Conshol: government stocks bearing interest. The term is an abbreviation of Consolidated Annuities, a term first used in the mid-eighteenth century. See Norman Russell, *The Novelist and Mammon: the literary representation of the world of commerce in the nineteenth century* (Oxford: Oxford University Press, 1986), pp. 39-40.

9.   *Shadrach*: a colloquialism for a Jew. In Daniel 1-3, Shadrach, Meshach and Abednego, three Jewish provincial rulers under King Nebuchadnezzar, are thrown into a furnace for defying his idolatrous religious practices. Miraculously, they survive.

10.   This list of worthies includes monarchs, republicans, writers, radicals and jurists:

Alfred the Great: (849-99), Anglo-Saxon king of Wessex who prevented the Vikings conquering the whole of England, negotiated the 'Danelaw' partition, and established the English navy.

Egbert: (d. 839), king of the West Saxons and reputedly the *Bretwalda* or 'sole ruler of Britain'.

Sir William Gascoigne: (?1350-1419), an English judge renowned for his integrity (legend has it that he imprisoned the future Henry V for violent behaviour).

Fortesque: Sir John Fortescue (*c.* 1385-1476), English jurist.

Coke: Sir Edward Coke (1552-1634), English jurist, statesman, and author of influential law books.

Bacon: Sir Francis Bacon (1561-1626), English statesman, philosopher and author of the classic pro-scientific polemic, *The Advancement of Learning* (1605).

Hale: Sir Matthew Hale (1609-76), English judge and author of books on the common law.

Sir Thomas More: (1478-1535), English statesman, executed for his opposition to Henry VIII's creation of the Church of England, and author of *Utopia* (1516).

Hampden: John Hampden (1594-1643), English parliamentarian who became famous for his non-payment of Charles I's ship taxes in 1635, and who died of wounds in one of the early skirmishes of the English Civil War.

Pym: John Pym (1584-1643), English statesman and compatriot of Hampden, defended the rights of Parliament against the excesses of royal power.

Sydney: Algernon Sydney (1622-83), republican writer and

parliamentarian in the English Civil War, who was executed for his supposed role in the Whig 'Rye House Plot' to assassinate Charles II.

Locke: John Locke (1632-1704), English empirical philosopher and author of the foundation text of liberal politics, *Two Treatises on Government* (1690).

Harrington: James Harrington (1611-77), republican theorist and author of the Utopian *Oceana* (1656).

Marvell: Andrew Marvell (1621-78), English poet and parliamentarian.

Shippen: William Shippen (1673-43), parliamentary Jacobite and an opponent of the Whig oligarchy in the early eighteenth century.

Hollis: Denzil, 1st Baron Hollis (1599-1680), English statesman and supporter of the parliamentary forces in the early stages of the English Civil War.

Milton: John Milton (1608-74), English poet and republican, author of *Paradise Lost* (1667).

Vane: Sir Henry Vane (1613-62), English statesman, republican writer, and a leading Civil War politician.

Fairfax: Thomas, 3rd Baron Fairfax (1612-71), led the Parliamentary forces in the Civil War until he was succeeded by Cromwell in 1650.

Prynne: William Prynne (1600-69), Puritan pamphleteer and supporter of Parliament in the Civil War.

Selden: John Selden (1584-1654), English jurist, historian and opponent of royalist absolutism.

Bolingbroke: Henry St John, 1st Viscount Bolingbroke (1678-1751), Tory politician and author of influential works on 'country' politics and 'patriotic' monarchy.

Chatham: William Pitt, 1st Earl of Chatham (1708-78), the 'Elder' Pitt, English statesman and advocate of the Seven Years War with France (1756-63).

Tooke: John Horne Tooke (1736-1812), English radical and reforming philologist, leader of the Society for Constitutional Information, who was acquitted of treason in the infamous trials of 1794.

Paine: Thomas Paine (1737-1809), English revolutionary propagandist and activist, whose most famous works are probably *Common Sense* (1776), *The Rights of Man* (1791-92) and *The Age of Reason* (1794-96).

Cobbett: William Cobbett (1763-1835), the leading radical journalist of the early nineteenth century, as reflected in his weekly *Political Register*, begun in 1802 and continued until his death.

Cartwright: John Cartwright (1740-1824), the 'Father of Reform', veteran English radical, who campaigned for universal suffrage from the 1770s to his death.

11. I discuss this theme in the Introduction.

Marcus: a reference to the Malthusian satire *The Book of Murder* (1839) by 'Marcus', a book which advocated infanticide as a solution to poverty.

Peter Thimble: a Malthusian philosopher in Cobbett's play *Surplus Population and the Poor Law Bill* (1831).

12. *Corn Law Catechism*: a reference to the work of the Anti-Corn Law League, established nationally in 1839. Many Chartists opposed the League for its *laissez-faire* economics.

13. *Canadian dwarf*: the precise meanings of this satirical encounter are unclear, but presumably there is a reference to the rebellion against British rule in Lower Canada in 1837-38.

14. *Primum mobile*: (Latin) 'prime mover' or first principle.

15. *Umbrageous*: shadowy.

16. *Buckram*: coarse cotton linen stiffened with gum.

17. A satirical catalogue of Evangelical societies. The Society for the Suppression of Vice, established in the first decade of the nineteenth century, was one of the leading reactionary cultural institutions of its day.

18. *LEGAL TENDER*: money which a creditor must accept for the payment of a debt.

19. *Exchequer Bills*: bills of credit carrying the authority of Parliament.
    Saving Scrip: see note 8.

20. *Quarterings*: a coat-of-arms with four emblems to represent an alliance of families.

21. *Escutcheons*: the coat-of-arms on a shield.

22. Ecclesiastical offices.
    Clerical benefices: a church placement or living.
    Pluralities: the holding of two or more clerical benefices at the same time.
    Prebendaries: the office of a canon in a cathedral.

23. *Stygian comfort*: gloomy or hellish consolation.

24. *Racing Calendar*: this guide to horse racing fixtures had been established since the late eighteenth century.

25. Though the precise references are unclear, this scene represents an attack on bogus solutions to the Irish problem, including capitalist speculation.

26. *Empiric*: a charlatan or quack.

27. *Corporations*: urban development plans and companies, particularly concerned with housing.

28. *Prog*: either a stab or thrust, or the supply of provisions.

29. *Axy*: untraced, but presumably meaning 'persuaded'.

30. *Cushy kye, from the Harmalyam mountains*: a cocoa plant from the Himalayas.

31. *A lump of fairy's butter*: presumably a reference to the small buns known as fairy's cakes.

32. *Gingham inexpressibles*: fashionable cotton breeches.

33. *Vertigoes*: giddy sensations.

34. *Exestuations*: boiling or overheating.

35. *Chops*: the mouth.

36. *Astringents*: medicine used to stop bleeding and contract body tissues.
37. The target here is clearly Owenism.
38. *"Tipp'ed with grey"*: possibly a misquoted allusion to Shakespeare, *Much Ado About Nothing*, 5.3.25.
39. Another satirical catalogue of banking jargon.
     Debentures: bonds issued for the repayment of interest on loans.
     Metaliques: possibly a reference to metal currency, or to the Turkish 'metalik' coin.
     India stock: money invested in the East India Company.
     Settling days: the appointed day when an account or debt is settled.
     Bear and bull account: not identified.
     Lame ducks: investors who default on payments.
     Pressures: presumably, financial squeezes.
     Bar gold: gold in the form of small bricks.
     Mint prices: the best or new prices.
40. A satirical mini-catalogue of institutions of financial speculation.
     Real del Monte Mines: South American mining interests.
     Equitable Loan Fund Societies: philanthropic money-lending companies.
     Railways to the moon: a reference to the railway boom of the 1830s.
41. *Spring Rische*: Thomas Spring-Rice (1790-1866), Whig politician and Chancellor of the Exchequer 1835-39. He introduced the penny post.
42. Famous writers on the law.
     Puffendorf: Samuel von Puffendorf (1632-94), German writer on jurisprudence and international law.
     Grotius: Hugo Grotius (1583-1645), Dutch jurist and politician, widely regarded as the founder of international law.
43. A catalogue of ornamental plants. The following have been identified:
     Savine: a kind of juniper.
     Rue: dwarf shrubs.
     Batchelor's buttons: a type of meadow buttercup.
     Bee-orchids: an orchid with a flower that has the colour and appearance of a bee.
     Love-in-a-mist: a blue-flowered garden plant.
44. *Noyeau*: a brandy liquor.
45. *Bellamy's*: a gentleman's club in London.
46. European explorers.
     Bruce: James Bruce (1730-94), Scottish explorer, who reached the source of the Blue Nile in 1770.
     Lander: Richard Lander (1803-34), English explorer, who traced the course of the Niger river in north-west Africa.
     Cortes: Hernando Cortés (1485-1547), Spanish conquistador and conqueror of Mexico. Darien is in Panama.

Sunshine and Shadow

Thomas Martin Wheeler

Editor's introduction

Sunshine and Shadow appeared in weekly instalments in the *Northern Star* between 31 March 1849 and 5 January 1850. Its author was the Chartist administrator and schoolteacher Thomas Martin Wheeler (1811-62). Some brief biographical details will show that Wheeler was well qualified for writing a historical review of Chartism's progress.[1]

Wheeler was born in south London, the son of a publican and wheelwright. From this respectable artisan background he went to school in Stoke Newington, and was later apprenticed to his uncle in Banbury, a haberdasher and woolcomber.[2] Some of this experience is echoed in the early career of his hero Arthur Morton, who is also apprenticed to an uncle. Wheeler soon left this trade, however, and embarked on a restless early manhood. He trained as a baker, tried his hand at gardening and spent several years wandering around the southern counties of England as an itinerant artisan. Eventually he settled in London and simultaneously became a teacher and a stalwart activist in metropolitan radicalism.[3] He rose quickly into the ranks of Chartist officialdom. Like Thomas Cooper and other Chartist intellectuals he achieved a measure of social mobility through self-education and political service to radicalism. His schoolroom soon became a political venue for meetings. He became the London correspondent of the *Northern Star* in 1840, a Chartist lecturer, and a member and later secretary of the Executive of the National Charter Association. He was therefore at the hub of Chartism's national organization and policy decisions. In 1845 he helped O'Connor formulate the Chartist Land Plan. He joined the Society of Fraternal Democrats, and in March 1846 he demonstrated his internationalist credentials in an address to the Friends of Poland. He is reported to have said, 'there is more glory in dying in defence of our country's rights and liberties than in a whole life of mean and truckling subserviancy'.[4] Later that year he resigned his post as secretary to the Charter Association to take up a new position as secretary to the Chartist Land Company. The Land Company was an intiative aimed at resettling poor, urban labourers on the land. The company purchased land out of weekly subscriptions and built fine cottages in generous allotments (many of these buildings survive to the present day). As a reward for his administrative work Wheeler was provided with the freehold of a cottage in the settlement called O'Connorville (built at Heronsgate, now part of Rickmansworth, near London). He resigned his post in July 1847, but this did not mark the end of Wheeler's activism. He participated in the National Convention in March and April 1848, where he argued that the Kennington

Common demonstration on April 10 should go ahead despite government opposition. Wheeler moved:

> That they should issue a proclamation, declaring their determination to hold the meeting on Monday next, notwithstanding the foolish proclamation of the Government, and notice of the police.[5]

On the great day itself Wheeler rode in the delegates' carriage alongside O'Connor, Ernest Jones and George Julian Harney. After the failure of the petition he retired to his pastoral retreat and spade husbandry. The break from official duties gave him time to write. In March 1849 the *Northern Star* published the first episode of the 37 weekly 'communions' which would make up *Sunshine and Shadow*. With this achievement behind him, Wheeler resurfaced in 'late' Chartism. He was elected to the National Convention in 1851 and worked hard to sustain the National Charter Executive. He wrote for *Reynolds's Political Instructor* (1849-50) and helped Ernest Jones set up the *People's Paper* in 1852. His last Chartist publication was a very brief life of O'Connor written to accompany the funeral oration delivered at O'Connor's burial in 1855.[6] Wheeler ended his days working for the Friend-in-Need Life Assurance Company.

An indication of Wheeler's aspiration to become a writer as well as an activist can be seen in a short series of articles he wrote for the *Northern Star* in early 1848. These form an account of a walking tour between several Chartist settlements.[7] The style of the pieces owes much to Cobbett's *Rural Rides*, interspersing topographical observations with historical and political disquisitions on the decline of the yeomanry and the rottenness of modernity. The major difference between Wheeler and Cobbett, however, is that Wheeler can look to the Chartist settlements as the Utopian solution to this problem. Sentimental nostalgia for the Saxon past is counterbalanced by equally sentimental praise for the Paradise Regained of the Chartist Land Plan. As a resident at O'Connorville, Wheeler constructs himself as the living proof that social relations have been restored to their 'natural state'. The settlements are the reincarnation of that lost cottage economy so beloved by Cobbett, but they are also beacons of hope and social transformation. When Wheeler notes that Lowbands is fertile in misletoe and O'Connorville in holly, he waxes lyrical about the symbolic value of these crops:

> Lowbands and O'Connorville — the misletoe and the holly — like them, may be green and flourishing amidst the decay and rottenness by which they are surrounded — like them may they, not only in Christmas season, but in every season, throw a gleam of joy and mirth around, and reciprocally unite and twine with each other.[8]

An oscillation between Quixotic emotionalism and radical diatribe is a hallmark of Wheeler's style.

Sunshine and Shadow has not received the critical attention it deserves for two main reasons: its inaccessibility and its form. Those left-wing critics who have sought it out tend to dismiss it as a thinly veiled piece of propaganda or journalistic reportage, lacking rounded characters and a coherent plot.[9] If those are the agreed requirements for good fiction then *Sunshine and Shadows* will certainly be deemed to be of low-grade quality. But the narrative requires a different set of reading principles, as Wheeler was writing for a Chartist audience.[10]

The date of composition is the first clue to the story's purpose, which is to take stock of Chartism after the turbulence of 1848.[11] This does not mean that Wheeler merely wrote an elegy for a defeated cause, as some critics claim. Indeed, Wheeler makes impassioned pleas for renewed efforts and remobilization. But equally important was to find a narrative method that would allow him to both present and assess the movement as a historical event. As he declared at the opening of the first instalment, the 'fiction department of literature has hitherto been neglected by the scribes of our body, and the opponents of our principles have been allowed to wield the power of imagination over the youth of our party, without any effort on our part to occupy that wide and fruitful field' (p. 72). In order to 'wield the power of imagination' successfully Wheeler decided to focalize a 'History of Chartism' through the depiction of 'one of yourselves struggling against the power of adverse circumstances' (p. 192). In other words Wheeler proletarianized the *Bildungsroman*, not only in placing a working-class hero at the centre of the story, but in opening up realism to social and political analysis, and using the story to mobilize the reader. Moreover, he constructs his hero's destiny out of the key moments in Chartism's development. Arthur Morton does not stand apart from history but is woven into its texture, personifying its contradictions and uneven progress. Arthur's immediate relevance is to show Chartism's 'high and generous inspirations' (p. 192) in a climate of post-1848, counter-revolutionary smears and misrepresentation.

Arthur conforms to the conventions of *Bildungsroman* heroism in being an orphan and underdog (we think of Oliver Twist, Jane Eyre and Alton Locke among a host of others). His uncle is a crass south of England wool-merchant, who lazily dispatches his nephew to a second-rate boarding-school. The one ray of sunshine in this experience is the friendship of Walter North, son of a wine merchant and school boxing champ (any resemblance to David Copperfield and Steerforth must be coincidental, as Dickens's novel did not commence serialization until May 1849). The North family take Arthur in, where he falls in love with Julia North, who is both educated and like himself a 'lover of liberty' (p. 91). Class forces soon assert themselves, and Arthur is separated from the Norths geographically and socially. While he is apprenticed to a printer, Walter goes to Liverpool to take over the expanding family business. Wheeler transforms the traditional device of the wresting apart of two childhood 'brothers' into a model of the class structure after 1832. As Arthur tramps for work in London, Walter becomes a merchant prince, 'a specimen of that large and influential class' set to 'dethrone the feudal aristocracy of the realm, and monopolise the political and social power of the empire' (p. 84). Talent and prosperity are inversely related. Arthur has a 'cultivated intellect' and a Shelleyan imagination. Walter is a philistine and so corrupted that he plots the seduction of Julia and her marriage to a West Indian island governor. Julia's Clarissa-like treatment provokes one of several outbursts in the story against Victorian sexual morality. Marriages of convenience are merely 'legalized prostitution' (p. 87). Although at other moments in the story Wheeler takes a traditionalist patriarchal line in being dismissive of women's public participation in the Chartist movement, his assault on bourgeois marriage and sexual hypocrisy owes much to Wollstonecraft and Godwin.[12] As the plot unfolds, it is clear that Julia has more in common with the exploited working class than her own exploiting class which betrays her.

The class polarization of Arthur and Walter gathers pace as Arthur tramps to Birmingham and arrives in the middle of the Chartist ferment of 1839.[13] Chartism provides his grievances with a voice and he becomes an activist and speaker. After the Bull Ring riots, which Wheeler attributes to *agents provocateurs*, Arthur is wrongly accused of arson and flees to Liverpool to take a boat to America. He almost seeks refuge at Walter's house, who is now a ruthless class enemy and would have certainly turned him in to the authorities. His sexual *rite de passage* begins appropriately at sea. His boat sinks in a storm and he and other survivors are picked up by a ship coincidentally carrying Julia to her new estate in the Caribbean. They embark on a liaison *manqué*. While Wheeler does not allow adultery to happen, he defends the lovers' feelings, and refutes the convention of the fallen woman:

> Love in her was no crime, albeit she was the bride of another, — it was the result of feelings as pure as nature ever implanted in human breast .... we produce human nature as it is — veritable flesh and blood, — glowing with warm and ardent feelings. (p. 105)

Almost half a century before Tess Durbeyfield, Julia is victimized by 'a false and slavish code of morals [which] still reigns in all its pristine barbarity' (p. 112). The same fate also afflicts Walter North's titled wife-of-convenience Clarence Fitzherbert. Like Ernest Jones in *Woman's Wrongs*, Wheeler highlights the oppressiveness of bourgeois marriage, though he does not extend this feminist consciousness as far as giving the women characters an independent narrative voice. Although Arthur manages to secure employment on her husband's estate, Julia dies of a broken heart (not guilt), surrounded by 'luxury and power' (p. 118). While there are echoes here of Heathcliff and Cathy Earnshaw, Wheeler's method of disturbing moral orthodoxies is very different from Emily Brontë's ironizing tiers of first-person narratives. While Brontë's approach removes narrative authority, Wheeler uses the discourse of direct address he has inherited from radical journalism to defend the 'sins' of his characters with an evangelical fervour. The love affair also mirrors the novel's literary unorthodoxy; both it and Arthur are trespassers on bourgeois territory, challenging its social exclusivity.

Arthur is now gloomier if wiser, and his reflections on his experience begin to merge with Wheeler's. He works in America for a while, depressed by slavery, but hopeful it will not be succeeded by the 'white slavery' of industrial capitalism. He then takes a gamble and returns to England, arriving during the 1842 disturbances. Once again his fortunes are revived by collective struggle and he is swept into a leadership position (one of the tale's weaknesses is not providing us with any examples of Arthur's oratory). Despite the failures of 1842 Arthur is now rejuvenated and a period of 'sunshine' ensues with romance and marriage. He and wife Mary (whom he meets at a Chartist rally) settle into a respectable life until unemployment blights Arthur's life for the second time — this time more ferociously as he is the 'breadwinner'.[14] His spirits deteriorate rapidly. Like John Barton in Gaskell's *Mary Barton* (1848), he personifies the tragic insecurity and precarious civility of life under *laissez-faire*. In a desperate last act to prevent descent into the workhouse (in working-class demonology this is hell-on-earth), Arthur robs a stranger. Wheeler again stretches the moral conventions of fiction by allowing Arthur to get away with this crime, which redeems his family from destitution. Arthur has to live with his own guilt, but for the reader's benefit Wheeler uses the artifice of plot-making to ameliorate the offence. The stranger Arthur robs turns out to be Walter North, newly knighted, and returning from a visit to a brothel. If Arthur cannot quite cleanse his conscience by applying a class-conscious analysis to his situation, Wheeler does it for him. On the other hand, this is the only occasion Walter is punished. As the villain of the narrative, we might expect further horrors to be in store for him, but it is clear that until the working class can arrest the tide of history, Walter's class is in the ascendent.

Despite his moral lapse, Arthur is renewed for a third time in the Chartist revival of 1848. Wheeler's analysis of the failure of this campaign is to identify the same pattern of state provocation and belated leadership that undermined 1839 and 1842. As the mass arrests begin, Arthur has to flee the country again. The story ends in a state of asymmetry, suspension and expectation. Arthur joins the flow of European political exiles like Mazzini and Kossuth. Arthur still believes that one day 'the glorious red banner, the emblem of unity and freedom, shall proudly float on the highest pinnacle of St. Stephen's' (p. 187). Only when that 'national jubilee' (p. 192) takes place will Arthur be reunited with Mary. Private and public history are not separable.

While *Sunshine and Shadow* undoubtedly has its callow aspects, Wheeler's achievement is all the more impressive when we consider that he constructed the narrative out of very small units: a weekly 'communion' of only a few thousand words. Wheeler was obviously keen to demonstrate his literary prowess by maximizing the opportunity to provide each small chapter with a variety of epigraphs. These quotations range from the mainstream to the obscure, and are a fitting testimony to Wheeler's literary labours, and the importance of literary culture to the Chartist and labour movement.

Notes

1. For biographical information about Wheeler I have drawn heavily on William Stevens, *A Memoir of Thomas Martin Wheeler* (London: J. B. Leno, 1862).

2. Dorothy Thompson notes that woolcombing 'contributed a number of leaders to the movement' including Wheeler (who moved on to other trades), John Snowden and George White (both active in West Yorkshire). See D. Thompson, *The Chartists: Popular Politics in the Industrial Revolution* (Aldershot: Wildwood House, 1984), pp. 228-9.

3. David Goodway calls Wheeler an 'outstanding activist' of metropolitan Chartism. See D. Goodway, *London Chartism 1836-1848* (Cambridge: Cambridge University Press, 1982), p. 42.

4. Stevens, *A Memoir*, p. 33.

5. R. C. Gammage, *History of the Chartist Movement 1837-1854* (1894; London: Merlin Press, 1976), p. 311.

6. Thomas Martin Wheeler, *A Brief Memoir of the Late Mr Feargus O'Connor, M.P.* (London: Holyoake and Co., 1855).

7. *Northern Star*, 5 February; 12 February; 1 April 1848. Years earlier Wheeler also published some poems in the *Northern Star*, 15 May; 31 July 1841. These were included in Y. V. Kovalev's pioneering *An Anthology of Chartist Literature* (Moscow, 1956), pp. 102-3.

8. *Northern Star*, 12 February 1848, p. 3.

9. See Jack B. Mitchell, 'Aesthetic Problems of the Development of the Proletarian-Revolutionary Novel in Nineteenth-Century Britain', in David Craig, ed., *Marxists on Literature* (Harmondsworth: Penguin, 1975). See also Martha Vicinus, *The Industrial Muse: A Study of Nineteenth Century British Working Class Literature* (London: Croom Helm, 1974), chapter 3, and her 'Chartist Fiction and the Development of Class-based Literature', in H. Gustav Klaus, ed., *The Socialist Novel in Britain: Towards the Recovery of a Tradition* (Brighton: Harvester, 1982).

10. According to Joel Wiener the circulation of the *Northern Star* in 1850 was 4,700. See Joel H. Wiener, 'Circulation and the Stamp Tax', in J. Don Vann and Rosemary T. Van Arsdel, eds, *Victorian Periodicals. A Guide to Research* (New York: The Modern Language Association of America, 1978), p. 172. While this figure is considerably below the *Star's* peak of around 50,000 in 1838, a circulation figure which outstripped *The Times* (see David Vincent, *Literacy and popular culture in England 1750-1914* [Cambridge: Cambridge University Press, 1989], p. 248), the national status of the paper, combined with the working-class custom of communal reading, provided Wheeler with a relatively large and captive

audience. On the other hand, there is no denying that he could have ridden the crest of a wave in 1838, but then he could not have written a 'history' of Chartism.

11.   This section of the Introduction draws on my treatment of the novel in I. Haywood, *Working Class Fiction: From Chartism to 'Trainspotting'* (Plymouth: Northcote House/British Council, 1997).

12.   Steve Devereux argues that the depiction of Arthur and Julia's love affair is artistically weakened by the conventions of romance, but he does not make the point that Wheeler is aware of such restrictions. See S. Devereux, 'Chartism and popular fiction', in John Lucas, ed., *Writing and Radicalism* (Harlow: Longman, 1996). Wheeler's more traditionalist views on gender are apparent at the end of Chapter XXVII, where he invites the reader to be dubious about the contribution of women orators to the Chartist movement.

13.   As noted in the Editor's introduction to *The Political Pilgrim's Progress*, this description of Birmingham produces a gratuitous anti-Semitic remark: 'here the thimble, emblem of industry, worn even to the wearer's bone in the still harder conflict of female industry against the Jewocracy of the world' (p. 90). The low intolerance of this remark must be contrasted with Wheeler's ardent admiration for the black Chartist William Cuffay (see chapter XXVII) and his revulsion of American slavery, which only demonstrates the near total lack of consciousness about Jewish emancipation in the Chartist mind.

14.   Jutta Schwarzkopf is critical of the tale's patriarchal construction of Arthur's marriage, though Jack Mitchell regards Mary triumphantly as the first working-class activist woman in fiction. See Jutta Schwarzkopf, *Women in the Chartist Movement* (Basingstoke: Macmillan, 1991), chapter 2, and Jack B. Mitchell, 'Aesthetic Problems of the Development of the Proletarian-Revolutionary Novel in Nineteenth-Century Britain'.

Sunshine and Shadow: A Tale of the Nineteenth Century

By Thomas Martin Wheeler,
Late Secretary to the National Charter Association and National Land
Company.

TO FEARGUS O'CONNOR, ESQ., M.P. FOR NOTTINGHAM.

RESPECTED SIR, — In dedicating this humble effort to you, I am actuated by
no sycophantic motive; words of mine can neither make nor mar your fame —
Time, the great arbiter, will do ample justice to both the Chartist party and their
acknowledged leader. The fiction department of literature has hitherto been
neglected by the scribes of our body, and the opponents of our principles have
been allowed to wield the power of imagination over the youth of our party,
without any effort on our part to occupy this wide and fruitful plain. Would that
some of the many talented minds acknowledging our tenets, would achieve that
supremacy in the novel which Thomas Cooper has done in the epic.[1] To
stimulate them to the effort, is the object of this attempt on the part of your
brother Chartist. THOMAS MARTIN WHEELER.
O'Connorville, March 24th, 1849.

CHAPTER I

Fair truth shall be my theme. Let others soar
To realms of fancy, seeking fiction wild:
Athwart my page, fair truth alone shall pour
Her charm:—a charm not always tame and mild—
E'en fiction never pleas'd unless it bore
The impress of truth: no heart was long beguil'd
To feel despite stern reason. For, in sooth,
Fiction's best dress is still the garb of truth.
Beste[2]

On a fine day, in the year 1831, at the door of a brick building, bearing the
lofty title of College House Academy, situate in the suburbs of London, stood
a stage coach waiting to convey the emancipated boys to their respective homes
in the great metropolis. Crack goes the coachman's whip, loud huzzas from the
joyous boys startle even the well trained horses, and the coach speeds on its

way. Quietly smiled the quaint old schoolmaster, pleased at the prospect of a month's release from the drudgery of the then system of scholastic tuition. Cheerful looked his buxom wife, the very pattern of domestic housewifery. Well knew she how to expend in the most thrifty manner the five guineas per quarter received with each boarder, so as to add each vacation a few more guineas to their scanty hoard; and now she, too, is released from the routine of duty, and the pleasure it gives is truthfully reflected in her countenance. Peace be with you, ye now ancient pair, may the cares of life fall mildly on you, and though the sunshine of existence is to you for ever past, may its shadows be devoid of gloom or danger.

Loud and cheerful were these boy passengers, life was to them a garden of pleasant flowers; true, they escaped not an occasional sting from the wasps of existence, but the venom was soon extracted, and the evening's shadow was always forgotten in the mornings sunshine. Oh! who does not look back with delight on his boyish days, when life was all enchantment; when, let the kaleidoscope be ever so varied, its colours were always bright, and each new combination more pleasing than the last. Time! what boyish dreams of fairy land hast thou destroyed — what rosy bowers turned to dungeon cells — what placid streams and gay trimmed barks have proved, alas! a treacherous ocean fraught with constant wrecks; thy smiling meads have been, indeed, an arid desert, without even the mirage of enchantment, to recall the blest waters of the past; the materials of the kaleidoscope are still there, but the enchanted glass is destroyed, and we have discovered that they were broken and valueless fragments.

Loudly sound the joyous huzzas from our heroes on the coach; they have reached their destination, the Flower Pot, in Bishopsgate street; little reek they of those sombre thoughts. Experience will come too soon, let not foreknowledge anticipate its date. Joy and hope are still with them, and friends and relatives await their arrival.

CHAPTER II

He owned the spell. Imagination woke
Within him and enthralled his willing soul.
The charm of music o'er his spirit broke,
And o'er each feeling held a sweet control.
Fondly he bow'd him 'neath young fancy's yoke,
Bade fancy make his sorrows and console,
Then the great song the blind man sang of yore,
Old Homer open'd all his sacred store.
                    Beste[3]

"Well, Arthur," said Walter North, addressing the only remaining tenant of the room, "all our companions are gone; our friends alone seem tardy."

"True, Walter, but their arrival brings our separation, and after three years' companionship, during which time I have looked up to you as an elder brother, I feel that I am about to be thrust alone into the world; you have parents, brother, and sister to love you, but I have only an uncle to look to, and he is so immersed in business that I fear I shall almost be forgotten."

"No, Arthur," said Walter, warmly, "while I live you will never be forgotten; my friends will be your friends; no change in circumstances will damp my friendship; my sister Julia will love you as a brother, and father and mother will be as proud of you as I am."

Arthur Morton was indeed a boy to be proud of. He was about fourteen years old, pale, light complexioned, and rather under the middle size, — his features were not regularly handsome, but of that cast which are generally termed interesting, — his eyes were hazel, and of remarkable brightness and intensity, and his whole countenance indicative of intelligence beyond his years. Left an orphan at an early age, and consigned to the care of a bachelor uncle, Ralph Morton, a woolstapler, residing in the dull region of Bermondsey, he had experienced none of those attentions and socialising influences which are generally the result of maternal or sisterly solicitude; he consequently grew up a shy and moody boy. Having naught else to feel an interest in, books became to him what society is to boys more advantageously situated; in them his whole delight was centred, they were the only medium through which he could give vent to his affections, and many a hot tear did he shed over the woes of the Madelines, and Rosinas, the Algernons and the Aubreys,[4] of the romances which adorned his uncle's scanty and ill-selected library. At eleven years old, more for the sake of ridding himself of an incumbrance than with a view to the boy's future welfare, our hero was sent to a second-rate boarding school; his progress here was rapid, and though his reading was desultory, yet it was sufficiently extensive and varied to give him a general acquaintance with most of our standard classical and English authors; poetry was his favourite study, and Homer and Virgil, Byron and Shelley,[5] would wile him away from his boyish companions, and wrap him in an elysium of delight, and yet he was not altogether a dreamer; there was in him, young as he was, sufficient of the iron of human nature to give something of a practical character to his most dreary reveries, and give promise that if hammered on the harsh anvil of human adversity it would emit sparks dangerous not only to his own safety but to the safety of others. This trait in his character arose from the habit of self-dependence which he had been impelled to acquire under his uncle's lonely mansion, with his one aged and uncouth female domestic.

School was a new era in the life of Arthur Morton, — the shy, reserved boy was now jostled in the uproarious Babel of some fifty candidates for the empire of the school dominions; willingly would he again have embraced the retirement of the lone house in Bermondsey, but he was compelled to endure the conflict, submit to the jokes and taunts of the wild urchins around him, until one insult deeper than usual aroused the iron in his nature, and he rained such a shower of blows on two of the most active of his annoyers that he speedily made them quail and shrink before the timid boy they had hitherto despised. This encounter drew upon him the notice of Walter North, the pugilistic hero of the school — their champion in all their broils with rival schools or surrounding suburbans — a "dunce at syntax but a dab at taw."[6] Walter was some two years older than Arthur, and of a very opposite disposition — he was as frank and free as the other was shy and reserved, — self-confident, and proud of his fine figure and raven hair, he was the self-constituted but undisputed leader of their every frolic and school-boy enterprise; from the hour Arthur secured his patronage he was exempt from all further annoyance, and gradually acquired self-confidence and self-respect, those primary qualifications to the respect and confidence of others. And Arthur, how his young heart bounded towards his friend; he was the first human being who had shown him more than negative kindness, the hitherto sealed up fountains of his affections welled up to his benefactor, — books were no longer his sole idol, — love for Walter begat love for all human kind, — the very features of his schoolmates assumed to his eyes a kindlier look, and their frolicsome deeds were no longer looked upon with disgust. Kindness was to him in boyhood what first love is to many in more mature years, it changed and coloured the aspect of his existence and created a new spirit within him. Oh! how we ought to inculcate lessons of kindness in youth; how often has the whole tenor of a life been changed and darkened by harshness blighting the early buds and tender shoots of youthful affection; the shy and reserved boy meeting with only insult and jeers from his companions, grows up the selfish and revengeful man, repaying back on his kind with bitter interest the harshness received in his early days, and scattering around him the seeds of that moroseness and hatred which early kindness would have eradicated or allayed; so true it is that love begets love, and happiness is born a twin, and cannot exist alone. From this period to that of their final leaving school, at the opening of our tale, the most perfect friendship existed between Arthur and Walter North; often thoughtless and exacting on the part of the latter, but ever self-sacrificing and trusting on the part of the former, the difference in their dispositions served only to cement this union by rendering their mutual good qualities subservient to each other's welfare; as the gases ejected by animal life give vitality and greenness to the vegetable world, and impart beauty and fertility to the whole, so did their opposite tastes give freshness and health to their friendship. Nature delights in such contrasts; the twining ivy clings to the supporting oak, — the modest primrose loves the shades of the umbrageous forest tree. At Walter's request Arthur had occasionally spent a portion of the vacation at his father's house, where in the company of his friend and his sister Julia, he spent hours of happiness, often afterwards recalled to his memory by unkindness and neglect; and thus the ideal of home and comfort, of female loveliness and domestic peace, became attached to Arthur's recollection of his youthful friendship.

CHAPTER III

Their counter is their idol, their till their God.
                              Chartist Oration.

Fair was her form, and flaxen was her hair;
Her red lips pouted like a wilful child;
Her blue eye flashed more meaning than you dare
Suppose it meant: and when she blandly smil'd
She won you to her feet and kept you there,
Bewitched, delighted, worshipping, beguil'd;
And when a sterner mood shot o'er her face,
Though not quite pleas'd, you thought 'twas some new grace.
                                             Beste[7]

The father of Walter North was a wine merchant in the City; he was a shrewd, though uneducated man — one of those characters common in the middle ranks of society — whose whole faculties are centred in the acquisition of wealth — devoid of principle, yet following the maxim, that "Honesty is the best policy," from a conviction of its truth, as evidenced by the events daily occurring within his circle; he would not be guilty of any open act of fraud, but was an adept in all the tricks of his trade. No man could manufacture such an unequalled port, or pass off acid Madeira for genuine sherry, better than Joe North, or drive a harder bargain for logwood chips, and the other etceteras of his trade; yet Joe North was, in the world's estimation, a respectable man — that is, he kept his horse and chaise, gave occasional dinners or suppers to his brother-respectables — had been only twice through the Insolvent Debtor's Court, and had never been detected in committing any flagrant breach of propriety. Such is respectability in the world's estimation. So long as the exterior decencies and moralities of life are moderately observed, the blackest villain that ever disgraced humanity stands well with society, and passes current through all its multifarious vocations, provided always that he has either wealth or its outward semblance; but woe to the poor wretch, however honest, however virtuous he may be, who is destitute of this essential qualification. The wife of Joseph North was a helpmate mete for such a man; originally cook in the same establishment where he served as butler, their combined savings enabled them to take a small public-house. Care and economy, at a time when these qualities were more attended with success than in these days of speculation, enabled them to embark in this more extensive branch of the business; and now that rolling years had brought competence and ease, the careful housekeeper was transformed into the dignified wife, forming a graceful accompaniment to his gig, a sharp mistress to his servants, and a kind mother to his children — and what did a plain man like Joe North need more? Being an excellent manager, without extravagance, she well supported the dignity of his establishment. An educated woman would have made him feel his own inferiority (for experience had taught him the value of a liberal education); she would have assumed too much the airs of a fine lady, and looked less after his servants in the cellar and the kitchen — so, at least, Mr. North informed his brother-respectables, on one of their picnic days, when the wine had well circulated, and the conversation grew mellow. Whether he believed this, or not, is a matter of slight importance to our tale. One thing is certain, he knew that under the present railroad system of commerce, education could not be neglected for the juniors; so Walter and Julia were, at a fitting age, sent to boarding school, to pick up such fragments of learning as their masters' skill and their own organisation would allow them to imbibe; and we have already said that, in Walter's case, his stock-in-trade of this commodity was small indeed. Possessing good capacities — shrewd and quick in ordinary affairs — he was too sharp, too clever a boy, (said Mrs. North), to need severe application to his studies; and Walter, finding himself the most popular boy in the school, and the idol of Arthur Morton — the best scholar in it — buoyed himself up with these reflections, and left College-house Academy with but a small addition to his previous stock of scholastic lore. His sister Julia was the reverse of Walter; the whole intellect of the family seemed to be inherited by her. True, the share was not large; but it was more than generally falls to the lot of females in her sphere of life. Girls of the middle classes are carefully initiated into all the accomplishments — so termed — of the upper classes; but their intellectual faculties are less cultivated than those of the small tradesman or mechanic whom they are taught to look down upon with contempt; and to frequent whose company, or to attend the same schools, would be to lose caste with their own rank in society; so strong is prejudice, that classes sprung from the same root, and not one generation removed, are as effectually separated, in all the social relations of life, as the god-descended Brahmin from the outcast Pariah. When will the middle classes learn their true interest, and combine their worldly influence and business habits with the strong sense, the sturdy independence, and the generous enthusiasm of the vast democracy beneath them? when will they abandon the False and Factitious for the True and the Real?

Julia North was a beauteous and well-trained flower, growing in a wild and uncultivated garden, possessing beauty of a rare order (beauty was indeed a characteristic of the whole family); there was still a nameless charm about her that it was impossible to trace to any mere combination of features; a form rather short than tall but most exquisitely proportioned, flaxen hair falling in ringlets on her delicate shoulders, eyes of the purest blue, and a complexion in which the rose and the lily were so completely blended, that art would try in vain to imitate it. Though there was nothing decidedly intellectual in the cast of her countenance, its beauty being of the order that would attract the attention of the sensualist rather than that of the philosopher, yet no one could gaze upon her and not at once pronounce that Nature could not have committed that anomaly of leaving so fair a body without a corresponding soul.

CHAPTER IV

Strange that the mind should ever dwell upon
Those years of childhood, ever fondly cling
To every dream that waits on memory's dawn,
O'ershadowing youth with gay imaginings;
Like wild flowers, 'neath whose buds live waters run,
Scented by tangled buds, that o'er them fling
An arch that hides their source, but bathes the tide
In sweets unmatched in all its wanderings wide.
                                                    Beste[8]

Arthur Morton found plenty of leisure in his uncle's lonely house to continue his studies, but solitude had lost its wonted charm; he longed for the presence of his bosom companion; he yearned to commence his career in the world, to relieve his relative of the burthen of his support. A spirit of independence is generally combined with a shy and reserved disposition; the mind naturally leans upon itself, it considers favours as heavy obligations, and, conscious of its difficulty adequately to acknowledge them, is anxious to avoid their incurrence. Arthur, therefore, requested that he might be apprenticed to some handicraft, in order to enable him to earn his future subsistence. This agreed too well with his uncle's wishes to be denied, and Arthur was speedily consigned for seven years to the care of a Mr. Austin, a printer, in a small town about thirty miles south of London. A parting visit was paid to his friend Walter and his sister Julia, and with many protestations of kindness and mutual remembrance, they parted, and years rolled by and Walter North had forgotten the very existence of his quondam friend and schoolfellow ere they met again.

Dear are the recollections of our schoolboy hours. Memory imprints the names, features, and remembrance of the prominent actors upon the tablet of our brain; though seas divide, though all trace of their existence is lost, yet can its potent spell collect the scattered family, and vividly recall the dear remembered past. But, alas for schoolboy friendships, how seldom are they lasting! How few of the number can we recall, even by name, when twice seven years have past! Love, the grand wizard, blots out the record, and the battle of life destroys its very existence. True, there are exceptions; and Arthur Morton, as far as the ordeal of time had yet been tried, was one. Never was the image of his friend entirely absent from his mind. In sickness and in sorrow he flew for consolation to the recollections of the past, and friendship supplied to him the place of parents and of kin. For some months a regular correspondence was maintained between the friends but by degrees it ceased on the part of Walter. Several letters having been unanswered by his friend, Arthur at length received one from Julia, informing him that her youngest brother was dead, and that Walter was taken into partnership with his father, and had removed to

Liverpool, to superintend a wholesale establishment they had opened in that town, and the neglect of Walter in not writing must be occasioned, she presumed, by the extra duties he was called upon to attend to, at the same time as urging him of the best wishes of her parents, and of her own undiminished friendship.

Welcome was this letter to our hero, the first he ever received from a female. Often did he gaze with fondness upon the neat handwriting and the pretty signature; and though he deeply felt the continued neglect of his friend, yet, with true faith in his friendship, he excused it on the ground that he was occupied with business, that he had many other ties, many other outlets for his affections, whilst he was alone in the world. Courteously did he reply to the letter from Julia, and enclosed one for Walter. An answer was returned, stating that she had duly forwarded it to her brother. Patiently did he wait for Walter's answer to this last appeal to his friendship; but it came not. He had no excuse to continue his correspondence with Julia and, being too diffident to frame one, all correspondence between himself and his only friends finally ceased.

Long and wearily did the seven years of his apprenticeship pass. His master was a demure, hypocritical pretender to sanctity. His youth had been passed in excesses, from which his constitution was now suffering, and, unable to enjoy pleasure himself, he detested even the semblance of enjoyment in others. His wife was a thin wiry woman, wrapped up in her own merits, and jealously alive to the demerits of all around her, not forgetting those of her demure rib. Family they had none, much to the chagrin of the self-sufficient Mrs. Austin, whose irritable temper kept the whole household in continual hot water. Such being his domestic position, with few acquaintance, and none intimate, no wonder that he relapsed into his old habits of reserve and abstract meditation. But a change had been worked in the character of his thoughts, chiefly wrought by the practical nature of his avocation. They printed the *County Chronicle*, a Liberal newspaper; and new views of society thus accumulated, he no longer pondered on imaginary dreams. He looked at the world by which he was surrounded, the laws, and the customs adopted. He saw the injustice of the former, and the general absurdity, of the latter, and wondered such things were. Oh! how often did he — when speculating on these things in his lonely rambles — give vent to the aspirations of his soul, and consciously fit himself for a future career, of which the idea had not then entered his imagination. The good people of M——, when they met the young enthusiast, and overheard his solitary but not silent musings, and observed his general absent manner, thought, and significantly said, that all was not right there, pointing to his head. But he was so good-tempered, so well-conducted, and inoffensive, that he was a general favourite. Attentive to his business, simple in his habits, never causing any anxiety or trouble, even his sour master and termagant mistress could scarce behave unkindly to him. During this time he only received a letter from his uncle at long intervals, which generally contained a small remittance. The last, containing a £5 note, informed him of his marriage, and that he must no longer look to him, but depend on his own exertions for his support. Arthur grieved not at this intimation — but the cold language in which it was conveyed certainly made him feel more lonely than heretofore. His friends had deserted him — his only relative had coldly cast him off; but he had sipped of sorrow until the bitterness thereof was destroyed.

In this manner passed his apprentice years, dark shadows with occasional gleams of sunshine. His character was fast maturing — he was emerging from the part of a dreamer to that of a worker. But a want was still gnawing at his heart. He was alone in the midst of a crowd — he longed to have some definite object to do, some satisfactory employment for his mind. He wept in very bitterness of spirit at the vague, unsubstantial nature of all that he saw, or was surrounded by. His spirit yearned for something, of the very nature of which he was yet unaware. He would have turned a religious fanatic (the ultimatum of many minds similarly constituted) but his shrewd sense had shown him the hypocrisy of the Austins, and further experience had not demonstrated to him whether religion was aught more than a cloak to vice, or, at best, a Sunday garment, worn because it was customary. Poor boy! the germs of young ambition were rising in thy soul, and thou wast unconsciously feeding that fire which more often consumes than enlightens. Like the bird charmed by the rattlesnake, thou flutterest uneasily before it, but cannot resist the spell. Thou seest naught but the fascination, and rushest blindly, yet wilfully, into its toils. Oh! why should high and lofty inspirations be productive only of misery and destruction to their possessor, causing him to sacrifice all that renders life endurable, in order that he may promote the good and well-being of that public, who, in return, either persecute or ridicule him, until death mercifully snatches him from their fangs! Oh! when will that true millennium arrive — that millennium of reason and liberty, which Voltaire and Rousseau were the prophets; Paine and Robespierre the harbingers;[9] and Shelley — the amiable and gloriously-gifted Shelley — the Messiah! Speed, oh! speed, its advent.

CHAPTER V

If to the city sped — what waits him there!
To see profusion that he may not share—
To see ten thousand baneful arts combined,
To pamper luxury and thin mankind;
To see each joy the sons of pleasure know
Extorted from his fellow creature's woe.
Here while the courtier glitters in brocade,
There the pale artist plies the sickly trade;
Here while the proud their long-drawn pomp display,
There the black gibbet glooms beside the way;
The dome where Pleasure holds her midnight reign,

Here richly deck'd admits the gorgeous train;
Tumultuous grandeur crowds the blazing square,
The rattling chariots clash, the torches glare.
                                        Goldsmith[10]

At the close of a fine July day Arthur Morton, the term of his apprenticeship
having expired, after seven years' absence, once more visited London. The
beauty of the evening had drawn forth the myriads of the metropolis from their
close-heated rooms and workshops to the streets and lanes of this giant heart
of the mighty centre of the world's civilisation; and as he traversed suburbs, and
mile after mile of glittering shops passed like a fairy scene before his view, he
felt something like regret at the opportunities of acquiring wisdom and
experience he had lost by passing his apprentice years at the small town of
M——, but with hearty resolution determined that future exertions should not
be wanting to distil the essence of wisdom in the vast human laboratory he was
now entering.

London! thou mighty shroud for misery and want, and equally mighty
emblazoner of luxury and pomp, who can look on thee after years of absence
and not feel amazed at thy stupendous concentration of all that is rich and rare
in talent, art, and science, and also all that is base, vicious, and degrading, so
mixed and mingled together that it would take the wisdom of a life to dissever
the pure from the impure! To thee fly the outcasts from all the nations of the
earth. The tyrant monarch, driven from his throne, and the patriots flying from
the despot's rage. Thou openest thy embracing arms to all; genius flies to thee
as the enlightened almoner to reward and extend her flight; poverty rushes to
thy embrace, that it may reap the reward of toil or die in thy enfolding arms.
In thy vast panorama what sudden changes of scene meet our view; one
moment the gorgeous palace, next the den of crime — the merchant's mansion
and the debtor's gaol — the senate house and the gallows drop — the gin
palace and the house of prayer. Each passing moment introduces new actors to
the scene; now the monarch great in her high-sounding titles, next the infected
courtesan, the titled lordling, and the adept in crime — the millionaire and the
starving artizan — the Christian bishop and the Atheist priest. All — all find
room in thy capacious bosom — all minister to thy greatness, and contribute
to render thee a world in thyself — a complete microcosm of humanity; thy
mighty arteries now bursting with excitement, anon gliding with the languor of
exhaustion, but, alas! seldom pulsing with the healthful glow of serenity.

With such reflections as these Arthur Morton pursued his way towards his
uncle's residence, but his reception there was so cold and chill, and the plea of
having no bed aired so iced with inhospitality, that he gladly turned his steps
to an inn for his night's repose, and, thrown on his own resource with but a
guinea in his pocket, was left to struggle with the mighty crowd of the mighty
town. Oh, that cant phrase, "thrown on their own resources," how glibly it
slides off the tongue of our sapient legislators, who never apply it but to the

industrial classes, whilst not a law is made, nor a custom enforced, but tends to dry up and cripple those resources. Ye legislators, wrapped up in the party-coloured raiment of your political economy; ye vile drones in the world's great hive, the day will yet come when you will, indeed, be thrown on your own resources, and then will the miseries that you have inflicted on others, have to be endured by yourselves. Day after day did Arthur wander from street to street seeking employment, but in vain; trade was unusually dull, and the country apprentice was not sufficiently initiated into the mysteries of London Trade Societies, to be a successful competitor with older hands acquainted with the ways of town. His few shillings were now gradually sinking into pence, starvation was in his thoughts and approaching towards reality; of friends he was utterly destitute, and his pride revolted against again seeking his unfeeling relative. Once his thoughts turned upon his old acquaintance, Walter North, but he was estranged and far distant; the image of his sister, the lovely, the tender-hearted Julia, crossed his imagination — it had often done so during the long wearisome years of his apprenticeship — for she was his first and only female friend, but he shrank from informing her or her parents of his destitute condition; and thus was he alone in that most lonely of all places to the poor and friendless — busy, bustling London. Oh, how changed was the current of his thoughts, from those with which he entered it but a few brief days previously. Hopes and anticipations of profitable employment, and vague dreams of future greatness, were then rife in his mind; now all was dreary and desolate, hope was sinking low in his bosom, and its reaction, despair, was fast usurping its place. London, the great nursing mother of the kingdom — he did not anticipate she would refuse to own and embrace him, and bitterly he felt his lot. Ah! little did he know the fickle nature of this wizard mother; she received all in her mighty womb — on some she lavishes kindness and favour, but her lodging houses in her courts and alleys could tell a fearful tale of the thousands who have died from the neglect to give them proper sustenance; yea, her pride, the mighty Thames, could give up hosts of pale and shrunken ghosts, who, neglected by this pitiless mother, have flown to her cold and watery embrace, from fear of that most direful of all spectres — famine gasping in the lap of plenty. Sad and awful spectacle; becoming, alas! too familiar to impress us with all its horrible reality. Were it not so, we should rush to the rescue of sinking humanity, and indignantly demand that the guilty record should be blotted from the annals of our land. Would that the grave could give back its unburied dead, and their gaunt forms pass in review before the eyes of our legislators, shouting in their terror-stricken ears, "Died from your neglect!" then might we wring from their fears that justice which they have denied to our repeated appeals. Ireland, thou sepulchre of famine's dead; what a terrific host wouldst thou add to this muster roll.[11] Numerous and hard-hearted as are thy enslavers, they would shrink before the host of their murdered victims, and thy dead children would burst those fetters which frantic efforts of the living serve only to strengthen and revive! Let this Golgotha[12] be removed from our sight.

Humanity sickens at the scene — our chill blood boils in our veins and we pray, as a last resource, that the wild justice of revenge may rid us of their and our oppressors; that the stain of thy blood — so deeply redly dyed — may be washed from our hands, that the crimes of centuries may be forgiven, and that we remain no longer the reproach and scorn of the world. Let the careless, and the lukewarm bear in mind, that "He who permits oppression, shares the crime," and awaken from their criminal apathy. Let not this withering reflection blight their latest moments that they might have saved their country — might, but would not.

CHAPTER VI

Read on, and thou shalt find fit speculation,
Deep as the depths of thy sagacity;
I will decry the present generation;
As portrait painter, show my small capacity;
Perhaps I'll make thee doubt my pen's veracity;
Perhaps I'll revel to things dead and gone,
But all I ask thee is, read on! read on!
                                        Beste

In a spacious drawing room in one of the best situated streets in the town of Liverpool, adorned with more profusion than warranted by good taste, sat Walter North. Nearly eight years have passed lightly over him since his introduction to our readers; the fine, frank, high-spirited boy was now become the polished citizen of the world, and reported to be one of the most prosperous merchants of this far-famed commercial city. Time had not effected many changes in the person of Walter North; he was what the ladies (God bless them) denominate a handsome man; tall, and well-proportioned, with fine black eyes, raven hair, and features rather remarkable for vivacity and good humour than for intelligence. He was still unmarried, though a prize in the matrimonial market that many were contending for; but Walter looked on marriage as he did on any other portion of his business — with the keen eye of a trader. He was still young; he could now command a match that a few years back he could not have dreamed of; business was fast increasing, and a few more years of single-blessedness might enable him to mingle his blood with that of England's nobility, so he heeded not the pits and trapfalls in which anxious mothers and maiden aunts sought to ensnare him, but pursued his ambitious schemes, smiling with self-complacency at their selfish views. His father had retired from trade, and was living in the suburbs of the metropolis; and under Walter's management the business had progressed — both in London and Liverpool — from almost a retail concern, to a gigantic mercantile establishment. Walter was the beau ideal of a merchant; open and candid by nature, the shrewdness and spirit of trade, that he had imbibed from his father, enabled him to make good merchandise of these qualities; careful without being penurious; enterprising without being rash; indifferent to the interests of others, yet careful, by attending to the decencies of life, to obtain their good opinion; he was a specimen of that large and influential class who, destitute of any high principles, and deficient in intellectual attainments, by their tact and readiness to accommodate themselves to the world, leave talent and principle far behind them in its estimation, succeed far better in securing to themselves possession of its treasured goods, and bid fair to dethrone the feudal aristocracy of the realm, and monopolise the political and social power of the empire.

Arthur Morton, with a cultivated intellect, with an enthusiastic love of justice, and an enlarged spirit of benevolence, is in danger of perishing from the want of the necessaries of life, whilst his quondam friend — deficient in all these qualities, but gifted with worldly prudence — is rich in the world's goods, and deemed an ornament to his class. Such is life, and such the qualities necessary for success! The generous, the noble, and enthusiastic are candidates for a life of poverty, and inheritors of an early and unwept grave; whilst the cold, selfish calculator, whose heart never warmed with love to God or man, rolls in wealth and luxury, and his fair fame is emblazoned by the chisel of the statuary. When such things are, can we wonder that the temple of virtue is devoid of worshippers? whilst the temple of Mammon is thronged by thousands of eager devotees, who, in their haste to offer homage at her polluted shrine, crush and destroy each other. Alas! strong indeed must be our belief in the doctrine of human perfectibility, and great indeed our trust in the principle of progression, or all would be carried away by the stream, and the world become one huge market, where youth, beauty, intelligence, and virtue would be bartered away for luxury and ease; and patriotism and independence be among the catalogue of things that were, but whose existence has ceased.

Sad and depressing as is this picture of human nature, faint not thou man of the Future, though pride and meanness fade away, for pride and meanness to succeed them; yet it will not always be so; the present transition phase of society is already passing away, and the bright future appears in dim perspective; then shall noble hearts, with noble feelings glowing within themselves, scatter blessings round them. The tree of ignorance shall vanish before the light of increased knowledge, and this fair globe become the happy region which Infinite Intelligence designed it to be.

Such thoughts and such studies engrossed not the attention of Walter North. Seated before a blazing fire, (it was a winter evening,) and occasionally sipping at the contents of a tumbler which stood before him, he seemed buried in thought, and from the cast of his features the subject of his cogitation was of an unpleasant nature, — at length a smile broke the gravity of his closed lips, and he muttered audibly: — "The silly fool, to refuse such an offer; a baronetcy, and £4,000 a year is no bad catch for the daughter of Joe North; true, he is double her age and a residence in the West Indies has not contributed to the strength of his constitution, but the better for the girl, she will soon be a blooming widow with a splendid jointure. Sir Jasper's name and connexions, will be of service to me in my matrimonial spec, and the match must come off". Again was the sombre hue of his countenance resumed, and the contracting brow and the listless sipping at the almost empty tumbler, showed that the mind was deeply meditating on the means to achieve this object; at length his thoughts again found utterance in words:— "I will write to Julia to spend a few weeks with me, and trust to my powers of wheedling to expedite this marriage, — should this fail, a little gentle force must be applied. Am I not her elder brother and the best judge of her true interests?" So saying, he rapidly rung the bell at his elbow, which was answered by a servant in livery, and ordering writing material, he speedily despatched a missive to "Joseph North, Esq., Oporto House, Brixton," with an enclosure for Julia, containing an affectionate invitation to spend a short period at his bachelor residence. Replenishing the tumbler from the decanter beside him, he applied himself vigorously to discussing its contents, — his feet are thrown upon the opposite chair, the fragrant scent of a cigar speedily perfumes the room, and Walter North is as happy and as free from qualms of conscience as though he had not been planning the ruin of his only sister. Conscience, thou art a very cheat! frighting the timorous, but playing the part of a sycophant to the bold! Thou arch tormentor of mankind! whipping their sin with a lash of their own entwining. Writhing beneath thy terrors, the murderer hath rushed madly to the scaffold; the weak-minded fallen a victim to the suicide's grave, or sought the worse refuge of a maniac's cell; whilst the strong-nerved and iron-hearted man of the world hath ruled thee as his slave, and deprived thy scorpion lash of its envenomed sting. Thou wast implanted by nature in the breast of man neither to be his serf nor his tyrant, but to act as a moral barometer, testing the weight and value of his good or evil deeds, and serving as a check to guide and regulate his actions. Custom has rendered thee what thou art, and formed thy meshes of such subtle but elastic material, that they encumber and crush the weak, but are powerless to restrain the strong; thus adding another link to the heavy chain which the bulk of mankind hug with such dreary pleasure to their hearts, fettering the freedom of their limbs, and causing them to fall an easy prey to their relentless oppressor, who laughs with Satanic mirth at their spasmodic struggles to achieve their natural freedom.

CHAPTER VII

Now, by two-headed Janus,
Nature hath framed strange fellows in her time;
Some that will evermore peep through their eyes,
And laugh like parrots at a bagpiper;
And others of such vinegar aspect,

That they'll not show their teeth in way of smile,
Though Nestor swears the jest be laughable.
                                        Shakespeare[13]

Even Love is sold; the solace of all woe
Is turned to deadliest agony: old age
Shivers in selfish beauty's loathing arms,
And youth's corrupted impulses prepare
A life of horror from the blighting bane
Of Commerce; whilst the pestilence that springs
From unenjoying sensualism has filled
All human life with hydra-headed woes.
                                        Shelley[14]

Sir Jasper Baldwin was a tall, dark man, of a stony and severe trait of countenance, which no smile ever relieved — corpulent as an alderman, and as bilious in complexion as he was in constitution. He was about forty-five years old, twenty-two of which had been spent in various of our West Indian islands, where from being an overseer to a plantation he had risen to his present dignity, and to the official station of Governor of one of the Windward Islands,[15] to which office he was but recently appointed, and was about sailing with the next man-of-war bound to that station, to take possession of his new dignity. During his short residence in London he had called on Joseph North, with whom he had dealings in his days of subordination, and was immediately smitten with the charms of the ex-citizen's daughter. With the promptness of a West Indian — in all that related to dealings in human flesh — he offered himself to her parents as their future son-in-law, and the offering was too flattering to meet with other than their cordial approval. Julia's consent was to him a matter of second-rate importance. Proud of his newly-acquired title and station, and backed by her parents' approval, he dreamt not of a refusal from the mild and amiable girl of his choice. Scarce could he credit his senses when, on making the application in as formal terms as though he were addressing the council over whose deliberation she was about to preside, he met with a firm and resolute negative to the honour he intended to convey on her. In vain did her parents exert their influence. Docile in all else, reason told her that implicit obedience was no longer a virtue; that no imperious necessity demanded a sacrifice which would result in misery to her, and procure no advantage to those she loved, but a momentary gratification of their pride, and then a separation — perhaps forever. Mr. and Mrs. North, unable to overcome the firmness of Julia, as a last resource, applied to her brother, whom she greatly loved, and yet stood greatly in awe of. The result was the invitation to Liverpool disclosed in our last chapter, and the lapse of a week saw Julia the inmate of her brother's mansion.

    Poor maiden! gladly had she accepted the invitation, thinking to escape from the unwelcome addresses of Sir Jasper. What, then, was her surprise, on the second morning of her visit, to see Sir Jasper enter the drawing room, and, with her brother's approbation, resume his odious suit. Day after day passed, and no entreaties or tears could induce her brother to give her any respite from Sir Jasper's wearisome presence. She had no female, or other acquaintance in Liverpool, to whom she could fly for a refuge from her persecutors, and her heart sunk within her at the treachery of the brother she had so loved. Walter North, finding that the time had nearly expired when the vessel in which Sir Jasper was to embark was about to sail, and that Sir Jasper, wearied with the coldness of his lady love, and his vanity wounded with his rejection, was about to abandon his suit, became afraid that the bird would take wing before his plans could be brought to bear, and, despairing of Julia's consent, took Sir Jasper into his confidence, and concocted an infamous scheme to induce the fair girl to agree to this ill-assorted marriage. Sir Jasper, inured to oppression as he was, shrunk at first from the proposal, but Walter, bringing his love and vanity into play, speedily gained his co-operation, and the villanous project was carried into effect. Walter North's bachelor establishment contained but two female and one male servant; these, under various pretences, were by Walter's contrivance, sent away from his residence one night shortly before the sailing of the vessel, and Sir Jasper, well heated with wine, was by Walter admitted to Julia's sleeping apartments, and, in spite of her tears, prayers, and entreaties, she became Sir Jasper's bride, for humiliated in heart and soul, all confidence destroyed in her brother, and fearful to what length they might carry their treachery, she became a passive instrument in their hands. All the favour she craved was, that she might be allowed to spend a few months in England, to visit her parents, recover her spirits, and prepare for the voyage, before she rejoined her husband. This request, at her brother's intercession, was granted, the more readily, as our West Indian had many arrangements to make ere he could instal his wife in that apparent pomp — but real slavery — which, in his estimation, his station as governor demanded. Bright shone the sun, merry rang the village bells, gay and cheerful were the spectators — even the very officials, in expectation of increased fees, put on their blandest smiles, when the holy bonds of matrimony united the lovely Julia, daughter of Joseph North, Esq., of Oporto House, to Sir Jasper Baldwin, Governor of one of her Majesty's colonies. Miserable mockery and profanation! Legalised prostitution! The saintly hypocrite and selfish worldling look down with scorn and contempt upon the unfortunate sisterhood who roam our streets, but to the mind of a philosopher, they are even less degraded than too many of those upon whose union the law has shed its sanction. Though driven by want to degradation, yet have they not sold their heart's pure affection for base lucre; though despoiled of virtue by those who should have supported and not betrayed them, yet have they fallen not so much by their own vices, as by trusting too much in the goodness of others; they have not put themselves up for sale to the highest bidder, the priest officiating as auctioneer. Deeply as they have fallen, they have not the additional misery of dragging day by day the weary chain of loveless wedlock, and appearing to rejoice in their hopeless misery. Thus Julia North — the intellectual, the liberty-loving maiden of our early story — became a bride. Ill-omened nuptials! Hymen's torch was but the feeble flickering ray that threw its shadow over the dense fog by which it was surrounded, and not the constant, cheerful light which warms, cheers, and illuminates. When will the union of the sexes be relieved from the miserable sophisms which superstition and prejudice have thrown around it, and become based on the principles of nature and morality. Had Julia loved another, no force, no treachery would have rendered her false to her first love; but having no sacrifice to make, save of her own person, for the sake of her own and her parents' reputation, she resigned herself to her fate, and returning to her parent's home, pouring her wounded feelings into her mother's heart, she sought that consolation and sympathy which none but a parent can impart. Bitterly did they regret the treachery of their son, but he laughed at their remonstrances and regrets, and buoyed them up with bright visions of the future, until they felt almost convinced that they had acted for the best; but Julia's waning health, and increasing lethargy of spirits, soon destroyed these visions, and with an aching heart did her mother expedite those preparations necessary to following her — shall we call him husband? to his far distant home.

CHAPTER VIII

Poverty hath a sharp and goading power
To wring the torture cry, and fill the breath
With frantic curses or despairing sighs;
But her cold withering grasp is deepest felt
By the fine spirit that endures in silence,
And trembles lest his shallow purse be sounded
By the sleek friends about him — him who dreads
The taunting mockery that ever waits
On sensibility, unwarranted by wealth.

* * *

  He does not show
The vagrant's rags, and tell the whining tale
Of doleful falsehood. He has never learnt
To shape his language in beseeching tone,
And stand a mendicant beneath the roof
Of some rich kin, who gives such good advice
To qualify the charitable gold,
That proud and honourable palms shrink back,

And rather grapple with the spectre hand
Of famine, than accept the boon so granted.
                                    Eliza Cook[16]

'Tis eve, and Arthur Morton has once more returned to his lodgings after
another day of fruitless application for employment, — his last shilling is
expended, — every available article of clothing has been disposed of, and no
resource suggests itself to his racked imagination save an application to his
uncle. Pride, which lingers long in the human bosom — which often proves
stronger than love of life — forbade his approach to his uncle's doors, but
conscience whispered, and hunger echoed the whisper, that it was a crime to
die of starvation while such a resource remained open to him, and ere he slept,
he determined to avail himself of this last barrier between himself and famine.
   Early next morning found him at his uncle's residence, where he was
informed by a young girl (the ancient dame had been discharged,) that Mr. and
Mrs. Morton were gone into the country for a fortnight. Arthur, notwithstanding
his pride, could scarce avoid tears as this last hope was rent from him; he,
however, explained his relationship, and was kindly asked into the house and
invited to partake of the girl's homely fare (she was on board wages). Arthur,
melted into weakness by her apparent kindness, explained to her his distressed
situation, and felt relieved by the audible vents thus given to his feelings; the
poor girl sympathised with him, and insisted upon his taking the remainder of
the loaf and cheese, and, unknown to him, wrapped up a shilling with it. Kind-
hearted Sally, it was thy only shilling, and will be needed before thy master's
return, but truly thou reasonest, that thou hast a shelter, and the reflection of thy
master's credit will enable thee to obtain credit also, and never could thy
woman's heart hear tales of distress and not, if it was in thy power, relieve it.
Type art thou of thy class! would that those calling themselves the middle and
upper classes, would profit by thy example. Honour to the working men and
women of England! poor and unable to provide against the future as are the
many; careless and improvident as are the few; never does distress fall with a
heavy hand upon a brother or sister of their acquaintance, but out of their
poverty they give with a nobleness of heart that redeems a thousand errors, and
outweighs a host of vulgarities. Oftentimes their method of rendering assistance
may be expensive and ill-judged — as benefits at theatres, balls, concerts, tea
parties, lotteries, raffles, &c.; but among what other class of society is such
active and devoted benevolence seen? And though the political economist,
buttoning up his pockets as though there was any danger of the money leaving
them, may assure us that indiscriminate charity is both vicious and impolitic,
yet it is a vice so near akin to virtue, that the working classes will be excused
by all but the said economists for indulging in it. And well does experience
teach, not only the professional beggar, but the really distressed, that it is not
at our west-end palaces, nor at our merchant's counters, or from our
shopkeeper's tills, that they will receive the dole of charity, but at the residences

of those who are but one remove from themselves, and whom the caprice of a master, a change in trade, and many other causes, may speedily place in as bad a condition. But Arthur, inexperienced in these matters, thought not of appealing to charity, or thought of it only as a last resource.

Tired of pacing the crowded streets of London, where, to his eyes, all seemed busy, all occupied, and he alone an unwilling idler, he turned his steps towards the northern suburbs, in the faint hope that the country would prove more fortunate to him than the metropolis had been. Hour after hour did he travel through the suburbs, inquiring for employment at every printer's, until the shades of evening came o'er him as he ascended the famous Highgate Hill, where, seating himself by the roadside, he undid his packet of bread and cheese, and was astonished at the sight of the shilling, — this was indeed a treasure to him. Oh! how he blessed the kindness of that poor girl. Those who have never felt the pangs of poverty, who have never been in a similar condition to our hero, cannot imagine the feeling of joy with which he gazed on that piece of silver; it was a mine of wealth that would enable him to reach Birmingham, where he hoped his wanderings would cease. With new vigour he arose and pursued his journey until nightfall, when taking advantage of a kindly haystack, adjacent to the roadside, (the shilling was too great a treasure to be spent for lodging,) he speedily fell asleep and dreamt of mines of gold, and steam presses, and newspapers printed with gold and silver type. Oh! what a blessing is sleep to the poor and needy. The beggar under its gentle spell can be as completely blessed during half the hours of his existence as he who heaps gold in his iron chest; yea, more so, for no pandering to a pampered appetite will bring visions of nightmare to his couch, — no fear of robbers at his treasured store cloud the brightness of his dreams. Despots of the earth! Mammon worshippers! who coin our blood and sinews into gold, thanks be to God, ye have no power in the realm of imagination, in dreams at least we are free; in the visions of the night we can for a while lose sight of the harsh realities of the day. So it was with Arthur; he was no longer a poor friendless outcast, with a haystack for his bed, his bundle for a pillow, and the damp dews of night for his curtain, but an eastern monarch, surrounded with gold and silver ore, which his slaves around were casting into dazzling type. The rising sun saw Arthur again resume his journey, and thus passed several days, during which time he lived on bread and water, and the heavens were his nightly canopy, but cheered by that bright phantom, Hope, he at length reached Birmingham.

Reader hast thou ever visited this mighty emporium of iron and steel, worked into every pattern, shape, and device that human ingenuity can suggest. Here is the metal forged that the warrior wields triumphant in the battle's desperate strife; here the thimble, emblem of industry, worn even to the wearer's bone in the still harder conflict of female industry against the Jewocracy of the world; here are wrought the ornaments which glitter on the dressing table of the wealthiest lady in the land; and here, also, every instrument, every tool that the professional man, the mechanic, or the agriculturist can require. Happy union of elegance and utility — of the arts of war and peace. Long has the versatility of thy trades saved thee from the extremes of indigence, too often felt by thy sisters, Manchester and Liverpool, Dublin and Glasgow. Long hast thou been the world's mart for all the devices of Tubal Cain,[17] from the plaything of the child to the weapon of the man! Look well to thyself thou city of swarth-faced and bare-armed artisans — thou parent of Cheap Johns[18] and mock auctions — or thy rivals in Saxony will beat thee not only out of the world's market, but even out of those of thine own land, and thy fame will only be a dream of the past. Such is the sure result of the policy of partial Free Trade, which thy merchants, thy shopkeepers have assisted to bring about, and in which too many of thy artisans have suicidally acquiesced. But we are not writing a political essay, and therefore must discontinue this theme, but Birmingham and politics were at the period of our tale almost synonymous. The iron-handed men of Birmingham, armed to the teeth by the Whig press, and arrayed in martial columns, were the magic which hurled Toryism from its throne, — sowed the most gallant aristocracy in the world, — gave the nation a delusive benefit in the shape of a Reform Bill, — and a real injury in raising to place and pay the Whig conjurors, for whose especial behoof the phantasmagoria of the Birmingham revolution was brought into existence.

Seven years had passed since that eventful period in England's history. The men of Birmingham — the men of England — had discovered they had been made tools in the hands of the Whigs and their *bourgeoisie* supporters, and defrauded of all share of the spoils of the dead carcass of Toryism; and in order to obtain from Whig fear what justice and gratitude should have immediately granted, they had banded together from north to south — from John o'Groat's to Land's End[19] — in one vast combination, to agitate for their political rights, and had embodied those rights in a document called the People's Charter. They had also elected forty-nine delegates to sit in London and enforce upon Parliament the adoption of these views. It was at this juncture that our hero arrived in Birmingham; fortune befriended him in procuring immediate employment in a printing establishment, whose proprietor was a strong advocate of Chartist principles. Here was a vast field of speculation open to Arthur, a passionate lover of liberty, as embodied to him in the dream of the poet, — the musings of the philosopher, — or the motley garb of the historian; he had never considered the details necessary to ensure and retain the presence of the bright goddess. His had heretofore been a dreamy worship offered at the shrine of a Deity enveloped in dim but glorious shadow, whose outline was too vast for contemplation, and whose features ever appeared to vary with the varying imagination. A study of the principles of Chartism gave form, proportion, and colour to the shadow of his imagination, and arrayed it in the garb of right, reason, and justice. A close and enthusiastic study of the subject soon made him perceive that a love for liberty in name only, without a careful application of its principles, was vain and delusive. Stern truth is there in the words of Algernon Sydney, "Britons have died in defence of Liberty without knowing what Liberty was."[20] Precious blood! lavishly, but uselessly, shed. They chased a goddess, but embraced a fiend. Heart and soul did Arthur Morton enter into the high wrought feelings which then characterised political agitation. Young, and enthusiastic, having no other ties to distract his imagination, he mentally vowed to dedicate every energy of his mind and body to the furtherance of these, to him, novel yet glorious principles. The dreams of his youth were awakening into realities; the seeds of ambition were springing forth in the genial soil into which they had been thrown; who shall say, whether to be blighted by evil passions, crushed by despotic rule, or ripened to wholesome fruition? Happy youth! the perils of the past were forgotten, or remembered only with pleasure, as obstacles surmounted. The void in his bosom was occupied. His yearning for the pure and beautiful was gratified. "Chartism, the foul fiend of mischief and anarchy," was the pure divinity of his soul, and all that tended to increase her worship was holy in his imagination. Bright and pleasing vision! too soon wilt thou awake and discover that "her altar is bedewed with tears of blood; that her worshippers are the contemned of the world, — the discontented and wretched outcasts of society; that to avow yourself a Chartist is to court persecution, transportation and death!"

CHAPTER IX

The sentiments of elder days inspire
His breast and lead him on. He nothing heeds
The lessons of the times. Let others hire,
And pawn, and sell their country. Modern creeds
That suit Britannia's modern heroes. Fire
More bright, warmed those of whom the scholar reads;
From them he learned his love of liberty,
From them he learned to conquer or to die.
                                        Beste[21]

With deathless minds, which leave where they have past
A path of light, my soul communion knew,
Till from that glorious intercourse at last—
As from a mine of magic store, I drew
Words which were weapons, round my heart there grew,
The adamantine armour of their power,
And from my fancy wings of golden hue
Sprang forth.
                                        Shelley[22]

A lapse of some months has taken place since Arthur Morton arrived at Birmingham, during which interval his leisure time has been devoted to the study of politics, with occasional attendance at the meetings, then almost nightly held. His shopmates, conscious of his abilities, had often invited him to address these public assemblages, but the inherent shyness of his nature had hitherto prevented his doing so. Meanwhile the political atmosphere was growing still more dense and clouded. The National Convention still continued its sittings in the metropolis, but their proceedings were not characterised by that unity of purpose which influenced those who had elected them. Oh! it was a noble, a heart-inspiring sight, to see the myriads of working bees in all our vast hives of industry, abandoning all sectional pursuits, forgetting all minor subjects of rivalry, actuated by one mighty impulse, sacrificing their time, their talent, their hard-earned pittance, and, in many instances, their employment, to one grand object — the regeneration of their country. Such union, such devotion, deserved, and would have ensured success, had their delegates in Convention been inspired by the same devoted self-sacrificing spirit. But the ascendancy in that body; composed of ill-assorted and hastily-combined materials, it had no coherency in it — all was rivalry and opposition. This rendered their proceedings a source of discord to their constituents; spreading the evils of disunion from the centre to the remotest limits of the Confederacy, reducing their moral and physical stamina, until they fell an easy prey into the hands of the government. Let not our censure be too sweeping — great and noble spirits were there in that Assembly. Men who were an ornament to that body, and to the class to which they belonged, but their influence was not sufficient to restrain the wild but honest ardour of the physical force party on the one hand, or the cupidity and selfishness of many of the moral force party on the other hand. The government, paralysed in the first instance, speedily regained assurance, and amidst its internal divisions, and the retirement of many of its members, the remnant of the Convention, distrusting their position in the metropolis, resolved to entrench themselves among the physical force men of Birmingham. But, alas for the reputation of Birmingham! it no longer suited the Whigs, not the Whig press, to parade the number, organisation, and military equipment of thy sons; thy phantasmagoria had achieved its object, the conjurors were seated at the helm; they needed not the illusion, so the spell was broken, the charm deprived of its power, and thou was transformed from a military citadel, bristling with guns and bayonets, into thy ordinary quiet and peaceful position, never again to regain thy warlike character.

On the evening previous to the expected arrival of the Convention, a large meeting took place in the Bull Ring. Densely crowded was that vast area, the dim lights showing in dark perspective the eager and anxious countenances of the assembled thousands. Speaker after speaker poured forth in angry invective, denunciatory of the middle-class leaders, who had betrayed and deserted them, and declared their fierce determination to dare the vengeance of the government, and rally round the remnants of their delegates. There is something tragic even in the excited passions and feelings of one individual — but when these feelings, these passions, are communicated to the multitude by the electricity of eloquence, the scene is majestic and overpowering in the extreme. All sense of individuality is annihilated — the unit is lost in the mass — the solitary billow merged into the raging ocean, which swells and foams as if in disdain of the laws which regulate its motion. So it is with the multitude, when once heart hath spoken to heart, and the sympathy of mutual feeling and mutual indignation has linked the speaker to his hearers.

Arthur Morton had been accommodated with a seat on the temporary platform. The spirit of the time and the hour was burning within his veins. A feeling of suffocation pervaded his frame. Unknowing what he did, and scarce conscious of his own identity, he sprang to the centre at the close of one of the speakers' harangue, and, casting a glance of fire on the agitated and troubled mass of human beings below him, gave utterance to the pent-up feelings of years, and poured forth such a torrent of fervid eloquence that the excited myriads before him were spell-bound with the potent charm. No longer swelled and roared that mighty living ocean. Motion itself seemed hushed, and the strained eyeballs glaring upon him, and the dense heavy silence which prevailed, were the only visible signs of the working of the spell.

A brief pause in the orator's burning words seemed to break the charm, the death-like silence quivered into voice, until the whole mass was redolent of sound. Again the voice of the orator falls upon their ears — hushed again is that stormy ocean. With the energy of inspiration, the speaker lays bare the miserable sophisms of the advocates of misrule, and laughs to scorn their blasphemous plea of right divine. The world's past history is thrown with lightning glance into his hearers' very hearts, and shown to be one red record of misery and crime wherever man's rights have been kept in abeyance; next his powerful eloquence vents itself on the treachery and deceit of those worshippers of the golden calf who would use the energies of his audience as the stepping-stone to their own advancement. The flimsy veil of their apparent co-operation is torn to shreds — the bitter mockery of their similarity of interest is laid bare with iron hand — their conventional hypocrisy is exposed in all its narrow and naked deformity, and earnestly and solemnly are they appealed to, to cast off all dependence upon others, to trust solely to their own energies, and leave the decision to the God of justice and the God of battle.

The audience still listened in breathless silence, but the orator had ceased; and while the echoes of their applause were still ringing in his ears, he was quietly treading his way to his home, overcome by this unwonted excitement. No after speaker addressed the meeting. It would have been but to little avail. The hoarded eloquence of an embittered life, the hard experience of hunger and of want, had been lavished upon them, and all meaner food would have been rejected.

Of all the varied gifts of man, the most powerful, the most fascinating, is the magic of the tongue, whether breathing soft whispers to beauty's willing ear, or commanding the wrapt attention of the listening senate — whether thundering in the pulpit, or pleading at the bar, its effects are alike potent. Would that its accents were only powerful in a right and just cause.

CHAPTER X

What if they failed! 'Twere glory e'en to dare
The proud achievement. Tens of millions brood
O'er human life in one penurious mood
Of paltry thought, and miserable care;
Then shall not these the palm of triumph wear,
A guiltless wreath by slaughter unimbrued;
For not by their own minds were they subdued,
But by the banded powers of ...

This was a fresh era in the life of Arthur Morton, one of those cycles of events on which the whole web of after-life seems to hang; the mute lyre of his soul had been touched by the finger of popular emotion, and gave forth sweet and sonorous music, of the possession of which it had hitherto been unconscious; but the lyre once touched, its vibrations ceased not until the fragile instrument was destroyed. In the exciting scenes that took place during the few days of the Convention's sitting in Birmingham, Arthur was a prominent actor; the irritating interference of a body of police, sent from London to preserve the peace, was the immediate cause of its being broken, and in the riots that ensued they would have speedily met their fate, had they not been sheltered by the military.[23] Arthur deeply regretted these transactions; enthusiast as he was, he would have shed his blood cheerfully in any struggle, however hopeless, which might possibly result in achieving the emancipation of the masses; but he was aware that mere sectional rioting would tend only to dispirit the friends, and exasperate the enemies of the movement; it was, therefore, with feelings of pain that he gazed on that grand and exciting spectacle in the Bull-Ring, when the pent-up passions of the mass bust forth like a volcano's lava, scattering flames and destruction around. The leaders of the Democratic movement are decried by their opponents as destructives, and incendiaries — men delighting in anarchy and confusion. Despicable falsehood! were it so, courage and opportunities have not been wanting, and England's mammoth cities might have been the funeral pyres of their oppressors, and blazing beacons of a world's warning against man's injustice to his brother man. Had the leaders of the people that night been the firebrands they are denominated, a new Birmingham must, Phoenix-like, have arisen from the ashes of the present one; but they, in common with the generality of Britons, have a respect for property, and a love of order, carried even to the extreme. Little, however, does this avail them; their motives must be impugned, and their characters maligned, in order that the thoughtless and the inert — the mass of the people — may be deluded and imposed upon, under the specious pleas of the rights of private property, and the reign of public order. The events that followed are matters of history, but of history that has to be re-written, to clear it of prejudice and calumny. Time, the great arbiter, will do all parties justice — more is needed not. The Convention, ushered into existence amid the sunshine of unity and hope, dissolved away amid shadow and gloom; many of its members were arrested, and the remainder, with few exceptions, dispersed or in exile; nor were the men of Birmingham suffered to go scathless — imprisonment and transportation was the lot of too many of her sons. Honest and true-hearted, they fell victims to the misguided enthusiasm of the moment. A tear to their woes, and a speedy termination to their exile! Had theirs been an impartial jury of their peers, they would have returned a verdict of "Temporary insanity, brought on by excess of zeal in a good cause."

Arthur Morton, deprecating this rioting, and taking no part in the firing of the houses in the Bull-Ring, had nevertheless become a marked man; he had displayed abilities too great to be suffered to go at large, whilst any plausible pretext could be found for ridding the country of him; he was, accordingly, one evening shortly after these events, arrested by Catchem and Holdem, two of the London police, and on inquiring the charge, was informed — "Arson." Arthur had seen enough of life to know that innocence was no protection in a court of justice when the political prejudices of a jury were appealed to; his resolution was therefore taken and acted upon at once. While the policemen were searching his papers and effects, he was descending the stairs to the street, with one of his captors in front and the other behind; he stooped suddenly down, seized the foremost by the legs, threw him headlong, jumped over his prostrate body, and succeeded in gaining the street before the hindmost officer could disengage himself from his companion, who, partially stunned by his fall, but having a dim consciousness of his duty, seized him by mistake for our hero. In vain did Catchem endeavour to convince Holdem that he had got the wrong man by the gripe; Holdem held convulsively to his leg, and it was only by a violent effort that Catchem tore himself from his grasp. Swiftly sped Arthur along the dark and narrow street, he has turned the corner, and no sound of pursuit falls on his ear; he slackens his pace to collect his scattered thoughts, but before he can arrange any plan of escape the shouts of the pursuers burst on his ear — darkness favours him, they see him not, but have traced him by the sound of his footsteps. Onward he flies, — now he emerges from the quiet streets, adjacent to his home, into New-street, and, walking quietly along, is lost to his pursuers amid the passengers that throng the street. In sooth to say, Catchem, in doubt as to the state of his brother officer, did not make any strenuous effort to continue the pursuit; feeling confident of a reward being offered, he rejoined his comrade, whom he found recovered from his insensibility. Holdem, whilst venting imprecations upon the prisoner's escape, laughed heartily at his own erroneous seizure; they then ascertained the route taken by Arthur, and suspended further active operations until a reward should enhance the value of their prey. Meanwhile Arthur, finding himself safe, hastened to the suburbs, and succeeded in reaching Wolverhampton in safety; he paused at the entrance of the town, thinking the lateness of the hour might cause suspicion, but anxiety to place the greatest possible distance between himself and his pursuers hurried him on, and during the whole night he tarried not, but pursued the northern road until he reached Stafford; here, pleading illness, he engaged a bed at a small public-house, and after partaking of tea, retired to the sleeping apartment and soon sunk into slumber; but sleep did not long exert its influence over him; the mind, perplexed and wearied, would not allow the body to repose; his was indeed a dangerous position, — with but a few shillings in his pocket — without change of raiment — destitute of even political friends, save those in Birmingham, with whom it was now dangerous to correspond, he knew not what course to take or where to proceed; with the natural instinct of courage he meditated upon returning to Birmingham, and meeting the unjust accusation, but reflection told him that it would be useless so to sacrifice himself, and that his flight would be looked upon as a strong confirmation of his guilt. After revolving ever various plans he at length decided upon travelling to Liverpool, and from thence writing to an acquaintance in Birmingham to turn the few things his savings had allowed him to purchase into money, trusting with the proceeds to reach America, that refuge for the world's criminals and the world's unfortunates, receiving daily the very refuse of Europe, — all who are discontented — all who are in debt — those who cannot, and who will not obey the laws of their native land — mingled with a few of its noblest spirits. Yet by virtue of thy Republican institutions purifying and refining these discordant elements, uniting all in the bonds of citizenship, and setting an example of order, economy, and prosperity to the nations of the Old World, and example which, sooner or later, they will be compelled to follow.

In safety did Arthur reach Liverpool, and from thence communicated with his friend at Birmingham. Day after day passed in suspense, during which time Arthur kept himself almost a prisoner in his room. One evening he ventured as far as the residence of Walter North, which he had ascertained from his landlady; half tempted was he to knock and see what reception he should meet from his old schoolfellow, but prudence bade him desist. He was a fugitive flying from the terrors of the law — his quondam friend was rich and prosperous, and seldom do fortune's favourites protect the felon or the outcast, so he sought again his quiet lodging, though he gazed long and wistfully at the splendid mansion he had left, and well was it for Arthur that he entered not that mansion. Walter North, a Whig economist in politics, and a bitter reviler of the vulgar Chartists, would have thought it his duty — that excuse for every mean and vile act — Walter would have thought it his duty to his country to sacrifice private friendship on the altar of public good, and would have gained golden opinions with his party for the supposed violation done to his feelings, and

Arthur would have been consigned to the grasp of the law. Our hero was beginning to despair of an answer from Birmingham, when happily it arrived, containing a £10 note, partly the result of the sale of his watch and few clothes, and partly a subscription from the few who were trusted with the circumstances. Arthur deeply appreciated the kindness of his friend; it would enable him to procure a few necessaries for the voyage in addition to the payment of his passage, and a few days saw him safe on board the "Camden", a fine American ship, sailing away from the land of his birth, the land that he would have died to benefit, but which met his devotion with persecution, and would have sentenced him to a felon's fate in her Australian world, had he not prevented it by self-exile. Such is the world and the world's justice!

CHAPTER XI

Boldly I venture on a naval scene
Nor fear the critic's frown — the pedant's spleen.

* * *

Thus the rich vessel moves in trim array
Like some fair virgin on her bridal day:
Thus like a swan she cleaves the watery plain
The pride and wonder of the Aegean main.

* * *

The sea-breached vessel can no longer bear
The floods that o'er her burst in dread career!
The labouring hull already seems half-filled
With water, through an hundred leaks distilled;
Thus, drenched by every wave her riven deck,
Stript and defenceless floats a naked wreck.
                                        Falconer[24]

   With mingled feelings did Arthur view the vessel's progress up the Mersey to its parent Ocean, all his bright hopes were dimmed and clouded, and he was compelled to seek in other lands that home which Britain denied him. Still he felt joyous at his fortunate escape, and the novelty of being on shipboard helped to amuse his thoughts; but no sooner did they clear the Mersey, and the wide expanse of ocean spread before them, than all other thoughts were buried in the contemplation of the grandeur of the scene. The sun was slowly setting, tingling the clouds and the sails of the vessels in the distance with its golden hues, whilst the crested waves shone sparkling in their emerald sheen, as their falling or rising billows caught its lingering rays, whilst the moon, rising in the opposite horizon, shed a flood of gentle light on all around. Breathing the spirit of calm and meditation, forgetting aught but the scene before him, Arthur thus gave audible utterance to his feelings —

"Oh! thou sublime, majestic ocean! thou mighty world of waters — which encompasses, beautifies, and fertilises the earth! who can view thee in thy grandeur and have no joy in thy magnificence! Earth has her gorgeous towns and castellated mansions, but the earth-encircling sea has spires and mansions more amazing still; men's volant homes — that measure liquid space on wheel or wing — that circumscribe the earth, and make it the highway of nations, and the grand agent of human civilisation! Oh! he who hath not gazed on thee hath not seen the sublimer portion of nature's kingdom, and can form no adequate notion of intensity or space."

With a mind calmed and elevated by these thoughts, he sought his cabin, and pondered over the events of his short but stormy career, since entering into manhood. Disappointed hopes had not yet deprived the glass of life of its silver plate; though its surface was beclouded and disfigured, his musings were still on his country's welfare. Harsh stepmother as she had proved to him, he still loved her with unimpaired devotion, and though he would correct her faults, and reform her abuses, yet harm from his hand would never fall on her. Type was he of his class. Our novelists — even the most liberal — can never draw a democrat save in warpaint. "Sincere, but stern and hard-hearted" — "honest, but blustering and insolent" — "ignorant, dogmatic, and fierce, but a lover of principle;" such are the characters they present to their readers, when they condescend to introduce so vulgar a being. They profess to paint from life; but they give us a daubed copy. Experience has never furnished them with an original; they cannot describe what they do not comprehend. Shades of the martyred democrats of all time; ye noble, but calumniated band! though dead, ye yet speak to the world, and attest that ye fell victims to your love of mercy — to your nobility of heart — in sparing those who never spared their fellow-man. If the aphorism be true — and of its truth there can be but little doubt — "that a political error is worse than a crime" — worse in its consequences — more enduring in its effects, of all the crimes that can be laid to the charge of Democracy, that of sparing its enemies when in its power is the most fatal to human progression. The last French revolution and its accompanying events afford a complete realisation of this fact.[25]

Speedily rode the vessel on her homeward course, bounding o'er the billows as though instinct with life and motion. Much did our hero find to admire — much to learn, on this his first entrance to a large vessel; all was novel, and entertaining. The weather was delightfully calm, and that most excruciating torment, sea sickness, had not yet laid hands on him; but on the second day of their voyage, just as the loneliness ever accompanying to a landsman the constant view of the water's wide expanse, had begun to supersede the emotion of admiration, the clouds began to look heavy and impending, and the vessel to roll and pitch in the trough of the sea. Arthur, who, in the spirit of curiosity, had been anxious to observe a storm at sea, had not the opportunity; but, alas! he, in common with the other passengers, was confined to his hammock in a state which none can imagine but those who have felt the sensation, and which no pretended remedies seem to have power to remove. The mighty element, over whose bosom they have been tranquilly sailing, almost forgetting they were not on the firm set earth, seems to take this gentle method of reminding the novices of her power and potency; happy are they who encounter her not in her wrath. Towards noon it blew what the seamen called a stiff gale, but to a landsman's apprehension, it was a perfect hurricane; gallantly did the vessel contend against the wrathful wind and waves, and with seaman-like alacrity did the crew perform their duty, but the storm increased to such a degree, that the loss of the ship appeared certain, the sea breaking so continually over her as to render incessant labour at the pumps necessary to keep her afloat; a billow, more mountainous than the rest, at length swept over the deck, and the tapering masts, and graceful yards, that so adorned the bird-like fabric, were whelmed beneath the waves, and the dismantled ship, no longer obeying her helm, was left floating at the mercy of the wild winds and raging waters, and gradually breaking up beneath their combined and powerful attacks. The passengers confined below, sick and exhausted, were but imperfectly acquainted with their true situation; nor until every means of saving the vessel was despaired of, were they informed of their awful peril. Oh, who could describe the feeling created in these heretofore almost inanimate beings! sixty human souls brought face to face with the insatiate monarch, Death, in one of his most terrific forms; one powerful emotion subdued all minor feeling, the nausea of sea sickness was forgotten, all was merged in the one sole idea of escape from present death. Men — bold men, who under other forms would have faced death without shrinking — were to be seen wringing their hands, and making no effort to assist in their own preservation. Women — delicate, modest women, half dressed — were clinging wildly to the sailors, praying them to save them, whilst they, with almost rudeness, threw off their embraces, and coolly but mechanically employed themselves in launching the boats, as their only means of escape. Darkness now added itself to their other evils, though it shrouded from view terrors appalling enough to shake the stoutest heart. Women and children shrieking loudly for hope, as the waves washed over their prostrate bodies; men maddened with liquor, flown to when all order was lost; or no less maddened by fanaticism, calling loudly upon Heaven for help, but neglecting to apply themselves to the human means. Arthur Morton, naturally brave and self-possessed, though far from being an assistance to the sailors, (this his want of nautical experience alone would have prevented), was sufficiently self-collected to exercise a restraining power over his fellow passengers and keep them in something like order, though all his efforts would have been unavailing, had they not been seconded by those of another passenger, a Lancashire farmer, and likewise by those of the officers of the ship. All the preparatory steps being completed, the passengers, with the exception of one man and two women, who were washed overboard, were safely stowed in the three boats, and the officers and crew, and what provisions and water could be hurriedly obtained, divided among them. Scarcely were they clear of the wreck when the ill-fated fabric, trembling as if with emotion, burst asunder, and plunged beneath the waves. The boats keeping as near each other as the darkness and their violent pitching would allow, steered for the nearest port on the Irish coast. As night fell the violence of the wind somewhat abated, but even the most hopeful had but a faint idea that they could survive until daylight, and then their only chance of safety was falling in with some vessel, as the hope of reaching any port was almost chimerical. In after life Arthur Morton often recalled the horrors of that night, and the dangers then endured and surmounted nerved his heart to minor troubles, and caused him to look with philosophical indifference upon the petty but harassing casualties of everyday life. The boat in which he, with twenty eight others, including the captain and purser, was stowed, was barely large enough to allow them to sit or lay, and their limbs were cramped and benumbed with their confined position; the waves kept continually washing over them, and the darkness and confined space preventing them from taking any effectual means to bale the water, they were consequently every moment in danger of sinking, and the intense cold added to their other horrors.

As daylight broke and discovered to each other their wretched plight, they saw with dismay that neither of the other boats was visible, — each looked aghast in his fellow's face, and anticipated the fate which had doubtless fallen on their companions. Out of twelve female passengers originally on board two had been washed over prior to embarking in the boats, eight were in the lost boats, and two in the boat with our hero; — the one, a fair girl of about nineteen, and the other about the middle age, and apparently her mother. In the darkness of the night, and the selfishness which absorbed all their own energies in the preservation of their own individuality, the females were forgotten, but returning daylight, whilst giving them fresh hopes, renewed within them the feelings of urbanity towards the weaker sex. Overcome by cold and fatigue they were nearly insensible, but a little wine being poured down their throats they gradually revived; but better far had they been left to sleep the sleep of death, for the loss of the other boats being abruptly communicated to them, heart rending were the shrieks they uttered. The youngest had lost a husband, to whom she had been but a few weeks united, and a father to whom she was tenderly attached; the elder had to mourn the loss of an affectionate husband, the Lancashire farmer previously mentioned, who, with his wife and youngest daughter and her husband, were about to proceed to Texas, and commence life anew in that El Dorado of the New World; separated from each other in the darkness and confusion, though united in life they were dissevered in death; the screams of these bereaved ones, though frightful at first, soon subsided into a low moaning; nature seemed exhausted, and to have imparted her last energies

to their convulsive grief; they never again raised their heads from their bosoms,
— all efforts to rouse them from their state of bodily and mental torpor were
fruitless, they never spoke again. As soon as daylight appeared a signal had
been hoisted, but no sail appeared in sight. Hours rolled on in misery and
almost despair; two of the passengers had died from the effects of fear and
cold, — noon was approaching; the storm had ceased — the waters were
becoming calm, and a bright sun was just beginning to beam upon them,
warming their benumbed bodies, and cheering their drooping spirits, when they
descried an outward bound vessel bearing direct upon their course. Oh! the
agony of suspense embodied in the next hour, a whole lifetime of emotion was
experienced in those fleeting moments, varying from the intensity of despair to
the wildest joy; as doubt no longer existed that they were descried, and would
speedily be rescued; this joy was not misplaced, as a few hours saw them safely
on board the "Esmeralda", a vessel bound for the West Indies, where they
received every attention from the captain and crew which their sad situation
demanded; many hours did the captain delay, in hopes to see something of the
other two boats, but in vain — they were never heard of more.

CHAPTER XII

Come over the sea,
Maiden with me,
Mine through sunshine, storm and snow;
Seasons may roll,
But the true soul,
Burns the same wherever it goes;
Let fate frown on, so we love and part not,
'Tis life where thou art, 'tis death where thou'rt not.
                                   Moore[26]

For long the wayward mind may not take part
In passion's dreams, nor feel the encroaching sway;
The ardent youth, whose buoyant untamed heart
In fancy's fairy regions dares to stray,
Not all unscathed, uninjur'd will depart,
But soon to passion half an easy prey;
Imagination may not idly rove
Through love's domain, nor feel the power of love.
                                   Beste[27]

The "Esmeralda", commanded by Capt. Wickham, was bound from Liverpool
to Barbadoes, and had on board two female passengers with their attendants,
and a planter returning from a visit to England; she had left Liverpool two days

after the ill-fated "Camden", and had consequently escaped the height of the storm, but the passengers were still confined to their cabins by sea sickness, which is usually the case for the first week of the voyage. On the following day the melancholy task of committing the two female and two male passengers to the waves was performed, at which ceremony the whole of the ship's crew, and those who were able of the "Camden", attended; Mr. Weeks, captain of the "Camden", officiating as clergyman. The next day being very fine and calm, the passengers, for the first time, made their appearance on deck. Arthur, who had suffered less from the effect of the shipwreck than many of his fellow-sufferers, was leaning against the ship's side when they ascended the ladder from the cabin; first came a stout elderly lady, the very personification of good living and good humour; she was the widow of a merchant residing at D——, one of the Windward Islands,[28] and had been to England to assist in celebrating the nuptials of her eldest daughter with the young Lord Cowpens, a nobleman who counted a long line of ancestors, each of whom for many generations had maintained the dignity of the name by decreasing the revenue of the domain, until the title was nearly the sole heritage left by the late lord to its present occupant; to remedy this inconvenience he consented to barter his title for the gold of the merchant's daughter, and Miss Selina Elkinson had lately become the Countess Cowpens, and Mrs. Elkinson was returning home not a little elate at the grand alliance she had contracted, and the increased importance it would give her at D——. The next figure that advanced up the ladder, — could it be a dream, or was it in reality the image that memory had indelibly imprinted on his brain, and associated with all the pleasing ideas of boyhood and youthful recollections. It was indeed his early playmate, Julia North, now Lady Baldwin, who, unable to obtain a longer respite, was about joining her husband, who was to meet her at Barbadoes, and who had entrusted her to the matronly care of Mrs. Elkinson, of whose journey to England he was aware; and proud was she to accept the office of *chaperon* to the lovely, though apparently drooping and low-spirited, wife of the new governor, Sir Jasper Baldwin. The first impulse of Arthur was to rush to Julia North, for he was unacquainted with her marriage, and renew their former acquaintance, but his natural reserve checked the ardour of his feelings, and he awaited a more favourable opportunity of discovering himself; this soon presented itself, for Capt. Wickham having acquainted the ladies, and Mr. Burke, the planter, alluded to, with the circumstances of the wreck, pointed out to their notice the captain, purser, and passengers of the "Camden", as constrained fellow-voyagers with them, unless, indeed, they fell in with a homeward-bound American, as his instructions did not allow of his in any way deviating from his course. Julia at once recognised Arthur, and greeted him with a warmth that surprised the good-natured Mrs. Elkinson, accustomed as she was to her usual quietness of manner. Long and interesting were the explanations which ensued of the years past since their last meeting. A recurrence to the scenes of her youth seemed to act as a charm on Lady Baldwin, and Mrs. Elkinson was delighted to see her in such spirits, and unacquainted with her history, attributed her prior dejection to the effects of sea sickness, from which she had greatly suffered. Owing to his being a friend of Lady Baldwin's, Arthur messed with the passengers at the captain's table, and being thus continually in Julia's company his boyish love was rekindled, but it was a pure and holy flame, unmixed with aught of selfish wishes. Julia never referred to her marriage, and when Mrs. Elkinson spoke of Sir Jasper her answers were cold but respectful. Arthur knew not of the constraint placed upon her affections, but his penetration soon told him she did not love her husband with that devotedness and energy of which he believed her capable; he therefore supposed that in this marriage she was guided as much by ambition as by love, and this reflection certainly lowered her in his estimation; but we never dwell long on the faults of those we love, especially when love is as it was with him, — a compound of early association, respect, and admiration. Day after day did he enjoy the delight of Julia's company, and though he evinced not by word or action the love that was hourly increasing within him, yet, almost unconsciously, his words assumed a softer tone, and his eyes a milder glance, when discoursing with his heart's idol, for such she was rapidly becoming; an idol to be worshipped in secret and in silence; at whose altar the votive gifts were sighs and regrets, the offerings of love's unfortunates. In Arthur's feelings of respect there mingled no thought of the difference in their rank or condition in life; he a fugitive from justice, she a rich and titled bride. Equally, yea more, would he have loved her had she been poor and friendless, — equally would he have respected her a poor man's bride as the bride of Sir Jasper Baldwin.

And Julia, for such we must list to call her — and Julia, what were her feelings? Forced into a hateful marriage, her thoughts towards her husband were a mingled compound fear and loathing. Constant intercourse might have worn the edge off this feeling, but absence had strengthened it, and naught but the positive injunctions of her parents, and a dread of the world's calumnies, would have prevailed upon her to join Sir Jasper. With a sad heart and fearful forebodings, did she leave her parents and her native shores, and not even the good humoured Mrs. Elkinson could raise a smile on her wan cheeks — her whole frame was jarred and unstrung. Passion of any description would have been a relief to her, for listlessness and languor were consuming her very soul. The unexpected sight of Arthur Morton (appearing, too, at a critical period, when the exertion of embarkation, and the effects of sea sickness, had disposed the mind to receive anything soothing as a positive boon,) gave a fresh tone to her mind, and struck a latent chord in the shattered instrument, which again spoke of life and beauty. Arthur, as a playmate, had been a favourite; in the long years that had passed he had never been entirely forgotten, and in her present isolated situation the remotest acquaintance would have been regarded as a link between her and the past, and a refuge from thoughts on the future; it was no wonder then that she looked upon him with feelings of no ordinary description, — his modesty, his intelligence, and let us not leave out, his interesting appearance, gave greater strength to the charm; there were none others to contrast with him, or cast his good qualities into the shade; and if idleness be the parent of love, what a host of young Cupids should attend a long voyage. Yes, gentle reader, Julia, if not in love with Arthur, had many symptoms of that disease, and time and opportunity were alone wanting to develope them, and of these they would have an abundance. Let not the censorious or the prudish blame my heroine. Love in her was no crime, albeit she was the bride of another, — it was the result of feelings as pure as nature ever implanted in human breast; the treachery of her relative, and the baseness of Sir Jasper, were the circumstances which caused it to verge upon crime — or rather, should we say, retributive justice. Let the saint and the hypocrite rail on — we write not for their perusal, we heed not their censure; we picture human nature as it is — veritable flesh and blood — glowing with warm and ardent feelings — feelings which are apt to overpower the judgment; but far better is it so than for us to fall into the Dead Sea waters of apathy, or wallow in the mire of cold and frigid selfishness.

CHAPTER XIII

I heard as all have heard life's various story,
    And in no careless heart transcribed the tale;
But, from the sneers of men who had grown hoary
    In shame and scorn, from groans of crowds made pale
By famine, from a mother's desolate wail
    O'er her polluted child, from innocent blood
Poured on the earth, and brows anxious and pale
    With the heart's warfare, did I gather food
To feed my many thoughts; a tameless multitude.
                                        Shelley[29]

Julia, Arthur, Mrs. Elkinson, and Mr. Burke were the usual occupants of the mess-room when the weather was not sufficiently calm to be on deck. Mr. Weeks and the purser were generally on deck with the captain. Mr. Burke was a tall, sallow-looking man, remarkable only for his devotion to the table and his careful superintendence of the ship's cook — he seldom spoke except at table, and then only relative to the good or ill qualities of the viands; after dinner he returned to the cabin, to sleep away the time until the next meal was announced. Mrs. Elkinson was likewise accustomed to an afternoon siesta: so that Julia and Arthur were generally left alone during the time between the dinner and tea bells. It was during these intervals that Arthur confided to Julia the minute particulars of his history; the dreamings of his boyhood — the reveries of his apprentice years — his struggles with poverty in the metropolis — his entrance into political life — the exciting scenes that occurred in

Birmingham — his unjust accusation — his flight, and the awful details of the shipwreck; these events, told in the eloquent and impassioned manner which Arthur could so well employ, were sweet but strange music to her ears — like Desdemona,[30] she loved him for the dangers he had past, and he loved her that she did pity him. In her eyes he became a hero of romance, and she longed to know the principles of Chartism and the motives of its persecutors; her heart truly informed her that the first were good and noble, or Arthur would not have adopted them, and the vindictiveness and injustice of the latter were then apparent. In forcible language did Arthur depict to her the wrongs endured by the people through unjust legislation, and the simple but complete means of remedy propounded by the Charter.

"Look around," said he, at the close of one of their conversations, "on the myriads of our fellow beings who yearly perish from hunger, or diseases brought on by hunger, whilst the boards of pampered idlers groan with the weight of every excess. View the dying thousands who feel that their lives might be prolonged by a few drops of those generous liquors which are maddening and destroying the lives of their possessors. See the thousands of honest artisans through whose ragged garments every winter's wind pierces like a dart, while yon sleek trades are well clothed in the raiment the others have created. Observe yon group of haggard females, compelled to desert their infant offspring, and sacrifice the joys of maternity at the shrine of the Factory Moloch. Glance at that crowd of women-men, inverting the order of Nature, and performing a mother's duties — nay, look not steadily at them, or their wan faces will blush with shame and anger. Trace the career of those deserted babes — see their stunted frames bending beneath their protracted labour, and their infant blood poured forth like water, that our millowners and manufacturers may become refined and luxurious. Gaze upon the white hairs of those ancient labourers, the venerable of the land, who after producing more wealth than would have kept themselves and their families in affluence — cheated of the result of their labour — are compelled to enter that hell upon earth a Union Workhouse, or turned adrift on life's dreary common, to starve and die."

Julia shuddered at these harrowing pictures, but alas! their truth could not be gainsayed.

"Does not such a state of society," continued Arthur, "need a change — a state where honest Industry starves, whilst bloated Idleness pants from excess — where Virtue and Patriotism hide their heads in hovels which shake beneath the carriage wheels of the sycophant and the sensualist — where millions are yearly wrung from the life's blood of the poor, that cormorant bishops and pampered parsons may preach the doctrine, that the rich man cannot enter into Heaven, and that passive obedience is the grand injunction of God? A state where ermined judges and silk-gowned counsellors sit in state to distribute the mockery of justice to him whom their laws have rendered criminal, and where more money is yearly extracted from the marrow of her sons, for the detection and punishment of crime, than would, if properly applied, for ever banish crime from the land. Yes, Lady Baldwin, it is for teaching these truths that I am rendered a fugitive from justice, an exile from my native land."

"Yet," said Julia, "surely it is but the designing few who support these monstrosities — the majority of the upper classes need only to have them pointed out to take steps for their removal?"

"Ah! Lady Baldwin; your charity leads you to judge them too favourably. Wrapped up in the mantle of their own selfishness, they heed not the destiny of those beneath them — they tread on a slumbering volcano, the lava of desolation surrounds them, but they have grown accustomed to the scene, and walk in fancied security. Providence, they say, had destined the many to poverty and labour, and it is useless for them to repine, and with this blasphemy on their lips they dismiss the subject, and proceed with their routine of existence — pleasure without enjoyment, revelry without mirth. If, perchance, one of their order should interest himself in so vulgar a subject, he is dubbed an eccentric or a monomaniac, and his presence is shunned as a bore."

"But the middle class," said Julia, "surely they should aid the working men in so noble a struggle — their interests are similar?"

"No, dear lady, their interests are not similar; they are as distinct as the positive and negative poles of an electric battery; they apparently belong to the same body, they are influenced by the same causes, but the effects on each are widely different — the interest of the working man is to sell his labour at the most profitable rate; the interest of the other is to reduce it down to starvation point; the one is benefited by the whole of his order being well employed and well paid; the object of the other is, by the introduction of machinery, and the encouragement of pauper immigration to the large towns, to cause a redundancy of labour in the market, that he may work upon the fears of the sensitive and the weak, and purchase their labour at his own price. Prior to the passing of the Reform Bill, there was one sole point of similarity in their interests — both were equally disenfranchised; but when, by aid of the energy of the working men, they achieved that measure, the chain of the labour slave was riveted still firmer; the employer was politically free, but the brand-mark was still deeper engraved on the brow of the employed; the ladder by which the middle class had risen was thrown down as useless, and they had ever since endeavoured, by every means in their power, to ally themselves to the upper class, and to build up a wall of separation between them and the working men. Selfishness is their ruling principle, — gold, the idol of their worship; to this divinity all must bow and bend. The shopkeepers and small tradesmen alone have a common interest with the working men, but they, too, are either so immersed in the hard struggle for bread that they heed not the sure method of obtaining it through good and cheap government, or so lamentably ignorant that they sell their birthright for a mess of potage."[31]

Julia replied not, but sighed deeply, her visions of the brightness of human nature were fleeting fast away, but centred still more firmly in the one, to her mind, perfect specimen before her.

Arthur continued: "No, fair lady, redemption for the working classes must spring from themselves alone; long experience has shown in every instance the credulity of depending upon others; and even among working men there are grades of aristocracy, who look down with contempt upon their equally useful brethren, who earn a few shillings less per week than themselves. Thus does the principle of aristocracy penetrate even into the heart of democracy, robbing it of vitality and strength, and causing the day of its deliverance to be afar off, for, of all enemies, the most deadly are those within our own ranks. But perhaps," said Arthur, mournfully, "it is a portion of our destiny that by sorrow, suffering, and persecution, again and again renewed, can we alone be fitted for the enjoyment of calm and peaceful liberty."

There was something in the tone and manner of Arthur that went to the heart of Julia, — she answered not, but thought of her own bitter lot, and that for her there was no ultimatum of enjoyment.

With such conversations as these did they wile away the tedium of the voyage. Julia drunk in the words of Arthur as from a fount of inspiration, — his sentiments became her sentiments, — his feeling her feelings, — and oh! how grateful to Providence would she have been if his lot, though one of poverty and danger, could have been shared by her also. Wealth and titles, what gaudy trappings ye are, how brilliant, but how unsatisfactory! Your votaries rush through every danger — dare every disgrace — spare neither age nor sex, friend nor foe, to clasp themselves in your embraces, and when success has crowned their exertions they find too late that your folds are venomous, and your embraces engender satiety and disease. Poor Julia! she sought not wealth nor titles, — a victim to family ambition, she must pay the penalty of others' vices. Poor players on the great state of humanity — we strut and fume away through our allotted parts, and vainly imagine that we are free agents and could act otherwise than necessity has determined for us. An atom struggling against a universe — a feather against the wind that wafts it — yet have we seen the feather, coquette-like, fluttering between contending breezes, as if choosing its own course — pleasant delusion, flattering to our vanity, but fatal to our happiness. Julia North, or rather Lady Baldwin, thinks that she could give up wealth and title to reside in a cottage with the chosen of her heart — that her destiny is in her own hands — that she has to choose between love on the one hand, virtue and matronly pride on the other. Poor moth! fluttering around the light, thy destiny is irrevocably fixed, thy mingled yarn is nearly spun, the sister fates will spare ye not.

CHAPTER XIV

From out of everything around he drew
A vein of deep and melancholy thought;

No plant more sprightly than its fellow grew—
No birds could sing their melody untaught—
No slightest object past unheeded by,
But furnish'd food for thought and minstrelsy.

* * *

His home, her home, how sweet the accents sound,
To every heart in every clime, they come,
With fairest dreams and visions interwound;
Dreams of past bliss enhancing present gloom.
How fondly in the exile's heart abound
Those o'erwrought fancies of the joys of home!
How fondly still he paints his native place!
How decks it out in charms none else can trace!
Beste[32]

Speedily the vessel neared the wished for port, — they had been five weeks at sea, and a few more days would end their voyage. The weather continuing calm, they often passed the forenoon on deck, gazing on the vast expanse of ocean, and noting with curiosity each incident that broke the monotony of the scene, — a cormorant chasing a flight of sea-gulls — a shark in pursuit of the boneta or flying fish — a tree borne down by the river from its parent forest and launched on the mighty ocean — each event was a text from which Arthur drew a homily, pleasing and instructive, or dark and chequered like his own fate, but all, all were tinctured with his political aspirations. The cormorant was a picture of the world, where the great preyed upon the small, growing fat and luxurious in the exact proportion that they ground down and oppressed those beneath them. The shark was an emblem of the law; the poor boneta was the victim, that, driven out of its element, sought shelter in its dry atmosphere, but finding it not was again speedily compelled to seek shelter beneath the waves, until chased and driven from one element to the other its weary wings can no longer sustain it, and it falls into the jaws of its stronger pursuer. The tree was an emblem of himself, that, torn from his parent earth by the whirlwind of power, was driven about by the waves of adversity, and knew not where his resting place would be. Thus did his ever active mind feed upon every aliment, drawing nourishment to his soul, and strengthening the bonds which bound him to his fair auditor.

Seated at dinner a few days prior to the termination of the voyage, Mr. Weeks, as captain of the "Camden", and bound to see the remnant of his crew and passengers to their destination, informed Arthur of his intention to take passage to New York for all those who chose to avail themselves of the opportunity, as speedily as a ship should present itself.

Arthur thanked him for the information, and trusted that when they next sailed in company their voyage would prove more prosperous than the last.

Mr. Burke seized the opportunity to call on Capt. Wickham for an extra bottle after dinner to pledge their prosperous voyage.

"I would thank you for a portion of the breast of that chicken," said Mrs. Elkinson to Mr. Burke.

"Chicken, madam, our voyage has been so long that it has positively got as tough as an old hen, though the cook assures me that he bred them himself; I fear that the rascal having a greater demand, owing to the honour of your company, (bowing to Arthur, Capt. Weeks, and the purser of the "Camden") has been serving us with the parents instead of their offspring."

"Shall I help you to a little of this loin of lamb, Mr. Burke," asked Capt. Wickham; "seeing you prefer the juniors of the family!"

"No, captain, in this instance, I prefer the parent. Mr. Morton, I will thank you for a portion of that haunch of mutton."

"Will you take turnips or artichokes, Mr. Burke?" inquired Julia.

"The turnips yesterday were ill-mashed, and the milk sour, I will therefore prefer artichokes. Ah! captain, I would certainly discharge your cook," said Mr. Burke, as he swallowed the first mouthful, "he has put sweet sauce instead of milk and butter to the artichokes."

Dinner being disposed of, and wine introduced, in many successive bumpers did Mr. Burke propose a prosperous voyage — abundance of provisions — and a good cook to Capt. Weeks and his companions when next they sailed. The wine flowed freely, for Capt. Wickham was a liberal man, who disdained not to worship at the shrine of Bacchus when his duties interfered not with his pleasures; all were elate with the generous liquor, and the speedy prospect of reaching port. Julia and Arthur alone were melancholy — they had so lived in the past that they thought not of the future, but this dinner conversation had roughly reminded them that the hours of their happiness were rapidly gliding away, and that a few days would in all probability dissever their destinies for ever, — bitter, indeed, was the thought, and no ray of hope from the future came to sweeten or soothe the recollection.

Their reflections were broken by Mrs. Elkinson inquiring of Arthur, "whether he should avail himself of Capt. Weeks's offer or remain some time in the islands!"

Arthur, in a desponding manner, replied, "that island or continent were alike to him; that his own exertions must create himself a home; but he presumed that America would offer the fairest prospect."

Mrs. Elkinson thought otherwise, and offered her interest to secure him an eligible situation either in her son's establishment, or on some neighbouring plantation.

Gratefully did Arthur thank the kind-hearted woman for this acceptable offer; a vague dim hope of future hours of happiness in Lady Baldwin's company insensibly animated him and dispelled the melancholy that brooded around him; and Julia, though she took no part in this conversation, with what feelings of delight did she listen to it! she could have fallen at the feet of her kind chaperone and thanked her for thus gilding the dark cloud that hovered over her fate. She had no hope for future happiness — no dream in which her fate could mingle with that of Arthur; but the thought that he would be an inhabitant of the same island — that she, perchance, might hear of his welfare, might even catch a glimpse of his presence, was a happiness which seemed great indeed when compared with the gloom which previously shaded her thoughts; and as she walked the deck that evening, leaning on the arm of her beloved, a calm and tranquil joy pervaded her bosom, and found utterance in her sweet and silver tones — she spoke of her childhood and the home of her infancy, of her loved parents, and her once adored brother; and though she had not many ties to attach her to Albion's shores, yet she feared that all the splendour nature had lavished on a tropical clime would not solace her for the recollections of home. And Arthur, he, too, partook of this joy, and grew eloquent as he replied to the gentle breathings of his childhood's choice. "Yes, Lady Baldwin, the green fields of our native land, its pleasant vales and rural villages, will live long in our imagination, becoming more bright and lovely as revolving years increase our absence from them; and though the land of the tropics may be rich and gay with plants and flowers, whose dyes seem steeped in Heaven's own beauteous arch, and its atmosphere glitter with winged wanderers, whose plumage shames the sober tints of the north, and though the regal sun shed its splendours over a sky whose beauty is unknown in colder climes, yet will our hearts cling to the past and pant to return to the land of the daisy and the primrose, the haunt of the redbreast and the nightingale; still shall we gaze on the cold star of the north and recall, in fancy's imagery, the happy English homes its beams enlighten.

Truly does the poet say —

"Oh talk of spring to the trampled flower,
Of light to the fallen star,
Of glory to those who in danger's hour
Lie cold on the fields of war;
But ye mock the exile's heart when ye tell
Of aught but the home where it pines to dwell."

Thus did this youthful pair give vent to their feelings of joy, — they dare not speak of each other, or trace their future lot, this would break the spell which binds them, and lay bare the rocks and shoals of misery and guilt by which they are surrounded, so they fall back on the past, and, in union of sentiment and commingling of recollections, nourish that love which, pure in itself, will, if madly indulged in, bring at least on one of them the world's censure and the world's scorn. Harsh and unfeeling world — how many noble minds have sunk beneath thy iron censure — how many gentle hearts have rushed into eternity rather than writhe beneath thy cruel scorn. Hard is the struggle and difficult the choice. Poverty and the world's reprobation, but love, blissful love, on the one hand; wealth and respect, but a blighted heart and an early grave on the other. Julia chose the latter, and the world's wisdom hallows her choice. Who shall dare to contend against it, let him prepare for buffets, sharp and severe, for he has an enemy to contend with who, once enraged, is hard to be appeased. Religion may boast of its devotion and philosophy, of its equanimity, but both, when severely tried, have bowed to the opinions and customs of the world, false and injurious though they know them to be! How long shall man remain a slave to this arbitrary rule! How long shall woman wither beneath its fiery breath! Alas! we progress in all else; the bands that bound the slave dissolved before the breath of public opinion; the sway of the few over the many is gradually losing its potency; even that dire monster, superstition, is fast losing its envenomed fangs; but the most fatal of all errors, a false and slavish code of morals, still reigns in all its pristine barbarity, diffusing its poison through every ramification of society; every effort to loosen its hold seems only to tighten the chain, — its martyrs are few and far between, none daring to encounter the awful fiend.

CHAPTER XV

The love of woman is a blessed thing,
    The heart of woman is a throne of power—
Fond, and more fondly still, it loves to cling,
    And grows more fond whene'er most dangers lower—
Constant beyond this world's imagining:
    Rich in all love — kind nature's bounteous dower:
Our guardian-angel — promise — guide in life—
    Our hope — joy — pride — grace — solace — home-star — wife!

A few more days passed in a similar manner brought the "Esmeralda" to anchor at Carlisle Bay, where, the vessel having been signalled the day previous, they found Sir Jasper Baldwin, Mrs. Elkinson's son, and a bevy of attendants, awaiting their arrival, to assist in unloading the luggage. Pompous and stately did Sir Jasper receive his young wife. There was naught in his manner to soothe her wounded feelings, or raise within her sentiments of affection or regard. It was such a reception as an Eastern Sultan would give to a favourite slave — pomp and splendour, destitute of love or respect. Sir Jasper was proud of his wife as he would be of a fine horse or a dog, or any other appanage of his estate, but it was the pride of ownership and not the pride of affection — it was vanity and not love.

    Kindly was the reception Mrs. Elkinson received from her son, and courteous the greeting he gave our hero, whom Mrs. Elkinson kindly invited to accompany them to a friend's residence until the morrow, when Sir Jasper intended to sail. Affectionate were the adieux Arthur gave to Captain Weeks and his late companions in misfortune. The next morning saw them under press of sail for D——. Arthur was now introduced by Mrs. Elkinson to Sir Jasper as an early acquaintance of his wife's, whom a most singular and awful calamity had again introduced to her.

Sir Jasper made a cold formal bow, and looked aught but graciously on his wife's acquaintance; nor was his good humour increased when he heard that Mr. Elkinson was about to appoint him to a confidential situation in his employ. Julia, who was in the cabin, knew not of this introduction, but, in reply to Sir Jasper's inquiries, with a palpitating heart and a confused air, told him of her brother's friendship for Arthur, their youthful acquaintance, and its unforeseen renewal. Nothing was there in this simple tale that could offend Sir Jasper, but nevertheless he felt irritated. He compared himself with Arthur, and felt that he gained not by the comparison. He, therefore, determined that this acquaintance should cease, and haughtily informed her that the wife of Sir Jasper Baldwin must not recognise an acquaintance in any one who filled a subordinate employment, and trusted that her ladyship would inform him that on reaching D——, their intimacy must for ever cease.

Had not Sir Jasper thus haughtily wounded her feelings, this blow would not have been felt so acutely, for Julia had pre-determined that Sir Jasper should have no occasion to reproach her with her intimacy with Arthur. Dear as he was to her, she had made her decision, and though in giving up his acquaintance she was parting with the last tie that linked her to happiness, yet the consciousness of rectitude would she imagined support her; but Sir Jasper's interference had deprived the sacrifice of all merit. It was no longer the offering up of her heart at the shrine of virtue, but an immolation of her soul on the altar of Mammon.

During the day she had no opportunity of communicating with Arthur, who seemed sedulously to avoid her. She, therefore, retired to her cabin, and after much hesitation and many tears, folded and sealed the following note:—

"Dear Arthur, — The kindness manifested by you during the voyage, has rendered that a pleasant recollection, which would otherwise have been a dull vacuum. The happy recollections of our youthful days, which have entwined your memory with all my past enjoyments, have made your presence contribute greatly to my happiness, but happiness and me are not destined to be companions. My husband's notions of dignity do not allow me to continue an acquaintance with one whose station is not superior to the one you are about to fill. To obey is my painful duty. Regrets are vain and useless. Perhaps this harsh mandate may be a real blessing. Believe me, that I shall ever treasure the recollections of your kindness, and though I may not again listen to the pleasure of your conversation, yet will the sentiments of honour and the doctrines of patriotism you have ever inculcated, remain indelibly impressed upon memory's tablets, until life's fitful dream shall end, and the dark unknown become a tried reality.   "Yours, sincerely,

"JULIA."

It was on the following morning that Arthur received this note. Again and again did he peruse it, scarcely conscious of his own feelings, but joy was uppermost, joy at the thought that his love was not expended in vain — that the idol he worshipped in secret responded, though ever so faintly, to his adoration; and though his fate could never be linked with hers, though the music of her voice might never more ring in his ears, though her beauteous form might no more meet his gaze, yet the thought that he had been a source of happiness to her, that his memory would still remain dear to her, this was a joy he dreamt not of, and a source of pride and consolation. In all the delicate feelings of the heart, in all the finer sympathies of our nature, how much clearer and stronger are the perceptions of woman than man. Julia knew almost by instinct that her presence or absence formed the sunshine or shadow of Arthur's existence, and this knowledge of its being reciprocated gave strength and vitality to her love, whilst Arthur knew not of the devotion he had inspired until Julia's farewell letter gave him a faint glimpse thereof. With such mingled feelings did he sit down to answer her epistle.

"Beloved companion of my youth, — With feelings of pain have I received my dismissal from the temple of my adoration, where I knelt — oh! how humble a worshipper — content with my lot, dreaming not of higher aspirations. Alas! even this happiness must no longer be mine. I must still continue to worship, but the shrine will be for ever removed, and my dark and chequered lot lose the only star that illumed its erratic course. Hard and unfeeling man, could not aught else have soothed thy pride without making shipwreck of my treasured happiness! Lady Baldwin, accept my hearty thanks for your kind remembrance, and if a love, holy as that of angels, pure as the dreams of infancy, be an acceptable offering, oh! receive the oblation. It will not tarnish the virtue of the altar, but will ascend as the grateful incense of a devotee to the shrine of the Most High.

"Ever yours,
"ARTHUR MORTON."

Such was the wild and passionate outpouring that Arthur gave in reply to the letter of Julia. The mandate of Sir Jasper had worked a spell on their young hearts. Writing beneath its effects, Julia had used certain expressions in her letter that her heart at another time would not have uttered, though deeply would it have felt them; and Arthur's love, that would ever have been kept as a treasured secret, burst from its hidden source with a violence proportioned to the strictness with which it had been pent up. Their eyes were opened, their love was no longer a secret. Happy was each in its consciousness, though its future enjoyment was for ever denied them. The blissful knowledge of first love, of love reciprocated, and rendered sweeter by the hazards that surrounded it, this was their happy lot. But such joy, though exquisite, is transitory and short-lived. The brightest colours quickest fade — the fiercest flame is soonest exhausted — the glare of the sun needs the darkened glass to view its splendour. The prophet of Horassan wore a silver veil to conceal the brightness of his visage[33] — so love needs the mantle of discretion to temper its warmth, and oft-time the veil of the prophet to conceal its deformity.

CHAPTER XVI

Nature imprints upon whate'er we see,
That has a life or heart in it — be free.
The beasts are chartered — neither age nor force
Can quell the love of freedom in the horse.
Cans't thou, then, honoured with a Christian name,
Buy what is woman-born and feel no shame!
Trade in the blood of innocence, and plead
Expedience as a warrant for the deed?
So may the wolf, whom famine has made bold,
To quit the forest and invade the fold;
So may the ruffian, who, with ghostly glide,
Dagger in hand, steals close to your bedside—
Not he, but his *emergence* forc'd the door,
He found it *inconvenient* to be poor.
                              Cowper[34]

A few days saw Arthur duly installed in Mr. Elkinson's counting-house, where his ability and readiness soon made him exceedingly useful, whilst his information and good temper made him a general favourite and a welcome guest not only at the table of Mr. and Mrs. Elkinson, but at many of the neighbouring merchants and planters; his duties at Mr. Elkinson's were light and agreeable, and he was treated more like a brother than a dependant. Occasionally his duties called him into the interior of the island, and he had many opportunities, in visiting various plantations, of acquiring information respecting the condition, domestic habits, and comparative happiness of the negro in his emancipated state,[35] also of what it had been in his state of bondage, the result of which assured him that liberty had created a *soul* in the negro *body*; that indolence and ignorance were being superseded by enterprise and intelligence; that if their energies had fair play, their habits of industry, their adaptability to the climate, and their system of brotherly co-operation, would speedily render them proprietors of those islands which they had so long tilled as slaves, and the Black Republic of the New World become, perhaps, as famous as the White. True, he heard complaints from many proprietors that since their emancipation they were lazy and would not work, and that their crops were spoiling for want of more hands; but Arthur soon perceived that if the negro would not work it was because he was not properly remunerated for his toil, and he approved of their policy of *light* labour divided amongst *all* hands. He found that there, as in Britain, the employers wanted to overwork the few in order to have a surplus of hands in the market, and thereby reduce the wages of the whole; for this purpose, also, was the Hill Coolies Emigration scheme patronised not only by the resident planters, but by our great proprietors and legislators at home.[36] This was a wily step to entrap the poor East Indian from his native home, and cause him to work hard and cheaper than his Western brother, thus enabling them to buy free labour cheaper than they could hitherto breed slave labour, and reduce the independent negro labourer to the level of the British artisan, — a chained slave at the heels of capital, selling his life's blood at the lowest possible price, fearful even then lest his brother slave should undersell him, and famine or the Poor-Law bastile be his lot. After experience in America fully convinced Arthur of the truth of these reflections. Deeply did he grieve at the mockery of a nation styling itself free, and yet retaining nearly three millions of its population in slavery; but for a Republican government to sanction this, — for men boasting of their civilisation to defend its justice, — for ministers of religion to connive at it, — for statesmen to enact laws to maintain it, was, to his imagination, such a monstrous anomaly that future generations would wonder, aye, would shudder at the very recital of its barbarous inconsistency. America, boasting of her free and liberal institutions — boasting that liberty, banished from the Old World, had there found, not merely a place of refuge, as safe asylum, but a wide and generous home, that worshipped in stealth by many faithful hearts in all lands, there, and there only, was her generous *regime* fully established. Deeper reflection and further experience rather moderated these feelings, and showed him that she could plead many circumstances in extenuation of her guilt, though none that could wipe away the indelible stain. The Republics of Old sanctioned and encouraged slavery; Athens, the pride of Greece, with but 20,000 citizens, possessed 400,000 slaves; Sparta, heroic Sparta, was still more disgraced by a similar policy; Rome, at one period was mistress of a horde of sixty million slaves. But those governments did not spring into existence like America, appealing to Heaven and earth that all men were equal, and therefore equally entitled to freedom and happiness. Those nations did not, like America, emblazon their standard with equality — fight for it — die for it — and when finally and triumphantly victorious retain in bondage a body of men, many of them sprung from their own loins — many of them daring participators in their struggle for liberty — all of them peaceable and useful subjects. He was, however, aware that a Briton should be the last to reproach America with this crime, for it was England that planted this foul weed in the otherwise fair garden of American liberty; it was one of the evil influences engendered by British misrule; it had grown with their growth, and strengthened with their strength, until it had become difficult, yes, dangerous, to hastily attempt its eradication. But Arthur likewise saw that if the same system of commerce and competition was continued in America, which was bringing ruin on his own land — if America continued madly to rush towards the vortex which was burying all that was free, manly, and national, in her parent country — then he saw that the system of slavery would eradicate itself, for the avarice of merchants and manufacturers would speedily discover that free labour could be procured cheaper and better than slave labour, for the slave will not work unless he is well fed, but the free man thinks half a meal better than none and when things come to that result (and that they speedily must, he felt convinced, for experience had shown him that in the West Indies free labour could be procured for twenty-five per cent less than was formerly paid for slave labour,) then compulsory slavery would cease, and free-labour slavery, as in his native land, supply its place. Actively did he exert himself whilst there to aid the real democrats in averting this impending evil; truthfully did he depict the barren supremacy it had established in England, heaping wealth upon the few, but misery and destitution upon the many; with pain was he compelled to acknowledge that their very slaves were better off, more cheerful, more free from calamities, better provided for in sickness and in old age, than his brother operatives in the old country; and that freedom purchased at the risk of sharing a British labourer's lot would be a curse and not a blessing to them.

CHAPTER XVII

What elegance and grandeur wide expand
The pride of Turkey and of Persia land!
Soft quilts on quilts, on carpets carpets spread;
And couches stretch'd around in seemly band,
And endless pillows rise to prop the head.

* * *

Here languid beauty kept her pale-faced court.
                                        Thomson[37]

Her cold unmeaning eye, her faded cheek,
How is she chang'd from what she was of old!
Her pale pale lips whence sighs unconscious break,—
Oh little those who every day behold,
Mark the sad change come on, and make a wreck
Of many a face that once so brightly told
Each happy thought that o'er the spirit played,
Casting a flitting light without a shade!
                                        Beste[38]

The mansion of Sir Jasper Baldwin was situate at ——, about twenty-four miles from the residence of Mr. Elkinson; it was a large pile of buildings, erected after the Eastern fashion, surrounded by a spacious garden, in which flourished every variety of tropical flowers and plants, — here the glorious rose unfolded its paradise of leaves, contrasting beauteously with the dark foliage of the ocynum; there the brilliant tropical lily and the scarlet blossom of the voluptuous bombex, intermingled their flowers with the sweets of the myrtle and the fig-tree; the tamarind and the date were seen side by side with the cocoa and the palm; the mango and the orange, intermingled their branches with those of the pomegranate and the citron; the sun and the shade, the flowers and the foliage, and the bright water glancing through the trees, all combined to render it an abode for the blessed. A dweller in our cold clime can scarce imagine the beauties of a tropical garden, where taste and wealth go hand in hand. Oh! that man's evil passions should mar the beauty of such fair scenes, that the slime of the serpent should leave such traces in the garden of Eden. A colonnade led from the garden to the rear of the mansion, and opened on a spacious apartment, sixteen feet square, the sides of which were covered with rich paper, representing the Loves of the Angels; the floor was covered with fine matting, which in the centre was overlaid with a magnificent Persian carpet; a low ottoman of beautiful workmanship stood at each end of the room; small but elegant marble tables were scattered about, on which were handsome vases filled with beauteous flowers; the windows at each end of the room were surrounded by a balcony, where the passion-flower climbed in fertile luxuriance, whilst a jet of water cast a delightful coolness on the air; the sides of the apartment were adorned with splendid mirrors and costly pictures, and a few books were tastefully arranged on an ebony table at one end of the room; and upon the ottoman near this reclined in sleep the beauteous form of Lady Baldwin, attended by two slaves or black servants, who, with fans in their hands, awaited the period of their mistress awaking. Upon the Persian carpet in the centre room sat, or rather lay, two mulatto females, strewing with careless hands the petals of the orange flower, that its odours might perfume the apartment. Pale and languid is the form that reclines on the ottoman, the dark crimson covering of which contrasts strongly with the white arms and slender hands that embrace its silken folds; the climate hath not yet had time to deprive her of that purity of colour so essentially northern, but its effects are already felt and shown in the extreme languor which pervaded her frame; but a malady more fatal is preying on her heart. For six months has she inhabited the prison-house of Sir Jasper's mansion — sumptuously is she apparelled — slaves await her every nod — her slightest wish is obeyed with mechanical precision — luxury and power surround her — yet her mind is chained, and the palace appears the prison. Sir Jasper, occupied in business in the morning, and in sleep during the heat of the day, usually rises with the rising of the sea breeze, and when no other resource presents itself passes the remaining hours of the day in his wife's apartment. He is kind to her, kind as his nature will allow him to be, — he interferes not with her pursuits or amusements — he is content to be the possessor of the jewel, to show it occasionally to his friends and dependents — he enshrines it in a costly casket, and surrounds it with gaudy trappings, but he knows naught of its hidden virtues, — it is for its glitter, and not for its qualities, that he esteems it. And Julia lay asleep on the silken ottoman, — the passion flower shaded her lovely brows — the water of the silver fountain fell murmuring on her listless ear — the perfume of the orange delighteth her not — the magnificence around her is unheeded. Her thoughts are far away, delightedly lingering in a small room in a dull street in the city of London — her parents, her brothers, are gathered around her — all is happy and serene — a youth enters the apartment, 'tis her playmate, 'tis Arthur, all is joy and sport; the scene changes amid hurricane and storm — she is dragged from her home to a far off clime, and they tell her she is married — she screams aloud at the dismal recollection, the slaves stare aghast at each other and fan the heated brows of their mistress; anon the scene changes, and she sits in fairy bowers, discoursing high and mighty truths with a seraph from above, but a rumbling is heard, the earth shakes, the seraph spreads his azure wings, and she is plunged into the yawning gulf, — she awakes trembling with emotion, and is scarce conscious whether it is the apartment or her frame that trembles and vibrates like the chords of a tempest-riven Aeolian harp;[39] and the passion flower still shaded her lovely brows, and the water of the silver fountain fell softly on her awakened ear, and the perfume of the orange diffused its grateful odours around, but they awakened no pleasurable emotion in the languid frame of Lady Julia, one dense cloud of mental haze enveloped her, and it was in dreams only that the faculties of her mind appeared to awaken from the torpidity of inaction.

During the six months that Lady Baldwin had resided with Sir Jasper she had never seen Arthur Morton; Mrs. Elkinson had been twice a visitor at the mansion, and from her Julia learnt of Arthur's welfare; and to hear that he was in health, and enjoying happiness beneath her friend's roof, was, indeed, a pleasure, but for her there was no corresponding enjoyment; the active employments of manhood may do much to rob the bitterest grief of its sting, but Julia had no such resource; the heat of the climate, and her lowness of spirits, equally combined to keep her from out-door exercise; the garden was the limit of her world, and even its beauties could scarce raise a pleasurable emotion. When sorrow hath darkened the heart, and the elasticity of youth is broken by the icy hand of apathy, nature in vain displays her charms — the sun loses its brilliancy — the moon its soft lustre — the stars do not smile from the heavens as they once did — the flow of the waters hath ceased its sweet music — the very flowers have lost their colours, and their sweets bring no incense to the heart — the towering forest trees are devoid of grandeur — the ocean itself is robbed of its magnificence. To the young, the innocent, and the light-hearted, nature unrobes herself, and stands confest in all her loveliness; but when despair hath brought on premature age, when crime hath scared the soul, when apathy hath benumbed the faculties, our perception of its beauties is for ever fled; we may, indeed, talk of them, but the feeling of bliss in their enjoyment is gone, no more to return; and Julia, once so light-hearted, who looked on every flower as her friend, and every tree as a companion, experienced this deprivation of feeling. She had no pleasure in society; to keep up an acquaintance with the few residents who had the *entrée* of Sir Jasper's mansion, was irksome to her, she had no feeling or sentiment in common with them; and though she sedulously performed her duty as the wife of the Governor, and saw that no rite of hospitality was violated, yet she shrunk with a feeling of morbid sensitiveness from any further intercourse with them than necessity demanded. Shut up in that splendid mansion with no companion but her own restless and dreamy thoughts, the society of Sir Jasper, which she at first loathed, became by degrees a relief to her, and his presence was no longer shunned. Strange and powerful is the effect of habit, blindly and imperceptibly do we yield to its influence, whether exercised for good or for evil. Prisoners who, when first introduced into their cells, have shuddered even at the thought of coming in contact with the vermin that infest them, have at length welcomed their society, and shed tears of real and bitter grief at death or other causes depriving them of the solace of their company. So it is with man and his fellow men; confine the two most bitter enemies in the same cell, prevent them from injuring each other in their first paroxysms of anger, and the love of society implanted in the human breast, combined with the force of habit, will speedily render them bosom friends; and, indeed, it is impossible for two persons, though mutual hatred may burn within them at the outset of life, to live long together on the terms of intimacy of man and wife, without habit supplying the place of love, more especially if no prior attachment exist to weaken its effect. Something of this kind was gradually creeping over the mind of Lady Baldwin, and had long life been allotted to her, and death or absence deadened the effect of her feeling for Arthur, she might, in time, have become an affectionate wife to the man she once loathed and dreaded. The passions of the human heart — dark, violent, and overpowering as they sometimes manifest themselves — are composed of more ductile elements than the world generally imagines, and it is well for our peace that they are so. Months rolled on, the summer was gradually waving into autumn, and Lady Baldwin's cheek waxed still paler, and her form more delicate and shadowy; in vain did the alarmed husband procure every medical aid that the island afforded; naught did it avail, the disease was beyond the reach of medicines.

> "Not the sage's skill, nor the leech's art,
> Can heal the wounds of a broken heart."

The lethargy of her mind, which the voyage had dispelled, now returned with deadening influence, and her intellect was gradually yielding before it; she would sit for hours in a state of almost torpidity, but a word, an accent, or even a scent that reminded her of the past, would operate like a charm upon her, and for hours she would live with renewed life beneath its spell. A sea voyage, and her native air was recommended by the medical attendants as a last resource; the idea of her return to England Sir Jasper would not listen to, but consented to her trying the effect of a few days' sail, and a residence upon his estate at Mount Pinto, healthfully situated in the highlands, about sixty miles inland. The voyage seemed to recall the drooping spirits of their patient; and Sir Jasper, who, with the physician, accompanied her, until her arrival at Mount Pinto, buoyed himself up with the hopes of long retaining his ill-gotten, but much prized treasure. Vain delusion, and speedily dispelled — it was the wizard power of memory that was tracing the faint bloom on his lady's cheek; almost unconscious of her present situation, she was revelling in joy with the companion of her childhood. Again were his lofty sentiments and pure aspirations ringing in her ears; again was he recounting the perils of his shipwreck, and his adverse fortunes in his native land; and by a strange hallucination she mistook her husband for Arthur Morton, and during its influence he gleaned from her their ill-starred affection, and the cause of Arthur's flight from England. Mad with jealously and revenge, he harshly upbraided his poor victim, but she heeded it not — his furious tones were music to her ears, and his violent upbraidings, the soft confessions of his love. Having seen his ill-fated lady safe to his country house, he re-embarked for his official residence, burning to revenge himself on his rival, by arresting him on a charge of "arson," and sending him to England for trial.

CHAPTER XVIII

Then, dearest, mourn not o'er my early fate,
It calls not for thy pity. I have been
Blest; and but grieve to leave thee desolate,
But thou wilt live in many a vanished scene,
Nor feel alone. Thou still wilt contemplate
These days of love though long years intervene.
We part not, dearest Arthur! still my love—
Warm — pure as now — shall bless thee from above.
                                                  Beste

Strange and unfathomable are the transitions of the human heart — to-day all is calm and serene — tomorrow some unaccountable fantasy pervades our feelings, and we are uneasy and disturbed — a gloom is on our spirits, and a thousand prognostications of danger seem to hang around us — prognostications too often the forerunners of evil. Can the subtle essence of which the mind is composed receive impressions, and be subject to sympathies which the bodily senses are not cognisant of, though they tremble uneasily beneath their influence? Will the doctrines of Mesmer,[40] or the marvels of Clairvoyance, yet lay bare the mystery of these positive and negative poles in the electric atmosphere of the human heart! Arthur Morton, occupied in his daily duties at the residence of his employer, or superintending the management of his property in the inland portion of the island, was fast recovering from the spell which the charms of Lady Baldwin had cast around him: her welfare was still dear to him, and it was with no common feelings of regret that he heard of her increasing languor and debility, still no violent emotion raged in his heart, it was a calm and melancholy regret; but suddenly his feelings experienced a complete revolution — his mind was racked with anxiety — nightly did he ride to —— that he might inquire relative to her welfare — covertly was he compelled to do this to avoid the suspicions of Sir Jasper — with alarm he heard of her voyage and removal to Mount Pinto. Restless and uneasy, he obtained a few days leave of absence, and morning's dawn saw him on his way to the residence of Lady Baldwin; he knew not his own motives or objects, but he longed to be near her, once more to gaze on her features ere the cold hand of death for ever shrouded them from his view. His ride was through a lovely part of the high grounds of the island: the breeze from the seaward played delightfully on his heated cheeks — the music of the birds and the murmurs of the waterfalls disturbed not the current of his thoughts — hours rolled by, and wrapped in his reverie he heeded not their flight — the sun beamed forth gloriously, and the breeze fainted away beneath its influence — the music of the birds was hushed, innumerable insects filled the air, and though his horse gave evident signs of weariness, still Arthur rode on, indifferent alike to all around him — filled with uneasy forebodings that he could neither repress nor account for. His horse suddenly stopping at a sugar mill in the valley into which he had now descended, recalled him from his reverie, and the surgeon of the plantation, with whom he was slightly acquainted, received him as his guest until the rising of the sea breeze spread its delicious odours and welcome coolness around, and wooed him again to recommence his journey. Nightfall found him at Mount Pinto, passing by the mansion of Sir Jasper; he rode to the adjoining negro village, and prior to retiring to rest wrote the following note, which he despatched to Lady Baldwin in the morning:—

"DEAREST LADY, — Impelled by feelings I cannot control, and alarmed by gloomy forebodings that I shall never again gaze on thy angelic face, I have come once more to worship the sun of my existence ere it for ever sets and leaves me in pitiable darkness. Pardon my presumption, heed not my forebodings, but admit to your presence the companion of your childhood.— ARTHUR MORTON."

Reclining on pillows on an elegant sofa, in a small but lofty apartment, lay Lady Baldwin. Oh! how changed from the Julia North of former days; her languishing eye, of Heaven's own azure, looked glazed and dim; the rose and the lily no longer contended for mastership in her lovely cheeks, but an ashy paleness supplied their place: a sweet smile still lingered on her countenance, but like a rose blooming amid snow, it seemed to mark still more strongly the desolation by which it was surrounded. Two days have elapsed since Sir Jasper returned to his residence. She was perfectly unconscious of the hallucination she was labouring under during the voyage, and the physician had thought it imprudent yet to inform her of it: her mind seemed calm, and to have recovered its former tone. Like the Eolian harp, it was mute and passionless, now the breath of Heaven no longer played around it. She is not alone, two attendants are with her; one is sprinkling the matted apartment with a decoction of orange and lime flowers: the other, an English girl, seated near her mistress, is reading aloud from a splendidly bound book, it is a novel by Washington Irving[41] — she hears in a kind of trance, for though its appeals to the heart are beautiful and impressive, hers feels them not, it is preoccupied with the romance of its own creation. A gentle tap is heard at the door, it is opened, and the note of Arthur is presented by an attendant. Slightly does the lady tremble as she recognises the hand, for though his last letter was speedily sacrificed to a sense of duty, yet the characters are still present to her memory; the contents of the note are quickly devoured — love and duty are harshly conflicting, but love assumes the mastery, and the attendant is dismissed with a note addressed to Arthur, containing the simple words:— "Come and see me, and let me bless you ere I die." What an impression did these words make on the sensitive spirits of Arthur Morton. With feelings of almost religious awe and respect did he enter that quiet room, — the English servant still remained in attendance, — he rushed towards the fragile form of the loved being before him, sunk at her feet and wept bitterly.

"Weep not, dearest friend," exclaimed Julia, "I am happy. Oh! so happy. I have had a long and fearful dream, but your presence has dispelled it, and I shall die in peace."

"Dearest lady, talk not of dying. Live! oh live long! to bless and cheer the hearts of your friends. My life is bound up with your own, I could not survive you. Oh! think of the hours of happiness we have spent together in our native land; think of the years of happiness that are in store for you, — young, beauteous, and blessed with every virtue, you cannot, must not die."

"Dearest Arthur, companion of my youth, why should I wish to live? Life hath lost its every charm, — my parents are no longer near me, and my brother hath treated me, oh! how wrongly, — my husband is kind, very kind to me, but I cannot return his love as I could wish. The only good on earth I could crave fate has denied me, and I would fain sleep and be at rest. Death hath no terrors for me. I have loved all mankind, and though I have been injured, yet do I forgive; they meant kindly, may they be all more blessed and more happy than I have been. One only grievous wrong have I committed in allowing my heart to love another than my husband; for, Arthur, I have loved you — dearly loved you. Woman's pride would fain have concealed it, but in these my last moments love is stronger than pride, and your image and your thoughts mingle with those of God and Heaven:" and she burst into a torrent of tears, while Arthur clasped her convulsively to his breast. "I know it is an error," she resumed, "but it is an involuntary one, and one that I cannot regret, though I trust that Heaven will deal mercifully with it, and that no part of the punishment will be visited on you:" and she sunk overpowered and exhausted on the sofa.

Arthur, gazing on the lovely wreck before him, was unable to give utterance to his thoughts, — his heart was bursting with love — wild, passionate love — which he felt it would be almost blasphemy to utter to the dying angel before him; he sobbed audibly, and wildly pressed her hands to his heart; slowly did he recover his calmness, and Julia once more rousing herself, and casting on him a look such as a dying mother might give to a beloved child, said: "Dearest Arthur, come, bid me farewell; I know that I shall no more see you in this world, I fear my senses have been wandering, but I thank God I have retained consciousness to see and bless you ere I depart. I shall confide to my husband this our last interview, if I see him ere I die — he cannot, will not, blame us. Kiss me, Arthur — it is our first and last kiss of love; may you be happy and prosperous as you deserve to be, and when sadness shall cloud your soul sometimes think of me, and if the spirits of the departed can again revisit this earthly sphere I will, in those moments, hover round and console you. Adieu! Adieu!"

Wildly, passionately, did Arthur press his heated lips to the icy cold ones of his beloved, and with eyes blinded with tears, and frame trembling with emotion, he gazed his last on his first love — the beauteous and lamented Julia North.

Reader, hast thou ever loved! Hast thou through sorrow and bitterness remained true to thy heart's first devotion! and when the blest consciousness has burst upon you that your love has been reciprocated, have your hopes been dashed to despair by the hand of death — the cup of joy turned into bitterness, and its very dregs poured into your soul! if thou hast experienced this, then canst thou comprehend the feelings of Arthur Morton. True, his love was unhallowed; neither religion nor custom would have sanctioned its indulgence; but when did love succumb to earthly ties — opposition but rivets its chain — it needs not the world's approbation to fan it into flame — it lives on its own elements, and burns the fiercer the more it is frowned upon. The enemies of Chartism assert that it is a coarse and vulgar doctrine, and that its advocates are destitute of refined feelings or imaginations; poor slaves of prejudice, they know not what they assert. Chartism is the offspring of imagination; the feelings must be aroused before reason will summons judgment to its assistance, and never was a cause more hallowed by refined feelings, by chivalrous devotion, and disinterested purity, than the Chartist cause. These feelings are the true essence of love; Arthur Morton is a type, a representative of his class — inheriting all their enthusiasm, inspired by all their devotion, and partaking of all their errors — wonder not, then, at his love, or that his love was unfortunate.

CHAPTER XIX

How blest could consciousness forsake his mind,
But vain, oh vain! Thought burning lingers on;
Thought bears him back to all he once designed—
To fond enthusiast hopes for ever gone;
Those glorious dreams for which he once had pin'd—
Ambitious visions scattered one by one;
What rail'd those proud aspiring energies!
He sees his fate — unknown, unwept, he dies!

* * *

Might she not flit around: and when his soul
Was wrapt in some sweet strain of earthly sound
Might not her whisper'd voice his thoughts control,
Thrilling amid the harmony around.
                                                    Beste[42]

He's truly valiant, that can wisely suffer
The worst that man can breathe, and make his wrongs
His outsides; to wear them like his raiment carelessly,
And ne'er prefer his injuries to his heart,
To bring it into danger.
                                            Shakespeare[43]

Slowly did Arthur retrace his steps to the village — all nature appeared dark and heavy to his sombre imagination — the noon day sun seemed enveloped in clouds and mist — joy and hope to have taken their flight, and himself and misery left alone on the earth. In this frame of mind he pursued his journey homeward, where he arrived at an early hour the ensuing morning, more indebted for his safe arrival to the goodness of his horse than to his own care or exertion. Upon making his appearance at Mrs. Elkinson's mansion about noon he was arrested by two officers despatched by Sir Jasper, and conveyed to the prison at ——, to await the sailing of a vessel to England. In vain did Mr. Elkinson exert himself to procure his release; in vain did he show the illegality of the seizure in the absence of evidence to support the charge. Sir Jasper, irritated against his supposed rival, heeded naught but the gratification of his vengeance, and our hero was immured in the worst cell of the filthiest hole ever denominated a prison, and his food was of a quality to match with his residence; but, fortunately for him, the frame of mind he was in made him heed not the combination of evils. He certainly wondered at his sudden arrest, as he had never mentioned the cause of his flight from England to any human being save Lady Baldwin; and being ignorant of the involuntary manner in

which she had betrayed it, he thought, when informed by his captors that the
charge against him was "arson," that his flight and subsequent adventures had
been traced, and that officers from England had been sent to apprehend him;
that Lady Baldwin could be the informant never entered his imagination. The
recollection of their last interview would have rendered such a thought
profanation to her memory. Day after day passed heavily away, and no change
came to his position: the lethargy of mind which rendered him indifferent to his
fate, on his first entrance to the prison, gradually subsided, and he became
restless and uneasy. His captors had said naught about his being sent to
England, and he hourly expected to be examined relative to the charge; vainly
did he endeavour to extract information from his gaoler, he either knew not or
was unwilling to impart it. Weeks rolled on, and Arthur was still a solitary
prisoner. Change of any sort would have been a relief to him, but suspense was
intolerable. Books might have served to solace his confinement, but these were
denied him. Often did he recall his last interview with Lady Baldwin, and
though it was a melancholy joy, yet its recollection was the only comfort he
enjoyed in his dungeon. When leaving her he felt assured that before many
days she would depart from this vale of tears, but now he felt confident that she
was still alive; his morbid feelings seemed to say that she could not depart
without a sympathetic nerve being touched in his own frame; had she not
assured him that her spirit, if allowed to visit this earth, should console him in
the hour of trouble: and sceptic as he was tempted to be, he felt confident that
she would not abandon him to die a victim to her husband's vengeance, for
gradually the thought had impressed him that she had confided their interview
to Sir Jasper, and his vengeance had dictated his confinement, perhaps perpetual
confinement, and the thought was dreadful. Death on the scaffold would have
been far preferable to him in his then state of mind. Oh! the agony of solitary
confinement — the misery it entails is dreadful — slowly the faculties of the
mind sink beneath its influence — the body may be imprisoned, even due
nourishment may be denied it, but give it the relief of employment — allow the
solace of books, or the company of fellow beings, and the soul will live and
flourish; but solitary confinement carried out in all its severity, is death to the
soul, — day by day is it deprived of nourishment until it either sinks into
annihilation, or starts into insanity: if these are its effects even upon enlightened
minds, upon those who have a world within themselves — a world of thought
and intellect independent of external scenes, what must be its effects upon those
who have no such charm to combat its influence — upon those who,
uneducated and brutalised by the vicious system which surrounds them, live
only on externals — delight only in the material world! wonder not that they
beg and pray for employment, and perish if they receive it or not. Yet this is
the system which our philosophers and legislators are anxious to introduce into
our prisons and penitentiaries, — a system which has utterly failed on trial in
America, — a system which is false in principle, brutal in practice, opposed to
every dictate of nature and every feeling of humanity.[44] Arthur Morton, the

child of imagination — the visionary enthusiast — who looked at mankind through the glass of his own pure heart, even he was gradually sinking beneath the baneful influence of this pernicious system. Hope was fast evaporating through his dungeon bars — the dreams of his youth became horrid fantasies to torment and rack his soul with their unsubstantiality — his overwrought visions for the improvement of his kind became dismal spectres haunting him with hideous mockery. Incipient madness was preying on his nerves, and the strength of his bodily frame alone averted the terrific evil. Oh! that those who make laws to operate on their fellow-beings could but even in imagination endure for a period the horrid realities they inflict upon others; if they have human feelings — if the milk of humanity is not entirely dried up in their hearts, they would ponder on the awful miseries they inflict, and cancel for ever from the statute book every arbitrary law, ever enactment not consonant with justice, and not essential to the safety and happiness of the community. Vain and idle dream — their existence is based upon the sufferings of their fellow-men — their splendour can only be maintained by his wretchedness. Were simple justice to be administered, privilege, with its hydra corps, must cease to exist; the judge and the magistrate, the gaoler and the policeman, would soon be among the rarities of the land — a consummation devoutly to be wished, but far, far from realisation; like vultures, they feed upon human carrion, and are interested in creating victims for their horrid repast.

CHAPTER XX

She died; but memory's wizard power,
With its ghost-like train had come,
To the dark heart's ruins at that last hour,
And she murmured, "Home, home, home!"
And her spirit passed with its happy dream,
Like a bird in the track of a bright sunbeam.
Picken[45]

Nearly a month had elapsed since the interview between Julia and Arthur, and day by day she grew weaker and weaker, but her senses seemed to have recovered their former vigour, and her mind to be more tranquil and assured. Sir Jasper had been often to visit her, and again flattered himself with hopes of her recovery. Seeing that she was ignorant of the occurrences during the voyage, he alluded not to them, nor to the arrest of Arthur; and Julia, often was she about to entrust her husband with her ill-fated love, and implore his pardon and his protection for Arthur, but her fear of displeasing him, and her bodily weakness, which rendered any species of exertion painful, prevented its accomplishment. In his last visit she expressed a wish to return with him to

D——; she would willingly die in the place that had first received her in the island, and which habit had endeared to her, he would then be always near to comfort and support her; and Sir Jasper, pleased at this display of tenderness, gladly conceded to her wishes, and by slow and easy journeys did they reach his mansion.

Two days have elapsed since her return, — she is in the room we have previously described. The leaves of the passion flower no longer shade her lovely brow, they have withered and died, and she mourns not, but rather envies their fate; the water of the silver fountain no longer sheds its coolness around, its murmurs have ceased, and the heated air from a stove supplies its place; the orange sheds not its perfumed odours around, but myrrh and aloes diffuse their fragrance in its stead. Winter hath succeeded to summer, and summer will again succeed to winter. The passion-flower will again bloom, and the orange-flower renew its blossom, but there is no renewal for the human heart once folded in the wintry embrace of death, — no succeeding summer can renew its glories, or give new growth and vigour to its once god-like frame; and Julia reclines on the ottoman, and the arm of her husband pillows her drooping head, and with low and trembling voice she relates to him the occurrences of her past life — of her childish love for Arthur — its involuntary renewal — her struggles to overcome it, and the purity of its nature. She then described her last interview with him, praying for pardon for them both, and the tears course fast and hot down her faded cheeks and fall burning on the face of Sir Jasper, kneeling at her side, and he, the unfeeling man of the world, inured by many years' witness of slavery to human misery, he is not proof against this woman's weakness, but his tears mingle with hers, and at length their hearts beat together in unison — his suspicions, his jealousies, are for ever dispelled — he cannot disbelieve the simple tale — his heart bleeds in listening to it — and worlds would he give that the love lavished on Arthur had been deserved and received by himself. Oh! it was a solemn sight to see that young and beauteous, though fragile form, lean so confidingly on the breast of that stalwart and careworn man, pouring forth its loves and its errors, and pleading so movingly for pardon — a pardon nobly and generously accorded — and the pure spirit of Julia seemed only waiting for the discharge of this, its last earthly duty, to take flight from mortality and care, for embracing her husband, she fell back on the sofa; he imagines her dead, and summons her attendants, but a sweet smile again illumining her countenance, shows that her spirit still lingers with him, but consciousness is fast leaving her, — she softly murmurs, "Husband — Arthur — pardon, Sir Jasper — father, mother, dear, I shall again see you — dear Arthur, I come."

> "And her spirit passed with its happy dream,
> Like a bird in the track of a bright sunbeam".

Sadly did Sir Jasper grieve over the fate of the being now become doubly endeared to him, — time had blunted his sensibilities, and a long residence in our slave colonies had seared the fresh and green emotions of his heart, but the seeds of love and generosity, though deeply buried, were still alive, and needed only a kindly cultivation and a deep stirring of the mould in which their fibres were entrenched to cause them to flourish with renewed vigour. Alas! that the cause of their revival should be of a nature to again blight them ere they could expand into maturity.

Had Julia lived she would no longer have been a splendid toy, jewelled and bedizened to gratify the vanity of an imperious lord, but a household charm to warm the heart and recreate the expiring humanities of an adoring husband; but she sleeps the sleep of death, and he is left alone and desolate, a prey to repinings and regrets, with none to cherish his awakened sensibilities, or guide him through life's stormy seas to the haven of domestic bliss. Oh! how poor and unsatisfactory are all earthly splendours when we have none left to share them with us: no wife in whom, as in a mirror we can see their brilliancy reflected; no child in whom we can retrace our own features, divested of all that is debasing and impure. Poverty hath its trials — oh! how many, and how severe! — but cheered by the ties of affection, and protected from positive want, it is more endurable than solitary grandeur.

Gentle reader, we have now concluded the first portion of our tale; like our own history it is full of errors and imperfections; let him that is perfect judge and condemn them. We have not plunged into the world of romance for our characters, they are the ideal representatives of known realities, — through them we have embodied truths of humanity which ever lie fruitful in the human breast, needing only the action of circumstances to start them into operation.

The Chartist world is blessed with many an Arthur Morton; and Julia, thou art no creation of the fancy, thine image hath often met our gaze; and though thou art for ever departed, yet many a Julia North is still in existence, doing penance to an ill-judging world for daring to exercise, without dissembling, the feelings which nature hath implanted in their breasts.

Our tale hath hitherto been one of hardship and sorrow, tinctured, perhaps, with our own bitter taste of poverty; but we have still faith in the future, and should the shadow depart we may yet revel in the sunshine of enjoyment.

We have been accused of prostituting our talent for the sake of filthy lucre; how false it is our own heart can best testify; but we heed not the revilers — truth will yet shine, and humanity rid itself of the load that artifice and custom hath heaped upon it — in this hope we will pursue our career, caring naught for the censure of enemies whilst blest with the approbation of friends.

CHAPTER XXI

Truth's something like champagne when brisk and bouncing,
Prone to explode, work mischief, and all that:

But still more like champagne when done with flouncing;
Because so monstrous few can bear it *flat*;
It stoops at folly like a falcon pouncing,
Therefore be cautious whom you fly it at;
If dull, 'tis scorned — mark many a holy thesis;
And if too brisk, it flies in people's faces.
'Tis dreaded like a monster with a sting to
Its tail, and voted on all hands an evil:
Kings hate, and prelates fear it: women cling to
Bland flattery instead — for it is so civil.
Thus you'll discover, 'tis a dangerous thing to
"Tell truth," (as Hotspur says) "and shame the devil;"
For like a thousand other things, the fact is,
'Tis more approved in theory than in practice.

                                                            W. Read[46]

Return we to Walter North. Elate with the matrimonial alliance he had achieved for his sister, and planning future schemes of aggrandisement, he scarcely thought of the treachery by which Julia's marriage was effected, and no feeling of sorrow or remorse visited his conscience: true he knew not of its fatal results, and if he had, he would have esteemed her death the consequence of aught save his own brutal conduct. Business was the absorbing passion of his mind, and all other feelings merged into the primary one of acquiring wealth, and through wealth, dignity and importance. Belonging to the new school of traders, who, emerging from the obscure but substantial manners of the past, no longer content themselves with wealth and retirement, but look forward to political honours, and the exercise of influence in wielding the destinies of the world, he entered actively into the political agitations of which Yorkshire and Lancashire were then becoming the arena. Imprisonment and persecution had, for a time, silenced the most active spirits in the Chartist movement; their champions, O'Connor, O'Brien, M'Douall, Lovett, Vincent,[47] and a host of others, were in Whig dungeons, paying the penalty for daring to be more honest, and more far-seeing than the majority of their compeers, and the middle class — with that spirit of tact and treachery which has ever distinguished their struggles for power — took this opportunity of consolidating the newly-acquired power which the Reform Bill had thrown into their grasp, and of dealing a death blow to their old enemies — the landed aristocracy. To effect this object, they saw the necessity of obtaining the co-operation of the people. Experience had shown them that, by themselves, they were unequal to the task of grappling successfully with their time-honoured opponents, to those legislative strongholds in which custom and prejudice were linked with their adversaries. Their leaders were aware that they were essentially a stand-still body, a balancing power between the aristocracy and the democracy, having no principle of motion in themselves, and that to overcome this *vis inertia* they needed the momentum of popular support. To bid for this was a necessary consequence, but the price was a matter of serious importance. The intelligent working men were conscious that the suffrage was the only measure worth their co-operation; but this was a sacrifice too great for the factions of the middle class, but lately admitted within the privileged pale. Already tasting its sweets they were anxious to monopolise them, and would not brook the idea of sharing these benefits with the mass. Impelled by self-interest to forego the universal they sought refuge in the sectional; they knew that poverty had rendered bread an Englishman's staple-food; to cheapen bread was a fascinating object, one which would catch the unwary artisan, and enlist the sympathies of the well-meaning, but ill-informed of all classes. The object was chosen with their usual shrewdness — it insured the support of the sentimental theorist, the sanctified hypocrite, and the paid hireling, and threw upon its opponents the odium of being the supporters of an acknowledged and admitted unjust monopoly. With the ground thus advantageously chosen, the repeal of the Corn Laws was the battle cry with which they rushed to the assault of the landlord forces,[48] who ill-marshalled, and destitute of any acknowledged leader, would speedily have succumbed to their opponents had not an unhoped for assistance — on the part of the farseeing Chartists — delayed their final overthrow, and imparted energy and excitement to the contest.

In the campaign Walter North was an active partisan. Destitute of the abilities necessary for the guidance of the combat, and but half admitted to the confidence of its shrewd concoctors, his wealth, appearance and apparent candour, nevertheless, rendered him a general favourite with the adherents of that measure, and gave his name a local celebrity which it otherwise would not have obtained: this was the chief object Walter had in view in joining this agitation. Of the hidden motives and wily calculations of its manufacturing fabricators he knew nor cared naught: he was content to be a puppet of the party, to echo their statements, and uphold their principles, on condition that their interest secured him a seat in the legislative assembly. To forward this object he purchased an estate near an adjoining borough, made it the centre of his Free Trade exertions, and assisted by the League influence,[49] was eventually the successful competitor for its parliamentary representation. He had now obtained one of the objects of his ambition, and trusted that the increased importance it gave him, and the extension of his circle of acquaintance would, combined with his really handsome person, effect his ultimate object — that of securing a noble and wealthy bride, and ultimately a patent of nobility to himself. These were lofty views for the retired publican's son, but his life had hitherto been a complete glow of sunshine, misfortune had never thrown her dark shadow across his successful career, and he therefore pursued his schemes, not doubting of their ultimate success. In the House of Commons, Walter North was not calculated to shine; the novelty of his election as a representative of the Anti-Corn Law interest, had for a time kept his name before the public, but he speedily sunk into the most obscure of all obscurities — a voiceless member of the British Senate. Without the eccentricities of a Sibthorp, the personal appearance of Muntz, or the cough and stammer of a Howard,[50] to relieve the tedium of his dullness, or point him out to public notice, his vote was aye ready to support the interest of his party, and the press was spared the trouble of reporting, and the public the waste of time in reading, his wise sayings and doings.

Of all legislative assemblies the British is the most dull, tame, and inanimate; deprive it of the Ansteys, the Urquharts, and other longwinded prosers, and it is a mass of unmitigated mediocrity, relieved only by the brilliant coruscations of a Disraeli, the eloquent sophisms of a Macaulay, the glowing eloquence of a Sheil, the sarcasms of a Roebuck, and the sound reasoning of a Peel, and the minor abilities of some dozen members of various factions.[51] For oratorical abilities it cannot for a moment vie with the French Assembly — for logical reasoning, with the German Diet, or States General — for animation, with the Cortes of Spain — or for despatch of business, with the American Congress — but in etiquette and precedence its claims are paramount. Happy the day for Britain when its cold contracted views shall expand with the infusion of new and vigorous blood; when the dullness of prerogative shall vanish before the glow of universality, and the chill of etiquette and the dogmas of prudence give place to the claims of utility, and the doctrines of humanity. Its atmosphere has become vitiated by stagnation; the effervescence of popular representation would purify it; its constitution has become torpid and emaciated by age and indulgence; the breath of revolution would infuse into it the vigour of manhood, instead of diffusing the pestilence of corruption, and spreading the curse of despotism, from the world's centre to its extremest bounds, earning the heartfelt maledictions of the brave and free in every clime; it would become a fount of liberty, from whence its pure streams would gradually diffuse themselves over the wide world, cheering the drooping spirits, and invigorating the care-worn frames of the sons of men. Never can we hope for this happy result until the claims of party are lost in those of justice and humanity; until the Walter Norths of the House of Commons are superseded by the men of the people, and the rights of the many triumph over the interests of the few: let us then all aid in achieving this desirable consummation.

CHAPTER XXII

"A hundred fathers would in my situation tell you, that as you are of noble extraction you should marry a nobleman. But I do not say so: I will not sacrifice my child to any prejudice."

Kotzebue's "Lover's Vows."[52]

Lord Fitzberbert was the eldest son of the Earl of Altringham, a peer whose ancestors came over with the conquering Norman, and whose possessions are recorded in the Doomsday Book of the succeeding reign: his progenitors are also honourably mentioned in the records of the battles of Cressy and Agincourt.[53] Lord Fitzherbert was now in his 45th year, and the father of as fine a girl as ever Dame Nature nursed in her fruitful bosom; left a widower at the age of twenty-seven, when his daughter was only a few months old, he devoted his whole time to the education of his only child, and to the improvement of his estate. To say that she was beautiful would be too common-place an expression to do justice to her charms. Her form was tall for her sex — features almost eastern in the rich olive of their complexion, and in the majestic style of their outline, her dark hair flowed in luxuriant curls over her ample shoulders, and her figure rather inclined to *embonpoint*,[54] but exquisitely moulded, was in perfect keeping with her large and oval countenance, and her full dark eye of sparkling brilliancy; a more gorgeous being pencil never painted, nor poet imagined, than Clarence Fitzherbert, now at the period of our tale in her nineteenth year. Brought up in retirement with her father, she possessed but few of the courtly graces of the fashionable lady, but in all the charms of unsophisticated loveliness she abounded. Pure and simple in her manners, as the sylvan tribes by which she was surrounded, she lived the life of a flower, glowing in the light but closing to the shade, flourishing alike amid sunshine and darkness, drawing the sweet elements of her beauty alike from both and both seemed to disrobe themselves of their harshness, and mingle their purest influences in her creation. She was truly Nature's child: she had no desires that the quiet retirement of Newland Hall would not gratify — no wishes which strayed beyond their domestic circle. Never was there a greater contrast than between the appearance and the manners of the wealthy heiress; her queenly brow and lustrous eye would seem to speak of homage rendered and admiration demanded, whilst her voluptuous form seemed moulded to exact a world's wonder, instead of hiding its brightness in a small village in Derbyshire. Since the death of her mother, her father could never be prevailed upon to quit the retirement of Newland Hall, which was endeared to him by many recollections. It was there his childhood had been passed ere his father inherited the family property, and there too he spent the short but happy period of his wedded days. Time had not dulled his passion, nor satiety effaced her charms, when the hand of Death removed its object; he was indeed a real mourner. His sole amusement was the infant Clarence; years passed on, and the lovely child unfolded new attractions to the doting sire — he was her nurse, her playfellow, her tutor and her physician; and beneath these united cares she gradually developed a form as perfect as it was enchanting, and by degrees the parent felt consoled for the loss of the mother in the charms of the treasure she had with her dying words bequeathed to his care. Until her fourteenth year her father was her sole tutor, and a more docile or affectionate pupil heart could not wish for; and it was only in compliance with the positive request of his parents, the Earl and Countess of Altringham, that he was induced to accede to the engagement of a governess for his youthful charge. Under her care she acquired the accomplishments thought essential to her future position in society, and rapidly matured from the gay and mirthful child to the gorgeous woman who won an admiring gaze from every passing observer; fortunate was it for the purity of her character that the complete retirement in which she lived rendered her inaccessible to the flattery and adulation that the world would have heaped partly on the handsome woman but chiefly on the wealthy heiress. In the world she must have learned that painful lesson to the young and pure girl — the language of deception; teaching her to hide her heart's feelings beneath the cloak of hypocrisy — to throw the mantle of pride over the features of Love — to burn with false shame if a tone of fondness or a glance of free delight escaped her bosom in the very artlessness of youthful feeling. But upon the world's teaching, rendering the fairest forms in creation the most deceptive and unreal, what can we expect in after life from those who, almost from infancy, are taught to cloak and disguise their feelings, and to smother feelings alike natural and honourable! Away with such deceit and double dealing! the pure love of a pure heart is naught to be ashamed of; if girlhood's bosom flutter at the name of her lover, it is a feeling as natural to her as in the opposite sex; and why should its expression be smothered to make it burn more intensely within, giving fresh fuel to that destroyer of her happiness — yclept, "womanly pride!" The daughters of poverty are exempt in a great degree from this false delicacy, and their social homes are far happier for this exemption.

But we must cease moralising, and proceed with our story. The Earl of Altringham was one of the few old Whig peers who supported "the Free Trade" policy. Walter North, prior to his becoming a candidate for Parliamentary honours, had been slightly acquainted with the Earl, owing to the similarity of their politics bringing them into contact in the county in which they were both resident, but is was that event which particularly introduced him to the Earl's notice. The borough he was canvassing was near the seat of that nobleman, and the property he had purchased was the adjoining estate, and in fact had once formed a portion of the Altringham property; it was owing, in a great measure, to the Earl's influence that his election was secured, and the connexion thus established between them soon ripened into something approaching to intimacy. It was during a casual visit at the Earl's that he first saw Clarence Fitzherbert — a brighter vision could not possibly have opened upon him; beauty, wealth and titles were combined in the lovely being he now for the first time beheld. To say his was love at first sight would be a perversion of the term: it was ambition, avarice and lust combined into one passion, developing all the power and intensity, but destitute of the softness and purity of genuine love. Exerting his every effort to please, he speedily wormed himself into the good graces of the calm and melancholy Lord Fitzherbert, and could not possibly have obtained a better passport to the good graces of the daughter, who loved her father with affection almost as great as his filial cares deserved. During the fortnight to which Lord Fitzherbert's stay was limited, Walter North was a constant attendant at the Earl's mansion, and so well did he improve this opportunity, that at the expiration of this period it would have been difficult to say in whose estimation he stood highest, that of the father or the daughter; unaccustomed to society, her father being her sole male friend, the handsome person, and the bland language of the young member of parliament, had an undue influence on her imagination. Love of homage and admiration, though hitherto undeveloped, could not fail to be latent in a frame like hers. Artfully did he raise these feelings within her, and minister to their gratification, whilst praise of the daughter was music to the father's ear; thus his suit prospered to his heart's content; and ere the visit expired he was formally invited to be their guest at Newland House, a favour denied to all save near relatives, since the death of Lady Fitzherbert. The Earl of Altringham, proud of his ancestral honours, would willingly have chosen a more exalted match for his loved grandchild, but gave way before the expressed wishes of the lovely Clarence, and Walter North was his neighbour and friend; his settlements were as liberal as could be desired, and his property combined with the Altringham estate, would re-establish the old family domains of the Fitzherberts, and repair the ravages which time and the extravagance of his immediate ancestor had effected upon the property; his consent was therefore speedily obtained, and ere a twelve-month had elapsed from his first introduction, Walter North led to the hymeneal altar the beauteous Clarence Fitzherbert — a prize which greater and richer men might have strove for in vain, but which without trouble, almost without exertion, fell into the hands of the lucky bridegroom. Fortunate man! thou has won a prize in the matrimonial lottery worth thy heart's true devotion — mayest thou prove thy gratitude by rendering her after years as peaceful and happy as those that have flown, ere she became thy bride! The cup of Walter's felicity was now filled to the brim — the stake for which he played was nearly gained; the lowly born publican's son was the son-in-law of an earl, and nobility to himself was a result almost within his grasp; he had but to throw off his allegiance to his League friends, and prove himself a devoted supporter of the Whig administration, and his ambitious projects would speedily be realised. Truly is Dame Fortune represented to be blind: her favours are showered indiscriminately around, worth is no criterion of posterity: industry cannot secure success; talent oft times is only a burthen to its possessor, whilst cringing mediocrity mounts the ladder of fame, and bland assurance reaps the harvest of undeserved promotion.

CHAPTER XXIII

"O! the grave, the grave! it buries every error — covers every defect — extinguishes every resentment! From its peaceful bosom spring none but fond regrets and tender recollections. Who can look down upon the grave and not feel a compunctious throb that he should ever have warred with the poor handful of earth that lies mouldering at his feet."

Washington Irving[55]

'To set me free !' he cried. With sudden bound
He rose; and with a vacant, 'wildered smile,
Sadly and doubtingly he gaz'd around
A moment; then cried with transport wild.

* * *

'Tis vain! The freshness of the morning light
That shone o'er youth is gone for evermore.
The heart has hop'd, the heart has known a blight;
It wakes bereav'd of Fancy's cherish'd store!
Vain, then, is every promise of delight—
Vain the dear dream it lov'd in days of yore.
Returning spring waft not thy balmy breeze—
'Tis vain, 'tis vain this world may not appease.

Beste[56]

Arthur Morton had been nearly a month in his solitary dungeon, when one evening, to his great surprise, he received a visit from Sir Jasper Baldwin, unattended by any of the officials of the prison. Tumultuous were the feelings that rushed to his heart at the sight of his persecutor, but respect for Lady Baldwin, and uncertainty as to the object of his visit, chained his tongue, and Sir Jasper was the first to break the silence. His voice fell so mournfully, yet so kindly, upon the prisoner's ears, who expected only threats and reproaches, that he gazed earnestly upon him, and his eyes gradually getting accustomed to the light which Sir Jasper had placed on the stone recess, which served him for seat, table, and bed, he saw that he was clothed in black, and that his countenance showed signs of deepest care. The chill of despair fell heavy on Arthur's heart, and banished all feelings of animosity. He knew that the wife of Sir Jasper was no more, he felt that his own unhappy love had helped to sadden her existence, perhaps to hasten its close; and quick and hurriedly as these reflections passed in his mind, yet Sir Jasper's accents had a second time fallen unanswered, save by the dim echoes of the galleries that led to his cell, ere Arthur comprehended or replied to the simple announcement "that he was free." A few hours previously freedom had been viewed as the most precious of nature's boons. Now the doors of his gaol were opened, but he still lingered in his cell, as though unwilling to quit it, and Sir Jasper gazed moodily on him, fearing that his penitence had come too late, and that the reason of his victim was wrecked. Arthur, at length, unheeding the presence of his companion, murmured,

"She is dead; and I, who alone knew her worth, not there to listen to her dying words, and receive the last pure tokens of her love."

Sir Jasper's blood coursed quickly through his veins; but, with a forced calmness which succeeded in arresting Arthur's attention, he said, —

"Young man, these are not words for a husband's ears; but I have done with wrath. I war not with the dead. Too late did I learn her worth — too late appreciated the struggles of her pure heart. Her dying words informed me of much of which I had previously been ignorant, and banished all suspicion from my mind. I pledged my word that you should receive pardon and protection. That pledge I now redeem. You were a prisoner — whether guilty or not of the crime laid to your charge your own heart knows best. I now set you free. I place only one restraint upon you. Choose your home without the bounds of this island and you shall have my blessing, and, if needs be, my purse also; but I dare not trust you within my power. Even now my angry blood rebels against my tongue; but for the sake of the departed — go, and go in peace. Three days hence a vessel shall await your decision as to your future home. I trust to your honour for the secrecy of this interview;" and thus parted — ay, in all probability for ever — the husband and the lover.

Arthur Morton, thus escaped from the fangs of the law, returned to the residence of Mr. Elkington, where his presence was hailed with feelings of unfeigned delight. His answers to their inquiries were necessarily evasive; but they gathered enough to know that his release had been conditional upon his leaving England, and that there were some grounds arising out of the state of political parties in England for his apparently strange and unprecedented arrest. Loth were they to part from him. His talents and urbanity endeared him to their hearts, and they manifested their kindly feeling by neglecting no step necessary to promote his welfare in the new home to which he was bound; for Arthur had decided upon carrying out his original intention of settling in America. This determination he had communicated by letter to Sir Jasper. Nobly and frankly did he pour forth the feelings of his soul to the bereaved man. Grief purifies and enlarges the human heart, watering and refreshing the gentler faculties of the soul, even as the dew of heaven refreshes and invigorates the flowers of earth drooping beneath the too regal influence of the sun. Oh! it is not in prosperity that we cherish the pure aspirations that nature hath implanted within us; sailing with the stream, looking with a holiday eye upon the world, we are apt to forget the great interests of humanity in the selfish enjoyments of the hour; but when grief falls on the heart, the mists that beclouded our vision are removed — our hearts beat in unison with the world's great heart — we draw nearer to the standard of our common humanity — the electric throb of sympathy links us to the vast human family, and we go forward on our mission to cheer, reform, and console.

The first era in the existence of Arthur Morton was now closed; with the death or desertion of our first love (not the mere attachment of boyhood, but the ardent breathing of early manhood when fancy is matured by judgment, and the curse of satiety is unknown) comes a change o'er our feelings and character, gradually, but not the less rapid and effectual. We no longer live in the present; the future, though viewed through the medium of a chilled and blight hearted, is still in the ascendant. The youthful freshness of the heart, which coloured

every object with its own rosy time, and peopled the stern globe with the bright
creations of a glowing fancy, is for ever departed; and the mind smiles in scorn
at the false idols of its former worship; no longer occupied in contemplating the
perfections of its beloved object, it turns its gaze inward, and acquires a deeper
knowledge of its own powers and nature, and forms a more correct estimate of
its relation to society, and the duties consequent thereon. If death has snatched
the loved object from our grasp, a tone of softness mingles with our bitterest
regrets; but if treachery hath robbed us of the prize, scorn and contempt mix
themselves up with our nature, and we become cynical and unjust. Time,
however, modifies and ameliorates these influences, and the elasticity of youth
again impels the heart gently, but irresistibly, forward to the regions of hope
and love. Through these various changes did the mind of Arthur Morton pass
— the ardent and enthusiastic youth became the melancholy and reflective man
— life was no longer looked at through the glass of enchantment, but beheld
in the dull sober colours of reality, its beauties not heightened, nor its
deformities concealed; he was becoming a fit companion to mix with his
fellow-men — with sensibilities blunted, and judgment matured, his loins were
girt up for the conflict with mankind. The shadows of misfortune had thrown
their dark mantle over the more glowing features of his character, and wrought
the sombre tints into more bold relief — he had become a more useful, though
a less amiable man.

CHAPTER XXIV

Spirit of Time! all silent power,
That grows with each succeeding hour,
To thee we bow — to thee we raise
A chorus of eternal praise.
Gladly thy dictates we obey,
Gladly we see thy power increase,
Sole ransomer from Fiction's sway.

* * *

True source of Joy, and Hope, and Peace!
Oh! thou at length — at length wilt show,
That Freedom is no faithless beam,
Whose flickering rays deluding gleam,
But a bright torch whose spreading glow,
Shall o'er the clouded future stream.

* * *

Proud spirit, whensoe'er thy birth,
Or wheresoe'er thy flight may end,
Still speed thee o'er our heaving earth,
Let speed upon thy course attend!
Though sailing oe'r us silently,
We feel thy grateful presence nigh,
And hail the motion of thy wing,
O'er us softly quivering.
Oh! speed thee, speed thee, hasten on,
Banish errors one by one,
Thou all-redeeming power, thou power without a throne.

Beste[57]

The fourth morning from leaving his dungeon, saw Arthur Morton sailing on
the blue waters of the Atlantic, towards the shores of the New World, and he
speedily arrived at New Orleans, where he had letters of introduction to some
of the principal merchants. The kindly terms in which he was spoken of by his
late employer, soon procured him a situation as a commercial traveller. And in
this capacity, during one and a half year's residence in America, he visited most
of its principal cities, and observed its varying traits of character — from the
phlegm of the descendants of the early Dutch settlers of New York, to the high
blood and bounding spirits of the sons of Maryland and Virginia; from the
shrewd calculations and stubborn spirits of the children of the Puritans of old,
to the new tribes, half-Indian, half-American, that constitute its army of
pioneers, subduing the wilderness and clearing the forest alike of its wild
animals, and wilder human beings. And everywhere he saw displayed that spirit
of enterprise — that energy of action carried into all the varying concerns of
life, which always distinguishes Republican Institutions — rendering them
famous in the annals of the world. Much did he see to admire, much also to
condemn in their customs and manners. And a clear inspection of their social
condition, soon convinced him that political liberty was only valuable as a
means to an end, that in itself it was powerless against the spirit of competition;
that the slavery of poverty was an evil that eats so deep into the human heart,
that even Liberal Institutions could not perceptibly mitigate the evil; tending
only, in some instances, to render it more conspicuous and glaring. There also
he saw the same elemental war of the natural feelings of man, rebelling against
the artificial codes by which he is surrounded, which raged in his native land,
and which will ever rage until conventionalities give place to justice, and the
real be worshipped instead of the fictitious. Even there he found that glorying
in the name of republicans they were cheated with the shadow, instead of
enjoying the reality of liberty. There, as in Britain, the mass of the population
was at the bottom of the wheel — the many dependent upon the capital of the
few. The aristocracy of wealth was becoming as dangerous as the aristocracy
of rank; the vices of the old world becoming naturalised under fresh phases in

the region of the new. The master-key of the whole social failure — "the monopoly of the soil" — was even there festering and cankering the very core of the heart of freedom; engendering and propagating the foul fiends of black and white slavery; disfiguring and disgracing the fair form of liberty, and causing its worshippers to avert their gaze from this land of promise, and seek, in other climes, to establish that *regime* of which the model exists yet but in imagination, but which, when realised, will throw into the shade the dreams of Plato, and all the visions of the Utopians; for what vision can be so bright as the spectacle of a great people living under the gentle rule of impartial law; each one's welfare equally cared for by the paternal state; each one possessing all the liberty that equal laws can give for the free developement of his own improvement and happiness; each one respecting himself and his fellows as moral beings subjects alike of the majesty of Heaven. No oppression bowing down the weak to the strong — the friendless to the favoured; no lordship of man over any of his species; no woman bowing beneath slavery's yoke; no power but for the common weal; no end but universal happiness. Before such a scene visions of crowns, and coronets, of patrician honour and baronial dignity, however highly wrought and richly coloured, must pale and fade away. Though Arthur could not but view the defect of the American institutions with the bitterness of regret, yet he saw no cause for despair. America, he reasoned, was still in the transition state — still contending with the evils implanted by European settlement. And, as yet, not perfectly gifted with the experience necessary for the cure of the evils she endured; their political education is but yet in its infancy, and bitter experience will teach them many useful lessons. They have the germ, the power within themselves for all improvement; all they need is the knowledge and the will to renovate themselves, ere the curse of wealth and distinction shall have penetrated so deep into the vitals of their social system as to render them unable to reform themselves, unless through the purifying power of a world-shaking revolution. He saw that America, with all her defects, was far in the advance guard of freedom; they possessed the fullest control over the machinery of the government — enjoyed the most perfect freedom of conscience — were well educated, and lightly taxed — extreme wealth, or extreme poverty, were rarely to be found — the laws were well executed and cheaply administered — peace and economy caused prosperity and order to abound — for the discontented and restless the New States opened an attractive field — literature and the fine arts were beginning to be universally cultivated — gambling and drunkenness were being fast banished from society. United within themselves they might bid defiance to the world, and speedily comprise within their dominion the whole territories washed by the Atlantic and Pacific waves. Whether such an accession would add to their real strength remains to be proved; each fresh addition of territory hitherto, has increased her strength, and begat a greater desire for aggrandisement. Who shall say how it will end? It is easy to prophecy — to indulge in black and dismal forebodings; but if past experience is to be a guide — if reason is allowed to

have unprejudiced sway — it would declare that the whole of the Northern and
Southern Continents — all that is comprehended under the name of America,
would be better governed, more in accordance with the feelings of the
inhabitants and the interests of the great human family, under the star-spangled
banner of the United States, than under the despots of Europe, or than they are
by their present insane and fleeting tyrants. The Free Land Movement had not
then commenced its career; that movement which, if honestly and skilfully
conducted, will prove the saviour of America, by distributing true notions of
man's inherent rights, and acting as a check to the overwhelming influence of
capital. All honour to the founders of that movement. Chartism, despised and
persecuted at home, has sent forth her martyred champions to America, who
have mainly aided in establishing this young and flourishing plant, which,
reckless of all party feuds, is spreading its roots in that generous soil, and will,
we trust, yet become the monarch of the domain, affording shelter and
protection under its luxuriant foliage to the denizens of the whole world.[58]

CHAPTER XXV

The sails are filled, and in pride she turns
From the red west where "The sunset burns,"
And the streamers have caught the glowing hue,
As they sport in joy o'er the waters blue.
Listen again to the gladsome song
Sent from the hearts of that joyous throng.
Welcome, ye waves, and thou restless sea,
Land of our birth, we return to thee!
The jarring elements unite to urge
The buoyant vessel through the boiling surge;
'Gainst adverse winds she holds her steady sway,
Nor calms retard, nor tides her course delay;
The skill of feeble man triumphant braves
The power of air, and lords it o'er the waves.
But whence that skill? let gratitude be given
Where it alone is due — to working men
Who had the sense that taught us to aspire,
To rule the world by water and by fire,
And nature's laws contracting to a span,
Plac'd power gigantic, in the hands of man.
                                        Persian tribute to Steam

I do not vouch the fact; but 'tis too clear,
Things are not as they should be; such as pause
To think upon these matters, cooly, swear

There never was effect without a cause;
And if old England be gazetted, there
Must be a —; well, I hope not! the new laws
Should keep the people quiet, or, as some
Are pleased to call the lower class — *the scum.*
The latter term is somewhat incorrect,
And, therefore one I wish my friends to drop;
For both by cook and chemist I suspect;
The scum is mostly found upon the *top.*
Indeed, without the slightest disrespect,
I may as well observe, before I stop,
That worth — like plumbs in pudding when we've got 'em —
If often apt to settle towards the bottom.
                                        Reade[59]

On a June morning in the year 1842, the sun shining as it shines only in warmer climates, and throwing its splendour far across the broad waters of the Manhattan, reflecting its rays on the crowd of sails that adorn this glorious bay of the New World, bringing into broad outline the whole surrounding coast, and the islands with which it appears to be indented, making it not far inferior in point of beauty to the proud bay of Naples itself, whilst in commerce, and as an agent of civilisation, it is fast outstripping its boasted rival, even in its palmiest days, Arthur Morton embarked on board the "George Washington" steam vessel, and left New York to return to his native land. There is some mystic tie that ever binds the heart to the land of its birth, to the home of its early recollection; and though Arthur had no friends to greet him on his return to England — though a felon's doom perhaps awaited him, and he left friends behind kinder than any he could expect to make in his own land — yet did his heart bound with joy at the thought of once more beholding the white cliffs of Albion, and again embarking in the arduous enterprise of achieving the long withheld rights of her injured sons. The residence in the New World, and the change of appearance incidental to the early stages of manhood, would, with a fictitious name, he felt convinced, entirely obviate any danger from his connexion with the Birmingham riots; and thus listening to the dictates of Hope, he left a good home in a free land, to return to the uncertain fate that awaits all the sons of labour in our own boasted country. The "George Washington" was a splendid vessel, fitted with every convenience that a residence even on land could contain, and contrasted favourably even with the comforts he had received during his voyage in the "Esmeralda". What a revolution has steam effected in the affairs of man! Steam, thou mighty agent, that hast more than realised the deceptions of the necromancers of old — thou annihilator of time and space, that clasps the whole world in the embrace that joins island to island, continent to continent, the Old World to the New — that art destined at no distant period to unite all the sons and daughters of men into one great family compact, in which neither king, bishop, nor noble will be named or known — great and varied as have been the advantages thou hast conveyed unto the capitalist and the worshipper of Mammon, and evil though thou hast inflicted on the sons of toil, who have strove in vain to compete with thee — flesh and muscle, against steel and steam (vain yet gallant struggle) — yet even the democrat can afford to sound thy praises, for thy true mission is only now commencing; like thy brother worker, man, thou hast been made the tool of the selfish and the designing, but thou art out-living the period of thy nonage, and becoming too powerful for thy masters — thou wilt not much longer obey the will of the few, but wilt minister to the wants, and crown the wishes of the many — no longer to them a curse but a blessing, thy end will be accomplished, thy mission fulfilled; steam, the regenerator, will have rewarded the exertions of those who invented and brought it into practical operation. Such were the reflections of Arthur, as the steamer triumphantly held her way through the blue waters of the Atlantic. Swiftly sped the vessel o'er the briny waves, and in less than a fortnight from leaving New York our hero was landed in Liverpool.

During his residence in the West Indies and America his accumulated savings had amounted to a decent sum; he had, therefore, no occasion to seek immediate employment. After spending a few days in Liverpool, he proceeded to Manchester; here, as in Liverpool, misery abounded, most of the mills and manufactories were running short time, and trade of every description was in a depressed state; in Burnley, Colne, and other parts of North Lancashire, the distress was still greater; thousands were unable to procure even bread sufficient for their sustenance — many actually died of starvation. The Anti-Corn Law League, taking advantage of this circumstance, had, at their various meetings, attributed the whole of this destitution to the working of the bread tax; and, in language of the most violent character, had called upon these men, whom misery had goaded to desperation, to rise and overthrow the tyrant aristocracy, and ensure cheap bread, high wages, and plentiful employment. Well was it for the peace of England that Chartism was the prevalent creed of the operatives in this district — that they knew the fallacy of the reasoning of their interested employers, and had too often been led astray by their pretended friendship to put trust in their physical force leadership. Still hunger was powerful, frenzy was beginning to supersede reason, and it needed all the influence of the Chartist leaders to counteract the insurrectionary doctrines propounded by the emissaries of the League. Nor was this state of things confined to Lancashire alone; the manufacturing districts of Yorkshire, subject to the same influence, were alike bordering on a state of incipient revolution. But it was in the mining districts of Staffordshire that the League influence was brought most actively to bear; there the prestige of their power was superior, because their characters as magistrates and employers was only partially known, and it needed but the tocsin of revolution to be sounded, to have thrown the whole district into convulsion. Artfully had these results been brought about;

aware that the Charter was the paramount object with the working men, they propagated their doctrines through the agency of Chartist orators and preachers — needy men, who had deserted the cause of principle for the pelf supplied from the coffers of expediency; and these men, but half renegades, so mixed up the two questions, and appealed so strongly to the religious and fanatical sympathies of their audience, that these poor dupes were easily led away by their promises of the Charter, and a repeal of the Corn Laws, within a few weeks, provided they carried out the measures propounded by the League.

Such was the state of the political world, in which Arthur Morton, under an assumed name, was about to embark. How changed the scene and actors, during the few years of his absence; scarcely one member of the Convention of '39 was now active in the Chartist movement; exile, persecution, desertion and death, had scattered that once formidable body. Frost and his companions were in exile; Lovett, Collins,[60] and Vincent (the beau ideal of his youthful aspirations), had sunk into the obscurity of mere sectional partisans; O'Brien, a victim to his own jealous feelings, was lost to the movement; O'Connor and M'Douall were the only men of note of that large array of enthusiasm and talent, that he found attached to the Chartist party. The Anti-Corn Law League had sprung into existence, and was then at the zenith of its power — strong in its organisation — rich in funds — powerful in talent — supported by the majority of Press of the kingdom — it soared to an equality with the government of the country, and seemed to challenge it to a trial of its powers. It had assembled 600 delegates as its representatives in Westminster, forming a rival Parliament to that of St. Stephen's; it assembled in February, continued its sittings for a month, again re-assembled in July, and broke up at the beginning of August. Argument gave way to declamation; threats of revolution were openly avowed; tracts and addresses of the most exciting description were distributed far and wide; the note of preparation was sounded, and the public daily expected the conflict would commence, but their leaders were men of talk, not of action, they wanted the advantages of a revolution in their favour, but they dreaded its risks. Amongst other plans propounded, was the strike of the colliers, to cause all other trades to come to a stand still, and the notable plan of a month's holiday, was again revived by a dissenting minister, a delegate from a town south east of London.[61] This latter plan was referred to a committee of the body, who never publicly reported thereon; nevertheless, after events proved that it was the plan adopted. Meanwhile, day after day passed, and no decisive steps were taken; the people would not rise to please these valiant talkers. Contempt was beginning to supply the place of fear, when they wisely broke up their Conference, and sought refuge among their constituency. Chartism was too powerful, the influence of the *Northern Star*, the organ of Mr. O'Connor, and the Chartist body too widely spread for the inflammatory speeches of the League orators to have their desired effect. Open rebellion having failed, the first act of the drama closed; meanwhile the riot proceeded, and a few weeks disclosed its many hued events.

CHAPTER XXVI

Men of England, wherefore plough
For the lords who lay ye low—
Wherefore weave with toil and care,
The rich robes your tyrants wear!
Wherefore feed, and cloth, and save,
From the cradle to the grave,
Those ungrateful drones, who would
Drain your sweat — nay, drink your blood!
Wherefore, bees of England, forge
Many a weapon, chain, and scourge,
That those stingless drones may spoil
The forced produce of your toil!

* * *

Sow seeds, but let no tyrants reap—
Find wealth, let no imposter heap—
Weave robes, let not the idle wear—
Forge arms, in your defence to bear.
                              Shelley[62]

'Tis morn, the sun is trying in vain to shine through the clouds of mist that envelope the goodly town of Manchester; its myriads of tall chimneys, each in itself a work of art, are disgorging their sulphurous vapour which, joining with the mist and becoming condensed, return again in showers, which would make you imagine that it never ceased raining in this metropolis of our cotton dominions. The streets are crowded with men, women, and children, hurrying to their respective factories, keeping time to the chiming of the bell, fearful lest it should cease ere they reach their destination, and a deduction be made from their already too scanty earnings. But many groups have collected together who seem not to heed the incessant ringing, or to participate in the general haste; rumours have reached them that the men of Hyde, Ashton, Stalybridge, and the surrounding towns, are about to enter Manchester and cause the factories to cease working until some definite object is achieved; some say, a rise in wages — some, a Repeal of the Corn Laws — whilst others maintain that the strike is to be continued until the Charter become the Law of the Land. The League masters had commenced their campaign; some more daring than the rest had actually closed their mills for a month; but the majority had given notices of heavy reductions in the rate of wages, thus throwing the responsibility of the strike upon the workmen — this trap had well succeeded. In all the towns surrounding Manchester the strike had become universal; in the words of the

Executive Address, "Within fifty miles of Manchester every engine was at rest, and all was still save the millers' useful wheels, and the friendly sickle in the fields."[63] The League agents were busy in propounding their scheme — that toil should cease until the Corn Laws were abolished and wages increased. Shopkeepers, manufacturers, all coincided in this preconcerted plan. Funds were largely subscribed — provisions distributed among the turn-outs — places of worship were opened for their meetings, and all seemed to bid fair to realise the League predictions. The magistrates, though fully aware of these proceedings, in accordance with the declarations of many of their body, refused to interfere, and secretly abetted the conspiracy. From the 26th of July to the 8th of August, continued meetings were held, and language of the most exciting description indulged in. On that day a League manufacturer proposed that they should march on Manchester, which, under the influence of Chartist councils, had hitherto remained quiescent, but not apathetic — for a meeting of Trades' delegates had been convened to deliberate on this momentous question, and a conference of Chartist delegates, in accordance with a long prior arrangement, was to assemble on the 16th of the month. On the noon of the day first mentioned, the 9th of August, the excitement, feebly demonstrated in the morning, has become intense; some thousands of artisans, marching in procession, have already arrived at Holt Town, and caused the factories to stop. Here they were met by two of the magistrates, who, placing themselves at their head, and dismissing Colonel Wemyss[64] and the military, seemed to give a semi-official character to their proceedings. Under his guidance they were conducted into the town. Everywhere on their passage work was abandoned, either voluntarily, or by the forcible interposition of the multitude. For three days and three nights was Manchester entirely under the control of this unarmed mass of people; nearly every town in the district was similarly situated, yet not one act of robbery or personal violence was perpetrated. Oh, what an answer is this to those who say that Chartism means robbery and spoilation. Tens of thousands of men were collected together — their passions inflamed — their power unbounded — the law seemed to have abandoned its supremacy, yet property was as much respected — human life was esteemed as sacred as if naught had happened to disturb the tranquillity of the town.

Meanwhile the object of the strike was still undefined. Some were in favour of a rise in the wages, others a Repeal of the Corn Laws, but the predominant feeling was in favour of the Charter; so long as opinions fluctuated — so long as there was a chance of the League object being achieved — so long did the authorities seem to forget that this state of things was not strictly compatible with their functions as justices and magistrates. But on the 12th this indecision was brought to a termination; for at a meeting of the delegates of the trades at Manchester and its vicinity — also of delegates from the chief towns of Yorkshire and Lancashire — it was almost unanimously decided that the strike should be prolonged until the Charter was obtained, and that delegates should be sent throughout the country announcing this determination to their fellow-men. This was a final blow to the League project, and it aroused them from their supineness; the monster they had created threatened to destroy their existence; they no longer directly or indirectly sanctioned the strike, but issued proclamation after proclamation, menacing all who took part therein. Meetings of delegates were forcibly dispersed — special constables were sworn in by thousands — military began to swarm in the streets, where hitherto a redcoat had been unseen. But a spirit was around that could not easily be quieted — meetings of trades delegates were still covertly held, and still did their placards announce their determination to persevere in the struggle for political power. All eyes were now turned to the assembling of the Chartist Convention; this body met on the 16th; here was a new element brought into action, or rather a gathering into one focus, of all the scattered elements previously existing. Had this body met a few days earlier, while the authorities were silently gazing around, the energy and enthusiasm they brought into the contest might have rendered it successful; but the crisis was past, throughout the whole district the magistrates were prepared for any emergency — the troops of the whole empire were fast concentrating upon the north — the blood of the people had already reddened the streets of Preston and Blackburn — the volcano had exploded in Staffordshire — and the people frightened at their own violence, had once more hugged their chains to their weary hearts. Nobly and manfully, notwithstanding these drawbacks, did the delegates proceed to their work; surrounded by hostile forces, they still proclaimed a continuation of the strike, their very words were words calculated to inspire a revolution. Listen to their glowing eloquence; "Brother Chartists, the great political truths which have been agitated during the last half century, have at length aroused the degraded and insulted white slaves of England to a sense of their duty, to themselves, their children, and their country. Tens of thousands have flung down their instruments of labour. Your task-masters tremble at your energy, and anxious masses eagerly watch this, the great crisis of our cause. Labour must no longer be the common prey of masters and rulers; and unless knowledge has beamed upon the mind of the bondsman, and he is convinced that all wealth and produce, — every thing valuable, useful, and elegant, — have sprung from the palm of his hands; he feels that his cottage is empty — his back thinly clad — his children breadless — himself hopeless — his mind harassed, and his body punished, that undue riches, luxury, and gorgeous plenty might by heaped in the palaces of the task-masters, and flooded into the granaries of the oppressor. Nature, God, and reason, have condemned this inequality, and in the thunder of a people's voice it must perish for ever. Therefore it is that we have solemnly sworn — and one and all declared — that the golden opportunity now within our grasp shall not pass away fruitless; that the chance of centuries, afforded to us by a wise and all-seeing God, shall not be lost; but that we do now universally resolve never to resume labour until labour's grievances are destroyed, and protection secured to ourselves, our suffering wives, and helpless children, by the enactment of the People's Charter." Again listen to the conclusion: — "Countrymen and Brothers,

— Centuries may roll on, as they have fleeted past, before such universal action may again be displayed; we have made the cast for liberty and we must stand, like men, the hazard of the die. Let none despond. Let all be cool and watchful — let your continued action be like a beacon to guide those who are now hastening far and wide to follow your memorable example. Brethren, we rely on your firmness; cowardice, treachery, or womanly fear, would cast our cause back half a century. Let no man, woman, or child, break down the solemn pledge; and if they do, may the curse of the poor and starving pursue them, — they deserve slavery who would madly court it. Our machinery is all arranged, and your cause will in three days be impelled onward by all the intellect we can summon to its aid. Strengthen our hands at this crisis. Support your leaders. Rally round our sacred cause, and leave the decision to the God of Justice and of Battle."[65] Such was the address put forth by the Executive on behalf of the Conference. Would that their machinery had been all arranged, but the hour had gone by. Division had already crept into their Councils. Mr. O'Connor, Harney, Hill,[66] and other influential leaders of the body, seeing the hopelessness of the contest, — fearing the ruin that would ensue, — were for abandoning the strike; the men of Wales who had abandoned their hammer and forge, seeing that the *Northern Star* was opposed to the movement, again resumed their employment; London and the West of England, where Chartism was still rife, were left destitute of any correct information how to proceed. One by one the delegates were arrested, or forced to fly; wholesale imprisonments became the fate of the poor and the unknown; treachery aided this fearful consummation; the chance of centuries fleeted from their grasp, and another link was added to the chain of despotism, — another scourge placed in the hands of the tyrants.

CHAPTER XXVII

Slaves, toil no more! Why delve, and moil, and pine,
To glut the tyrant forgers of your chain?
Slaves, toil no more! Up from the midnight mine,
Summon your swarthy thousands to the plain;
Beneath the bright sun marshalled, swell the strain
Of Liberty; and while the lordlings view
Your banded hosts, with stricken heart and brain,
Shout, as one man, "Toil we no more renew,
Until the many cease their slavery to the few!"

* * *

Slaves, toil no more! Despite their boast, e'en Kings
Must cease to sit in pride, without your toil;
Spite of their sanctity, the surplic'd things

Who, through all time, have thirsted to embroil
Man with his neighbour, and pollute the soil
Of holiest mother earth with brothers' gore;
Join but to fold your hands, and ye will foil
To utter helplessness; yes, to the core,
Strike their pale craft with paler death. Slaves, toil no more!

For that these words of truth I boldly spake
To Labour's children, in their agony
Of want and insult; and, like men awake
After drugged slumbers, they did wildly flee
To do they knew not what, until with glee
The cellar of a Christian priest they found,
And with its poison fired their misery
To mad revenge; swift hurling to the ground
And flames, bed, cassock, wine-cup of the tippler gowned.

For that I boldly spake these words of truth,
And the stared multitude to fury wrought,
By sense of injury, and void of ruth,
Rushed forth to deeds of recklessness; but naught
Achieved of Freedom; since nor plan, nor thought
Their might directed. For this, treason foul
'Gainst evil tyrants, I was hither brought
A captive, 'mid the vain derisive howl
Of some who thought the iron now should pierce my soul!
                                                    Thomas Cooper[67]

While these scenes were being enacted in the North, the League emissaries had produced a similar result in Staffordshire; labour was universally abandoned, upwards of 30,000 colliers were on strike in Hanley, Burslem, Lane-End, Stoke-upon-Trent, and nearly every town in the district. The shops were closed, and one universal holiday prevailed here, as in the North; so long as the Charter was kept on the back ground, so long did the great League masters secretly abet the strike; but when Thomas Cooper, Ellis, Richards,[68] and other Chartists defeated the League plot, and made it a purely Democratic movement, then were the terrors of the law launched out against the rioters; blood flowed freely in several encounters, which the exasperated people were driven into with the police and military; still their numbers were so overwhelming that the military, fatigued and harassed with marching and countermarching, could not avoid their holding complete possession of Hanley, Shelton, and other towns in the district; and, unfortunately, the prudent counsels of the Chartist leaders were not attended to, for, in the madness of revenge they fired the houses of several of the obnoxious gentry in the neighbourhood, including that of the Rev. E.

Atkins, and, brutalised with the wine with which his cellar was stored, many of the rioters fell victims to their madness, and perished in the flames. This state of things could not long exist; Cooper left for Manchester, to attend the Convention, and, arrested at Burslem, was fortunately discharged, though ultimately he received two years' imprisonment, and narrowly escaped that transportation to which Ellis, and many other good men were doomed, for a presumed participation in this destruction of property. Hundreds were condemned to various periods of imprisonment, and prescription and terror fell with annihilating influence upon the Chartist body, who had to bear the whole weight of magisterial and government prosecution, combined with League malice and persecution. Thus ended the League drama, bringing destruction upon thousands, who, though not blinded to its treachery, yet thought themselves powerful enough to turn it to their own holier purpose; experience proved the fallacy of this hope, and the oppressors of labour again triumphed.

On the Sunday following, the 16th of August, Arthur Morton, after three years' absence, again arrived in London; misery and disappointment sat heavy at his heart, for he had been no idle spectator of these exciting events. Fortunately, for his personal safety, he was unknown; and, thus taking no responsible position he escaped that danger in which too many of the active spirits in the Chartist movement were involved; circumstances, however, had introduced him to some members of the Executive Committee, and being about to start for the Metropolis he was charged with a confidential communication to the Secretary of the Metropolitan Delegate Committee, at that period, next to the Executive Committee, the most important organised body in the movement. On inquiry he was conducted by a friend to a long narrow room, up a flight of stairs, in that portion of the town call the Old Bailey, opposite the celebrated Newgate Prison. The clock had just struck three, and the chair being taken, about fifty delegates answered to their names — the room, capable of holding about 200, being densely crowded with spectators. Communication after communication was received, detailing the posture of affairs in the North, and the dispersion of the members of the Executive Committee. Reports were also received of the various meetings which had been nightly held in the metropolis, and arrangements made for their continuation. The most unbounded enthusiasm prevailed, which even the reverses, throughout the country, seemed only to increase. Aware of the necessity of an accredited head, a *pro tem* Executive of five persons was elected until such time as the fate of their late leaders should become known, and an address passed, couched in terms of the most daring defiance, to the government. William Cuffay[69] was a prominent actor in this body; appointed by acclamation to the newly-formed Executive, he for the first time attracted the attention of Arthur Morton, who gazed with unfeigned admiration upon the high intellectual forehead and animated features of this diminutive Son of Africa's despised and injured race. Never during his residence either in the West Indies or America had he met with such an intelligent specimen of the coloured race born in England. Though the son of a West Indian and the grandson of an African slave, he spoke the English tongue pure and grammatical, and with a degree of ease and facility which would shame many who boast of the purity of their Saxon or Norman descent. Possessed of attainments superior to the majority of working men, he had filled, with honour, the highest offices of his trade society, was an auditor, and one of the Executive Committee of the Ancient Order of Druids; and had that day been elevated by the unsought voices of his fellow-men to the highest office in the Chartist ranks, who knew that in the hour of danger no man could be more depended on than William Cuffay — a strict disciplinarian, and a lover of order — he was firm in the discharge of his duty, even to obstinacy; yet in his social circle no man was more polite, good-humoured, and affable, which caused his company to be much admired and earnestly sought for — honoured and respected by all who knew him. Alas, poor Cuffay! the enthusiasm of the moment — the madness of the hour — hath driven thee to pass the remainder of thy days under the ban of society — a transported felon — yet am I proud to acknowledge that I was once honoured with the felon's friendship — that I shared thy noble enthusiasm, and that fortuitous circumstances alone, in all probability, saved me from sharing in thy fate. I acknowledge that it was madness that brought thy fate upon thee but it was a noble, a god-like madness — a spark of that electric fire which shook the dynasties of Europe to its extremest bounds — that caused the olden power of monarchy to tremble and bite the dust — that created, by its magical breath, a race of free men and free institutions, and caused Old Time almost to suspend his flight to gaze in admiring wonder upon its glorious march. Yes, Cuffay, should these lines ever meet thine eyes in thy far-distant home, yes, my friend, though thou hast fallen — thou hast fallen with the great and noble of the earth. In every land the dungeon encloses the bodies of the free. But their spirits yet float in the air, anxiously searching an abiding home. In every land the earth is red with the blood of those who, like thee, were afflicted with this glorious madness, and their yet wet blood cries aloud to Heaven and their fellow-men for vengeance. The noble structure of freedom, which seemed to rise in much grand and fair proportions before the eyes of an astonished world, is swept from the face of the earth, and all lands again groan in darkness and in misery. But faint not, mine old companion, the darkness of the present time will but render more intense the glowing light of the future. The experience now learnt will but sharpen our weapons for the conflict that must again, ere long, rouse the world. But we digress from our tale, — Arthur Morton speedily became intimate with Cuffay and other active London democrats, and assisted in keeping alive that spirit of enthusiasm which existed in London during this period, and which was the more beneficial to the cause, as persecution and imprisonment had so thinned the ranks in the northern and midland counties, that Chartism might be said to sleep the sleep of death. The establishment, by Mr. O'Connor, of the *Evening Star* newspaper, tended greatly to promote the spread of Chartism in London;[70] and the appearance of several female orators on the Chartist platforms,[71] by attracting curiosity and the strictures of the press, also gave increased publicity to Chartist principles, and made it a subject matter of common conversation. Whether the labours of these female orators were beneficial or not to the cause we leave others to decide. During this attendance at the London meetings Arthur was particularly struck with the enthusiasm, good sense, and propriety displayed by the numerous families who attended these gatherings, and argued well for the future success of the movement from this, to him, auspicious event.

CHAPTER XXVIII

Love, oh Love!
Thou art the essence of the Universe —
Soul of the visible world — and canst create
Hope — joy — pain — passion — madness or despair,
As suiteth thy high will. To some thou bring'st
A balm — a lenitive for every wound
The unkind world inflicts on them; to others
Thy breath but breathes destruction, and thy smile
Scathes like the lightning: now a star of peace,
Heralding sweet evening to our stormy day,
And now a meteor with far-scattering fire,
Shedding red ruin on our flowers of life.
In all —
Whether arrayed in hues of deep repose,
Or armed with burning vengeance to consume
Our yielding hearts — alike omnipotent.
                              Alaric A. Watts[72]

Oh! beautiful it is to look
Upon a guileless maiden's eyes,
When mirror'd clear, as in a brook,
Each feeling of her young heart lies;
When joy is radiant in her smiles,
Or sparkles the ingenuous tear,
Ere yet corrupted by the wiles
Of this dark world, her bosom clear
From aught of falsehood, or deceit,
Its every inmost thought displays,
With calm serenity does meet, —
In conscious innocence — the gaze:
'Tis said from such a maiden's eye
E'en beasts of prey will daunted fly.
                              Nemo[73]

It was at one of the London meetings that Arthur Morton first became acquainted with Mary Graham, the daughter of a shoemaker who had for some years been active in the democratic movement. Attending all the Chartist meetings, she had often attracted his attention, and, by a kind of fascination, his eye always sought her, and wandered uneasily round the assembly if she was not visible. Yet he had never spoken to her, not even made an effort to court her acquaintance, which he could easily have effected, for never was maiden more free from affectation, or of a more open and friendly disposition, than Mary Graham. Inheriting from her parents an ardent and enthusiastic disposition, to be a Chartist was sufficient to claim a share of her friendship, and it was displayed with a warmth and impetuosity that, had it not been general to all, and the evident offspring of a heart free from guile, might have rendered her liable to the charge of coquetry — a charge entirely misplaced and false. Often had she wondered at the silence preserved towards her by Arthur even when circumstances had so situated them that silence might be construed into actual rudeness; it evidently was not shyness, for Arthur had entirely overcome this tormentor of his early years; and it could not be rudeness, for though no words fell from his lips, yet his features expressed a kindly feeling. Arthur Morton having enshrined the image of Julia in his heart, vainly supposed that he was proof against any future attacks of Love; but fearful of putting it to the test, he shunned the company of the young of the other sex, with a degree of morbid sensitiveness, entirely at variance with his usual manner. Circumstances at length forced on him an acquaintance with Mary Graham. A grand lottery was got up for the benefit of the Victims; in conjunction with other females Mary was appointed to superintend the distribution of the fancy portion of the articles; Arthur was also upon the committee; common politeness, independent of business considerations, forced them into conversation, and the ice once broken there was no after reserve — their feelings, their ideas were similar, both were connected with the same movement, and both impelled to action by the same hopes and aspirations. Can we then wonder that their acquaintance speedily ripened into intimacy? Arthur was still young, and though Mary, who was scarcely eighteen, was much his junior, yet the discrepancy was rather in favour of the creation of Love than otherwise — in her glowing spirits Arthur could retrace the freshness of his own youthful feelings, and she could look up with admiration to his superior wisdom and experience; and the charm of his conversation, the amiability of his manners — so different to the coarse behaviour of the generality of his sex she had hitherto met with — was not lost upon her, for she speedily loved him with all the warmth and enthusiasm which her young heart was capable of. It was Mary's first initiation into the great mystery which sways all our destinies; the void which had hitherto existed in her heart was now filled to overflowing — the warmth of feeling which had in vain endeavoured to expend itself on the exuberance of friendship — which she lavished on all she came in contact with — had now found a novel yet legitimate outlet. Of a light, buoyant disposition, the gravity and passiveness of

Arthur's demeanour threw a mystery around him, that never fails to interest a woman's heart; it is not the gay or light-hearted, the jovial companion or the witty guest that finds most favour in the eyes of the gentle sex; a sigh and a tear, even if breathed and shed for the love of another, is a greater passport to their hearts than aught that mirth or cheerfulness can essay. This may in some instances be incorrect, but with Mary Graham it was a veritable fact.

Slowly did Arthur yield his heart to the seductions of Mary's attractions; but day by day the defences with which he surrounded himself were sapped and undermined, until in an hour when past feelings and associations were painfully vivid on his imagination, he related to her the ill-starred fate of his first love; the sympathy it drew forth from the ever pitying heart of Mary, and the tears — of love and sisterly pity that mingled with his, entirely completed the conquest, and henceforth their two hearts became one. Oh! how rarely is it that female errors or weakness meet with pity or forgiveness from their own sex. How have we grieved to hear those whom we thought all gentleness and love, dwell with bitterness and acrimony upon the faults of a sister, whilst they overlook, or treat with indifference, far more heinous faults in the male sex. How unlovely, how unfeminine is this, and to what base suspicions may it not give rise; 'tis a fault in the education, — an error in the morality of our females, — productive of equal injurious results with those it affects to condemn. Mary Graham, — almost destitute of education, owing but little to the experience of others, but acting according to the dictates of her heart, (always just and true in the young and the innocent,) — was as far above the women of the world in true morality as she was inferior to them in art and finesse, and yet they, envious of her good qualities, would fain slander her fair fame; for young as she was, — pure as Arthur believed her to be, — the liveliness of her manners, her enthusiastic attendance at Chartist meetings, and her open and fearless disposition, had given a handle to the strait-laced, the sly, and the demure; and oh! to their shame, be it said, seldom do men attempt to check this disposition, but rather (especially if their vanity is flattered thereby,) do they encourage and attempt to give a seemingness to the untruth, — often, oh! how often, to the injury of those whom, in their hearts, they esteem, but who fall a sacrifice to this cowardly system of detraction, — their fair fame destroyed, they lose their own self-esteem, are careless of the consequences, and ultimately become the character they were represented to be; Arthur Morton was aware of all this, and it was thus he moralised. Reader, reflect on this also.

Hitherto we have dwelt on the character, and have neglected the portrait of our heroine. She was about the middle height, with a form as symmetrical as an artist could desire; a profusion of glossy raven tresses fell around a face, rather round than oval, whilst a delicate tint as of morning's first blush illumined her cheek; her eyes were large and brilliant, and of the richest brown; her lips were as the ripe cherry, and seemed never to part but with a smile; if not supereminently lovely she was sufficiently so to attract general attention, and to constitute her the pride and delight of her parents. Being the eldest of a large family, whose means of livelihood were but scanty, she was early initiated into the secrets of domestic economy, and devoted her whole time to the comforts and attentions of home, her sole enjoyment and recreation being her attendance on public meetings, whither she was generally accompanied by her parents. Though brought up in poverty, and compelled to undergo the many privations, and to make the many shifts which ever fall to the lot of the poor, yet she had contracted no mean or debasing habit of thought or feeling, and had thus escaped one of the evils which poverty too often inflicts on the poor — rendering them careless of the amenities and courtesies of the more fortunate ranks of society, and too often engendering in them a want of self-respect, which is the parent of a host of evils, and a sure accompaniment of a slavish disposition. How true it is that evil engenders evil; and though poverty is no sin, yet it is the parent, the incentive to a thousand crimes that a competency would have saved the perpetrators from committing. How much have our legislators to answer for in this respect! They make laws which by keeping the bulk of the community in poverty induces crime; and then with relentless hand they punish the child of their own creation; for, alas, the poor criminal finds no pity; but respectability is a great softener of the law's austerity, and society goes hand in hand with the law in shunning the poor, and in endeavouring to mitigate the rich offender's punishment. Mary Graham was fortunate in possessing a mother who united in herself all the qualities necessary to form the character of a young maiden in the class to which she belonged; frugal and a good housewife, yet possessing sufficient energy and romance in her disposition, to prevent her ever becoming a domestic drudge — possessed of a strong mind, and owing some slight advantages to education, she seemed by instinct to comprehend any subject which attracted her attention. Amongst these was politics; and in correctness of reasoning and a happy appreciation of, and expression of ideas, few men could compare with her; but it was only in private company, or in the domestic circle, that this faculty was observable; for though a great frequenter of public assemblies, her character was of a retiring nature — more fitted to adorn home than shine in public. Arthur Morton, when increasing intimacy had admitted him as a visitor at their humble home, watched with admiration the development of these qualities, and ever entertaining the highest respect for the judgment of the matron, it formed a strong link in his attachment to the daughter, that she was brought up under the eye, and had imbibed the principles of this excellent woman. Week after week passed away and Arthur, who had obtained employment at his own trade, became more and more a visitor at Mr. Graham's; he was Mary's constant escort to all the meetings of the Chartist body; and the image of his lost Julia, though still dear to his remembrance, was sometimes forgotten in the rapture of present enjoyment or, if remembered, it was with a calm and quiet feeling as near akin to joy as grief — like the faint reams of past sickness recalled to memory in the hour of buoyancy and health.

CHAPTER XXIX

How merrily the Wedding bells rang on!
The parting guests mov'd homeward to the chime.
Two hands were joined whose hearts had long been one;
And life look'd glad as Spring in rosy prime.
And life renew'd, when this should all be done,
Look'd brighter still — beyond the reach of time.
Is it not sweet to think the bond of love
Contracted here, will yet endure above!
                                        Beste

The Camp may have its fame, the court its glare,
The theatre its wit, the board its mirth;
But there's a calm, a quiet Heaven, where
Bliss flies for shelter — the domestic hearth!
If this be comfortless — if this be drear,
It need not hope to find a haunt on earth;
Elsewhere we may be reckless, gay, caressed—
But here — and only here — we can be *blessed*!
                                        Read[74]

Arthur Morton had been in constant work during the four months that had elapsed since his residence in London, and having the promise from his employer of a regular situation, he felt justified in making a tender of his hand to her who already possessed his heart. He might not have been thus hasty in his proposal, but he dettested long courtships, and knowing that owing to the slackness of work, experienced by her father, Mary was thinking of going to service, he preferred, rather than this alternative, taking her to a less comfortable home than he had otherwise wished to provide; and Mary, without any false delicacy, accepted his offer, and there being no rich relations to consult — no lengthy legal settlements to be drawn up, they speedily became man and wife. Merry rang the marriage bells — merry were the select few present at the wedding feast; care and dark anticipations were, for that day at least, banished from their thoughts, and joy and cheerful mirth presided. Mary, though adoring her husband, could not but regret leaving the home of her youth; the children she had been almost a mother to, and the parents who had ever treated her with kindness, and whom she loved and reverenced; but her husband's devoted attention, and a pretty cottage neatly but plainly furnished, in the suburbs of London, soon reconciled her to the separation; and by her industry and cheerfulness, she soon rendered Arthur's home what home ever should be — a pleasant retreat from the cares of business — a spot where strife and unkindness can never enter — a heaven where all is peace and love. And Arthur Morton, oh, he was truly happy; never before had he known the thousand charms comprised in the word "Home." Left an orphan to the care of his austere relative — never experiencing the comforts of female management or domestic felicity, prescribed in his own country — thrown a wanderer on the wide world — received at length into the haven of domestic bliss, it was a haven of delight compared with his past bitter experience. Politics were almost forgotten in the honeymoon of his bliss — indeed, a complete lethargy had fallen upon the whole country. The Sturge Conference[75] had aroused the Chartists of the Empire from their former torpidity; but its failure, though hailed as a triumph, served only to widen the breach between the different shades of Reformers — a reaction had taken place, and all had again sunk into inanimity. In home, therefore, all his joys — all his desires were concentrated, and happy is the man who can boast of such a home, and resolve to enjoy himself therein; for though we may experience gaiety and pleasure in the thousand amusements of the world, it is at home — and at home only — that a man can be truly blessed; and Mary, surrounded by naught but pleasant associations, each day unfolded new attractions to her admiring husband. Possessed of an excellent voice, and having a slight knowledge of music, she sung with a degree of feeling that, in Arthur's estimation, made ample amends for any deficiency in scientific execution; and he could sit for hours listening to her sweet voice now warbling forth the melodies of Moore or of Burns,[76] anon delighting his ear and gratifying his vanity by trilling his own democratic words to the airs of her favourite music. Possessed of a good taste and a fondness for reading, she plied the busy needle with increased agility and delight, whilst Arthur read to her the glorious stanzas of the immortal Byron — the inspired readings of the divine Shelley — the splendid utilitarianism of Lytton Bulwer[77] — or the heart-arresting, home-breathing tales of Dickens; nor were other works of a more scholastic character wanting to complete their studies.

Thus employed, the winter evenings glided rapidly away, and under Arthur's instructions, Mary rapidly progressed in intellectual attainments. The company of a few democrats of their mutual acquaintance and occasional visits from the parents of Mary made a pleasant variety to their studies, and served to increase the sum of their enjoyments. The dark shadow that had so long rested over the fate of Arthur Morton seemed to be flitting away, and a gleam of sunshine gilded his existence. Early spring was now beginning to displace the chill of winter, and under its genial influence and Mary's care the little garden attached to their residence bloomed as bright as its master's fortunes; and here, every evening, might Mary be seen improved in all the graces of womanhood, and looking as lovely as Flora herself[78] in the midst of her flowers; her bright eyes ever glancing down the road that led to the river side, watching for her husband's return from his employment in the city, and receiving him after his day's absence with a fondness that knew nought of satiety. "Few and simple are the annals of the poor"[79] — so sings one of our sweetest bards, yet if feelings — if emotions are matters of history — if love — love uninfluenced by rank or wealth — be the poet's theme, where would he find materials so complete, so pure, as among the sons and daughters of toil! If penury, want, and the thousand dire associations connected therewith, the matters which bring the passions of humanity into grand yet fearful action, where could the novelist or the tragedian find fitter subjects for illustration! Fiction sinks into insignificance when compared with the strange yet fearfully tragic and comic scenes which are every hour occurring in the very heart of the great metropolis. Oh, that those who see and dwell amongst them had but the pen of a Bulwer or a Dickens to record these strange truths — more of the intricacies of the human heart would be laid bare to the gaze of the philosopher — more of the springs from whence the rapid rivers of vice and crime take their source would be exposed to the view of the moralist; a truer picture of humanity in all its phases, now gloriously bright, anon fearfully dark, would be given to the world, than can ever be gleaned from the thousand fashionable novels which now form the delight of the youth, ay, and of the middle aged of both sexes.

Summer succeeded to spring, and still found Arthur and his wife the happy tenants of their peaceful abode; whilst the increasing beauty of the plants which adorned the little raised platform under their prettily curtained windows, looking out upon as green a bit of turf as ever adorned a suburban residence; relieved by the scarlet geraniums, with which the centre and each corner were adorned, and the few additional ornaments which decorated the rooms, showed that fortune was still favourable to their exertions. A change too had taken place in their domestic arrangements; the young bride no longer looked with a watchful eye towards the smoke that ascending from the steamers gently floating in the air, showed the direction in which lay the mighty Thames; her place was supplied by a younger sister, for the bride had become a mother, and increasing domestic arrangements caused the care of the garden to devolve on the former; but the love that prompted Mary's to be the first eye to greet her husband's arrival had not evaporated, it had only found a fresh variety of display; the little Arthur — for so the infant was called — had to be decorated to receive its evening's kiss from its pleased father; and thus a new attraction was created from home, a new stimulus given for industrious exertion, and a novel, yet endearing tie, formed between the happy pair, in addition to those heretofore existing. And thus in calm retirement, undisturbed by any of the rougher gales which too often wreck our fairest prospects, passed the two next years of Arthur's life; the only incidents that created any intensity of excitement, was the birth of a daughter named after its aunt, Fanny, and an event as painful as the former was pleasurable — the death of Mary's mother. This last was a heavy blow to both Mary and Arthur, for she was endeared to them by a thousand acts of kindness, and was respected by the husband as much as she was loved by the wife. Peace be to her manes; a better wife, a more devoted mother or a truer democrat never existed; those that had the pleasure of her acquaintance, or recognise her portraiture, will long sorrow for her loss; cut off in the prime of her existence, she sleeps in peace, and has been thus spared many a bitter pang which has fallen heavily on those she left behind. This was the first knell that broke with its dismal echoes upon the peaceful serenity of their domestic bliss; and Arthur's heart shuddered uneasily beneath its influence, and feared, almost with a superstitious fear, that his career of happiness was ended — it was one of those presentiments that reason in vain endeavours to combat — which return again and again until they almost create the evil which their agency seems to portend.

CHAPTER XXX

Dost know what hunger is? not appetite,
The rich man's blessing, but the poor man's curse.
                              Anon

He also is a prey to care,
To him 'tis said, "starve thou or borrow!"
Grey grows betimes his raven hair,
And to the grave pursues him sorrow!
With hard compulsion and with need,
He, like the rest, must strive untiring,
And his young children's cry for bread,
Maims his free spirit's glad aspiring!
Ah! such a one to me was known!
With heavenward aim his course ascended;
Yet deep in dust and darkness prone,
Care, sordid care, his life attended;
An exile, and with bleeding breast,
He groaned in his severest trial;
Want goaded him to long unrest,
And scourged to bitterest self-denial.

* * *

At length his spirit was subdued!
The power to combat and endeavour
Was gone, and his heroic mood
Came only fitfully, like fever!
The muses kiss sometimes at night
Would set his pulses wildly beating;
And his soul soared towards the light,
When might from morning was retreating!
                  Ferdinand Freiligrath[80]

The spring of 1846 saw Arthur Morton and his wife an inmate of the same abode, but a look of dulness seemed to hang about the cottage, — the turf no longer looked the pattern of neatness, — the geraniums were withering and dying away, — misfortune had laid its heavy hand on the inmates of this once happy home — for months past Arthur had been out of employment, — his late master had failed, the business was disposed of, and Arthur had been unable to procure another situation. Day by day had their little savings melted away; week by week some prized ornament, or some article of clothing disappeared; still they did not despond, — hope, that false flattering spirit, still cheered them on, and listening to her specious tales, they still lingered at the home endeared to them by so many touching associations; a gleam of their former enjoyments — a scintillation of the past still remained with them, and under its influence they still continued their studies. Still did Arthur compose tales of love and romance, and still might Mary's voice be occasionally heard singing the songs of "Auld lang syne;" but when month followed month and no change of prospect appeared in view — when the struggle to maintain their respectability merged into the struggle for mere bread — then they left their pleasant cottage, which seemed like bidding adieu to hope, and took a room in a dull street in Chelsea; here, lost to their friends, and sheltering themselves from every prying gaze, they managed to live for some weeks upon the sale of the remnant of their goods; when this was exhausted, then came the hour of trial. Hitherto Arthur had fought manfully against his adversities; failing to procure employment at his own trade, he had endeavoured to procure it in any of the multifarious branches with which commerce in London abounds, but fate seemed to delight in frustrating his hopes. Often had their morning's scanty meal been cheered by the fair prospect of at least a certainty of its renewal, but the evening saw them again downcast and desolate, — the hope had passed away, — some fatality had befallen, and the weary search for labour had again to be renewed. Mary supported these disasters with greater fortitude than falls to the lot of many inured to poverty in her early years, — thrifty in her domestic arrangements, she made their scanty stock of money seem almost inexhaustible, but sickness seized on the children, and the doctor's bill made sad inroads on the little stock; when this was all spent she parted without a murmur with all the little keepsakes and ornaments that a husband's fondness had in happier days bestowed upon her. Arthur's own clothes were the last things that were sacrificed, — the appearance of respectability was kept up even while hunger was ravaging the inner man. It were a painful task to trace them in their downward flight into the deep recesses of the dismal haunts of poverty, — the change from abode to abode, each one more dreary and comfortless than the last, — the day, the weeks, that were almost passed without food, how passed, unknown almost to themselves, — the hours that were spent in vainly endeavouring to sleep away the sharp pangs of hunger, — the craving for bread, a luxury denied them, oatmeal being their only food, their stomachs often rebelling against its reception, and the nausea of sickness, added to the pains of exhaustion. Mary, by unremitting exertion at her needle from morning's dawn till the midnight hour, could not earn sufficient of even this coarse food to supply the wants of her husband and the children, who clung in their very helplessness to the hearts that cherished them, and repined not until the heavy hour when the little that suffered to sustain them could no longer be supplied, then burst the hopeless sob from the mother's bosom, — then rebelled the proud spirit of the father, — his manner changed, — he became morose and taciturn, — temptation, like a thing of sin and death came creeping round his heart, and Mary saw with sorrow that he was no longer the perfect being her young heart had worshipped. Occasionally she procured a day's washing, or some other domestic employment from some of her neighbours almost as poor as himself, for the poor are always kind to each other; this was indeed a godsend, and in the evening, her frugal meals, almost untasted during the day, were shared with her family. On these occasions Arthur had to remain at home to attend to the children, who were yet too young to comprehend in its full extent the misery in which they were involved; never till gazing on these children, clad in the vestments of poverty, asking, but in vain, for the little enjoyments they had been used, — never until then, did he regret that he had listened to the dictates of love, and made Mary his bride. Had he been alone in the world he could have battled with poverty, or if the struggle became too painful he could easily have withdrawn from the conflict, but his wife and children now bound him to life, he had their lives and welfare to protect, with the maddening knowledge that he was unable to perform it, — that he was a drag upon his wife's energies, a recipient of the infinitessimal sum that is doled out to the poor semptress, and to reflect upon it was to endanger the sanity of his intellect. Misery had set her mark upon him, — the terrible struggles of his mind were visible in his features, — his former acquaintance would not have recognised him, in the emaciated and haggard-eyed shadow that might occasionally be seen wandering through the streets of the metropolis, seeking bread but finding none; exploring, with ardent gaze, the very pavement of the streets in the vain hope of finding something that would procure a meal's victuals. How bitterly the extreme of want is felt when surrounded by opulence and plenty, — how hideously grand seemed the splendid domain of Belgravia to the hunger-pained artisan as he passed its splendid mansions, wending his way into the heart of the metropolis. With what a spirit of mockery the bakers, provision, and cook shops, crowded on his eye, seeming to taunt him with his inability to purchase food for his famishing family at home; how he envied the condition of all he met, — all seemed prosperous, — all intent on business or pleasure, — he alone was a wretched outcast, — the thought drove him to madness, and he would rush madly homewards, fearful of being tempted to some act of desperation. At length his misery reached its climax; Mary sunk beneath her exertions, and was unable to leave her bed; Arthur, their eldest born, — the child of its father's hopes, — sunk suddenly into the grave. Arthur, overcome by this fresh calamity, — stupified by sorrow, — knew not what to do; he applied to doctor after doctor, none would attend him at his miserable abode, but referred him to the parish surgeon, and his child died in the interim. It was the first time Arthur had recourse to parochial aid, but his spirit was too far broke, and the necessity was too urgent to admit of further delay, and under the doctor's care — a rough but benevolent man — Mary soon recovered, for it was want of food more than disease that had laid her on a bed of sickness.

Of the thousands that annually fall beneath the dire disease of hunger, — yes, let it be rung in the ears of all who will listen that the victims to hunger are neither few nor far between, — though no record of their fate be given in the bills of mortality; though no inquest be held upon their murdered remains, — murdered by the vile ordinances of society, — yet have they, nevertheless, died of hunger. Shame to the country that allows it, — shame to the men who permit themselves to fall its victims. Is it not a wonder that the fair daylight structure of society reposes so tranquilly, girt round, as it is, with this abyss of dark and unutterable suffering: surrounded, as it is, with the elements of all that is rash and discordant, — all that is vile and loathsome. Can we wonder that from this ocean of misery and despair by which society is encircled, terrific waves should at times surge up, wrecking and stranding human souls, and laying bare the rocks and shoals of our false, though gilded civilisation; not until this occurs does society take cognisance of those wretched outcasts, and then only to cast them off from her bosom for ever.

Fortunate is it for our conventional system, but unfortunate for outraged humanity, that extreme misery begets apathetic dullness, — that the body being unhealthy and debased, the soul of the victim becomes stupified, — the type of humanity is lost, and a dull state of animalism supplies its place, — were it not so the violent and reckless deeds which sometimes shock society would be repeated *ad infinitum*, until their reverberation electrified the social fabric into a state of convalescence. The economist may tell us that those extremes of misery need not occur; that parochial relief may be had by all who apply for it; true, — but coupled with such conditions — surrounded by such limitations, and environed by such indignities, that the sensitive and the high-minded sink into the sleep of death, or rush headlong into futurity, rather than encounter the difficulties of procuring this provision, guaranteed by English law, but despoiled of its beneficial tendencies by the irresponsible decision of an arbitrary power, new to the annals of British jurisprudence. There are other reasons why men shrink from applying to the workhouse for relief. In the words of the poet Thom,[81] they know that if once they fall into the abyss of pauperism "they never hold up their heads in the world again;" they are degraded amongst those who are almost as deeply stricken by poverty as themselves; their names are erased from the books of men; they become bound hand and foot to their degraded situation; and the few remaining links between them and their fellow-men are severed at a blow. Few, very few, are the cases on record, where men once accepting the enforced charity of their fellow-creatures, — once becoming inmates of a Poor-Law Bastile, — ever return for any lengthened period to honest labour; they have sunk in their own esteem, — they have fallen in the estimation of others, — the brand is upon them, and they can never again rise in the social scale. This should not be: but though writing fiction we deal with facts, — we speak from experience, and know that it is too true.

CHAPTER XXXI

I shall not struggle more
Nor longer strive for food,
I've lost all vital power
And energy of blood.
I sink apace, and feel
The stillness of the grave,—
To whom can I appeal,
Or what is left to save!
Still I want bread, and bread I crave,
Or scraps or dusty crumbs,
Until my senses rave,
Or madness numbs.

Oh Heaven! and thou art kind,
To grant a soft release
By waste of flesh and mind,—
By gradual decrease,—
Not torn away in pride,
Nor mow'd in fulness down,
Not frenzied out to suicide,
By intellect o'erthrown.

I sigh'd for bits of bread,
Oft thrown unto the dogs;
And gnaw'd my gums until they bled,
At victuals mask'd for hogs;
And fancied that this earth
Was barren to mine eye,
Where beasts could fatten from their birth,
And man with hunger die.

What pangs I felt when pain'd,
My first desire for food,
As if my stomach drain'd
My arteries of blood!
And then I raved and wept,

And long'd with starving glare,
Until exhausted nature slept
'Midst banquets rich and rare.

Why dread the angry cloud
Of thunder, tempest, rain,
When there's an element as loud,
That rages in our brain!
When dizzy ears no more
Can hear the howling cry
Of famish'd organs, in their roar
For hopeless charity!

By genius was I cursed,
By passion undermined,
Or was I in that cradle nursed,
Which desecrates mankind!
No matter, let me glance
Above, below, around,—
Oh! where, save mimic countenance,
Can charity be found!

Nought left, but to desire
That in another life
No more can hunger dire
Promote such vital strife!
I have no use for stomach, jaws,
Teeth, gums, or bowels — let it be,
As here I fail'd in nature's laws,
I need them not eternally!
Still I want bread, and bread I crave,
Or scraps or dusty crumbs,
Until my senses rave,
Or madness numbs.
      Sick bed, Manchester, 8th July, 1848

Return we to the house of desolation and mourning: during the time of Mary's illness, Arthur was too much absorbed with grief to attend to any domestic cares; he had fallen into a state of torpid apathy, more fearful to contemplate than his previous moroseness. By the doctor's agency a nurse had been provided, and all arrangements completed for the child's funeral, and it was not until the corpse was about being borne from the house that he showed any signs of being conscious of the loss that had befallen him; then Nature awoke within him, and he exclaimed, "My beauteous boy! thou too dead," and sunk senseless on the coffin — with difficulty the bearers conveyed him to his room. The pauper funeral then proceeded, and the body of the prized and petted infant — the child of many hopes — was laid in its mother earth without a single mourner to weep over its early fate; no father's tear to water its lowly grave — no mother's sob to waft her prayer to Heaven and beg a welcome for her babe — yet does he sleep as soundly in the pleasant churchyard of Brompton, and the grass grows as green over his quiet grave as though he was buried in all the panoply of grief, with the dark plumed hearse, and the hired mourners following in its wake, making still more bitter by its solemn splendour the genuine grief of those whose hearts really wept his fate. Oh! the mockery of human ceremonies, the hired ostentatious action of grief! Can they recall the dead to life! can they assuage a single pang of those whose hearts bleed in secret! Yet do they so cling to humanity that the poor victims to their delusions will spend their last shilling — endanger their credit, ay rob the survivors of their daily bread — rather than the bitter mockery should be withheld, and their pride gratified at the expense of their real comforts; but such thoughts found no echo in the bosoms of Arthur or Mary Morton: she, the disconsolate mother, grieved in silence as only a mother can grieve, that she was denied the privilege of seeing the last duties performed to her lost child, and her sick bed was indeed a bed of weariness; and Arthur — he who should have been to her a shield and a consolation in this, their day of mutual tribulation — he was a frantic madman, raving continually of past joys, embittering the sorrow of the present hour, by insane reminiscences of by-gone hopes. Slowly did his mind recover its former tone — the unceasing attentions of his sick wife alone prevented his falling a victim to insanity, and to what a world of misery did he awaken. With the recovery of Mary, the benevolence of the doctor towards them ceased, and hunger once again stared them in the face, yes, took actual possession of their bodies. Mary's illness caused her to lose her employment, and deprived of her scanty earnings, charity was their only resource.

Reader, hast thou ever known the pangs of hunger? hast thou ever heard thy infant cry for food, and turned away thy face in hopeless agony? Being in all probability one of Arthur's class in life, thou hast doubtlessly experienced want and privation, or thou hast been more fortunate than the majority of thy brethren. But if thou hast not, in the literal sense of the word, felt the pangs of hunger, thou hast but little conception of the despair that raged in Arthur's heart — his faculties were strung into a state of frantic excitement — bread must be had if he perished in obtaining it — he rushed from the scene of hopeless desolation that his home presented, through courts and alleys, wretched and filthy, where the sun never shone in its splendour to cheer the misery that dwelt there; he wended his way until he gained the open thoroughfare, when he paused not knowing where to bend his steps. It was a cold evening in the month of December, the rain came drizzling down, and the north east wind swept in triumph through the almost empty street. The rich and the respectable were safely housed in their snug domiciles — misery and want were alone abroad — several wretches, poor as himself, hurried by him, striving by an increased pace to warm the blood that want caused to stagnate in their frames — it was a time when misery seemed to be alone in the streets — taking counsel with despair how to avenge the wrongs that society committed upon it. Arthur heeded not the biting blast, nor the strange companions that flitted by him — rage had warmed the blood that despair had so long chilled — he felt that he was treated as one of the offal of humankind, and he longed to avenge himself on those who scorned him; onward he passed until he came unto the usually crowded thoroughfare of Pall Mall. A gentleman was gaily conversing with a courtesan; Arthur implored him for charity, and was answered with a jeer; his blood boiled within him; he rushed on him as a wild beast on his prey, hurled him to the ground, and ere the astonished woman could give an alarm he was gazing, with almost childish glee, upon a glittering heap of gold and silver that he had wrenched from the grasp of the man he had assailed; with the instinctive cunning of crime, he evaded pursuit and reached his own abode in safety; he paused at the door; he could not face his own loved Mary and his innocent child without some plausible excuse for being possessed of such, in reality, untold wealth; he felt it would be degrading them to his own level to make them conscious of his crime — reflection had supplied the place of rage — and though he neither regretted the act he had committed, nor dreaded its consequences, still he felt that he had sinned against society; he could no longer look down with scorn upon the depravity of his fellows; he had been sinned against, but he had returned evil for evil. While these thoughts were busy in his mind, his eye glanced uneasily around, fell upon one of those haunts of vice glittering in splendour disseminated Gin Palaces; he speedily sought refuge from his conscience in this sanctuary, and drowning remembrance with repeated draughts of brandy (a luxury long untasted), staggered home in a state of moody intoxication. Our hero had now realised the fact of crime and drunkenness — subjects which his imagination had often dwelt uneasily upon, but of whose dead sea fruits he had never hitherto partaken; he had now made a fresh experience — he had become a link in that great chain of outcast humanity which is continually clanking in our ears, and enfolding victim after victim in its iron bands.

Crime under our present social arrangement seems in some shape or other to be the inevitable inheritance of the whole family; the rank of open criminals belongs to no distinct class of society, its recruits are mustered from every grade of mankind. Rich and poor, young and old, are alike its votaries, no distinction of sex is known; beauty and intellect fall beneath its sway equally with deformity and ignorance; still it is true that the majority come from that class who have to endure the most privations, and enjoy the fewest pleasures; nor can this be wondered at; it would be strange and more appalling were it otherwise; it would argue that man was naturally depraved, that vile cant of the religionist, whereas we can now trace the evil to its true source — the unequal distribution of wealth — the opulence of the rich acting as a powerful temptation to the poverty of the poor — it is an effort of nature to restore a due balance amongst the varied members of her giant body; and though these eruptions and excrescences are loathsome and unsightly, and the safety of society demands their removal, yet are they analogous to the blotches thrown outward by the human frame in its efforts to restore the body to a state of health and vigour. This doctrine may be unfashionable, may irritate the prejudices of many; but we believe it to be true; it does not advocate the cause of crime; it merely points out the source from whence it flows; it recognises the man even in the criminal, and points the finger of hope to the future; it is from this feeling of sympathy with the man, but detestation of the crime, that springs that morbid curiosity for criminal literature and for the possession of relics of great offenders; we feel an interest in their fate. We long to know the steps by which they became lost to society, what temptations, what passions and necessities, have driven them to their fate, and we thrill with sympathy if the magnitude or nature of the temptation, touch a similar chord in our own bosoms; for how many, who now maintain a fair character, must, if they dare penetrate into the recesses of their hearts, admit that it has been more owing to a concurrence of happy circumstances, than to moral fortitude or rectitude of principle!

CHAPTER XXXII

She was a thing like thee, that seemed
Almost too glorious for desire;
And all of which romance had dreamed,
Tamed all that passion meant to fire.
Look round — and where the bright — the holy —
The dawn-star! fallen from the skies:
And after vice and craftier folly,
Where nobler natures weep — despise.

* * *

In that false world to which thou'rt chained,
Who sins not is too tame to reign;
And custom in an hour hath gained,
What vice for age had stormed in vain.
And duller, colder sins shall mar
The gloss upon thy spirit's pinion;
This sorcerer world but makes the star
It most invokes, the most its minion.
And all the pleasures which possess thee
But dim thy heart while they caress thee;

And truth will lose her virgin beauty;
And art shall mould itself to duty;
And all that fashion bids thee follow,
Leave love foresworn and friendship hollow.
I would not meet thee when some years
Have taught thy heart how folly sears,
And trifles now so tempting fluttered
Away the youth they but embittered,
When all our fancies most adore,
Cling round that joyous form no more.

                              Lytton Bulwer[82]

The clock has just struck eight, the night is cold and drizzling, the wind sweeps in fitful gusts through the streets, and is heard moaning as though in grief at nature's desolation; in the parks of St. James and Hyde, the region around seems dull and untenanted, but it is high noon in Belgrave-square, — gilded lacqueys are hurrying to and fro, the carriages are setting down their richly dressed occupants at a mansion whose blazing lights and bustling appearance seem to indicate that some unusual revelry is taking place within: two policemen are at the door to keep order among the rival servants, each asserting their owner's claims for place and precedence; the stately groom of the chambers is bawling the names of the titled visitors as they are ushered into the splendid suite of rooms; the mistress of the mansion, the beauteous Clarence Fitzherbert, now Lady Maxwell, is busily employed in receiving her guests, and going through the routine of aristocratic ceremony; how changed from the pure-hearted girl of our former chapters; the simplicity of girlhood no longer hangs around her, she has emerged into the blaze of resplendent womanhood, — she is the fashionable leader of the *ton,* — the cynosure of all eyes, and the admired talisman that attracts a thousand beating hearts, — her brow seems loftier, though paler, than of yore, and her voluptuous form, attired in all the splendour of lace and jewels, seems to dazzle the beholder; yet a careful scrutiny of her countenance would show to the most inapt observer that all is not peace under that gay exterior, — her eye no longer swims in the liquid light of unaffected happiness, — her footsteps have not the lightness of their former tread, — her gaze, when unoccupied with receiving the meaningless compliments of the gay flutterers who surround her, is absorbed and vacant, — she is a splendid mistress of a gorgeous mansion, not the loved wife of a happy home. Her husband, Walter North, now a peer of the realm, has been elevated to the Upper House with the title of Lord Maxwell, as a reward for his subserviency to the Whig Cabinet: his quondam friends and supporters, the Corn Law League, occasionally receive his support, but in all essential respects he has become a mere tool of the ruling faction; his services are ever at their command, and his mediocre abilities better suited to the dull region of the Peers than to the more active arena of the so-called House of Commons; his father-in-

law and the Earl of Attringham are both immured in the tomb of their
ancestors, and in right of his lady he has become possessor of their extensive
domains; his career has been one complete gleam of sunshine, the height of his
aspiring hopes has been attained, and his whole soul glories in his success; still
his happiness is not without alloy: his lady has twice brought him a son and
heir, but death has claimed them as his prey, and his ambition frets and chides
itself, that whilst every cottage on his extensive domain is crowded with
starving children whose parents waste their strength in vain efforts to support
them, whilst his baronial hall, where more food is wasted than would supply
the wants of the whole hamlet, is destitute of a child to share its plenty, or
transmit the honours of the lord to succeeding generations. Marrying from
motives of pride and ambition — destitute of the genuine feeling of love, —
when a few short months had passed, passion was exchanged for satiety, —
home ceased to have charms in his eye; used to the active pursuits of trade he
could not enact the simple but dignified part of a country gentleman, and the
retirement of Newland Hall (for the fond father had insisted upon their living
with him whilst in the country,) was too irksome a restraint to be long endured
by one whose every wish had hitherto been gratified. Attendance to his
parliamentary duties being a valid excuse, his home was but seldom visited, and
speedily quitted, without any symptoms of regret, and his once flattered bride,
the lovely Clarence, in the depth of her heart was forced to admit that she had
pledged her affections to one who was careless of the value of the offering;
vainly did she try by every solicitude in her power to charm back his wayward
heart, but immersed in business or pleasure, he heeded not her attractions; and
love for her father, whose declining health would not permit his removal to
London, still kept them estranged from each other until the death of Lord
Fitzherbert, when they removed to their town establishment in Belgrave-square.
Devotedly attached to her father, Clarence mourned his loss with no common
grief, — he was to her a dear companion and a sincere friend, — and when
bereft of him she felt still more keenly the unkindness of her husband; but once
introduced into town life, the novelty of the scene — the glitter and refinement
with which she was surrounded — awakened the dormant passions of her soul,
and she plunged recklessly into its whirlpool of gaieties, and sought to hide her
domestic grief in the chaos of dissipation. Young and lovely — admired and
flattered by all — she strove, amid bustle and gaiety, to fill that void in her
heart which unrequited love gave birth to, but in vain did she seek to satisfy its
cravings; in the dance and the carousal she was the giddiest of the gay, but in
her deserted chamber she felt all the lone bitterness of a slighted heart. True,
she was flattered and caressed, and many were the voices that whispered to her
of love — false, adulterous love — but though the fulsome adulation gratified
her and duly awakened vanity, and whiled away the tedium of the hour, it
never reached her heart, — her education had been too pure, — her nature too
unsophisticated, for the poison to sink deep or the careless husband might have
wrecked his inattention to his fair bride.

If our fashionable novelists paint truly the scenery of high life, how vapid and unsatisfactory are its pleasures! — how fruitful its tendencies for vice and crime, gilded though they be by artifice and refinement! Love — genuine love — can scarce survive in its baleful atmosphere; virtue is scorned, or treated with ridicule — still its outward show is maintained, but, like all hotbed productions, its blossoms are false and deceitful, calculated to please the eye and gratify the palate, but unsubstantial and worthless, compared with the genuine fruit. Yet these are our legislators and rulers — these are those who govern by right divine, whose authority so to do it is treason to question. On the night with which our chapter commences Lord Maxwell had taken for the first time his seat and the customary oaths, on presenting himself as a member of the Upper House, and a brilliant assemblage (so called, we presume, from the jewels that sparkled among them) was met at his residence to congratulate him on the auspicious event. But, alas! the lord of the mansion appeared not — hour followed hour, and his carriage came home empty, the servants being unable to trace their master. He had ordered his carriage at the Reform Club-house, at eight o'clock, intending to walk thither from the House of Peers. Elevated with the new honour which had been conferred upon him, and having partaken freely of wine, he had fallen in with a fair Cyprian,[83] and thus occupied was attacked by a maniac, robbed, and left bruised and insensible: the girl having given the alarm he was conveyed to the nearest doctor, and some hours elapsed before he was sufficiently recovered to make known his name or residence. Reader, the school-fellows had once more met. The peer had encountered the outcast — the favourite of fortune had sunk beneath the hunger-smitten rage of his quondam acquaintance. What a tangled web of arbitrary arrangements do the affairs of this world appear. Good and Evil, Right and Wrong, are so mingled together, that we cannot trace the principle that governs it, nor find the clue to its varying threads. Cause and Effect seem to have abandoned their unity, and the whole to be composed of vast fragments of one mighty chapter of accidents. We see vice triumphant, and Virtue in adversity; Genius in rags, and Mediocracy in power. How calculated is this to raise a doubt of the superiority of the existence of a beneficent superintending Power. In the world of Nature all is harmony and beauty — all is in accordance with known natural laws; the planets roll through space without infringing on each other's spheres; the seasons rise and fall in due succession — every tree, every plant, is placed in a soil and situation suited to the development of its peculiar properties; all is order — all is regularity. But when we turn to man, how sad is the contrast. Boasting of the lights of revelation and philosophy, proclaiming himself an emanation from the Deity, he spreads around himself chaos and confusion. With bitter malignity he seems to delight in heaping evils on his own head and on those of his brethren; the fair world around him he curses with his passions, until he makes it one scene of desolation. He dwells in an atmosphere of corruption and calls it a metropolis of civilisation. He shuts out the pure light of heaven, and defiles the very air he breathes, in order that he may have the pleasure of paying physicians to torture and to rob him. He invents laws innumerable, and by his devices renders it impossible for them to be obeyed, in order that he may have the malicious satisfaction of punishing those that break them. He places power in the hands of those whose interest he makes to abuse it. He invents a religion, which, professing peace and goodwill, spreads warfare and animosity wherever it penetrates. He delights in war and massacre, and worships it under the guise of patriotism and glory. He denies instruction, yet punishes ignorance. He brutalises his fellows, and then scoffs at their want of refinement. In a word, he makes a man a monster and then shrinks in terror from his own handiwork, and not content with these evils, by his false training he sophisticates his mind, and makes thought — that living God — an incarnate Demon, torturing him with a continuity of suffering, adding to present torments the memory of past evils, and embittering them with the prospect of a still increasing future store, until he renders himself a fit inmate for his priest's hell, and the earth a fit dwelling for such a demoniac being. While humanity is so constituted, — whilst those who would fain improve it, and bid the Evil Spirit avaunt, are treated as fanatics and impostors, who can but despise himself that he belongs to such an insensate herd, and count it wisdom to join in the wild revel of humanity, rob and despoil all who come within his reach, wrap himself up in the mantle of selfishness, and laugh at the mingled folly and atrocity by which he is surrounded?

CHAPTER XXXIII

But lovely is a woman's soul,
And e'en when sorrow spurns control,
Its selfishness she smothers;
And Mary, though perchance the dart
Had entered deeper in her heart
Ev'n than her husband's breast; yet cherished
The thought that in *his* grief had perished,
The thought, the sympathy for others!
So, roused at moments from her bow'd
And brooded sorrow, she surveyed,
Alarmed and anxious, the strange cloud
That o'er her husband cast its shade.
Too pure, too guileless to discover
The barb and mystery of his soul,
She dreamt not she beheld a robber,
In him compassion would console.

* * *

But oft, when Mary with her sweet
And her delicious beauty, stole
Athwart his presence — seemed to fleet
The demon from her husband's soul!
With a fixed and charmed eye,
And a quick and startled sigh,
Would his panting heart pursue her!
As if to use the fairy words—
That passion tuned to fancy's chords—
He yearned to meet her silvery feet,
His soul to pour unto her.

* * *

Yet sometimes e'en her magic failed,
And a darker power prevailed,
Then a cloud came o'er his air,
Or a swift and angry glare
In his gloomy eyeball glittered,
And low words he strung embittered,
By the passions of a breast,
Roused — a tempest from its rest.

                              Lytton Bulwer

Arthur reached his desolate home, if an almost empty garret in a filthy
Metropolitan alley deserves to be recognised by that name; his wife was
anxiously awaiting his return; no cheerful blaze illumined the grate — no
candle shed its pale ray around — she sat by the remains of what had once
been a window, gazing vacantly on the roof of the opposite house, and listening
to the rain as it pattered on the tiles, and dropped heavily on the remnant of the
pavement below; grief was heavy at her heart, — the enthusiasm which once
glowed in her bosom was for ever chilled, — misery had dimmed the beauty
of her countenance, and the voice that was once melodious in the song, and the
step that was once so light in the dance, were now sad and heavy, their
harmony and elasticity had for ever departed; with sensitive frames the volitions
of the body depend greatly upon the temper of the mind; continued sorrow acts
as an opiate on the body, chilling and benumbing its faculties, until the soul
departs from it, and the mere mechanism remains, injured — disfigured and
bereft of its pristine vigour. Intent on her sombre meditations, she heard not the
footsteps of her husband, and his intoxicating accents were the first harbingers
of his return; he threw down a quantity of silver on a box containing their
scanty wardrobe, which served them for a table, and bade the astonished
woman fetch wherewith to eat and drink; in utter astonishment she silently
obeyed, and the poor outcast threw himself on the bed, and was soon lost in

slumber. The wife, in her innocence, imagined, when sufficiently collected to think upon the subject, that he had applied to some former acquaintance and procured this timely supply; and of the handful of silver which he had scattered on the box but the smallest modicum was expended, and she speedily returned with a loaf and the necessary ingredients for making tea, and was followed by a boy bearing a small quantity of coal and wood. With unaccustomed cheerfulness she was soon busily employed in preparing this frugal meal; the child, their darling Fanny, was awakened to partake of the welcome treat, but the husband still slumbered, and the poor wife, though longing to partake of the smoking beverage, was unwilling to disturb his slumbers. O the patient virtues of womankind, how they shine when compared with man's selfish engrossments; never does sympathy with the distress of others forsake the breast of woman; never does their own grief make them callous to the feelings of their fellow-sufferers. For upwards of an hour did Mary wait in patience the period of her husband awakening, unwilling to lose the pleasure of his participating with her in their cheerful meal, and Arthur, when he awoke, was parched and feverish, — the conflicting emotions of his mind, and the unusual quantity of liquor he had partaken, caused him to feel lassitude and depression, and to Mary's inquiries relative to his possession of so much money, he replied, that he had found the purse in the street, and that delirious with joy, he had partaken of brandy, and becoming stupified, had not yet examined his prize; he then handed her the purse, which she took without the remotest suspicion of the truth of the narration, and emptying its contents, found, to her astonishment, upwards of twenty sovereigns, in addition to the silver she had previously received; this was indeed a perfect mine of wealth as compared with their previous indigence, and though Mary spoke of the loss it would be to the owner, yet she felt no scruple of conscience in applying it to satisfy their wants, but seemed rather to regard it as a kind gift of Providence to remove them from the temptations of misery. Arthur, pleased with the success of his stratagem, and anxious to avoid further questioning, pleaded illness, and was soon in the world of visions, but joy kept Mary long awake, — a thousand ways had she to consider how the money might be most advantageously laid out, until the bitter reflection came over her that had this treasure been theirs but a few weeks earlier her lost Arthur might still have been nestling in her bosom, and the vain regret bestowed her pillow with bitter tears, and more than balanced her previous pleasure. Joy and sorrow are so mingled in the cup of human existence that the sweets of the one are oft neutralised by the bitters of the other; seldom indeed can we empty the chalice of its divine nectar but the poison lurking in its dregs insidiously mingles with the draught, and the balm is turned into gall.

A week has elapsed, they have removed from their former filthy abode, the pawnbroker has been visited, and they are again clad in decent apparel, and Arthur being now enabled to appear in the face of day has received the promise of a situation; the glow of health begins to appear upon their haggard cheeks,

and Mary's spirits rise proportionably with their improved prospects, but it is
not so with Arthur, he is no longer the even-spirited character of our former
tale, — a weight seems hanging upon his mind, which all the endearments of
Mary serve not to remove, — he had ascertained, by a report in some
newspapers which he had borrowed to look at the advertisements, that the man
he had robbed was Walter North, Esq., who that day had been created Lord
Maxwell; the particulars were too minute — the time and place too accurately
engraven on his memory — to leave him a shadow of doubt, that the friend of
his early years — the brother of his once adored and lamented Julia — had
been the victim to his necessities, and the knowledge of this fact imparted
additional uneasiness to his mind; he morbidly conceived that he had trampled
upon the memory of his lost love, and insulted her in her grave by committing
this outrage upon her brother; he knew not to the full extent how treacherous
that brother had proved to her, — he dwelt only on the insult to the dead, and
even fancied he could hear her upbraid him with it. Conscience, what cowards
thou dost make even of the strongest minded, until familiarity with crime begets
indifference, and success or punishment alike has taken off the novelty of the
first plunge into the turbid waters of criminality. The man who, driven by stern
necessity, has committed one crime, is harassed by vain remorse during the
remainder of his existence, whilst the man of many crimes is hardened and
indifferent; but better far to our ideas of religion and morality is the victim to
one great and solitary crime, than the man of the world, — the respectable
villain, whose whole life is a series of meanness and hypocrisy, unrelieved by
magnanimity of any description, — true, he evades the law and the law's
justice, but he is none the less a villain, — the gold that he accumulates may
be encrusted with the gore of his starving victims, — the respectability of
which he boasts may be based on the ruin and prostitution of hundreds, — the
blighted hearts he has trampled upon may be thickly strewn about his path, —
but he recks it not, the world smiles on him, he has no remnant of natural
religion in his soul, and he knows no remorse; with demure and sanctified
countenance he worships in the temple of his God, and boasts, with the
Pharisee of old, "that he is not a sinner like other men;"[84] well might the
glorious Byron sing, "Oh, for a forty parson power to sing thy praise,
hypocrisy."[85] Arthur Morton, driven by poverty to crime, endured more mental
anguish from this one unguarded act than he had ever experienced during his
many and appalling privations; in vain did reason plead, that though he had
broken the conventions of society, yet had he but obeyed the first great law of
nature, self-preservation; that the gold he had stolen, though life and wealth to
him and his family was but an atom from the store of his former schoolfellow,
— an atom that would have been dissipated in vice, or squandered in frivolity,
— it nevertheless haunted him like a spectre, and cast a still darker shadow
over his dreary fate, and yet he was no victim to religious fantasies; it was no
supernatural terror that prostrated his mind, it was his high sense of rectitude
— his poor feeling of morality — which had been broken and disturbed, and

the wound bled the more inwardly from its outward concealment; and when time, that great opiate to all cares, had modified his feelings of regret, and restored somewhat of serenity to his mind, in the irregular impulses of his after career an astute psycolist might trace the working of some secret crime which had deranged the balance of his mental faculties, and threw its perturbing influence over his conduct. Oh ye sages and philosophers who affect to trace the hidden springs of the human mind, — to picture its strength and its weakness, its growth and its decay, and to outrival the religion of old, — have ye no balm to bestow on a wound like this? is there no restorative in your mental pharmacopeia for a guilty conscience? can ye not compete with the priest and the confessor, and speak peace to the shaken mind? can ye give no absolution to the erring but repenting mortal? if not, vain is your craft. The grand impostures of former times were more in accordance with the feelings of frail humanity, — more soothing to the hopes and aspirations of the bleeding heart than the stern wisdom of the present day, — they, with all their seeming pride and austerity, felt more nicely the pulse of the great human heart, — dived more absolutely into its hidden intricacies, and restored its beating to a more healthy tone than all your boasted philosophy can effect, — hence the ascendancy they gained over the minds of men, — hence the vast empire they erected in the human soul, the ruins of which still strike us with awe and wonder. Vast fragments of a mighty fabric, destined, perchance, under a new phase, and with the lights of a new experience, to again regain the empire of the mind, and, Colossus like, bestride the portals of the soul, making puny the crafts of the present age, for what is Communism[86] but a new organisation of the disjointed fragments of the gigantic past, — a fresh breathing into the dying clay of past existence, a resurrection of the soul of decaying humanity, divested of the grossness and impurities of its former material being. In a word, a new earth created from the ruins of a former world, purified by the fire of revolution, and rendered sacred by the blood and martyrdom of its founders.

CHAPTER XXXIV

Ill fares the land to hast'ning ills a prey,
Where wealth accumulates and men decay;
Princes or lords may flourish, or may fade;
A breath can make them, as a breath hath made;
But a bold peasantry, their country's pride,
When once destroyed can never be supplied.
A time there was, ere England's griefs began,
When ev'ry rood of ground maintain'd its man,
For him light labour spread her wholesome store,
Just gave what life requir'd, but gave no more;
His best companions, innocence and health;

And his best riches, ignorance of wealth.
                                        Goldsmith[87]

But He, who serves all earth — whose mind
Stars the dark wanderings of mankind;
And from lone thought's empyrean height,
Exalts the soul, its glories light,
For him no grateful memory lives;
No justice weighs, no love forgives;
For him, the Universal Eye,
Each heart he cheered has grown his spy.
The very lustre of his fame,
Betrays the specks upon his name;
The columns of his triumph stand
As Pasquins[88] for each vulgar band.
For him the wonted shades which hide
Home's reverent secrets, are denied,
Exposed, dissected, canvassed o'er,
Each household word and hidden sore;
His very heart hung forth a prey
To the sharp-tongued remorseless day;
The temple he hath built will yield,
For him alone no shrine to shield;
Nay, round the altar where he flieth,
The coil'd and venomed slander lieth,—
Crush'd by the serpents of his doom,
Behold his temple walls his tomb.
                                        Lytton Bulwer

The winter of 1847 saw Arthur Morton and his wife in comparatively flourishing circumstances, but the remembrance of his difficulties had left its traces on his once fair and open brow, and gave a tinge of sadness to his conversation; the love of home, which once characterised him, existed no longer, it reminded him too bitterly of the past, and he flew with avidity to the excitement of politics; if he was a better citizen he was no longer so affectionate an husband; his heart beat as warmly as ever for the welfare of his fellow-men, but he no longer viewed their destinies through hope's enchanted glass, he felt that the evils which surrounded them were stern and stubborn facts, which would not yield to the fiery heat of enthusiasm, or melt beneath the glowing breath of eloquence; to effect their removal he saw that it needed the iron weapons of reality, — the demonstrative power of practical experiment; impressed with this belief he viewed with pleasure the progress the Land Agitation was making throughout the country;[89] holding firmly to the opinion that the land was national property, — that England's soil was the joint property of England's sons, — he nevertheless saw that to induce them to claim their rightful share in this common inheritance they must be taught its inestimable value, — they must be shown that it was the golden stamp which gave value to all other commodities, — that land was made for man and not man for the land, — that divorced from the soil man was an emasculated helot, a victim to his own necessities, and a slave to minister to the wants of another, — that the laws were made for the protection of the land, surrounding acres with a triple shield, but leaving industry weak and unprotected; that for land the Corn Laws famished their yearly victims, — the Game laws demoralised whole districts, — the law of Primogeniture defeated the law of Nature, and the law of Entail set aside the claims of Justice;[90] that land held in the hands of the few, governed, taxed, and Atlas-like,[91] weighed down the many; that the law of the land was the law for the land. He wished them to be imbued with the love for the land so excellently described by that great French historian, Michelet, who says:— "That to get land in seven years the Alsatian sells his life, and goes to meet death in Africa: to have a few feet of vineyard the woman of Burgundy tears her breast from the mouth of her own child, puts a stranger in its place, and weans her own; 'too soon, my child,' says the father, 'either you will live or you will die, but if you live you shall have a bit of land.' Is it not cruel, nay almost impious to speak thus? reflect well before you decide. You shall have a bit of land means, you shall not be a mercenary, to be hired to-day and turned adrift tomorrow; you shall not be a serf for your daily bread, you shall be free. Free! glorious word, comprising indeed all human dignity. There is no virtue without liberty." Truly are the words of this glorious Frenchman, "Liberty without land is a soul separated from the body, — a vain chimera, which if it exists at all can produce no fruition, but is barren and unprofitable."[92] It was, therefore, with no common satisfaction that he watched the gradual development of the National Land Company. Faint and feeble in its infancy, it needed all the cares of its founders to prevent its being strangled by the hands of an ignorant and hostile press; but once emerged from its swaddling clothes, — once fairly placed before the British people, — its success was unprecedented, demonstrating that the Company, aided by Mr. O'Connor's pen and influence, had distributed correct notions of the value of land, and its primordial influence upon the welfare of the community far and wide, and that which in England had hitherto been a question presumed to effect only farmers and landed proprietors suddenly became the question of the day, — the grand palladium which was to insure the continued prosperity of these islands, and which ultimately will effect that grand desideratum, a national demand for its speedily becoming the property of its rightful owners. Never did a Company, established for any sectional or commercial purpose, ever affect such a revolution in public opinion as that effected by the National Land Company; and though the political furore caused by the events of February, 1848, in France, and April in England, threw into comparative obscurity the minor interest of the Company;[93] though the tide of popular support has long ebbed and left the giant fabric almost a deserted hulk on the bleak shore; though its nationality has become a thing of naught, yet hath it performed its work in the channel of Progress, and out of its timbers may yet be hewn the vessel which shall ride triumphant into the harbour of Success. The principles on which the Land Plan was founded have stood the test of the time; each succeeding fact, — every fresh incident, — has but shown more strongly their solidity; that the details of the scheme may have been faulty, — that the experimentalists may have been unfitted by their prior pursuits in life for its beneficial working, — that the seasons have been unpropitious, and that the members have failed in performing their stipulations, are facts that will scarcely admit of doubt, and on these circumstances and not on its principles, or the motives of its founders, ought the blame of any apparent failure to be laid; but such is the inconsistency of men, that instead of taking shame to themselves for the failure of any cherished project, they denounce and abuse the very persons whom by their criminal neglect they have incapacitated from the power of serving them; no falsehood is too base, no personal attack too vile, to administer gratification to their wounded hopes and self disappointments, — from such men good Lord deliver us; but the prayer is vain, it is a penalty public men must arm themselves to submit to, and clothed in integrity, and fortified by the co-operation of the just minded, they need not shrink from the contest, painful and mortifying though it be.

At the period of our tale all was enthusiasm and prosperity, — no idea of failure had entered into the minds of its members, — even the Press had ceased its vain opposition, and the Plan was fast attaining universal celebrity. In the political world all was calm and quiescent, but it was the calm of thought, — the calm of reflection, and not the calm of despair, — like the dull heavy clouds that presage the coming storm, it presaged the approaching political commotion which threw all minor projects into the shade. As the year closed strange and unusual heavings took place in the sister isle; the war notes of resistance seemed to ring in every gale; the spirit of freedom began again to breathe in Gaul, and its potency to disturb even the calm visage of the Citizen King;[94] still England slumbered on, but the distant murmurings of revolution began to rise louder and higher upon our ears, — ardent hearts again began to speak in hopeful language, — the spirit tongue of liberty swelled the accents of Ledru Rollin, or Mitchel, Meagher, Blum, Kossuth, and Mazzini,[95] until at length its glorious tones were heard above the din of war and strife, louder and more thrilling than the clash of swords and the cannon's roar, proclaiming in triumphant notes that the tyrant of France had fallen, and that the reign of "Liberty, Equality, and Fraternity" was at hand. Tyrants in every land trembled and fled aghast at the sound, the vile traffickers in human misery shrunk terrified into their obscene dens, and prostrated humanity revived from her long trance, shook her limbs like a mighty wrestler, and stood prepared for the combat; the electric shock thrilled through every vein of the British Empire, and startled the sons of Erin into convulsions of insanity. Alas! that they were not earlier prepared for the rending of the old *regime*; had they thrown off their apathy but a month, a short month earlier, the Ides of March might, as in Rome of old, have changed the whole destiny of the empire, but their slumber was prolonged until the electric influence of the glorious days of February was frittered away, and so reduced in potency by April, when the National Convention met, that its small voice, neither bass, nor treble, had neither the war tones of Revolution, nor yet the gentle accents of Peace, Law, and Order; composed of two distinct elements, those of war and peace, which it vainly endeavoured to amalgamate, it was powerless for either, and thus served only to irritate the public mind; the parent of a mixed progeny, it named as its successor and executor the National Assembly,[96] and closed its career in obscurity; nevertheless let us do justice to its memory, — its members had an arduous part to play, and discharged their duty with firmness and courage. The 10th of April, 1848, that day made so memorable by the preparations of the government, as ridiculous as they were pompous, — that day when the middle class of London, and the empire generally, showed their love for Democracy by arming themselves for this slaughter, — that day when the President of Republican France[97] became a gallant special to support Whig misrule, is a day to which the Democrats of the Metropolis, and of the Empire, through its representatives, can point to as a bright one in their annals, — a day which was neither disfigured by cowardice nor disgraced by turbulence. Many have wished that the triumph had been greater; that Kennington Common should have seen the Sons of Freedom marshalled, and marching back to the City's heart in the same order as they came; but the peculiar position of Feargus O'Connor, their great Parliamentary champion, and the awful responsibility it would have entailed upon the Convention in perchance leading an unarmed people into collision with an armed force, furnished with every requisite for slaughter, made them decide otherwise; and the good organisation and discipline of the people was more strongly evinced in acting according to the instructions of the Convention, and was productive of more lasting terror to the government, than any more temporary success which the people might have achieved in a street conflict. It is order, discipline, and a yielding of their own impulses to the commands of their leaders which shows a determined organisation among a people, and when the oppressor sees this he feels that the hour of retribution is arrived; that the hand-writing of his destiny is written on the wall of millions of human hearts, and that they only need a fair opportunity to achieve their freedom. Under circumstances of the most unfavourable character did the National Assembly meet; dissension had arisen in the Chartist camp, and was spreading its baneful influence in the ranks, the People's petition had been pronounced as a gross imposture, and the Press teemed with calumny and misrepresentation; destitute of sufficient funds, — at war with some of its own members, — deserted by the bulk of those whose co-operation it counted upon, — it lived in tumult, and died from exhaustion. Much undeserved calumny has been heaped upon it; many who were once its defenders are now suffering for their temerity in exile and persecution, — it would, then, ill become us to join in this denunciation: it contained noble-hearted men, though varying in opinion; for weeks it proclaimed truths eternal as justice, — truths dangerous to society as at present constituted, yet truths that find an echo in every honest heart, and which will one day ring the knell of expiring despotism; for weeks it braved the opponent; and though Alien Bills and Gagging Bills were fulminated against it,[98] its members stirred not from their course; and weak and powerless as it seemed, not one of its members was arrested until after its dissolution, and even then the government would have paused ere it let loose its wrath, had not the "Moderates," that name which in politics will be eternally identified with treachery and deceit, taken advantage of the weak-mindedness of the true Republicans in France, and gained the upper hand in the government;[99] then did the cowardly Whigs recover from their terror, and dreading no longer Republican France, caused England and Ireland to wail in anguish the loss of many of their truest sons. In all these events Arthur Morton was not merely a spectator; though belonging to the physical force school, he yet respected the opinions of his opponents, and ofttimes admired the proofs of moral courage which they displayed in fearlessly propounding them when popular opinion ran so strongly against them; for in those exciting days it required more moral courage, ay, and at times more physical courage, to brave the opposition of a people excited to desperation than it did to dare the wrath of an irresolute government.

CHAPTER XXXV

Ye stubborn recusants of right — and worse,
Daring apologists for wrong — know ye
How bitter 'tis to earn a nation's curse,
That execration wrung from misery.
Go — learn it from the millions who rehearse
The foul deeds which sum up your infamy;
Go — read it on the tombs which mark the grave
Of myriads whom you could but would not save;

That curse is stamped upon the haggard face
Of starving multitudes throughout the land;
E'en in the countenance of babes you trace
The mark as though impressed with demon hand.
Britannia's self is pale at the disgrace
Which taunts the morals of her native strand,
And History turns her mournful face aside,
The gushing fountain of her grief to hide.

God do thy thoughts sleep, while England moans
Beneath this Whiggish sway. Shall mortal dare
Thus to make men anticipate the groans,
The pains, the agonies of hell, for where
Is vengeance to be looked for? Must the bones
Of those who died of hunger be laid bare,
And brought as damning evidence to show
Who were the authors of this fearful woe.

Oh that the great arch orator, whose tongue
Made Verses tremble, could return again
To vent on ye the indignation wrung
From every honest heart, to taint — to stain —
And to besmear your names, ere they be flung
Forth on the moral dung heaps that remain
Throughout all ages to perpetuate
Those dread examples which we execrate!

They starving stand upon the land
Wrought fruitful by their hand alone;
Around them, halls made rich and grand
By them — who have for bread a stone.
Shall the producers have *this* share
Of the rich produce of their toil?
Shall the consumers never bear
The labour, yet devour the spoil?
Behold the plight of men by whom
Your rights of property have birth!
What do their *prior rights* become,
Whose *duties* give the soil its worth?
They ask enough to house and feed,
From hand to mouth, their babes and wives,
No hoard of all the wealth they breed
For the weak age of toil-worn lives.
                    Francis Worsley[100]

The National Assembly, after propounding a plan of organisation more suitable
to the genius of the French than the English people, a plan which needed
discipline almost military in its strictness, and a good faith in the honour of our
brethren, more famed, in this instance, for its breach than its observance,
dissolved itself, and the easy, comfortable, every day world, after being for
months terrified with dreams and omens of revolution, were at length allowed
to slumber in quiet, whilst the government filled the public ear with loud
huzzas upon the victory they had gained, and the Press and the Legislature vied

with each other in commending the wisdom of the Executive, and the loyalty of the people, which had averted the impending evil of revolution from our heads; but their triumph was premature, they had scattered the elements of revolution, not destroyed them. The sons of Erin had looked with no careless eye upon the proceedings in London, they received with enthusiasm Ernest Jones and Samuel Kydd,[101] who waited upon them, requesting their co-operation with the Assembly, and elected several delegates to attend the meeting of that body, but owing to the dissensions respecting the legality of its sittings, only one, Michael Doheny, (whose adventures in connexion with the late rebellion would form a romance in itself),[102] ever attended, and the leaders seeing no chance of a powerful diversion in England in their favour trusted to native ranks and native swords, and embarked in a noble but hopeless struggle, — a struggle in which priestcraft dominated over patriotism, and treachery and ignorance marred the efforts of enthusiasm and intelligence; a struggle in which the dastardly Whigs, outvieing in infamy even the Tories of old, by blood money and spyism of the most nefarious description, succeeded in entrapping their destined victims, and then, may burning curses ever blight their names, brought the same agency to bear on the Chartists of the Metropolis.

It was at this period that Arthur Morton was delegated by a few ardent spirits to make a tour of the country, and collect a transcript of the state of public feeling, more especially in the north of England; during this tour he visited the several estates of the National Land Company, and became more than ever impressed with a love of the natural over the artificial state of society; the interests of his mission prevented his making a long stay at any of these happy retreats — those verdant oases in the surrounding agricultural desert, — but the elegance of the cottages, and the beauty of their respective situations, made a lasting impression upon his mind, coming as he did fresh from the turbulent scenes which the Metropolis then displayed; nevertheless he could not but observe with regret that the slime of the serpent had penetrated even to these abodes of bliss; society had become so thoroughly vitiated by the long dominant power of wealth, that it was impossible even there to contend successfully against it, unless favoured with more capital than fell to the share of most of the inhabitants of these fairy abodes; and the majority of the occupants had been so trained in the vicious customs of looking to a capitalist for their Sunday's meal, that it needed both mental and physical energy to withstand the evils they had to encounter. With a mind filled with these reflections he quitted these peaceful abodes, which will ever remain a monument of the power of the masses to do much, even under adverse circumstances, towards achieving their own emancipation;[103] when he contrasted their situation with that of the surrounding agricultural peasantry, he thought that, even with all their privations, he could be happy and contented with such a lot, so forcibly did their advantages shine by contrast. He saw the peasant in his master's fields consuming life and strength in the ungrateful task of turning up the clods of jealous mother earth, who will yield her treasures only to unremitting toil, and at the close of the day, a dry black crust was his only recompense, the rich harvests he produced, the noble animals he fattened, were not for him, they were reserved for the table of his employer, who worked not, but consumed in luxury the results of his labour. He saw him with downcast head and stooping gait, too much oppressed, too poverty stricken, and too certain of his ultimate fate ever to think on the beauties of nature, or listen with delight to the melody by which he was surrounded. What to him are the charms of scenery, the delight of hill and valley, wood and stream, tower and waterfall, they are only one universal blank, representing his master's acres, from which by hard toil he can scarce extract his six, eight, or ten shillings per week; one-sixth of which goes to find him a home — if a wretched hovel less comfortable than his master's pigsty deserves that name — his life is one dull round of tedium, enlivened only by the village alehouse, when so favoured, as to be able to enter its threshold; domestic love and enjoyment are not for him, they reside not with penury and wretchedness; his lot is, indeed, one of toil, softened only by ignorance and apathy, for hope to him is unknown; wake him not from his trance, attempt not to educate him, for you will only increase his misery; let him rest in peace, a memento of the brutish state to which thoughtless loyalty, priestly rule, and want of education can reduce a human being. And yet, where is the man who should be so happy as the peasant? Nature is no niggard of her bounties, she is ever young, beautiful, and generous — poetry and loveliness dwell in her domains, and cannot be separated therefrom. It is the eye, the intellect, the unbroken spirit, that alone is wanting in the labourer, to enable him to understand and appreciate her beauties: the most blessed of beings should be that man, who possessing a mind, enriched with knowledge, cultivates his own little domain, and accures happiness and liberty to himself and family, by the exercise of his strength applied to Nature's garden, protected from want by his own industry, independent of the power of capital, working when the sun of Heaven cheers his labour, reposing when Nature dictates repose, surrounded by all that is calm, serene, and beautiful, he would, indeed, be a *man*; living in the essence of poetry, yet mixing sufficiently with the world and his fellow labourers to shield him from insanity; he would, indeed, be a poet — ay, and a philosopher — for too far removed from the bustling world to be subdued by its glare, yet sufficiently influenced by it, to watch with emotion its ever varying phases, he could calmly reflect on its features, and analyse their worth and defects. And Arthur saw that all this, and much more, might be attained by the members on these estates, provided their first difficulties were overcome; he saw in them the leaven that was to infuse light and activity into the benighted population, by which they were surrounded, and ultimately become the regenerators of our agricultural population; and so bright did the prospect appear, that he sighed in bitterness of spirits, even at the supposition of its failure; he feared it would throw back the cause of social progress for years, for he well knew the avidity with which its opponents, ever on the watch to misrepresent would seize upon such an event and turn it to their own vile purposes; perhaps the view he took was too desponding; but misfortune upon misfortune had been so heaped upon him, that he feared to look with too sanguine an eye, lest his disappointment should be the more severe.

Impressed with these feelings, he wended his way to the busy hives of industry in the North; how he succeeded in his mission it is not for us to tell; the events are too recent, and the prominent actors too well known, for the subject to be now broached, suffice it to say that everywhere he found misery and distress, trade languishing, artisans starving, indolence rioting, industry pining; everywhere the seeds of incipient revolution were rising; but in such profuse disorder, that, if a struggle came, it needed no seer to foretell the inevitable result. Of all the struggles that Time hath yet witnessed, that will be the most dire where a monied and landed aristocracy are combined against the people. Between a people roused into wrath and a despot, the contest is soon decided, but in a country like Britain, where capital and its interests penetrate into every fibre of the social frame — in a country like Britain, where the aristocracy have shared their privileges with the bulk of the middle classes; where talent in every class (provided it is subservient enough to the powers that be) can penetrate even into the highest offices in the state; a country where all who do not labour enrich themselves by keeping the labourer dependent and voteless; in such a country where all are so interested in the stake, the struggle will be one of life and death; ay, and even should the people prove physically victorious, the combat will but then have commenced, for the enemy has been so long in the ascendant that he has a fortified camp in every guild, an army in every abuse, sentinels and guards, even in the heart of the army of progress; but so long have we bowed to wealth and influence, that there is traitor even in every man's heart, and when the struggle comes — and come it must — the least vacillation, the least treachery — misnamed mercy and moderation — will at once break down the barriers, which have shut out oppression; and the hot blood, which has been so freely lavished, the privations, which have been so heroically endured, will have been shed and endured in vain, another cycle of oppression will commence, and the hopes of bleeding, tortured humanity will again have been blighted. Oh that the veritable democrats of England may read aright the lessons of the past, that the example of prostrate France may not be given in vain, but may the slaughter and banishment of her glorious sons ultimately eventuate in achieving a world-wide freedom; then will their misery not have been endured in vain, for the fire of their persecution will have become the beacon light, to show the shoals and sandbanks on which they have foundered, and guide us in triumph to the rocks of liberty, equality, and fraternity. Heaven speed the day.

CHAPTER XXXVI

Time when it lowers on states, inspires
Some thoughts above self's low desires;
And if I speak of hope, the weed
Hath scarce the construing of the herd;
Since nor with careless glance — my soul
First gazed on dark Time's riddled scroll —
First conned the food of Truth and wrought
The chyle of memory into thought,
Is my still heart I learnt to rear,
Beyond all lowlier hope or fear,
Beyond the harlots of the hour,
The lusts that burn for wealth or power,
The snake-like arts, that while they wind
Aloft, are tracked in slime behind:
Beyond the day's brief praise or blame —
Beyond the smiles of kings — the loud
Not lasting, worship of the crowd —
Beyond all, — save the heart's — applause;
Oh God — Oh Earth! your common cause.
                              Lytton Bulwer

Close by those ever burning brimstone beds,
Where Bedloe, Oates and Judas hide their heads,
I saw great Satan, like a sexton stand,
With his intolerable spade in hand,
Digging three graves — of coffin shape they were,
For those who, coffinless, must enter there
With humblest rites. The shrouds were of that cloth
Which Clotho weaveth in her blackest wrath.
The dismal tint oppressed the eye that dwelt
Upon it long, like darkness too it felt.
The pillows to those baleful beds were toads,
Large, living, livid, melancholy toads,
Whose softness shock'd! — worms of monstrous size
Crawl'd round — and one upcoiled which never dies.
A doleful bell, inculcating despair,
Was always ringing in the heavy air;
And all about the detestable pit,
Strange headless ghosts and quartered forms did flit.
Rivers of blood, from dripping traitors split,
By treachery stung from poverty to guilt.
I asked the fiend for whom these rites were meant:—

"Those graves," quoth he, "when life's brief oil is spent—
When the dark night comes, and their sinking into Hell,
I mean for Davis, Tinley, and Powell."
                                        Charles Lamb[104]

Upon his return to London, Arthur found the greatest excitement prevailing,
Ernest Jones, the Meagher of the Chartist movement, had been arrested,
together with Sharp, Williams, Fussell, Vernon, and other active London
Democrats, under the provisions of the Gagging Bill; they were speedily found
guilty by middle class juries, and sentenced to lengthened periods of
imprisonment; John Shaw, Bezer, and many talented provincial leaders, quickly
shared the same fate;[105] revenge began to actuate the minds of the warm-
hearted, and desperation usurped the place of judgment. In the metropolis, this
feeling was very prevalent; Ernest Jones, John Shaw, John Fussell and other
victims, had been long known, and highly respected; the former was almost
adored by the disciples of the physical force school; of a warm and poetic
temperament, gifted with great eloquence and an impassioned style of delivery,
by birth and education a gentleman and a scholar; yet withal, so urbane and
condescending, he acquired a magic ascendancy over the young and the
enthusiastic; to obtain his release or revenge his fate, they determined to hazard
any measure, however apparently hopeless. The vile Whig government, taking
advantage of this feeling, and of the absence of the old school Chartists from
these meetings, introduced among them their base tools, Powell, Davis, Tinley,
and others, who by their accursed arts blew the flame until the mine exploded,
and involved many true hearts in its ruins; but none, whose fate is more to be
regretted than William Cuffay's — long will the democrats of London miss his
services — cautious and cool-headed, yet brave and enthusiastic, the excitement
of the time overcame his usual sound judgment, he was entrapped in the snare,
and fell a victim; but so disgusting was the treachery by which the government
had lured him and his fellows to their fate, that not by the Chartist body alone,
but by the public generally, they were regarded more as martyrs than criminals,
and the Whigs will never efface the odium which their spy system has heaped
upon them.

   Arthur Morton had been too intimate with these men to have any chance of
escaping their fate; enlinked with Cuffay by the ties of friendship, like him he
refused to save himself by flight; fortune, however, favoured him, for by some
fortuitous circumstance he escaped denunciation from any of the government
tools until the trials were proceeding, when timely information being conveyed
to him, he acted on the advice of his friends, and once again became a fugitive
from Justice. We must not dwell on these events. Attached to some of the
metropolitan victims by ties of the closest friendship, we mourn their lot; two
of their number have fallen beneath the murderous system of discipline to
which they were subjected; their blood will not sink in those dungeon vaults,
but will rise to heaven demanding justice on their murderers; the rest still wear

their chains, and may yet experience the fate of the martyred Williams and Sharp, — to assist them is almost impossible, to pity them is useless, — the only help we can render is to support liberally their wives and families, — to rouse up the scattered elements of the democratic party, — to rally public opinion round the principles which they are embalming by their sufferings, and thus convince those of them who may re-appear amongst us (for alas! years may elapse before the exiles will return,) that we have been active in working, while they have been passive in enduring, and that the war between the oppressed and the oppressor has not, nor ever shall cease, until substantial justice shall be impartially administered to all. Arthur Morton, assisted by the good and true, after many perils escaped to the continent, where he yet resides awaiting the hour when the glorious red banner, the emblem of unity and freedom, shall proudly float on the highest pinnacle of St. Stephen's; then will the woes, and the woes of his compatriots be recompensed; the shadow will then fall from his visage, and the sunlight beam on his countenance. His fate, though hard, hath been a common one; endowed with genius and patriotism, they served only to embitter his lot by setting him at enmity with the world and the world's laws; ardent and sensitive, he felt keenly evils which would have passed lightly over a willing slave; he roams in exile in a foreign land, uncheered by the wife of his bosom, or the child of his affections, yet in the far distance he hears the melody of freedom breathing among the green hills and the lovely valleys of his native land; and though its sweet sounds fall faintly on his ear, yet his heart vibrates to their tone, and the soul of the wanderer glows with the hopes of hereafter. Sometimes the melody floats to his ear in the simple words of freedom's song, and the music lulls his cares to rest; anon it bears the lofty tones of paeans for Italy's regeneration, and his heart leaps at the inspiration; again it bursts on his ear in the war songs of Hungary's triumph, and his lips echo with gladness; but ah! the melody is hushed! woe is me! Italy has fallen! Hungary is ravaged! and the mournful dirge falls on the poor exile like the knell of departing hope, for the sun of Kossuth and Mazzini hath set in clouds and bloodshed — like him, they are wanderers and exiles. Still the spirit melody deserts him not, but whispers hope on hope ever, and the heart attuned to the sacred sound, dwells fondly on its far off echoes and the stricken soul revives again.

If genius has its evils it has also its charms; there are hours when every thought comes clothed with verdure, when naught is too bright to hope, and naught too high to dare, when the veins seem to flow with blood too subtle to be of earth, and the thought of despondency is unknown, then we leave the dull highway of the world, and leap at once to fame and glory; then night and solitude are charming, the soul becomes intoxicated with deep draughts of pure delight, and if language could then convey the heart's felicity, what dreams of spirituality would it pour forth, what whispering of wondrous voices, thousands of dim and fairy feelings flock around that would perchance lose their very charm in the revealing; then the earth is no longer a plague spotten world, but a verdant paradise; the heavens above are clear, not a cloud dims their beauty, new feelings and a new heart seem created within, all the duties of life seem heightened and ennobled, refined and softened, the sense of self is lost, and we glow with feelings for others; the heart swells with more generous emotions than priest or prophet ever penned, the soul feeds luxuriously on its own creations, and all is love and gladness. Such hours have given more names to immortality than whole ages of plodding life, when with careworn brows we drive away the lofty impulses of our nature, and dwell only with the gross matter of fact world; but alas, such joys are transient, and disappointment hath a venomed sting, fated from their birth; they die an early death, age looks back with mingled joy and sarcasm upon the visions of its early days, the heart grows accustomed to the iron cage and harsh bars which enclose its once fond anticipations. Yes, the soul that can wing its way from this cold world into the region of enchantment, is not all starless in its path, though oft it droops its weary wing among the clouds of darkness and uncertainty, for "genius is a blessing twin-born with a curse."

These reflections apply strictly to Arthur Morton; for though our hero was tried in the fire of adversity made still more fierce by his sensitive nature, yet his doom was not all misery, it had its sunlight intermingled with its shadows; and though a wanderer and an exile, living a life of misery and want, uncheered by aught save fond recollections and hopeful anticipations, yet is he less to be pitied than his early associate Walter North, who has attained his ambitious height, and now looks around on a world that despises while it flatters him; for he has earned the curse of satiety; he has no hopes for the future, the past to him is one vast blank, from Dan to Begrabeba all is vacuity;[106] the impulses which should set the generous blood in motion are frozen at their fount, and his lot is more unendurable than the patriot exiles, for the depths of misery may be sounded, but the gulph of satiety is bottomless, and the soul sinks lower and lower in its dark waters until annihilation itself would become a relief, but the soul is powerless even for its own destruction.

CHAPTER XXXVII

By Mary's side, her hand in his,
Her Husband kneeleth,
And from that hand his heartfelt kiss
Still to her ripe cheek stealeth.
But Sorrow pales its wonted hue —
She feels not now the thrill,
The Glow — that roused and yet subdue;
Her heart lies mute and chill.
And he — ev'n he — the while he sought
Her grief to comfort or to chide,

Ev'n he felt one o'er powering thought
Of anguish stifle all beside.
"Be soothed", he said, "we part, but yet
One Hope our severed soul will cheer,
And all the past we most regret,
Shall chase away the future fear.
Oh! while in distant lands I toil,
And Exile breathing Freedom's sigh,
Thy thoughts, like dew, shall bless the soil,
Thy love, like stars, smile from the sky.
And never, love, believe me, never
Did those who through all changes bore
The heart unchanging — fate so severe
But that they met — we'll meet — once more!
I do not say, "Be true to me,"
I know that deep and tender heart!
I only tell thee — Live to see
How lov'd — how truly lov'd — thou art.
Oh! what are years to those whose thought
Can bear them o'er the gulph of space.
By grief itself my soul hath bought
The right to fly to this embrace!
Methinks, if when, once more we meet,
The form be bowed, the looks be thin;
'Tis but thy welcome eyes to greet,
To light Youth's camp once more within!
Age is not made for us! No! all
The Past defies its withering breath!
The snows of Time on Love may fall,
And only warm the soil beneath.
Well weep — weep on! for hearts like ours,
Me thinks, 'tis sometimes wise to weep!
For if our love had flowed o'er flowers,
It ne'er had been a stream so deep!
If Joy the Fancy most beguiles,
'Tis Grief that to the hearts endures;
Oh! slight the love which springs from smiles,
To that which has been nurst in tears!"
He ceased — for many feelings rushed
Upon him, and all language hushed.
                    Lytton Bulwer

Return we to the home of Arthur Morton; the language even of the poet fails
to describe the parting scene, when forced by imperious necessity he bade a

long, yet hurried adieu, to the wife of his bosom; he had loved her with a love which was the only outlet of the hoarded and passionate musings of his romantic life; upon her had lavished all the tenderness of a heart, overflowing with love towards all mankind; but which mankind rejecting with scorn, the torrent flowed with the greater force towards the only being who appreciated it; and now she is left in sorrow and loneliness, to brood over his fate and mourn his absence; all the ties of memory, all the consecrations of regret, wind themselves round her heart, and issue forth after the companionless Exile. Her only consolation is her child — her Husband's child, the little Fanny now turned four years' old, inheriting all her mother's beauty, and her father's talents, she is, indeed, a treasure to her mother's widowed heart; and while gazing on her speaking countenance, and listening to the prattle of her soft melodious voice, she wipes away the tear of misery from her eye, and owns she is not all desolate. Child as she is, she is loved, yea almost worshipped, by her mother; for the tones of her voice vibrate on her heart, and remind her of him who is absent; they have the same low deep tone, and yet sound so cheerfully on her ear that hope unconsciously mingles with the image, and she rejoices in the hope of yet presenting the child to the father. And the little Fanny, with an intellect far beyond her years, will sit for hours by her mother's side, listening to the recital of her hopes and fears for her father's welfare. She is thoughtful and serious beyond her years, yet at times the joyousness of childhood will burst forth; and the youth of the mother beams forth from the laughter of the child; and months have glided on; yea, season has followed season — two Autumns have fallen with their sear leaves upon Mary's heart, yet she despairs not, her husband is still a wanderer, but she hears of his welfare, though at distant intervals; and the knowledge that he is free, cheers her in her loneliness. Respected by a numerous circle of democratic acquaintance, their kindness in procuring her employment, protects her from actual wants, and she has been too much inured to the common hardships of the poor to repine needlessly at her lot; the enthusiastic visions of her youth are not all fled; she still rejoices in the name of a Chartist, and reflects with pride upon the devotedness of her husband's attachment to a cause which is hallowed in her memory, by the suffrage of its martyrs. From her lips we have gained much information relative to the earlier career of her husband, and have listened with no common feelings to her lifelike description of the dark hours of their period of adversity, and have left her humble abode with higher notions of woman's fortitude, and woman's devotion, than we had hitherto imbibed.

Oh, how much of the glory of humanity is hid from the observation of the world; scenes are every day being enacted which, were they recorded, would reflect credit upon our common nature; victories are everyday being achieved over evil — triumphs over temptation — which have no pen to record the results, no sympathies aroused to cheer or support the victors; and though their space is but the small arena of a human heart, yet all in nature that is great or good beats in unison with them, and the vast future depends on their results.

Compared to these victories those of the warrior conqueror are indeed worthless; his privations are cheered by the hope of fame, his sacrifices are accompanied by national gratitude; his triumphs bring to him wealth and power, but the triumphs in the battle of life, though chronicled too often by increased misery and wretchedness to the victors, are more glorious for humanity, are productive of more real good to the community, than all the hollow victories which have ever desolated the world's wide plains. If we survey mankind — if we look with a calm and a stoical eye upon the scenes and actors by which we are surrounded — we see everywhere what would appear to be the great law of nature, all preying upon each other. We find it so in nature, in commerce, in religion — and in politics — all prosper in proportion to the downfall they occasion others. The spider lives by entrapping the fly, the manufacturer thrives by impoverishing the artisan, the Protestant flourishes upon the decay of the Catholic, and politics have hitherto been only an engine by which the few have been enabled to enrich themselves at the expense of the many. When you meet with a solitary exception to this great rule, you meet with a man whom the rest agree to trample under their feet, as an alien to the creed professed by themselves. No talent, no morality, no virtue can enable him to evade this fate, they then rather hasten him towards it. Is it not enough to make man doubt the existence of virtue, and drive him, even for self-preservation, into the common vortex?

Arthur Morton and his wife, from their youth upwards, had devoted their best, their freshest feelings, to the dream of serving their country — to this great end all minor attractions had been made subservient in pleasure and in popularity; in the intoxication of love, and in the depths of despair, this one object had never been forgotten; in the lowest abyss of squalid misery into which they had been dragged, this hope had never deserted them, for their prayers for other's welfare had ever mingled with those for their own, in sickness and in want; its practice had ever been continued, for they had shared their last cup, and broken their last crust, with those who, perhaps, needed it far less than themselves; and if, in the dark hour of temptation, when nature itself played them false, when a temporary madness usurped the place of reason, if in this perilous hour Arthur proved false to the creed of his life, and sank, however, gently into the great gulph of vice, by which he was surrounded — let us not dwell too harshly on the fault, if fault it be, for a desperation too powerful for humanity to cope with, impelled him onward, and years of remorse have wiped away the crime. Surely, there must be something in virtue more potent than our moralists have yet discovered — something in patriotism more powerful than hath yet been developed, or its votaries could never stand firm in their faith, whilst all around them, and even their own feeble frames, are reeling and rocking in the shock of that earthquake which threatens to swallow up all that is pure, generous and noble in humanity. If it is a phantom of which they are in pursuit, it is a glorious deception, outvieing in power the noblest conceptions of reality. There is a majesty in extreme misery, when the mind falls not with the fortune, which cannot be looked upon without emotion; and it was a glorious sight to see that youthful couple battling with misfortune, and proving victorious, even in defeat, for while the heart bled at the sight, it could not withhold its admiration; want never debased them; poverty never rendered them selfish; though existence was stript of its every charm, they still clung to their faith in the goodness of humanity; though all the poetry of life had vanished, yet their affection to each other was as pure and undimned as in the hour of its creation — the depths of misery had but served to render still more strong the ties which bound them to each other. Looking in vain for support from the world, they flung themselves more devotedly into the arms of each other, and when the storm beat loudest, they drew close together, until their hearts became one. Then came the shock which rent them asunder, and it needs no delineation to picture its force; but the same hope, and the same devotion, which had hitherto supported them, failed them not even in this dread trial; and they have yet confidence that they shall again meet in happiness, and share in that national jubilee, which shall commemorate the downfall of oppression, and the annihilation of those social conventionalities which have bowed the just to the unjust, and the virtuous to the adepts in vice — which have caused man to doubt the supremacy of goodness, and shaken his faith in the glorious doctrine of progression, forgetting the great fact that, though virtue cannot shield us from the ills of fate, that its power can support us under them, and soften their roughest aspersities.

Gentle reader, our tale is ended. For nine long months we have held weekly communings with you, and have endeavoured — though feebly — to depict one of yourselves struggling against the power of adverse circumstances; his fate is still enveloped in darkness, what the mighty womb of time may bring forth we know not. The spirit of despotism is still in the ascendant, and we still bow beneath its influence; but all hope is not lost, the earth still labours in the pangs of travail, and will ere long give birth to a new and better era; the spirit of freedom is again taking wing. Men walk wistfully abroad, and hold their breath in the deep ponderings of suspense. These are not the hours to waste in idle dalliance; we must be up and doing, or when the time comes, we shall again be found unprepared. In quitting our simple tale, we seem like parting with friends, and with these reflections delay the minute of final separation. We have endeavoured to prove that Chartism is not allied with base and vicious feelings, but that it is the offspring of high and generous inspirations — that it looks not to self but to mankind; that whilst working for the present, it holds the future in its grasp, that it is founded upon justice and truth to nature, and, therefore, must ultimately prevail. We might have made our tale more interesting to many, by drawing more largely from the regions of romance, but our object was to combine a History of Chartism, with the details of our story. We might have made it more piquant, by delineating the portraits of the active minds in the movement, but for this the time has not yet arrived; written under unfavourable circumstances, its failings must be forgiven; it hath wiled away many an hour that might have been occupied with unpleasant retrospections, and if it has amused or instructed any, its purpose is fulfilled, its object accomplished.

Notes

1. A reference to Thomas Cooper's *The Purgatory of Suicides: A Prison-Rhyme in Ten Books* (London: Jeremiah How, 1845).
2. For his mottoes Wheeler uses a number of quotations from John Richard Beste, *Cuma, The Warrior-Bard of Erin, and Other Poems* (London: Longman, Rees, Orme, Brown and Green, 1829). Wherever possible I have given the page reference from which the quotation originates or seems to originate. Wheeler's acquaintance with minor nineteenth-century poets is both idiosyncratic and indicative of the expansive literary tastes of Chartist intellectuals.
3. Beste, *Cuma*, p. 93.
4. Arthur weeps over imaginary and real characters.
    Madeline: the heroine of 'The Eve of St Agnes' (1820) by John Keats.
    Rosina: probably a shortened from of Rosalind, a popular name for a romance heroine, as seen in Shakespeare's *Love's Labour Lost* (1595) and *As You Like It* (1599).
    Algernon: Algernon Sidney (?1622-83), republican martyr.
    Aubrey: either John Aubrey (1626-97) the biographer, or a misprint for 'Audrey', a country wench in *As You Like It*.
5. *Homer*: the supposed author of the Greek epics the *Iliad* and the *Odyssey*.
    Virgil: (70-19 BC), Roman author of the epic poem the *Aeneid*.
    Byron: George Gordon, Lord Byron (1788-1824), Romantic poet.
    Shelley: Percy Bysshe Shelley (1792-1822), Romantic poet.
6. *Taw*: a game of marbles.
7. Beste, *Cuma*, p. 46.
8. Beste, *Cuma*, p. 99.
9. Enlightenment and revolutionary writers and thinkers.
    Voltaire: François Marie Arouet de Voltaire (1694-1778), French author and satirist.
    Rousseau: Jean Jacques Rouseau (1712-78), French philosopher, essayist and novelist.
    Paine: Thomas Paine (1737-1809), English republican theorist and activist.
    Robespierre: Maximilien Marie Isidore de Robespierre (1758-94), Jacobin leader in the French revolution.
10. Oliver Goldsmith, *The Deserted Village* (1770), 311-24.

11. This is a reference to the Great Famine of 1846-48, in which around a million Irish either starved to death or emigrated.

12. The site of the crucifixion of Jesus, also known as Calvary.

13. Shakespeare, *The Merchant of Venice*, 1.1.50-56.

14. Shelley, *Queen Mab*, canto 5, 194-201.

15. *Windward Islands*: the group of Caribbean islands comprising Martinique, Dominica, St Lucia, St Vincent, and Grenada.

16. Eliza Cook, 'Silence. A Fragment', 1-10, 17-26. Wheeler could have read the poem in the *Weekly Dispatch*, a paper to which Cook contributed regularly. Or he may have found the poem in *Poems by Eliza Cook*, 3 vols (London, 1848), vol. 2, pp. 65-6.

17. *Tubal Cain*: a periphrasis for weapons (iron tubes which kill fellow human beings).

18. *Cheap Johns*: a cheapjack is a hawker of wares.

19. *John o' Groat's to Land's End*: the extreme northern and southern tips of Britain.

20. Algernon Sydney (?1622-83) was executed for his part in the Rye House plot, a conspiracy to assassinate Charles II.

21. Beste, *Cuma*, p. 92.

22. Shelley, *Laon and Cythna* (1817), canto 2.20.6-13.

23. A serious riot took place in the Birmingham Bull Ring on 8 July, 1839.

24. The lines are from William Falconer's poem *The Shipwreck*, first published in 1762. Wheeler could have read the poem in the *The Poetical Works of William Falconer* (London: William Pickering, 1836), part of the popular Aldine Edition of the British Poets series.

25. Wheeler refers to the defeat of the 'red republican' faction of the French revolutionary government in June 1848, and the ascendancy of Louis Napoleon.

26. From Thomas Moore's popular air 'Come o'er the sea', one of Moore's enormously popular *Irish Melodies* (1808-34). Wheeler could have read the lyric in *The Poetical Works of Thomas Moore* (London: Longman, 1845), p. 192.

27. Beste, *Cuma*, p. 95.

28. Dominica or Dominique, a British colony since 1805.

29. Shelley, *Laon and Cythna*, canto 2.9.2-10.

30. *Desdemona*: the heroine of Shakespeare's *Othello* who is captivated by Othello's accounts of his travels.

31. The proverbial saying can be traced to the Genevan Bible's chapter heading to Genesis, ch. 25: 'Esau selleth his birthright for a mess of potage'.

32. Beste, *Cuma*, p. 94.

33. *The prophet of Horassan*: probably a reference to Thomas Moore's popular series of oriental tales in verse which went under the title *Lallah Rookh* (1817). The plot of the first story, 'The Veiled Prophet of

Khorassan', has some parallels with Arthur and Julia's situation. The beautiful Zelica is lured into marrying Mokanna and dies during the rescue attempt of her lover Azim.

34. From William Cowper's anti-slavery poem 'Charity' (1782), 169-72, 180-89.

35. Britain abolished slavery in 1833.

36. *Hill Coolies Emigration Scheme*: a reference to the importing of 'East Asian' labour to British Caribbean colonies after the abolition of slavery in 1833.

37. Not traced.

38. Beste, *Cuma*, p. 25.

39. *Aeolian harp*: a musical instrument resembling a guitar which makes a drone when air passes over it.

40. *Mesmer*: Friedrich Anton Mesmer (1734-1815), Austrian physician and founder of a hypnotic treatment named after him.

41. *Washington Irving*: (1783-1859), American writer and diplomat.

42. Beste, *Cuma*, p. 128.

43. Shakespeare, *Timon of Athens*, 3.5.31-35.

44. Wheeler attacks the 'solitary system' used by most English prisons from the 1830s onwards. Prisoners were confined to their cells and not allowed to associate with other prisoners. For a useful summary of the Anglo-American controversy about this aspect of penal reform, see Michael Slater, ed., *Dickens's Journalism. Volume II* (London: J. M. Dent, 1996), pp. 212-14.

45. Andrew Picken (1788-1833) was a Scottish poet, the son of a draper. This quotation has not been traced in Picken's *Miscellaneous Works* (1813), but Picken published quite extensively.

46. The quotations used for this chapter and for Chapters XXV and XXIX come from William Read's poem about the evils of gambling, *Rouge et Noir*, 3rd edn (London, 1830). For these lines see Canto 1, stanzas 1-2. *As Hotspur says*: Shakespeare, *King Henry IV, Part 1*, 3.1.62.

47. Chartist leaders who were imprisoned for periods of up to two years.
O'Connor: Feargus O'Connor (1794-1855), Chartism's principal leader.
O'Brien: James 'Bronterre' O'Brien (1805-64), one of the leading Chartist intellectuals.
M'Douall: Peter Murray McDouall, Manchester Chartist.
Lovett: William Lovett (1800-1877), a veteran of radical movements from the 1820s, one of the founders of the London Working Men's Association which published the first Charter in 1838.
Vincent: Henry Vincent (1813-78), Chartist orator and agitator.

48. The Corn Laws were abolished by Peel in 1846.

49. The Anti-Corn Law League was established in 1838.

50. Contemporary politicians.
Sibthorp: Charles de Laet Waldo Sibthorpe (1783-1855), MP for Lincoln

1826-55.

Muntz: George Frederick Muntz (1794-1857), MP for Birmingham 1840-57.

Howard: George William Frederick Howard (1802-64), 7th Earl of Carlisle, held numerous government posts including Irish Secretary and Viceroy of Ireland.

51.   Contemporary politicians.

Anstey: Thomas Chisholm Anstey (1816-73), MP for Youghal 1847-52.

Urquhart: David Urquhart (1805-77), Scottish diplomat.

Disraeli: Benjamin Disraeli (1804-81), Tory statesmen, leader of the 'Young England' movement in the early 1840s, and sponsor of the Second Reform Bill in 1867.

Macaulay: Thomas Babington Macaulay (1800-59), popular political journalist and Whig MP.

Sheil: Richard Lalor Sheil (1791-1851), Irish dramatist and politician.

Roebuck: John Arthur Roebuck (1801-79), MP for Bath and Sheffield at various times, Chairman of the Administrative Reform Association in 1856.

Peel: Sir Robert Peel (1788-1850), Tory Prime Minister 1841-46.

52.   Wheeler quotes from the popular play *Lover's Vows*, translated by Elizabeth Inchbald in 1798 from the German of August von Kotzebue (1761-1819). The play has become famous for the place it occupies in Austen's *Mansfield Park*. The speaker is Baron Wildenhaim, who is agreeing that his daughter can marry the penniless tutor Anhalt rather than her wealthy suitor Count Cassell. The Baron is making amends for having seduced a peasant woman in his youth. Wheeler could have read the play in the popular series *Cumberland's British Theatre*, vol. 17 (1829).

53.   These famous battles in which the English defeated the French were fought in 1346 and 1415.

54.   *Embonpoint*: stoutness (French).

55.   From Washington Irving's essay 'Royal Funerals' in *The Sketchbook* (1820). Wheeler omits the words 'even of an enemy' after 'look down upon the grave'. The essay can be found in *The Works of Washington Irving in Ten Volumes* (London, 1853), vol. 2, pp. 99-108, though this is not the edition Wheeler is quoting from.

56.   Beste, *Cuma*, pp. 133, 28-9.

57.   Beste, *Cuma*, pp. 140-41.

58.   Probably a reference to the campaign for land reform organized by the expatriates Chartist Thomas Ainge Devyr and George Evans in the 1840s. An account of this can be found in Ray Boston, *British Chartists in America 1839-1900* (Manchester: Manchester University Press, 1971).

59.   William Read, *Rouge et Noir*, Canto 6, stanzas 3-4.

60. John Collins the cabinet-maker, who was imprisoned with William Lovett in 1839.

61. It is unlikely that one individual steered the Anti-Corn Law League in the direction of organizing a manufacturers' lock-out, but Wheeler could be thinking of Alderman Chappell, who is identified in the *Northern Star* on 20 August 1842, p. 4. It would be interesting to know whether Wheeler relied on memory or his own 'archive' for such historical details.

62. Shelley, 'Song to the Men of England', stanzas 1-3, 6. This poem was one of a group of 'Popular Songs Wholly Political' which Shelley wrote in 1819 in response to the Peterloo massacre. None of the poems (including *Mask of Anarchy*) were published until after Shelley's death.

63. The 'Executive Address' was issued by the Executive of the Chartist delegate conference held in Manchester on 16 August 1842. A brief report of this meeting was published in the *Northern Star*, 20 August 1842, p. 5. Wheeler quotes more extensively from the Address later in the chapter.

64. *Colonel Wemyss*: deputy commander of the northern district.

65. See note 63.

66. *Harney*: George Julian Harney (1817-97), 'red republican' Chartist who emigrated to America in 1863.
    Hill: William Hill, the first editor of the *Northern Star*.

67. These are the opening stanzas from Thomas Cooper's prison poem *The Purgatory of Suicides* (1845; see note 1). Thomas Cooper (1805-92) received a two-year prison sentence in 1843 for his speech to the Staffordshire miners, though an earlier charge of having caused the arson attack referred to in the quotation was dropped.

68. Cooper, Richards, Ellis, Moses Simpson and W. Ridgway were the Chartist cadres sent to agitate in the Potteries.
    Ellis: William Sherrat Ellis, a young potter and socialist, transported for 21 years for his part in the Staffordshire riots. According to Dorothy Thompson, Ellis was sentenced on 'perjured evidence'. See D. Thompson, *The Chartists: Popular Politics in the Industrial Revolution* (Aldershot: Wildwood House, 1984), p. 300.
    Richards: John Richards, Chartist shoemaker.

69. *William Cuffay*: (1788-1870), the prominent black Chartist, transported to Tasmania for his part in the Orange Tree Conspiracy of 1848 (see Chapter XXXVI). Wheeler clearly knew and admired Cuffay, and wrote a profile of him for *Reynolds's Political Instructor*, 13 April 1850.

70. O'Connor edited the daily London *Evening Star* from August 1842 to February 1843. Although he had long nursed an ambition to edit a daily Chartist newspaper, heavy losses meant the *Evening Star* closed after six months.

71. *Female orators*: a list would include Susannah Inge, Mary Anne Walker, and Caroline and Elizabeth Blatherwick. See Dorothy Thompson, *The*

Chartists, chapter 7, and Jutta Schwarzkopf, *Women in the Chartist Movement* (Basingstoke: Macmillan, 1991).

72.   Alaric A. Watts, 'The Broken Heart. A Sketch', stanza 12, 13-28. Wheeler could have read the poem in *Poetical Sketches with Other Poems*, 4th edn (London, 1828), p. 22.

73.   *Nemo*: a pseudonym for Henry Gardiner Adams, though I have not traced the quotation.

74.   William Read, *Rouge et Noir*, Canto 3, XVII.

75.   *Sturge conference*: Joseph Sturge, the Birmingham reformer and leader of the predominantly middle-class Complete Suffrage Union, organized a conference in December 1842 which held out the promise of an alliance with Chartism. He was defeated by O'Connor and Lovett, who refused among other things to expunge the word Chartism from the title of any new association.

76.   *Moore*: Thomas Moore (1779-1852), popular Irish poet and lyricist.
      Burns: Robert Burns (1759-96), the national poet of Scotland.

77.   *Lytton Bulwer*: Edward George Lytton Bulwer (1803-73), English novelist and MP.

78.   *Flora*: an ancient Italian goddess of flowers and fertility.

79.   Thomas Gray, 'Elegy Written in a Country Churchyard' (1751), 32.

80.   Ferdinand Freiligrath (1810-76), German poet and political refugee after the collapse of the 1848 revolution. See Rosemary Ashton, *Little Germany: German Refugees in Victorian Britain* (Oxford: Oxford University Press, 1986), chapter 2. Ernest Jones reprinted Freiligrath's poetry in *Notes to the People* (London, 1851-52).

81.   Willie Thom, the Scottish handloom weaver and poet who achieved a measure of fame in the mid-1840s, partly through his friendship with Thomas Cooper. He died in poverty in 1848.

82.   The quotations from Bulwer Lytton used for the epigraphs to Chapters XXXII, XXXIII, XXXIV, XXXVI and XXXVII have not been traced but they are probably from an early version of *The New Timon*, first published in 1845, which contains a tragic heroine named Mary.

83.   *Cyprian*: a prostitute.

84.   The Pharisees were an ancient Jewish sect renowned for the strictness of their worship, but the term had become proverbial for sanctimonious hypocrisy.

85.   Byron, *Don Juan*, 10. 34. 1.

86.   *Communism*: Owenism or another communitarian philosophy.

87.   Oliver Goldsmith, *The Deserted Village*, 51-62.

88.   *Pasquins*: Roman columns upon which satirical graffiti was written.

89.   Wheeler's praise for the Chartist Land Company and Chartist settlements flows from his own experience as secretary to the former and inhabitant of the latter.

90.   *Law of Entail*: the control over the settlement of property.

91. *Atlas-like*: the god Atlas was punished for his part in the revolt of the Titans by having to support the weight of the earth on his shoulders.
92. *Michelet*: Jules Michelet (1798-1874), French historian.
93. Wheeler refers to the February revolution in France and the great Chartist demonstration of 10 April 1848, both mentioned later in the chapter.
94. *Citizen King*: Louis Philippe (1773-1850) was the son of a nobleman but changed his name to Philip Egalité during the French Revolution. He became King of France after the revolution of 1830.
95. Leaders of revolutions and insurrections in Europe in 1848.
     Ledru Rollin: Alexander Auguste Ledru-Rollin (1807-74) was a believer in universal suffrage and a member of the revolutionary provisional government in France in 1848. He led an unsuccessful uprising in 1849.
     Mitchel: John Mitchel (1815-75), Irish nationalist and 'Young Ireland' leader who was transported for allegedly writing treasonable articles in his paper *The Nation*. Like Meagher he escaped and fled to America.
     Meagher: Thomas Francis Meagher (1822-67), Irish nationalist and one of the founders of 'Young Ireland', who was transported for life after his involvement in the Irish uprising in the summer of 1848. He escaped and became active in American politics.
     Blum: Robert Blum (1807-48), German agitator and bookseller, who was arrested and shot for supporting the uprising in Vienna in 1848.
     Kossuth: Lajos Kossuth (1802-94), Hungarian revolutionary and governor of the Hungarian republic in 1849.
     Mazzini: Guiseppe Mazzini (1805-72), Italian patriot, member of the brief republican government in Rome in 1849, and leader of 'Young Europe'.
96. The Chartist National Assembly met for only eight days in May 1848.
97. The provisional government's president was Dupont de l'Eure.
98. *Alien Bills and Gagging Bills*: repressive measures introduced in 1848.
99. The first 'free' elections in France in April 1848 produced a mixed conservative and 'moderate' government, largely due to the rural vote.
100. Francis Worsley: from Francis Worsley, 'The Labourer's Gathering', published in *Douglas Jerrold's Shilling Magazine*, 3 (January to June 1846), pp. 145-6. Worsley was the author of poetical and historical romances such as *Waltheof, the Last Saxon Thane* (1843).
101. *Ernest Jones*: (1819-69), Chartist writer and one of the leaders of 'late' Chartism, who was imprisoned for two years in the summer of 1848.
     Samuel Kydd: (1815-92), Scottish Chartist, like Jones a lawyer, and an important propagandist, speaker and organizer in 1848. See Stephen Roberts, *Radical Politicians and Poets in Early Victorian Britain: The Voices of Six Chartist Leaders* (Lampeter: The Edwin Mellen Press, 1993), chapter 6.
102. *Michael Doheny*: Doheny was an Irish nationalist delegate at a meeting with O'Connor and other Chartist leaders in Manchester on 17 March, 1848. See Stephen Roberts, *Radical Politicians and Poets in Early*

Victorian Britain, pp. 114-15.

103.   See Wheeler's articles in the *Northern Star*, 5 February, 12 February, 1
       April 1848, describing a walking tour of Chartist settlements.
104.   Charles Lamb, 'The Three Graves' (1820). The poem carries the subtitle
       'Written during the time, now happily almost forgotten, of the spy
       system'. This epigraph is one of Wheeler's most sophisticated and ironic
       uses of intertextuality. His 'Author's note' for the quotation reads: 'A
       slight liberty has been taken with the last lines of the original'. This is a
       cryptic way of indicating that the names of the spies in the last line have
       been updated. Lamb's original refers to 'Castles, Oliver and Edwards', the
       infamous *agents provocateurs* of the Pentridge rebellion in 1817, and the
       Cato Street conspiracy of 1820. Wheeler's spies figured in the trial of the
       so-called Orange Tree plotters in 1848. Lamb could hardly have known
       that his poem would be revived along with the spy system he believed
       was 'happily forgotten'.
       Bedloe: William Bedloe (1650-80), a spy who profited from informing
       on Catholics.
       Oates: Titus Oates (1649-1705) caused a national alarm in the early
       1680s when he alleged that a Catholic insurrection was imminent. He
       was later convicted of perjury.
       Clotho: one of three Fates of Greek folklore, she held the distaff of life.
105.   Ernest Jones, William Sharp, Joseph Williams, John Fussell, W. J.
       Vernon and John James Bezer were some of the London Chartist leaders
       arrested in May 1848.
106.   *Dan to Begrabeba*: Laurence Sterne, 'In the Street— Calais' (third scene)
       from *A Sentimental Journey through France and Italy*, vol. 1 (1768): 'I
       pity the man who can travel from Dan to Beersheba and cry, "Tis all
       barren."'